Dominic's Nemesis

D. Alyce Domain

This book is an original novel self-publication by the credited author, D. Alyce Domain.

This is a work of creative fiction. Names, characters, places, and incidents are either a product of the author's imagination or are used fictitiously, and any resemblance to actual persons, living or dead, business establishments, events or locales is entirely coincidental.

Stock Photography by: Captblack76 | Dreamstime.com

ISBN-10: 0996926712
ISBN-13: 978-0-9969267-1-3

DEDICATION

I dedicate this book to my life-long friend Nadia Galloway Dickson who was the first person to read my book and to her husband Dwight who prodded me along to finish and publish my first novel.

CONTENTS

ACKNOWLEDGMENTS

I would like to acknowledge the unconditional love and undeserved blessings that I receive from God and his precious son Jesus Christ. Without his saving grace nothing in my life, not even my life itself would be possible.

I send a special thanks to my very supportive very patient parents, Charles and Eunice Domain who believed in me without fail.

I also thank all my long-time friends and family who have sent me positive thoughts, without which I would not have been able to focus and complete my writing goals.

PROLOGUE

Italy (1800s)

He lay on the pit floor, limbs stiff from lack of movement. The crawl space no longer accommodated his length. With no light to guide him, he planned each movement to avoid scraping against the granite. First, he shuffled his legs, then rolled his shoulders to bring back the circulation. His skin pulled and itched like the devil. The gouges must be scabbing over, he thought.

He hadn't tried to stand in a while, but he knew from the last time that he was almost tall enough to reach the pit's lid. Just a little while longer and he'd try again. He was preserving energy and hoping to be healed enough to try jumping. She would come soon, he knew. For now, the darkness was reassuring. It calmed his mind. As long as he was alone in the dark, nothing hurt him.

He didn't hear her approach. He never did. Light peeked through the pit's lid, casting the iron bars in distorted shadows around him. He trembled and buried his eyes in the bend of his arm. Panicked, he struggled to shove his gangly, pubescent body into a crevice between two outcroppings. If he merged with the granite walls, maybe she wouldn't be able to find him and do more damage.

"Come, come, now, little fiend." Her voice cast a lure like the nectar of a carnivorous flower.

3

The boy squeezed his eyelids tight despite the arm shield. He knew who awaited him above. He squirmed further into the jagged stone. The taut scabs on his shoulders cracked open and bled. He did not bother to scream or beg. Nothing ever saved him from whatever agony she came to inflict. Instead he prayed, "Help me, God, please. Do not let her see me this time. Hide me."

"Where are you, little fiend?"

He felt her mind rummage around for him like a blind man groping for his cane. Something new, he thought. Didn't she know where he was? Couldn't she see him? The pit was a scant six-foot cube and she waved the candelabra close enough so that hot wax splattered atop his forearms.

"Come here you little fiend!" Her voice turned shrill. "Give me back what's mine!"

Her ham-fisted attempts to locate him left him halfway between fear and confusion. Why couldn't she see him? Or touch him with her mind? By now, he should be frozen, mid-air with tangled clops of hair his only clothing. Fear ebbed into curiosity. He dared to lower his arm and peel his lids open. Even with his head still bowed, the candle-glow forced him to squint.

Here lay the true test, he knew. If his tormentor really couldn't see him or sense him, she wouldn't react to his gaze. He'd learned long ago to avert his eyes in her presence. He hadn't glimpsed his tormentor up close in six years. The boy swallowed the upsurge of fear and snapped his head back before he lost his nerve.

He blinked several times to sharpen his vision. He recoiled, scraping the skin at the point of his hip. Another blink, then he relaxed. Hair. Her obsidian tresses dangled down between the iron grate, seeming to reach for him. Her face was contorted from its cloying perfection, but not in reaction...more from anger or maybe frustration he guessed. He continued to stare, shocked, not sure what to do. How long would her...blindness or whatever it was, last? She started to screech obscenities and jab around with her mind. The violent brush of her mind jerked him from his stillness. He used the jagged wall behind him to pull himself upright. Gaunt, with wobbly knees and a hobbled gait, he crept close enough to fan his hand in front of her eyes.

"Mama?" His voice sounded croaky from non-use.

No reaction.

Then, he caught sight of his arm, the arm that should have been fanning before him. There was only empty space. With a huff of amazement, he glanced around him. His body cast no shadow. It was as if he had faded from existence, become part of the void.

ONE

Eden had been at the St. James' country estate less than a week, and her cousin Millie had already enticed her to attend a weekend Hen party. She tried to cry off, sighting the strict rules of mourning and her lack of party spirit. But, Millie insisted that this was her last outing before the baby, pointing out that she wouldn't be available to chaperon for at least five months. Millie did not want her cooped up with grief for another half-year. Eden did not want Millie to worry, so she'd given in.

"Why must we have chaperons at an all female gathering, anyway?" She whispered. The only men present were the footmen and even they were banished when the party retired to the upstairs parlor.

"Shhhh!" Millie swatted at her. "The next game is about to begin."

The room mirrored the Grecian style, complete with faux columns, a bust of Caesar and leering satyrs in each corner. Eden, Millie, and ten other ladies were instructed to gather around a low table in the center of the room. They sat on leg-less chairs, flush with the floor. For comfort's sake, Eden folded her legs behind her. She guessed that the table and its bizarre chairs were a temporary addition since it neither matched nor complemented the room's theme.

"Ladies, is everyone familiar with 'Spin the phallus'." Lady Haversdale cocked a brow.

Eden listened, as their host explained that they were to take turns twirling a mosaic glass rod with a pointy end and a blunt end. When the 'phallus' stopped spinning, the lady on the blunt end of the rod was allowed to ask whichever lady unlucky enough to be on the pointy end a question. This, Lady Haversdale explained, was to allow everyone to become acquainted. The questions started out harmless, favorite color, and the like. After several turns, the questions veered into gasp-worthy topics...first kiss, biggest fears, and with whom one would most like to dance the waltz. Eden stammered to answer the former of the three.

"Well I, eh...have not been kissed." She colored scarlet. "Yet."

Millie poked an elbow in her side. "I know you're enjoying yourself. You cannot deny it."

"This is *scandalous*." Eden felt a smile threaten even as she whispered the words. The risqué element shocked her out of her doldrums.

The ladies broke off into murmured conversations as the phallus game ended. Lady Haversdale's niece sat on Eden's other arm. The triplets, buxom girls each with chocolate eyes and curly hair, sat on the left half of the table. The red-haired sisters filled out the rest of the circle.

"I hope you do not take offense. Aunt is very *modern*." Lady Haversdale's niece was the first besides Millie to address her outside the games.

"Yes, very." Eden agreed.

The girl ducked her head. "I just thought I should warn you, as you are the only one who may be ignorant of her more eccentric ideas."

Eden smiled to set her at ease. "Nothing could be so shocking as sipping from my tea cup only to find it brimming with sherry."

"Aunt does not agree with denying herself the same liberties…and vices…that gentlemen enjoy."

Eden did not have the chance to respond. Just then, the room began to darken. She swiveled to see the redheads dousing the sconces, as their host exited the room. Haversdale returned with a Grecian wreath encircling her head and her hair hanging unbridled down her back. Her frock, she'd traded in for a white billowy gown. Maybe she was aiming for Mother Nature, but she looked more like Lady Godiva. No wonder the sisters had dimmed the lights, Eden thought.

The only illumination left was a flickering candelabrum at the table's center. Her nostrils flared as a piquant aroma burned her nostrils. The candles must be scented, Eden noted. She glanced to her right, not sure she was having fun anymore. *"Millie—"*

Lady Haversdale broke into the circle between her and Millie, cutting her off. "Ahh, ladies, our final activity of the evening will be a table turning. If everyone will link hands and concentrate on the candlelight we can begin."

The ladies giggled and fumbled around to comply with their host's instructions. Eden felt both ladies on either side of her grasp her hand. Haversdale's niece, on her left, must have somehow sensed her unease; she gave her palm a reassuring squeeze. Eden's apprehensions abated a little when she closed her eyes.

The miss who had questioned her during spin-the-phallus piped up. "Who in Hades are we supposed to be contacting? Shouldn't we know so everyone will conjure up the same entity?"

"Shhh! I will act as a medium and recite the invocation." Their host commanded. "Empty your mind ladies…"

"A feat easily achievable by some." Her niece murmured near Eden's ear.

Eden coughed to stifle the laugh that bubbled up. She

quite liked Lady Haversdale's niece.

"Now, concentrate...and center yourselves on promoting a safe, inviting atmosphere for benevolent spirits."

Unconvinced, the bold redhead persisted. "But what will we do once it gets here? Offer it tea?"

"Certainly not." One of the triplets joined in the jest. "Its the dead of night. A glass of port, or some brandy perhaps."

Lady Haversdale sighed. "Each lady will have a turn to address the spirit. Try to think of a matter on which you need advice or guidance."

"Humph." Huffed the redhead. "I do not think it wise to discuss private matters with an unknown spirit."

"Particularly after it's had a glass of port."

A chorus of giggles followed.

"All eyes closed." Haversdale ordered. "We must evoke a harmonious, spirit-friendly environment, if we have hope of making contact. Even your breathing."

The room grew quiet. Eden glanced around the circle of shadowed faces. After a moment of indecision, she sighed, and closed her eyes. In through her nose and out through her mouth—she tried to empty her mind of morose thoughts. She concentrated on her parent's souls reunited in the afterlife and pictured herself joining them in heaven.

A tremor ran up her arm when Lady Haversdale began murmuring something...a chant she realized after several successive recitations. With each incantation, the words became more forceful. Eden began to sway to the pull of the words, and the lulling scent in the air. She found herself chanting along with their host. The other ladies joined in until they were all chanting in unison.

Eden felt the sensation of being an observer instead of a participant in her mind. She heard herself...speaking, but the words were different from the chant. There was no rhythm to them, and they did not feel calm. She could not discern what she said but knew that the words were desperate, her existence or *someone's* depended on the message she conveyed. And then, she felt slack, as if being released from a grip. The sensation vanished with no warning, her consciousness slammed back into her mind like a stampeding horse. She heard herself scream, and her arms come up in a protective cross over her face as the fleeing sensation ended.

Eden awakened sprawled on the floor with her arms in a defensive position. She slit her eyes to find the room over-bright. She blinked, and experienced a moment of vertigo, then blinked several more times. When her head cleared, the first thing she saw was a cushion contraption in a heap nearby. Hers?

"Look! She's come out of it."

The others ringed her as if approaching a rabid animal. Expressions ranged from horror to confusion.

Millie hovered nearest, a deep furrow in her brow. "Eden?"

"Ms. Prescott?" Lady Haversdale stepped forward.

She jerked at the sound of her name, and peek at their host through the cross of her arms.

"Miss Prescott, please speak if you are coherent."

"What...happened?" She lowered her arms, feeling silly. "Why is everyone staring at me?"

"Her voice is back to normal." She heard someone murmur.

"Time enough for explanations later." Millie bullied her way back to the forefront, bending to offer assistant. "I take it, Lady Haversdale, that this is the end of the festivities."

* * *

"Psychic phenomena, gentlemen...and ladies, is our topic this evening." The speaker tipped an imaginary hat to his audience.

Burlington's Lecture Hall bustled near capacity. The crowd consisted of gents with the odd flock of thrill-seeking ladies sprinkled here and there. The smoldering lanterns built into the baroque architecture threw off more shadows than light adding a mystical quality to the proceedings. A contrived effect, no doubt, Dominic thought.

The lecturer was Professor Davide Greyson. An American, Dominic was surprised to learn...and also younger than he'd imagined. Judging by the lean build and silver-free hair, Greyson could be no more than eight and twenty.

Careful not to call attention to himself, Dominic edged the spectacles off the bridge of his nose to study the speaker as the younger man tilted his brow and smiled at a giggly threesome several rows out from the mahogany podium.

"Psychic phenomena. We are all familiar with the term, but do you know what it means? What comes to mind? Mesmeric trickery. Table-turning in the parlor. Spirit photography. These social amusements are just that...amusing. When I, as a scientist, approach psychic phenomena, I am speaking of mental awareness and in extraordinary cases, mental influence over external objects without physical means." Greyson spoke in a voice as eloquent as his attire, employing graceful gestures to illustrate his points. "I further believe that, *Adepts*, people gifted with such abilities are not a myth, but a reality. There is no reason to be frightened or distrustful of adepts. They are people just like you or I, but with the ability to utilize a greater portion of their brain."

Just then, a haphazardly dressed gent ejected himself out of his seat. "Then where are they, mister?" He pitched this way and that. "I say, I could use a bit of parlor trickery to get me senses reelin'."

A few snickers followed, but for the most part, the drunkard was treated to a good many annoyed glares. He seemed to realize the audience around him was hostile and collapsed down into his seat. Dominic glimpsed neither anxiety nor hesitation from Greyson. He ignored the outburst and dived back into his topic with gusto.

"The problems lie with manifestation and control. Think of the human brain as a locomotive engine. Having worked primarily with—"

Dominic left off listening as he caught sight of a familiar figure making a laborious trip down the aisle towards him. He sat at the very back of the lecture hall and had struggled to maintain an empty seat on either side of himself, but the effort was in vane. Cael was alone.

His gaze remained trained on the podium. "You're late. And where is Ethan? I thought he was coming with you."

"A midnight lecture, Dominic? This is a little perverse even for you."

He let the comment go. Cael, like Greyson, was American after all.

"Where is Ethan?" He branded his younger brother with as hard a stare as he could manage through the tinted barrier of his spectacles.

Cael returned the stare without flinching. "Why do you persist in donning that ridiculous eye-wear? It's the middle of the night in a darkened auditorium. No one is likely to—"

Dominic tensed. "Where. Is. Ethan?" He shoved the spectacles back up the bridge of his nose and turned away. The cravat restricted his movements somewhat, but he could still catch his brother's profile out of the corner of his eye.

Dark blond brows and amber eyes registered defeat as though he'd just remembered to whom he spoke. "Settle down, Dom. I haven't the vaguest notion of Ethan's whereabouts. He muttered something about madcap colonists run amok in polite society just before he commandeered my hack and thundered off. I did however insist upon his promise that the endeavor was not life-threatening."

"Good." Satisfied, Dominic returned his attention to the podium. "The midnight venue was the only one where our presence here would not draw attention...or questions."

Cael glanced to the speaker before looking back to his brother. "You still have not explained why you wanted us here."

"Just listen." Dominic raked a hand through tar-black locks, which hung over the back of his collar. Ethan would have just listened. Cael demanded more. He always had.

"Who is he, Dom?"

"An American radical. He is university-trained, and has published multiple articles on science, medicine...and spiritualism."

His brother's head snapped to face him. "*He's* a spiritualist?"

"No." Dom frowned. "His publications regarding Spiritualism are not supportive. I'm surprised you haven't heard his name before."

"Perhaps I would have if you did not object to my applying for membership into the Royal Society. All the respected practitioners-"

"Please do not change the subject." Dom cut him off. The last thing he wanted was another convoluted argument about the validity of that scientific gossip club.

Cael exhaled a long-suffering sigh. "Dom. The Society promotes the improvement of knowledge in the natural sciences."

"It's an unholy mixture of science, politics, and gossip." He snapped. "But that's neither here nor there. I called you here because this assembly of his is the first in a series of academic campaigns promoting the acceptance of a new field of science. Psionics. The study of psychic deviants...*us*. His ultimate goal is anyone's guess."

"I see." Cael returned his attention to the speaker. "You think he's a threat."

"You don't?" Dom groaned at his brother's toneless reaction. He knew he wouldn't get an answer from Cael. The man was impossible to read when he chose to be.

TWO

The ladies piled into Eden's chamber like children eager for a bedtime story. Millie fussed around her while the bold redhead and Haversdale's niece each sat at her right on the bed. The remaining redheads and the giggly triplets alternated between whispering to themselves and gawking at her. They were all agog to see what would happen next. Eden did not blame them. She'd be intrigued too, were she not the object of their fascination. Lady Haversdale, armed with a stern expression, resumed her questioning.

"Now then, tell us the last thing you remember."

"I remember chanting along with everyone else. I...eh..." Eden hesitated, not sure how to explain the other impressions she'd experienced.

"Do not fret." Lady Haversdale smoothed, reading her fears. "No one here is likely to label you a heretic or a madwoman."

"Aunt is right." Her niece concurred. "We all participated. By accusing you we would incriminate ourselves as well."

The others dutifully nodded their heads.

Assuaged, Eden labored to explain. "I remember feeling disconnected...from myself. As if, something else had control of me and I was just the vessel it used to speak. It did speak, did it not?"

"Yes." Their host confirmed. "Quite forcefully."

Despite her increasing fear of knowing just what had happened to her, Eden's curiosity got the better of her. "What did I say?"

Her question caused an uneasy silence in the room.

"Well, tell her." The bold one ordered. "Or I will."

One of the triplets spoke up. "Your voice was...different. Husky. The sound of it took us by surprise...my sisters and I. I'm Primrose, by the by."

Eden eyed her, then the two on either side of her. She found their alikeness rather dizzying.

"The point, Prim, get to the point." One sister ordered.

"Yes, of course. You...the other you, I mean, garbled something about sins and punishment. You sounded sort of eh, desperate."

"Hysterical more like."

"Hysterical then." Prim amended. "Over and over again, perhaps with a few variations. Then, the most frightening thing happened."

Enraptured, Eden leaned towards her.

"For an instant, only an instant mind you, you did not look like yourself. An energy of sorts emanated from you. Then, your plaits were undone and flying around. Your hair is so ashen...eh, it appeared to...glisten...a little." She rushed on as if apologizing. "It could have been just a trick of the light, because you're...also pale."

The sister to her right took over the re-telling. "That is when Lady Haversdale ordered us ladies to break the circle and put out the candelabrum. We heard an awful crash in the dark and then Prue, Prim and I helped re-light the lanterns. I'm Sephie...its Persephone, really, but who could be bothered to say all that. Anyway, we found you on the floor next to what was left of your cushion seat."

"Has anything of this magnitude ever happened before?" Their host asked.

"One might ask the same of you." Millie snapped. "Aren't you the professed medium?"

"No." And Eden hoped it would never happen again.

* * *

A multitude of low-burning sconces lined the walls, mirroring the shadowy atmosphere of the lecture hall. Dominic stood alone, dead center of the room, sipping brandy and debating the wisdom of loitering about in society. He longed to discard his specs so he could get a clearer image of the people around him, but he dared not. Cael had gone off under the guise of fetching himself a brandy. Where the devil was he? Dom suspected he'd been ditched until he spotted his brother's dark blond head a few yards away.

Members of the audience aggregated in smallish groups. Cael stood near one of two drink tables...a discreet distance behind Greyson's six plus frame. The gent in conversation with him was older, with meager hair scattered over a shiny scalp. Dom watched as his brother inched closer. Eavesdropping, no doubt. The twosome was deep in conversation. So, Cael could be expressive when it suited him, he thought. Curious of the odd mien marring his usual poker-face, Dominic began to pace towards his brother.

"What did you say your business was, Mr..."

"Montgomery. Matthias Montgomery. Perhaps the name is familiar."

Dom watched Greyson shrug at the comment. "No. I can't say that it is."

"Pity." For an instant, his eyes hardened.

Upon closer examination, Dominic noted that Montgomery's garb was quite a bit more common of style and thread than the others around them. No waistcoat, or cravat either. He wore a rough charcoal jacket over a shirt of equally dull color and would have been considered stocky if he were shorter. Standing next to the picturesque Greyson cast him as an impoverished cousin waiting in the wings to inherit a better lot in life.

"Actually, Greyson, you an' I is in the same business. I just 'andle a different leg of it, you might say." He edged closer, nudging Greyson's arm. The gesture implied a camaraderie that did not exist between the two men, if the younger gentleman's puzzled expression were to be believed.

"How's that, sir. Are you an anatomist?"

"I runs a lunatic asylum for the upper crust Lords and Ladies wot don't want a blemish ruining their social calendar. I used to get about as a Bow' Runner in the old days, but found this line of work much more rewardin' financially...and personally too, you understand. Wot's a body to do wit the odd uncle that goes off the deep end? They'd have a right nasty time of it in Bedlam's general population. This way is more humane. But if it's like you say, some of 'em ain't so much touched in the head as they are adept at otherworldly things, perhaps we could strike a bargain—"

Greyson cleared his throat without preamble. "Mr. Montgomery. As much as I appreciate your enthusiasm and unique...eh, view of cerebral abnormalities, I do not think that we have enough goals in common to be true colleagues. I am however honored at your faith in my work. Stay as long as you wish. There are, I believe some leaflets available, which you might find of interest. Do excuse me."

Without giving the gentleman an opportunity to renew their dialogue, Greyson departed. He did not stop or look around, but joined a group of eager-looking ladies halfway across the floor. Montgomery fumed at the cut before snatching a brandy glass from the table and stalking off in the opposite direction.

Dominic meandered to close the gap between him and Cael.

"I did not like that gentleman." His brother confessed.

"Greyson?"

"The other one."

"Yes." Dominic mused. "There was something disquieting about him, but he is no fool."

"It might be better for Greyson if he were."

"Do not waste your sympathies. Greyson is no fool either."

THREE

Dominic grimaced at the swath of disheveled papers before him. Deeds. Creditors. Unpaid debts. A vaguely threatening magistrate's letter. Damn. He needed a break. Like the funeral, he had hoped to leave the settling of his father's estate to the Italian branch of the family. But, events transpired such that he was forced to play at least a cursory role in Lucca Ambrosi's affairs.

Dominic abandoned his desk and meandered around the study, shoveling his hands through the already disarrayed waves atop his head. He came to stand beside the hearth, shed his jacket and waistcoat...and longed for a bath and a shave. Afternoon had not yet resolved into evening, but he was restless enough to consider retiring to his suites. His grandmother was due the following morning, and he'd no doubt need a day and a half's rest to deal with the old dragon. He dreaded her coming, but he was resigned to it.

Dominic abhorred visitors in general. He could narrowly tolerate the skeleton crew of servants required to keep up an estate the size of his countryside residence. Where there were people, gossip and innuendo were sure to follow. The Ambrosi' could ill-afford whispers and murmurings.

Just then, a muffled commotion captured his attention. Startled, he dashed for the desk to don his spectacles before heading for the door. In the foyer beyond the main entrance, Dominic spied Cael and Ethan haggling with his wiry butler. Dominic dispatched Renfred to his quarters and invited them to join him in the study.

He knew the instant the door closed that they bore dire news. Ethan, a paler, older version of himself with warm eyes and chocolate hair, took up pacing in front of the fire. Cael, a sturdy port in any storm, came to stand opposite Dominic with the wide expansion of desk in between.

"I received a summons from the University." Cael stated without buffer. "There's been an *incident* involving Stephan and several other students."

So, it had finally happened, the thing he had dreaded since he'd first located his two American brothers. "How bad?" He heard himself ask.

"It's uncertain if one young man will ever recover from his injuries." Cael informed him. "But there is no talk of witchcraft or sorcery...yet."

Good. That's good. Maybe the damage is still manageable.

"The headmaster wants him off the premises immediately." Ethan inserted mid-stride. "There was mention of involving the magistrate. It will take no small level of finesse if we have any hope of keeping it quiet. We must be off post haste."

Dominic groaned. "I cannot."

"You have a more pressing matter to attend to than the possible incarceration of our brother? Do tell." Cael injected just the right amount of censure to get his point across.

Dominic avoided his gaze, knowing his next words would not be well received. He didn't feel like arguing with Cael tonight, but it seemed fate superseded him.

"Nonna descends shortly from Italy to help settle some

concerns regarding the Ambrosi legacy. Gideon informed me of the Conte's ill-health some months ago and promised to handle things there, but—"

"Conte Ambrosi...is dead?" Ethan paused in his pacing.

"Your father died?" He felt Cael amber's eyes digging into him. "When?"

"Ahh...A month, perhaps six weeks ago." He fanned his fingers at the uselessness of the question. "Does it matter? Gideon said—"

"To hell with Gideon." Cael snapped. "Your father died a month ago and you didn't mention it? Did you attend the services at least?"

Ethan came to stand beside Cael. Dominic imagined he was accustomed by now to playing the arbitrator.

Dom sighed. "I was not overly attached to the man. You know this. Is it such a shock that I would not mourn his passing?"

"Say what you will, Dom, but it is unnatural not to feel something...bitterness even...at the death of a parent."

Ethan's voice sliced through a tension thicker than pea soup. "Cael, that is unfair. Everyone grieves in their own way."

Both brothers ignored him.

Dom's gaze held fast to the fire burning in the hearth. "If you mean to say that I am an abomination, do not bother. I have always been aware of my place in the world. I am, however, saddened to learn Stephan has fell victim to the Ambrosi family curse. I had prayed that you and he at least would be spared."

"You know, Dom, cutting yourself off from society will only hasten the madness that you are so afraid is inevitable. God did not create man alone." Cael ran a frustrated hand through his hair. "I am going for a walk." He turned to address their other brother for the first time. "Ethan, be ready to leave when I return."

* * *

A tranquil breeze whistled through the scattering of trees, causing the loose foliage on the ground to flit upward in spiral patterns. The blue-grey sky far off on the horizon provided a serene backdrop. Unmoved by the picturesque surroundings, Eden wondered at the irony of such a beautiful place being the setting for such tragic events. Fate was a cruel mistress, she thought.

Evening crept in through the trees. Eden knew she should start back towards the house. Instead, she ambled along a trail of sorts that carried her beyond the St. James' country estate. Some time later she found herself lost in a dense patch of forest. After a minute or two of scanning the area, she slumped in acceptance. She felt as if her spirits were lost as well, cast to the wintry breeze with nothing to anchor them. The St. James' had been her last refuge. What would she do now? Where would she go?

Her shoes, inadequate for long walks, kept getting snared under tree roots and low-lying vines. After the third misstep, she kicked the troublesome things aside and continued on barefoot, savoring the sharp cold of the soil. She might have to spend the night in the woods since the approaching twilight left little chance of finding her way back. She kept walking out of futility rather than hope. Lord Linley would be more prone to bar the door than send a search party. A hysterical laugh bubbled up at the thought.

She stopped short. A clearing. A sizable clearing. It slanted downward into a pond. Well, it was more of a marsh, Eden deduced when she came nearer. Wind rustled through the trees, roughing the surface of the pond. Curious, she crept closer, her eyes drawn to the murky, moss-colored water. It called to her, some unseen thrall, luring her ever nearer...to the water's edge, where a grotesque thought entered her mind.

What if all the pain could be over? It would be easy,

quick, perhaps not painless, but a lesser torture in the grand scheme of things. The soggy ground oozed up between her toes. Eden continued to stare at the reflection in the water's surface; her hazel eyes were owlish and unfocused. Wisps of chestnut hair spilled out from the bun at her nape. To her mind, the lady in the pond resembled a tragic maiden caught in the cross-fire between two warring Gods.

Come home to us, Eden. We will take care of you.

Wait…Chestnut. Her hair should be blonde. She was knocked off-kilter. The ripples in the water's surface calmed as the wind died down. Something…someone, an eerie unfamiliar face…or vestige of a face took shape…a face not her own. In the bowels of the pond, Eden spied feminine features obscured by tentacle-d hair and the water's natural murkiness. That of a smaller, child-like image continuous almost with the pond lady hovered near. *Eden. Come with us.*

Eden did not know when or if she made a conscious decision to hurl herself in the water. She only became aware of herself when she inhaled a mouthful of viscous liquid. Her eyes stung terribly as she flailed around. She gained little headway towards the surface for all her frantic movements. Disoriented from lack of air, she grew tired. Her mass of skirts helped weigh her downwards to certain doom. Resigned, she ceased struggling and let herself sink, graceful almost, into oblivion. Her life did not pass before her. Eyes closed, arms outstretched, Eden's last conscious impression was that of a man…with olive-skin, black hair, and the oddest expression she could ever imagine.

* * *

In the thirty or so minutes since Cael had stalked off, Dominic plunged into silence. As he sat motionless on the couch between the desk and the hearth, he could sense that Ethan knew not what to say to him.

"Dom?"

Dominic smiled at the shortening of his name. Cael and Stephan started the trend. Before them, Ethan would have been scandalized at the mere notion of a nickname. Ethan was as English as the Queen.

"Do not apologize for him. Cael meant every word."

"Tell him the truth."

"Given the choice I think he'd prefer the illusion. Besides, his knowing will change nothing."

"But at least then he would understand."

"Perhaps *I* prefer he did not know." Dominic stood abruptly and faced his brother. "Ethan, as a physician it is in your nature to heal, to fix things. Your ability enhances that instinct. You helped to heal my body as much as possible, and whatever fragment of my soul that still remained. Be content. My spirit, however, is lost. Cael will learn that soon enough with no outside help. Then, he will turn his efforts to Stephan where they belong."

Ethan acquiesced for the moment, but Dominic got the distinct impression that this particular debate wasn't over.

"Where is Cael? He should have returned by now."

Dominic frowned, not liking his extended absence either. "I'll find him." He closed his eyes to concentrate on his brother's life force. It took him but a moment to locate him…or rather, *them*. "Cael is not alone. There is another entangled with him."

"Who?" Ethan stiffened.

"I don't know, Ethan. I cannot read minds."

"What are they doing? Does the other one seem hostile?"

"They are stationary. I doubt if the one with him is hostile. The essence is weak, fleeting almost." Dominic walked around the back of the couch. "Stay here and wait for me. If I do not reappear in ten minutes, assume something is wrong." With that, Dominic's corporal body shimmered from a solid form to a flicking hologram and finally to a two-dimensional likeness of Dominic before he winkled out of existence completely.

Dom reappeared in a crouched position at the edge of the clearing in the grove. Cautious not to expose his unorthodox mode of travel to anyone who might happen along, Dominic stood, glancing about to ensure there were no prying eyes. Once he was standing he spotted Cael. His brother emerged from the pond, sopping wet, with the unknown person in his arms. Dominic approached to help him exit the water.

"Ethan was worried. What happened?"

Cael panted as they placed the limp woman on the ground. Her head lulled to the side. Yards of clinging, algae-covered hair obscured her features. "Isn't it obvious what happened?"

"It's obvious you pulled her out of the pond. It is not obvious who she is or what she is doing here. Or how you happened upon her in the first place. This pond is at the south boarder of the property."

"Later, Dom." Cael bent over her ruined bodice to listen for a heartbeat. "Weak, but still beating."

"She is not breathing right." Dom voiced, watching the frail chest sputter like an engine running low of coal. Each breath sounded as if it might very well be her last.

"I am surprised she's breathing at all. I had a devil of a time fishing her out." Cael sat up, worry etched on his face. "It's a long walk back to the house."

"Ethan's waiting. I will take the woman with me." Dominic stood, centered himself and took a long deep breath. "When I tell you to, hand her to me."

Cael registered surprise, but he did not argue. He bent to lift the woman in his arms once more, and waited for the word from Dominic. He watched as his brother's continence shimmered and then began to winkle out of sight.

"*Cael.*"

He stepped forward and released his burden into his brother's transparent arms and stepped back.

Her head fell forward, burying her face in Dominic's disappearing chest.

* * *

Dominic shimmered into the study to apprise Ethan of the situation. "Cael is fine. Meet me in my suites." Satisfied he had imported all necessary information, he shimmered out again.

Breathing heavily, Dominic deposited the woman on the satin counterpane of his bed. Her weight was negligible, but piggybacking with her through the astral realm still took its toll. He began removing her soaking clothing. He went to remove her shoes, only to realize she wasn't wearing any. Odd. Next, he rolled her on her side to tackle the dress. He had gotten her down to her underthings when the door opened to admit Ethan. His brother had wisely procured several blankets and towels—from one of the servants, he assumed.

"What happened?" Ethan asked as Dominic stepped out of his way and allowed him to take charge.

"You'll have to ask Cael when he gets here. He fished her out of the marsh in the south grove."

Dominic hovered a few feet away, watching his brother with a mixture of awe and pride. He loved to see Ethan work. Ethan first stripped the woman of the last of her wet clothing, rolling her too and fro to make the task easier for them both. Her breathing did not improve, but grew more ragged and sporadic. By the time Ethan cast the last garment aside, she was twitching like a leaf in the wind. Ethan covered her nakedness with the blankets and rolled her onto her stomach so that her face hung off the edge of the bed.

"She swallowed something more substantial than water." He declared, as he pulled back the blanket to expose clammy bluish skin. "It's lodged in her throat."

Dominic could see the delicate bones of her shoulder

blades arch upward as Ethan used his hands to knead the area stiffly, thumping her on the back. A minute or so later, she gave a great rattling gag and coughed up a wad of gray-green moss. It landed with a soggy clunk on the floor. Delicate yet deep breathing sounds resumed, even and unhampered.

"Ahh…much better." Satisfied, Ethan pulled the blanket back up and shifted her to the middle of the bed. "Now, then, let's get that hair out of your way."

Dominic handed him the last of the towels. Ethan wiped and patted her face, removing the wet clumps of hair masking her features, and wrung the length of them with the towel to remove the excess water. Dominic staggered back a step when his gaze fell on her face.

Her ethereal beauty hit him like a punch in the stomach. Her skin was the tone and texture of fine porcelain…no, marble. Her damp hair, now semi-free of mud and algae, was the palest blonde he's ever seen. Even her fly-a-way brows were ashen. Her cheeks, he noted, grew pink, as if she were somehow aware of his scrutiny. He wondered what color her eyes were. The thought reminded him of his own atrocity and he reached up to make certain his spectacles were in place.

"She is quite insensible." Ethan, who had been watching his reaction with some interest, turned back to his patient as he spoke. "She could not have seen them even if you hadn't been wearing the spectacles."

"The woman will have to be removed to one of the guest chambers immediately." Dominic averted his gaze from the patient, not sure why he felt so unsettled by her. He'd gazed upon attractive women before. "I'll not have her stumbling about my private rooms."

"I was rather curious why you brought her here in the first place."

Not having a good explanation, Dom did not bother to make up a bad one. "Cael looked a bit winded. I think a few hours delay would be a good idea."

"I'll suggest it to him. Though I doubt he will accept my advice. The situation with Stephan needs to be handled straight away."

"Then demand a detailed explanation about the woman, and make sure you delay him. I would do so myself, but he wouldn't believe that I had any interest in her well-being."

He felt his brother's dubious expression leveled at him. Damn. Dom wondered if his reaction to the woman was that blaring. Cael, he could never fool, but he'd become skilled at sidestepping Ethan.

FOUR

The following morning found Dominic closeted off in his study with his grandmother and his late father's mousey solicitor.

"Conte Ambrosi—"

Dom bristled. "Please. I am either Dominic or Signori Ambrosi."

"Forgive me, Signori, but the estates may, if you wish, be placed in trust for your heirs, just as your father—"

"There will be no heirs."

"Yes, but are you *certain*—" The solicitor persisted. "—absolutely certain that you wish to transfer ownership and deeds to all your father's lands, the family estates, the vineyards, and the country province to your brother?"

The little toad of a man annoyed him. "Yes, as soon as it can be arranged." Dominic felt restless to have the business finished. He had other issues on his mind, the sodden beauty lodged in his bedchamber for one. "I have no idea of ever returning to Italy. Gideon was apprised of my wishes regarding our father's estates. He has agreed to assume all responsibilities. Since my father's title was set forth in such a way that it is inherited by all male heirs, there is no legal reason why the estates wouldn't be transferable as well. A portion of the profits from the vineyard and properties will be diverted to me. You may also allot a percentage of revenues into a trust of some kind for any future nieces and nephews, if you like. The rest I leave at Gideon's discretion."

Dominic left the man hunched over a desktop awash with papers, while he joined his grandmother by the mantel.

"Nonna, you could have handled this yourself and sent the final papers by messenger for my signature." Although Dominic preferred to avoid all matters Ambrosi, particularly ones that involved him traveling to the family estates in Italy, he admired his grandmothers' shrewdness. He oft times wished his father and uncle had inherited the trait.

"Si'." She agreed without hesitation. "But then I would not have had the pleasure of seeing my favorite grandson."

Nonna was not given to tender emotions. "And?" He prompted.

"Always such an intuitive child, you were." She smiled as if he pleased her in some small way. The smile faded, and she spoke next in a hushed tone. "A warning, Dominic. Fausto was quite put out at having his title and lands revoked by the Consulta Araldica. He's been up to some mischief of late. I cannot be certain this tirade of his will not extend to you. You are, after all, your father's son. Fausto's envy of Lucca knows no bounds…even in death. Like Cain and Abel, they are."

Dominic agreed with her on the last point. "I once heard Nonno say, 'If Lucca died tomorrow, Fausto will undoubtedly be livid because death would be just another deed his brother accomplished that he could not'."

"Aye." Nonna Ambrosi looked even more imposing than usual bedecked in the traditional mourner's bombazine and black crape. Black eyes, much like his father's, narrowed on him with intent. "Dominic, it is unwise to stay squirreled away in your English countryside.

You are needed at home. Gabriel is...ill again...and Gideon is beside himself. It is your duty as both the eldest son and the firstborn grandchild. The family is fragmented, vulnerable. Lillian saw to that with her ceaseless philandering. All will never be right with the Ambrosi legacy unless you take your rightful place at the head of the family."

"Gideon is Conte Ambrosi. Given the proper encouragement the tenants will learn to respect him as such. Very soon he will hold the legal and financial rights to the legacy. He is more than capable of rebuilding therefore I suggest you champion *him* as your savior."

"It is not his place. He merely assumes it in your absence."

"I will not return to Italy, Nonna." Dominic spoke with finality. "I did not return to bury the old Conte, and I will not return to become the new one."

"You could make up a bit for your mother's...peculiarities." Her taunt features reeked of distaste. "She spread her legs far and wide, daring to put the Ambrosi name to her ill-gotten brats."

Dominic's eyes hardened behind the spectacles. He met his grandmother's accusation without flinching. "She is not the first, nor last, woman to 'spread her legs' far and wide...and they have nothing like her excuse to absolve them."

"Stubborn Ox." She shrugged her age-bowed shoulders, conceding a momentary defeat. Ever the gracious loser, she put on a polite showing. "How are the...*others*? I hear from Gideon that the youngest lad is finishing up at University this year."

"Yes, Stephan is quite academic." Dominic cut off any further discussion with a curt 'ahem'. "Forgive me, Nonna, but there is a matter which demands my attention. I leave the finer points to you and the Signori."

Dominic bowed his respects and exited the room.

* * *

Eden awakened little by little, becoming aware of the rawness in her throat. She swallowed once to dislodge it, only to have the ache worsen. A cough formed deep in her throat and erupted from her chest, leaving a horrible throbbing sensation in its wake. Breathing was agony. Each breath seemed to trigger the start of a new coughing sensation, which worsened the throbbing in her chest. Muffled voices reached her through the haze of coughing, throbbing and breathing. She wondered to whom they belonged.

An intense wave of coughs seized her, jarring her awake…and rolling her over onto her side. A moment later, she felt cool hands on her cheek and arms restraining her with gentle pressure. After the worse had passed, the hands helped ease her into a sitting position with well-placed pillow-props.

"Thank you." Eden almost did not recognize the frail croak as her own voice. She blinked at the hovering gentleman, before taking quick stock of her surroundings. The nightshirt she wore was not her own, and from what she could tell was made for an above-average sized male. The great circular bed she occupied was not her own back in Boston nor was it the guest room at Reginald and Millie's. The room beyond seemed to blink back at her, equally curious at its unknown occupant. A large pine wardrobe loomed in one corner, while a paw-footed tub waited for an introduction on the opposite side of the room. The bed dipped as the dark-haired gentleman sat. She was glad not to have to crane her neck.

"Here," he cupped the back of her head and put a mug to her lips. "Take a sip. Your throat is on fire."

Eden wondered how he knew that, as she allowed herself several soothing swallows of the spicy-sweet elixir.

"How do you feel?" The dark-haired gentleman asked.

"Groggy, I-"

Eden started to answer when something stirred. Her eyes collided first with a floor-mounted avian roost adjacent the window. Then, she gasped as the olive-skinned Adonis uncoiled from the window seat into her line of sight. The gentleman at her side might as well have vanished, so arresting was the other's presence. His attire, complete with coat, matching waistcoat and trousers, conveyed a stiff formality belied by his lithe movements and unruly wavy locks. He remained silent, seeming content to impress upon her the knowledge of his existence. Tinted glasses obscured his eyes, but Eden still felt their piercing stare. Though she was sure she had never met the man, he was the one thing in the room acutely familiar to her.

"What is your name?"

Eden snapped back to the man at her side. "What?"

"Your name, do you remember it?"

"Yes." Her eyes darted back to the window seat before she identified herself. "Eden Prescott."

He smiled back at her with eyes that reminded her of warm chocolate. "Good to make your acquaintance Miss…or is it *Lady* Prescott?"

"Lady, however, I prefer *Miss*. I am American and unmarried." The silent one stirred at this revelation, but he neither spoke nor moved from his perch.

"Dr. Ethan Raine, and that is my brother Dominic Ambrosi. Aside from the sore throat and lead chest, how do you feel?"

Making a concerted effort to keep her eyes from straying, Eden did her best to describe the rung out feeling in her limbs. A well-placed growl from her stomach announced her hunger. When she glanced down at her hands, she was embarrassed to find them wrinkly and pale from her 'swim'…more pale than normal even for her.

She hadn't gained her weight back from the three-month bout of seasickness from the crossing and now she had nearly drowned. Cringing, she realized she must look ghastly. No wonder the silent one stared at her so. He probably had never seen a more pathetic creature in all his life.

* * *

His spectacles in place and the length of the room between them, Dominic watched Ethan tend to the woman. His thoughts ranged from the perverse to the profane. Despite the visceral reaction her presence claimed on his senses, even she was a welcome reprieve from his grandmother's dominating ways. Ahhh, hazel. Her eyes were hazel, he realized with a burning satisfaction he did not understand. If she knew the true direction of his thoughts then she would probably cringe.

* * *

"Do not worry." The doctor was saying. "I have already sent for a light soup. Now then, can you remember what happened? Were you alone? How did you land here?"

Her throat felt better, less scratchy, when she spoke. "Where is here?"

"My brother's country estate."

One quick glance, then Eden took a deep breath and launched into her story, her lungs not so heavy anymore. "I went for a walk on my cousin's grounds back of the house. I suppose it must border this estate. Perhaps you know him, Reginald St. James, Marquis of Linley. My cousin is…" She trailed off, not able to finish.

"I am familiar with the family name, yes. The wife recently died in childbirth. A physician friend of mine attended the…birth." The doctor paused awkwardly as if just realizing something. "Please allow me to convey my condolences on your loss."

"Thank you."

He eyed her, brow arched for her to continue.

"Eh…" Eden faltered, not sure how far she wanted to take her explanation. She wasn't sure she knew what happened to her at the pond or why she'd jumped in. "I, eh…lost my way and then dusk began to settle. The clearing seemed a god sent, but then I saw…a woman, in the water. She was drowning, I think."

The doctor exchanged a glance with the other one. Eden didn't know what to make of it since she saw neither man's expression. "I leapt in on impulse to save her."

"Can you swim?" The doctor asked bluntly. "Because from what we could ascertain, it did not appear so."

Eden donned a sheepish expression. Best to straddle the fence on this one, she decided. "Yes, but I am not a strong swimmer. I became disoriented, looking for her. My skirts weighed me down. I did not think to cast them off beforehand."

Her story must have sounded at least plausible because he nodded. "Well, I am glad my brother was present to attend you. It would have been a shame to lose one so young. May we contact St. James? He must be quite concerned for you."

Eden sighed. "I doubt Linley would care to be saddled with an ailing in-law who's existence he just became aware of two months ago. Besides which, I have already made plans to relocate to town as I am unmarried and now so is he."

"Your father and mother then?" He offered.

"Mama…" She averted her eyes and took another fortifying breath. "…died just before Michaelmas last year. A fever that lingered too long, the doctors said. Papa passed not two years before of an arrest of the heart. It was sudden."

"More distant relatives, an aunt or uncle perhaps?"

"There was a carriage accident last summer before mama took sick. My aunts…I do not know the particulars except to say that it was fatal for everyone involved."

"Oh dear."

The good doctor seemed perturbed by her plight. Eden sensed in him a compassionate man, given to great acts of kindness. His brother, her attention migrated back to the window seat, emanated power mingled with a sort of aloofness that set her on edge. A strange tension was building between them, since she first became aware of him. He felt it too, she knew. Why couldn't he at least speak? Seated there so still and mute, yet she sensed him tracking her every movement behind the tinted glass. He gave her the impression of a predator stalking the runt of the litter.

A faint knocking broke the thread of silence. "Yes, that will be Nell with your breakfast." With that the doctor stood from the bed. "We will leave you to dine and rest. And when you are ready, Nell will attend to your bath."

His brother took the cue and straightened from the window seat to follow him out as a nervous maid hovered with the tray.

Seized by an impulse, Eden addressed the silent one. "Ahem. Mr. Ambrosi."

He halted. She thought for a moment that he would ignore her and resume walking. Instead, he turned.

Seconds ticked by and Eden fumbled with her hands trying to think of something to say. Why had she called his name? Besides rabid curiosity and blind impulse.

"Thank you." She shifted her eyes to include Dr. Raine in her statement. "Thank you both for saving me."

Nothing. No smile. Nor did he remove the spectacles when he did speak. "Thank Ethan and Cael. I had no hand in it." With that, he resumed his exit.

His voice flowed over her like a hot breath. She almost sighed.

"Who is Cael?" She thought to ask just as he crossed the threshold. He continued out the door as if he hadn't heard.

So, naturally, Eden took up questioning the maid the second the door closed behind them. Eden deemed her

'Nervous' Nellie. She would certainly need a bath when Nellie finished feeding her. As much of the soup went down her nightshirt as went into her mouth. Eden feared the poor girl would faint.

"Is there a lady of the house?"

"No, Miss." Plop! Another spoonful of soup.

"Mr. Ambrosi, what manner of man is he?" Eden mopped up the damage with her napkin as she spoke.

"A strange one, for sure." Her voice lowered to a hush. "Keeps company with a hawk, fierce eyes and a nasty sharp beak. Talks more to it than any other."

"Mr. Ambrosi mentioned someone by the name of 'Cael'. Do you know him?"

"A sibling I think, Miss. Master Ambrosi has quite a few." Nellie's hand faltered. Eden's gown got doused with another spoonful of soup. This time, Nellie hurried to dab a napkin at the increasingly transparent cotton. "Sorry, Miss, but I shouldn't be telling ya private things about the master. He won't like it none. Dismissed three maids just last month for gossip-mongering and invading the restricted areas."

"Oh please, just one more question."

Her brow furrowed as if she longed to say no, but could not quite bring herself to deny her betters. "What is it you wish to know, Miss?"

"His eyes. What color are they?"

She shrugged. "Always wears the specs. Cook says his vision must be very poor; uses the hawk to see for him."

"But I haven't seen him with a bird."

"If you stay around long enough you will."

Then why wear *tinted* spectacles? Eden mused. She feigned a headache and let poor Nellie off the hook.

"Yes, Miss. I'll come up in an hour or so with warm water for a bath."

"No need, just show me where..." Eden scanned the room, frowning when she saw nothing.

"There is no bell pull." Nellie informed her. "The

master does not allow strangers in his private suite. Even us servants are allotted specific times and days to clean them."

"Is this the bed...er, the chamber I mean where Mr. Ambrosi sleeps?"

"I dare say it is, Miss."

* * *

"You seem unsettled by her."

"Weren't you?" Sans his spectacles, Dominic avoided his brother's gaze.

"Not over much."

He pivoted on the pianoforte seat to let his fingers flit over a familiar composition of Verdi's. His music room, like his bed, reflected non-traditional taste. The grand pianoforte occupied the central space in the room, and was bathed in direct sunlight from the circular glass section of ceiling. The rest of the room lay in shades of light and shadow, with no other windows or wall-mounted torches to illuminate the corners. The pianoforte served as a private island, a safe haven away from the darkness. The effect at night was even more dramatic.

"There are no undercurrents in the pond." Dominic informed his brother. "She should not have been in any danger of drowning."

"Yes, I know. Cael said she stood gazing in the clearing and then leapt in the water and sank like a stone."

"An attempted suicide."

"Most like. She has lost her entire family in the space of two seasons. Alone, the world can be a scary place. Awash with so much grief, death must have seemed like the perfect solution."

Dom eyed the other man askance, wondering if his brother knew just how well he identified with the woman's situation. There was a time when he would have gladly taken his own life if he thought it would have afforded him some peace.

"Let's not contact the Marquis just yet." Ethan continued. "At least not until Cael returns and he can assess her mental stability. She may well succeed the second go round."

"So, you think she will try again."

"Her situation has not changed. She is still alone and grieving."

"Whatever you think is best."

"She will have to remain here, for a time at least." He clarified, seeming to expect something.

Dominic shrugged, cutting his eyes to catch the reaction to his next words. "Send for Kathleen."

Ethan's brow rose. "*Three* houseguests inside of a week. Should we have the ballroom aired?"

He ignored his brother's wit and pivoted back to the musical piece in front of him. "Nonna was not invited. She will be leaving within the hour. And your wife is hardly a guest. She will serve a purpose. The woman is unmarried. She needs a chaperon and a diligent watchdog. I'll not have her harming herself under my roof." The mere thought of her coming to further harm put him in a tetchy mood. Dominic was anxious for her safety, annoyed with himself for caring, and angry at her for affecting him so. He was loathe to explain how or why his signature indifference, cultivated over a span of years, crumbled at the thought of one slip of a girl with sad hazel eyes and a name that literally meant heaven.

"You could always watch her yourself."

A wave of heat hit him at his brother's suggestion. Lascivious images exploded in his mind. A wall of silken white blond hair cascading down around naked alabaster skin as she stepped unawares from his nightshirt and into a waiting steam bath... Something broke open deep within him, some primal craving betrayed only by a staccato tick in his jaw.

"You've a queer sense of humor, Ethan."

His brother shrugged. "I will bring Kathleen with me tomorrow."

"Yes, and see to it that the woman is removed from my chamber and housed in one of the guest rooms."

FIVE

Eden had taken to bathing in the evenings before dinner. Now that her voice was back and she had more color in her cheeks, she was allowed out of bed and took dinner with the doctor and his wife in the dining hall. Mr. Ambrosi did not join them. In fact, Eden had not laid eyes on him in the three days since she'd awakened from her ordeal. He was avoiding her of course. The thought depressed her. She found herself longing to see him again. Each night at dinner she bathed and dressed as best she could under the circumstances. There weren't a lot of flattering options to employ with widow's weeds. Kathleen was gracious enough to procure the proper mourning attire for her. The wardrobe brimmed with black crape and bombazine.

Sitting in a steaming bath with her head lolling on the rim of the tub, Eden let her eyes drift closed. If he meant to avoid her for the duration of her stay, why didn't he simply send for the Marquis and have her removed. She was fully recovered. Even Dr. Raine ceased to treat her like a patient.

"Ya much too thin. Do they no' feed tha lasses in America?" Eden opened her eyes to find Dr. Raine's buxom, red-haired wife staring down at her. "'Tis no surprise ya are no' wed. Put some meat on those bones and you'll be beating tha lads off with a brick."

Kathleen tended toward bluntness. Eden learned quickly not to take offense.

"I haven't been at liberty to socialize much." The truth was, she'd never met a man she found more than passably interesting even before death and mourning limited her social engagements. Her thoughts flicked to Dominic Ambrosi. Until now, that is. There was something unnerving about him... and yet he still appealed to her.

"I know dis must be a difficult time but might I offer a word of advice."

She nodded as Kathleen lowered herself eye-level with Eden.

"Do no' grieve too long. Is no' healthy ta dwell upon death. And they would no' want dat for ya."

The older woman went on to relate her own experiences with tragedy. Settling into the steaming water, Eden bent her knees so that they stuck up out of the water and slid down to rest her neck back against the rim of the tub. Kathleen lectured about the evils and expectations of the world. Eden heard only a fraction of what she said, savoring her voice more than her words. She almost felt home again. Her mother and aunts had often attended her bath, to chat, gossip or impart cautionary advice.

* * *

Agitated, Dominic paced the length of his bedchamber. He could almost smell her. Two days had passed since she'd last occupied the room. He'd instructed the servants to discard the bedding and swab the chamber from floor to ceiling. Yet, he still picked up minute remnants of her essence in the room whenever he shimmered into the astral realm. The faint colors he'd first glimpsed with Cael had since blossomed into an intoxicating swirl of lavender and twirling violets immersed within evolving geometric patterns. Dominic felt the tug of her like a fish ensnared in a lure. He did his best to make himself scarce, but to no real end. She saturated his mind. What was she doing? How did she fare? He yearned to be near her. Unable to resist any longer, Dom shimmered into the astral plane of the universe.

The astral plane did not exist in normal time and space. Just as twilight marked the hazy time between day and night, the astral marked the shadowy realm between life and afterlife. The senses... sound, smell, touch, and taste were meaningless. Mind-sight defined reality. Before learning of the dangers of the astral realm, Dominic spent copious amounts of time there. The ability to disconnect from his corporeal body afforded him a measure of peace he never seemed able to achieve in the physical world. He'd once lost six months in the astral realm.

The passage of time was near impossible to quantify. There were no landmarks, no buildings, no ground, sky, water, animals, nor trees...only an infinite many body-less souls dotted the airless void. A year, an hour, a decade might past in the realm that time forgot. The traveler would be unawares and in danger of being permanently disconnected from the physical world. Dominic sojourned there when necessary and sometimes used the realm as a rapid mode of travel, but he was careful never to linger.

At the moment, Dom's jagged dance of dark and white light sought out Eden's alluring purple-violet vortex. He halted a short ways from where her essence hovered, watching the color patterns mingle in harmony with a second essence he recognized as his sister-in-law. Curious, Dom exited the astral world and slipped into invisibility. He stood just inside her bedchamber, present in both body and spirit, but not visible to either woman.

* * *

"Mama was afraid if we wrote to papa's parents in London of his death, they would descend upon us and take me away. My grandparents are powerful people from what I know of them and not at all happy to have their heir married to an American nobody." Eden paused in her oration. Her hands stilled in mid-plait and she turned her head slowly to scan the room.

"What is it, lass?" Kathleen followed her gaze, puzzled.

"Nothing. I just felt a...draft." Her brow furrowed as the 'draft' sent a prickling sensation over her skin. She jerked as a disturbing notion occurred to her. What if they were no longer alone? "Papa...and mama would always say that that was the reason they had made the choice to live in Boston, to avoid their controlling ways. Ironic it seems that in the end, mama begged me to seek refuge with them."

"How then did ya come ta be with tha St. James'?"

"I could not face turning up on their doorstep, begging for sympathies from two people I would not recognize if I stumbled over them. Instead, I threw myself on the mercy of Millie and Reginald." Unnerved still, Eden shivered and sunk lower in the tub.

"Is tha water cooling off, then? Let me see wat is keeping Nell."

"No, no, please. There is no need."

"Nonsense. We canna have ya catching a chill. One more ordeal might just finish ya, wee one." Allowing no further argument, Kathleen excused herself. Eden found herself alone... with the unseen conjuring of her mind.

It approached from the side of the bed, watching her as she drew herself into a tight ball and cowered so low that her nose hovered just above the waterline. It slowed the approach to a crawl. Why was it here? What did it want from her? The most terrifying question of all, what would it do once it reached her? Eden cringed as the presence stalked closer still. Every muscle in her body grew taunt with fear and dread. Inch by inch it came, feeding off her stark emotions and pinning her to the spot. Her breath hitched. Eyes wide and staring, stiff fingers clutched the sides of the porcelain tub…

When at last the thing reached the far edge of the tub, Eden opened her mouth to scream. The next instant she felt the gentle touch of …hands, reaching beneath the water, fingertips fluttering against her skin. They applied a soft pressure to the sole of her foot, in vague circular motions. The administrations were smooth, unhurried, and pleasant even. She rose a little, eyeing the foot in question, with a disbelieving hazel gaze. Her fear dissipated.

The presence pulled a little at her foot and she complied. He (it must be a 'he' she reasoned) set the right foot over the edge of the tub at the knee and stepped closer to grasp her left foot from beneath the water. She felt the brush of a body between her legs at the knee. Languid she became aware of an odd tingling blossom in the pit of her stomach. Eden allowed her left leg to be lifted high on the diagonal, unperturbed by the intimate view of her person this position gave the unseen him. Could a virtuous woman be ruined by a figment of her imagination?

She must be losing her mind. A sane woman had no cause to ask such questions. The fact that she conjured up a seduction-bent presence to raid her bath and do wicked things to her feet was probably proof enough of escalating madness.

Lulled into a sensation-seduced daze, Eden closed her eyes and slipped beneath the water's surface…lay with her torso flush against the bottom of the tub. Taking full advantage of the extra leverage, the hands slid further to kneed her calf with the same soft, soothing motions. The tingling in her stomach sharpened to a vague longing for something she could not name. Her hands clutched at the sides of the tub. This time the action born of yearning, not fear. Images of herself in a similar position flashed in her mind.

At first, they came as staccato flickers of her body. She was unclothed, but not in the bath...somewhere else. The second wave of images lingered longer, were clearer, like photographer's stills running one after the other to produce disjointed motion. She occupied a bed, her pale naked skin and flaxen hair at a drastic contrast to the ink-black sheets. Her head arched backward, hair lay fanning the pillow, her mouth open in a pose of sensual fusion of pleasure and pain. A dark figure loomed over her, his face hidden in shadows...

His chest bare, as broad as she was narrow, undulated above her. His voice moaned in what could only be described as ecstasy. "E—DEN..."

That voice! She recognized it even in her head. Eden shot up so fast the movement sent choppy waves splashing over the tub's edge. She sat ramrod straight breaking contact with her unseen molester, as she realized what the images likely represented...and with whom.

"Dominic."

And then, she was alone.

* * *

She sensed him. She'd known he was there the instant he'd materialized from the astral realm and cloaked himself. *Amazing.* Seeing Eden as he had imagined so often, languid in a scented bath, aroused him to the degree of pain. Touching her was a mistake, he knew it the second his fingertips brushed against the slight curvature behind her ankle. Temptation, once realized only intensified. The throbbing fullness between his legs only ached more, not less.

He froze when he heard the door of his music room open. He waited, watching as Ethan walked into the circle of light.

"Dom?" His brother eyed the empty pianoforte, almost as if he expected a response. But how could he? His

47

attention dotted along the black-lacquered surface following the tiny rainbows dancing in the light. "Dominic, I know you're in this room somewhere."

With a muffled curse, he uncloaked himself. "How the devil can you possibly know that?!"

Ethan stepped onto the raised area. Dom was seated on the bench with his head bowed over the keys, sans his spectacles. He did not look up.

"I know because you refract light when you're invisible. The next time you have a mind to avoid me, hide in a hall of mirrors."

"And where did you pick up that tidbit...Cael?"

The good doctor smiled, proud of himself. "He and I attended a lecture series a few months back. Physics is such a fascinating topic. I wonder now that I chose to study medicine."

"Why is he so damned anxious to explain away my... abnormalities... with science and natural law?"

"Perhaps, because you still think of them as abnormalities, while he thinks of them as characteristics that make you unique. He and I are in complete agreement on that front." His brother laid a reassuring hand on his shoulder as he spoke. "Do not isolate yourself so much and maybe you would see that you're just another person, born no better and certainly no worse than any other."

Frustrated and angry with himself, Dominic struck the keys with a fisted jab. The brief cacophony voiced the turmoil warring between his struggle for self-preservation and the new and overwhelming desire for intimate contact. "Tell me what you bloody well want and get out of here!"

"Is it such an annoyance conversing with your own brother?"

"Forgive me, Ethan." Dominic sighed. "I am not used to stumbling over so many people. I prefer solitude. You know that." His agitation had nothing to do with the doctor or his wife and everything to do with a certain blonde. How the bloody hell could she both *see* and *recognize* him? First *her*. Now Ethan, and probably Cael too. He was beginning to feel exposed, vulnerable to prying eyes...in his own sanctuary.

"It was not my intention to intrude but circumstances being what they were..." Ethan trailed off and began anew. "Actually, this might come as a relief. I came to tell you that I would be detained for several days in town. So, there will be one less person to despoil your peace."

"Ethan, do not go."

"You just said you were bothered by too many people milling around your house. I would be one less."

"Take Kathleen and the woman with you and there would be three less."

Ignoring Dominic's almost comical spite, he continued. "Our patient is—"

"*Your* patient."

"Our *guest* then."

"*Interloper* works best, I think." Dom said with an acid smile. "Now, what is this pressing matter in town?"

"House calls. Several of whom are long-standing patients."

"Put them off."

"I cannot put them off any longer. Plus, it might interest you to know that Cael is back in town with Stephan."

He swiveled around, surprise etched on his face. "How do you know that?"

"If you ever bothered to stir from your hidey-hole, you would know it too. Cael sent a message this morning."

Dominic had the decency to grimace before he snatched his face away. Ethan's serene expression hadn't changed in the brief moments when their eyes met. It never did. But then, Ethan was one of very few people whom he occasionally allowed to see him sans his spectacles.

"The boy is having a rough time of it, Dominic. Among the injured was a close friend. You might consider inviting him to stay."

"Stephan is rash and too excitable. He could learn a thing or two from Cael. Certainly more than I can teach him."

"He worships you. At least go see the lad."

"Perhaps." He made no promises. Dominic ran a clenched hand through his hair. He was on overload since the 'bath' earlier, and didn't know if he could handle another incident. With Stephan, nothing ever transpired without incident.

SIX

"Mr. Montgomery—"

"No sense puttin' on airs. 'Matthias' will do just fine. That's wot me friends call me."

The other man cocked a brow. "Rather presumptuous."

"Optimism is a necessary thing in me line of… work." Matthias sized up his newest off-the-books client. Foreign, most like. The gentleman did his level best at concealing the accent, but no dice. French maybe. Moneyed. The ruddy blush reeked of a soft gentleman, who over-indulged in fine wines, rich foods, and classy whores. He guessed by the tailored lay of his waistcoat and high-kick boots that he could roll the gent right now for a couple of hundred pounds at least. The stiff posture, bespoke a certain haughtiness. Probably thought himself too good to have dealin' with a lowborn proprietor of a paranormal asylum. The prig.

"An wot can I do for ya on this 'ere fine evening." In truth, it was an ungodly hour of the night. The sparse office area they occupied abutted a stone structure housing the inmates. A hum of activity, punctuated by the odd thump or bang, radiated from the asylum proper belying the hour. "I reckon you ain't 'ere to pay a penny and see the 'freak show'."

"Some other time perhaps."

The gentleman offered a half-smile at the notion. Intrigued, not horrified, Matthias noticed. He retained total composure even with the knowledge that the only thing protecting him from a hundred lunatics, many with 'abnormalities', was a blotchy, paint-bare wall. Good. Matthias found that encouraging. The more amenable his clients were to the seedier side of life, the more willing they were to pay to distance themselves from it.

"I've come on a rather delicate...family matter." He approached the subject with the same caution one might use if he were attempting to cross a bridge of questionable construction. "The problem is such that it requires an...impartial party, and your ...services...well that is to say, I have reason to believe that my late brother's heir...heirs, but that's neither here nor there."

Family affair, ha! Matthias knew his game; he saw it often enough. The sneaky bastard meant to poach his brother's inheritance by having the legitimate heirs declared insane. Not original, but effective, in his experience. If their situations were reversed, he'd probably give it a go as well.

"Their mother was a certifiable lunatic, you understand. The woman broke every natural law in the Good Book: bigamy, adultery, sorcery, and eventually suicide. She died an inmate at Bedlam. One of the younger sons has been on the path to madness for years...but we had hoped. Ah well."

"You wish my help shakin' the family tree 'til all the nuts fall out...that 'bout it?" Get on with it. Matthias grew tired of his charlatan act.

"Yes, and no. The oldest...eh...legitimate son is a recluse. No one's seen him for years. With my brother's passing, the title plus all adjoining properties and monies...the family legacy is being laid at the feet of a trio of madmen. And I will not stand for it."

His composure slipped, Matthias spied the twisted lip that revealed not concern for his nephews, but envy and hatred for their luck of birthright.

"That evil, lying...I will not stand idle while that bitch ruins the rest of the family the way she ruined my brother."

"So, wot is it ya require me to do Mr..."

"Ambrosi."

"Ambrosi, then." Ah, Italian.

"The younger two began exhibiting bizarre behaviors in early adulthood. They can wait. First, I want you to find my oldest nephew, Dominic Ambrosi, now Conte Ambrosi. He is here in England somewhere. Find him...he is stark raving mad at his advanced age. Find me the evidence first. And then I want him removed to a suitable facility in Italy, where he can be watched."

Fool, Matthias concluded. To play such a dangerous game was folly. One heir could have an accident or be discredited with relative ease...but three? Folly. But, who was he to turn away an easy mark.

"As ya wish." Matthias' eyes twinkled with malevolent greed. "'Tis the matter of—"

"No need to quibble. A handsome sum is yours upon the receipt of any damning evidence."

"Then, I'm at yer service."

SEVEN

Seated alone at a table fit for a party of thirty, Eden went through the motions of eating dinner only because she could ill-afford to skip a meal. She was relieved at not being forced to keep up pretense in front of the all-too-intuitive Kathleen. The doctor had departed for London, so no probing questions from that direction either. Dominic abstained as usual. And there were no footmen because their host preferred not to have people leering about while he ate. Since he never seemed to darken the dinning hall, Eden wondered why he cared who occupied the room.

Dominic. He became a virus in her mind, spreading until all her thoughts were infected with him. Even the strange...Hallucinations? Visualizations? She knew not what to call the oft disturbing bend her conscious mind seemed to lead her these days. Whatever they were, they were saturated by shades of Dominic. Dominic straddled above her spread-eagled body on a circular bed of black satin. Dominic standing over her in the bath, gasping her leg high in the air, with parted lips hovering millimeters from her wiggling, pinkish toes. Dominic writhing in agony and shame as some unseen force rent deep slashes across his flesh.

The latter image distressed her even though she knew it to be just more bizarre evidence of her declining lucidity. The strangest thing was, outside of the fleeting images and the unnatural circumstances that had provoked them, she felt sane and rational. But what if she wasn't? What if she were going soft in the head? How long before someone suspected, Dominic, the doctor, or both? Would they toddle her off to Newgate or worse yet, Bedlam?

* * *

Several days later…Determined to reclaim some measure of normalcy, Eden decided to take Kathleen's advice and discard her mourning clothes. Sporting a bright-colored, if voluminous day dress, she wandered about the second floor halls looking for a worthy subject to sketch. She adjusted the parchments and tin of charcoal under her arm as she strolled past another dull oil portrait and about the fifth podium-ed vase. All were much too commonplace to warrant an artist's attention. Twenty minutes later, lost and weary of banal art, lifeless tapestries and Spartan architecture, she headed for the third floor.

She stopped short when she rounded an unfamiliar corner. There stood a massive set of double doors, adorned with exquisite metal relief. A stained-wood plaque hung over the threshold. She couldn't read whatever language the words were written in, but the stark, black inscription evoked a note of warning. Probably, a promise of doom to the travelers who failed to heed the warning, which could only mean one thing…Behind these doors lay Dominic's private lair. She'd stake her life on it, and would probably have to if he caught her sneaking around the restricted wing. So then why did find herself pushing open the great doors.

She nearly jumped out of her skin when the hinges creaked. The door itself seemed to protest her entering.

Eden inhaled a courageous breath and skidded forward to take a bite of the forbidden fruit. The first thing that struck her was how different his domain was from the rest of the house. The room was large, but stark and empty. The walls bereft of art. The space naked of furniture. No rugs adorned the polished oak floors. No windows broke the monotony of walls. She deemed it 'the music room' because there was but one object present. A pianoforte.

Eden came closer to admire the instrument. The lacquered grand occupied a raised circular stage in the center of the room, hauntingly illuminated by a beveled glass window blinking down from the ceiling. Most of the rest of the room fell in shadow as the sun at the moment hung directly above. Eden envied the brilliantly contracting effect achieved by the light descending upon the ebony pianoforte in a perfect circle whilst leaving anything outside the central sphere chained in darkness. The scene was an artists' wild fantasy. She longed to sketch it at dawn…hmm, maybe twilight…no *midnight*. Tempting but with her appetite so wetted, Satan himself could not stop her from exploring further.

Sliding her hands along the length of each wall, she located a knob-less door in the wainscoting. Beyond it, she gasped. *Beautiful.* Hundreds, thousands surely, of books lined the five…no six walls in the hexagonal room. A second and even third layer of jam-packed shelves ran upwards to an impossibly high ceiling. No blinking eye gazed down at her though. Instead, diagonal rectangles of paned glass spanned the perimeter so that the window appeared to be one long diagonal stair-step that ascended one level with each side of the hexagon. This allowed the bookcases to exist undisrupted on all six sides and afforded the central reading area a unique panoramic distribution of sunlight. Eden imagined spending hours, days lounging in the radiance, reading the classics atop the ottoman, sketching admit the luscious-looking throw pillows dotting the rug-ed floor, dosing in an armchair before the fireplace.

Awe-struck, Eden abandoned any notion of leaving the room. She bypassed a lamp table without thought and stepped onto the rotary ladder, her bundle of sketching paraphernalia still clutched under an arm. Excited, she climbed up one-armed, wanting to get a glimpse of what sorts of treasures lay in the wealth of bound volumes. Who knew when she'd ever have another chance to visit.

She almost reached the third level—stopping to skim a title or two—when disaster struck. The bundle under her free arm slipped. Had she let the items fall to the floor, she would have been fine. They were just paper and chalk, after all. The fall couldn't have damaged them. But, she acted on reflex. She reached to 'save' them, upsetting her balance. Eden felt herself tilt backwards in slow motion, cognizant of impending disaster but unable to prevent it. A beat later, she knew the ominous weightlessness of freefall.

* * *

Dom stood in the dressing room adjoining his bedchamber, his hair still damp from the bath. Pants on but barefoot, he was buttoning his shirt. A stifled sound seized his attention. Like someone smothering a scream with a pillow, he thought. His body slid from corporeal to astral on instinct.

All other senses faded to naught, honing his mind-sight a hundredfold. He latched on to her at once. Distress morphed her usual rich purples and violets into a blinding shock of indigo. Dom melted his own life force with hers just before he exited the astral realm.

* * *

"Umph!" Eden landed hard on her back, atop something soft...in comparison to the hardwood floor, anyway. She did not remember anything on the floor near where the ladder attached to the shelf-wall. Only temporarily winded, Eden let out a long sigh of relief and began to test each limb for injuries. She gasped anew when the thing she had landed on also began to stir beneath her...enfolding her in solid, sinewy arms dusted with wiry black hairs.

"Oh..." Realizing that she'd landed on a 'who' and not a 'what', Eden scrambled even harder to extricate herself. "I'm so sorry. Are you—"

"Keep still." Dom ordered, shifting beneath her.

Dominic! She squirmed around to see for herself. She'd landed on the enigmatic host himself. Could her luck get any worse? Or better...she did not yet know which category to file their latest encounter under.

He made some adjustments to his position, removing her hindquarters from his groin. Plop! Her bottom slid ungracefully to the floor. He moved again, detangling their arms, flipping her forgotten hem down. She was able for the first time to turn fully around. The bun atop her crown pick that instant to crumble and unleash a cascade of hair over her face, but not before she caught a glimpse of his gapping shirt and lack of spectacles.

A mangled noise escaped her throat at what she saw, sickening patches of ruined olive flesh and scar tissue marred his chest and extended above his collarbone. Just like in her hallucinations...only, the damage was done to his back and shoulder blades. It couldn't be...real, could it? What happened? Who could have possibly done such a thing to him? Annoyed at having her view obstructed, Eden shoved at the blond mass, but in the few seconds it took to dislodge her hair he finished buttoning his shirt. Single-minded, she scooped forward, hands outstretched.

"Such terrible scars." The whispered words slipped from her lips. "What happened?" She reached for the collar of his shirt.

Dom jerked away from her as if he thought she meant him harm. Eden lifted her gaze from his torso to his face wanting to see him...and gauge his expression. Blast! The spectacles were back in place. Did he *never* forget the damned things? Why hadn't she thought to get a look at his eyes when they'd been unshielded? She frowned. Because she'd been too busy gaping at the heinous scars on his chest.

"Well-bred young ladies do not cavort alone with any man other than their husband." This he said whilst he stood, offering her a hand up as well. Damp clumps of hair spilled across his forehead and cheeks.

"And, well-bred gentleman do not shun their house guests for days on end." Eden ignored his hand and stood of her own accord...padding her dress and hair as best she could.

"Guest?" He mocked her. "Strange, I don't recall extending an invitation to...eh, what did you say your name was again?"

Not to be outwitted, Eden squared her stance, stepped closer and through down her name like a gauntlet. "You invited your brother and his wife and you shunned them too."

When he didn't retort immediately, Eden tilted an expectant brow at him. "Well?" She invited. Still he did not speak. She imagined he was sizing her up. He shuffled his feet a bit...ahhh, he didn't tower over her as he'd expected, she realized. She guessed him to be an inch or two above six feet, which meant he was only four or five inches taller.

"My brothers do not await an invitation to visit me." Dominic informed her. If he dipped his head a few inches he could catch her blush-colored lips with his own hard seeking mouth. It would be so easy, so satisfying. His breath quickened a beat.

"Ahem." He cleared his throat. "And Kathleen is here out of necessity, as a chaperon...and doing a rather poor job of it. Where the devil is she, anyway?"

He scanned the room as if he expected his sister-in-law

to burst forth from the woodwork. "How is it that you're loose to hurl yourself off of ladders and such?"

"There is no need to be rude. She wasn't feeling herself this morning." Eden pulled a face and gestured to the forgotten parchment. "I was bored and thought I'd find an interesting subject to sketch. Are you going to answer my question?"

"About?" His gaze settled back on her. The expression did not waver, that she could tell. Eden felt at a distinct disadvantage not being able to see his eyes.

"What was your question about, Ms. Prescott?"

Her focus lowered, to his now shirted-chest. Again, almost involuntarily, one hand edged upward, seeking yet hesitant to try for his collar. "The scars. Were you in the military? How did you—"

"There are no scars." He followed the path of her seeking hand with his shaded gaze.

"But I saw, just now when—"

"A trick of the light." He dismissed it with a flippancy that annoyed her.

He must think her stupid. "You, sir, are lying." Never in her wildest dreams would she have thought of calling anyone, much less her host, a liar when she'd been snug and cosseted back in Boston. But the new, reckless, world-weary Eden possessed a streak of boldness. And she took exception to his highbrow attitude. "I know what I saw."

"Do you, now…" The one daring brow, arched above his spectacles, was all the warning he gave. The next instant, buttons flew in all directions to join the forgotten sketching supplies scattered about, as lightening quick hands ripped the shirt open in one jerk.

There his stood, a sculptor's flawless muse, broad chest bared to show her ripped musculature and taut enticing stomach, giving way to a beckoning spiral of hairs…Eden's mouth dropped open. Each breath forced in and out through sheer will power. His was the body from her visions…sans one detail. There were no scars, just like he'd said. What impetus would cause her to imagine such a hideous thing? Wait, maybe...

She glazed up at his masked eyes. He seemed to read her thoughts. The shirt fell to his elbow and he turned gradually, never breaking eye contact with her until the very last moment when he dropped his head and sloped his shoulders for her inspection. With nothing to stop her, Eden approached, unbidden.

* * *

Dominic resisted the urge to bolt, and instead planted his bare feet in the rug. Seconds ticked by and he waited, wondering if she would do the one thing he both craved and feared. Ahhh...she touched him. Her gentle, jittery fingertips played along the tops of his shoulders, perhaps testing his willingness to accept the contact. Dom shuttered, savoring the pleasure of soft hands on his skin, and in the same moment trying to shut out the past pain. Her palms flattened out and slid lower, caressing his blades and lightly kneading the muscles there.

She had seen what she needed to see. He should stop her, step away. He couldn't. Not yet. He wanted a memory to store and relive for when she was gone and he was alone again. One luminous sunrise to blot out a lifelong eclipse. He brought his head up to rest his chin on his left shoulder, as she continued to explore him.

Her hands curled, possessively, around his torso to flit over his pecs and down to his stomach. He nearly relinquished control amid the sea of mounding arousal. He must compose himself...at least enough to stop her. *Impossible.* His breath hitched as he felt the stirrings of a new and aching need, soon to tent his pants. *No...*Dominic pulled the scattered fragments of his self-control together, and stepped sharply forward out of her grasp. He jerked the linen back over his body in an ominous gesture. He did not face her, merely spoke over his shoulder in profile.

"Leave." The word hung in the air like a noose. "*Now.*"

"The house?"

"My library, my...space. Never invade it again." He spoke in clipped, warning tones.

Enthralled and confused alike by his mercurial mood, Eden stared with searching hazel eyes. "Are the doctor and your other brother allowed to visit your space?"

"You are not my brother." He snapped, breathing several times before he spoke again. "I come here to be alone...find peace. You're an intruder and I will treat you as such."

"Alright." She would go, but not before she left him with something to think about. Coming forward, she stood on her tiptoes and murmured directly in his ear. "I know that was you, Dominic...in my bath the other day."

He stiffened.

"If you don't want me invading your space, then stay out of mine."

* * *

Good night! What had possessed her to say such a thing...goad him almost. What impulse propelled her to touch him...molest his person so liberally, and enjoy it *so thoroughly*, heaven help her. Even their verbal sparring held a certain amount of thrill and enjoyment. Dominic Ambrosi, for all his insolence, moodiness, and secrecy, proved to be by far the most interesting man Eden had ever met. And he brought out a side of herself that she never knew existed and wasn't quite sure she liked. She perched in front of the vanity, running a brush absently through her flaxen hair. For once she was grateful her mama and papa weren't here to witness her...make a cake of herself. Or a wanton, more like.

Another thing she just could not wrap her mind around, the scars. "I *know* I saw them." They were there in the visions, well one of them anyway. In the other vision, with her and Dominic in *flagrante delicto*, his torso front and back had shone smooth.

"Come to think of it—" She stopped mid-stroke, replaying the entire library interlude over and over in her mind, picking up new clues with each re-do. How did he happen along just as she lost her footing? Why hadn't her landing atop him harmed him? Winded him even? He must have entered at the very second she fell to be standing at that exact spot when she came tumbling off the ladder. Blast! Why couldn't she think of these things at the most opportune time? Now she'd never know…no way could she bring the incident up in the future. Judging from the end of the conversation it did not appear as though he would be conversing with her again any time soon.

EIGHT

Normally, Dominic would have shimmered to town. Cael was one of few people whose essence he could track to very specific locations. It wouldn't do to attempt astral travel with so many wild emotions. Plus, he needed a cooling off period before he faced his brother. Otherwise Cael would notice his upheaval, and knowing him, ask questions Dominic did not want to answer or rather had no answer for. So, he instructed the coachman to saddle up one of the greys. Dominic road the beast with vigor and did not stop until he reached Southwart, a semi-seedy district south of the Thames where Cael had chosen to set himself up professionally.

The austere facade lay nettled in a square with several other fledgling trade stores, including thankfully a livery stable. Beyond the square lurked a dense wasteland of decaying riverside warehouses, intermingled with teaming slums, and the occasional pub or house of ill repute. The air writhed with a chill of eager misery, ready to swallow whatever unfortunate soul lurking near enough to tempt fate. Dockworkers, ladies of the night, beggars and pickpockets, young and old alike, filled out the canvas. Dominic abhorred the place at night, when one was rarely able to take two steps without enduring solicitations of one vice or another.

Later afternoon was settling into evening when Dominic housed his mount at the livery and strode the scant distance to his destination. Cael greeted him at the door.

"Dominic. This is a surprise." He ushered him inside. "What brings you to town? And during the season."

Dom shrugged, noncommittal. He took a haphazard turn about the serviceable room. Along the way, he eyed the certificates and licenses adoring otherwise bare walls, more interested in appearing nonchalant then the framed medical credentials. Cael followed him as he meandered about, until Dom stopped stalling and came to roost on the desk's visitor chair. His brother paused, standing beside his chair. Dominic felt the all-seeing amber eyes watching him, no doubt trying to size up what had drove him from his haven in the country.

"Are you sure more pressing matters didn't prompt this…eh, visit?"

"I'm not one of your mental cases, Cael."

"Sorry, old habit." He ceased the scrutiny and sat opposite him behind the folder-piled desk. "It's just that you're not a social butterfly. So, when you turn up here for no obvious reason and wander around my office like you need a road map to find the chair-"

Dom shifted in his seat. "Ahem, Ethan mentioned that you and Stephan had returned to town."

"Yes, two days ago." He confirmed with a nod. "I wondered when you did not accompany him."

"How is Stephan?"

"Ahh…as well as can be expected." Cael tried for a weak smile. "He is no more fond of my analyzing ways than you are."

"There shouldn't be any lingering problems with the University. I instructed Renfred to settle a very sizable donation on their redevelopment fund, care of the illustrious Conte Ambrosi. The Ambrosi name seems to have doubled in impact and importance since my rise to peerage. Even hermitic foreign nobles are all the rage these days."

Frustrated hands mangled dark blonde locks. "I am more worried about how the incident is affecting Stephan. He will not discuss it." The restless movement and bleary eyes echoed a thread of uselessness and despair. "There is an enormous amount of pain and guilt he is concealing. Too much, I fear."

Dom frowned. Despite always being at odds with each other, he did not like to see Cael so defeated and unlike himself. "Perhaps the season will distract him." He suggested, but he knew as soon as the meaningless words left his mouth that they were best left unsaid.

"A young man of Stephan's intelligence and depth will not be mollified by a few dances and a tryst with some silly, round-heeled debutant."

Cael always did wield the truth like a sword. "No, I suppose not."

Dom stumbled awkwardly in their reversed roles. Cael did the cajoling and advice-giving and Dom shot him down. That was their long-standing routine.

"My biggest fear is that there is another cause for his guilt, something we don't know."

"Perhaps, I could be of service." An idea alit his mind...of mutually beneficial design. "Ethan mentioned something before he left. About me, maybe hosting Stephan for a few days in the country. I don't know how much good it will do. I am not one for exposition—"

"Come again?" Liquid amber eyes burned a hole in him.

"Well, don't look so aghast." It somehow piqued Dominic to spy his brother's mouth hanging open. "You're gaping for all the world like I just eloped to the Orient with a peg-legged actress."

He blinked. "Forgive me, Dom. It's just...never mind."

Shaking his head, he closed the book on the subject. "I've been meaning to visit myself. How is the patient?"

Exasperation clashed with raw desire whenever he thought of her. "Back on her feet...and too much underfoot. Ethan is delaying her leaving so you may assess her state of mind. He's mentioned her situation, I'm sure."

"Yes. A string of recent tragedies left her with no family."

"Ethan and I agree. The dip in the pond amounts to a suicide attempt."

Cael nodded, resolute. "Survivor's guilt. It drives some to take their own lives. I have seen similar cases with patients who have lost all to scarlet fever."

"So, she is not altogether well?"

"I'll not know that until I speak with her first hand, but yes, there is a possibility that she still harbors unhealthy thoughts."

"Ethan thinks she will attempt to harm herself again." Urgency heightened Dominic's words. "Earlier today, she threw herself off a ladder in my library."

"You saw her jump?"

"No. I broke the fall."

"I've been in your library, Dom." Amusement flittered across Cael's face for the first time. "Leaping from the shelves is not sufficient enough for suicide. A broken leg, perhaps."

"Broken neck, more like." He muttered.

"She probably just lost her balance. What was she doing there anyway?"

"Sketching, she said." Dominic admitted, with some reluctance. "There was chalk and parchment scattered about."

His brother shrugged. "Sounds reasonable enough."

"Kathleen is a poor watchdog." Dominic, eaten with a sudden agitation, stood from the chair, and paced about the office. "I cannot be everywhere at once. Ethan has run off to handhold with rheumatism-ed old biddies. I haven't the fortitude to deal with her, Cael. You must come immediately or send Stephan."

"She must be quite a handful." Amused in earnest at Dominic's harassment, Cael grinned. "I promise to drop in soon. I would have before now, but this thing with Stephan...*and* I've been looking into those two characters from that queer lecture we attended a couple of months back."

Dominic froze. Shocked into stillness. "Why would you—"

"Greyson somehow got wind of the incident at the University. He is resourceful and well-connected. He contacted me, regarding Stephan."

"Contacted you, how?"

"Wrangled an introduction from a mutual acquaintance at a social I attended."

Dom scoffed. "And you wonder why I abhor cavorting in the ton."

"He was quite polite actually." Cael reflected. "Knew his science and seemed to want to help."

"What did you tell him?"

"Nothing. I knew little about him save for what I learned at the lecture and what he told me for himself."

"But?" Dominic braced himself.

"I think cultivating a relationship with him could benefit Stephan. There is no predicting how his newfound capabilities are affecting his mind. And Greyson seems to have a genuine interest in severing the link between adeptness and mental instability."

"Adeptness?"

"Greyson's terminology. *Adepts* are people gifted with psychic abilities, like yourself. *Adeptness* is the abilities themselves. According to Greyson, control is the key to side-stepping the psychological and emotional damage that wielding such enormous amounts of psi energy inflicts on the mind." Cael hurried on in fascinated prattle. "I also discovered rumors that he runs a very queer sort of household."

"What of his background?" Dominic inquired, suspicious but considering. He himself ran what could be construed as a 'queer sort of household'.

"I found nothing sordid or questionable. He's awash in trade-wealth, with no living relatives. Savvy investments perhaps, since no apparent family business exists, here or in The States. He's respected in the scientific arena and among the ton, with the normal sprinkling of highball enemies and well-connected friends. Several peers sponsor his research activities. And he is on the board of social reform."

"Tell me more about this household of his."

"I couldn't find out much. Just that it's a sort of haven for social outcasts…according to the rumor mill, mind you. I haven't the chance to—"

"I've heard enough." Dominic silenced further discussion. "As I suspected, Greyson is dangerous. He isn't to come within a mile of Stephan."

"Dom…"

"Stephan is intelligent, stable, and grounded in reality…if a bit volatile. His sanity is *not* in question, and I will not have him poked and prodded by some quack bent on giving him a complex."

"He accidentally *maimed* his closest friend. He has a complex already—as do you, I might add. Is that how yours came about, a *quack* like Greyson or myself?" Cael again donned his analyzing mien. "You never share about your early life, Dom. Why is that?"

He sidestepped the issue like a puddle in the road. "I have lived with…adeptness—as he calls it—since adolescence and I still possess my full facilities. Stephan will adapt as I have."

Cael grimaced. "I wouldn't wish your method of adapting on him."

"I am sane." Dom countered flatly.

"And paranoid of encroaching madness."

"A legitimate concern, considering our origins."

"No." Cael stood and walked around the desk so that they were eye to shaded eye. "Being concerned is not the same as living the life of an exiled monk, nor is it healthy."

"*Discretion*, not exile." Dom argued. "Protecting myself and my brothers from public ridicule and accusations of heresy—"

"By the by, how is Gabriel?" Cael made no attempt at tact or subtlety. "Did *adapting* serve him well?"

Cael hit his mark. Dominic's chest caved; the words impacted him like an arrow to the heart.

NINE

For an instant, the image staring back at her from the mirror was not her own, but that of a beguilingly beautiful woman with obsidian eyes and a glossy mane of hair framing the visage. Her mouth twisted into a cruel smile as if she enjoyed a jest at Eden's expense. Eden sighed, another nameless specter to taunt her. The lady in the mirror winkled away into her own frowning image.

Just as she was about to turn away from the mirror, a fleck of something caught her notice. She shifted a handful of blonde tresses and leaned in closer. Poking through the strands, she picked out several dark aggregates marring her ashen mane. How odd. Dismissing it, she quickly twisted her hair around itself and secured the knot atop her crown.

Eden abandoned the vanity table. The same too-loose dress from her earlier jaunt tangled about her legs as she moved. The room gave her a creepy awareness of sorts. She'd found it spotless upon her return...bed made, vanity organized, fresh flowers hung in the window ledge, chamber pot emptied. Yet, she hadn't seen Nell or any other maid or manservant since the previous evening, and evening had nearly rolled around again. Apparently, Dominic's dislike of underlings lurking and spreading

71

gossip extended to the entire house, not just his quarters.

How can he stand it? The isolation. The death-like silence. She felt trapped inside her own mind, with naught but empty space and echoes ringing in her ears. It clawed at her insides like hunger pains in her stomach. Her heart craved contact, companionship, and love. A softly spoken word to a friend. A hearty chuckle between siblings. A warm hug from a lover. Sound, movement...Something. Anything... to ensure her grief hadn't crushed her spirit and cut her off from the world...and any hope of happiness.

On the edge of screaming just to hear a live voice and fearful of another vexing vision assailing her, Eden quit the room in haste and went searching for Kathleen. Armed with a knap sack brimming with sketching materials, she found the pretty redhead dosing before the fire in the second floor study with a half-eaten plate of sweets tilting off her lap. Eden removed the plate and set it aside, smiling at the cozy picture Kathleen made. Hmph. The good doctor probably did not know it yet, but he would be welcoming a little stranger before the end of the year. Sleepiness, increased appetite, and she never saw Kathleen ahead of ten in the morning. Having attended her cousin Millie, Eden recognized the signs.

"Kathleen?" She nudged softly.

"Hmm..."

"Forgive me for waking you, but I was wondering if you would care to take a walk with me?"

Kathleen stirred, rubbing sleepy eyes. "Wat of dinner?"

Eden bit back a grin. "I thought we could have a late supper. Otherwise, I'll loose the light."

"Oh." The redhead un-tucked her feet, ambled upwards, and straighten her skirts. "Aye, I suppose a wee stroll might do us both some good. Let's be off then."

Impulsively, Eden nipped forward to hug her as she'd done so many times to her aunts whenever they caved to her requests. "Thank you, so much. The country is so lovely and I've been cooped up much too long."

"Poor lass." Kathleen gave her a pat on the shoulder. "Come along and let's put some roses on those cheeks. And ya really must insist Dominic hire a true lady's maid. Forgive me for saying so, but such lovely hair is shamed by dat wash-woman's knot."

Eden wondered that Kathleen thought her in any position to 'insist' Dominic do anything much less procure her an exclusive maid. Perhaps she'd broach the matter with the doctor…if he returned. It *would* be nice to look the part of a marriage-minded maiden again.

* * *

On a well-marked path centuried on either side by mammoth trees, Kathleen and Eden approached the ivy-hung gazebo beckoning in the distance. The skies shone a happy blue, while the wind kissed their skin with welcoming breath.

"Would you mind terribly posing for me when we reach the gazebo?" Eden shot her companion a shy smile.

"An honor, t'would be."

They continued in a comfortable silence, punctuated by lyrical birdsong and trilling dragonflies flitting through the trees. At the gazebo, Eden positioned Kathleen in a seated repose, with the dense green forest in the backdrop so that the waning sunlight set her flaming red hair ablaze with highlights. She arranged herself and her chalks and charcoals on the opposite bench. Parchment poised on one raised knee, eyes narrowed on her subject, Eden stroked across the page with form-defining lines and contours. It felt good to be sketching again.

When Kathleen reached to massage her neck, and then snatched her hand away, Eden knew a moment of guilt. "There is no need to sit as still as a statue. Just so long as you hold the general position."

"Oh bless ya, I thought me back would snap soon."

"Kathleen." One hand darted to and fro on the paper, making a line here, a shadow there while the other held the parchment steady. Eden's artist's eye flitted from her subject to the burgeoning portrait as she spoke. "Tell me something about Dominic."

"If I can, wee one."

"Why does he always wear the spectacles? Have you ever seen him without them?"

"Oh dear me, no." Kathleen chuckled as if the thought were ludicrous. "Ethan tells me his eyes are light sensitive. I donno believe him at first, but I canna think of another reason ta hide them...so perhaps 'tis true."

"Has your husband seen them?"

"Certainly."

"They are close, then."

"Aye. So much so dat I think Dominic resented me a wee bit when Ethan and I were wed. In time, he realized he had naught ta fear of me betraying him or taking Ethan away. He's quite considerate nowadays."

Eden nodded, while adding a longer shadow to the background foliage. "So he isn't always this cloistered. He's circling the wagons because of me."

"Donno take it ta heart." The conversation eased into a reluctant seriousness. "Dominic is 'no given ta trusting anything unfamiliar ta him, particularly people. His early life was... difficult...and it has shaped tha man dat he is."

"How so?" Anxious for more answers but mindful that she probably wouldn't get them if she appeared too eager, Eden forced herself to maintain blithe movements and mannerisms.

"I..." Kathleen hesitated. "I canna say exactly. 'Tis no' me story ta tell. Be patient, lass. All things reveal themselves in time."

Disappointed and intrigued alike, Eden let her shoulders sag. "What about the other brothers? Nell says they are quite numerous."

"Aye, a brood of six, there is. My Ethan is tha oldest.

You'll likely meet Cael and Stephan before long."

"Are they all...like Dominic? I mean, your husband seems well-adjusted."

Kathleen laughed on a sigh. "My Ethan, bless him, was 'no tha man he is today when we first met. He was 'no tha same as Dominic, but just as much a victim is many ways. Dom, he bore tha brunt, but none escaped unscathed. Now then, enough of dis talk."

* * *

Dominic stood with his back to his brother.

"Dom?" Cael repeated, softer tone, exuding genuine concern. "How *is* Gabriel coping?"

"Badly. He dreams constantly now. Gideon is beside himself." Dominic silently cursed Cael's uncanny ability to read people and the situations around him, particular himself. "How did you know?"

"Ah, you look tired. Been spending a lot of time in the astral realm lately, monitoring his life force, I gather."

Dom conceded with a nod. "Patients must find that all-knowing thing you do infuriating."

"Actually many of them profess to find it comforting...not being forced to string together words to express their misery. In this case—"

"Is that how...you think of me?" Dom spoke, hesitant, whispering as if he were afraid or ashamed to voice the thought. A shaky hand hovered over his face and finally stripped his eyes of the specs. He turned. "Of us? Gideon, Gabriel and I. Are we as so many head-cases...a mass of problems to be...worked through and solved...or abandoned as hopeless and left to self-destruct."

"No, Dominic. Never that." Cael stared at his brother, humbled.

Dom forced himself to hold his brother's gaze, seeing a virtual torment of emotion darken his familiar amber eyes. Eyes that he rarely saw unhindered by shaded glass.

"I think of you as reflections of myself, whom I will never allow to self-destruct." He admitted. "Dominic, I've never told you this, but I often wonder what sort of man I would have become if I'd had…an indifferent up-bringing. I see a lot of myself in you."

Dom nodded his understanding and donned his spectacles once more. He ducked his head momentarily, gathered his strength, tucking the little boy back into that tiny crawlspace in his mind where he'd be safe from the scrutiny of a harsh outside world. "Ahem. Gabriel's ability is more a curse than any of us have had to endure."

"We don't yet know the extent or context of Stephan's ability." Cael reminded. "Forgive me for asking, Dom, but why haven't you gone to Italy? If not for Lucca than surely for Gabriel's sake."

"I…can't." Too many ghosts lurked there to haunt him. "Gideon will alert me if my presence there becomes…imperative."

He nodded. "Gabriel aside, it is absolutely necessary that Stephan master his ability. English society is not so forgiving of those with mental illness."

Dom exhaled when he didn't push. For once, Cael seemed to accept that there were certain things he just wasn't ready to voice.

"Paranormal asylums have begun to emerge, born of fear and ignorance, the likes of which are run by cruel opportunistic charlatans like Matthias Montgomery. That abomination of his—"

A sharp rap stilled the conversation. Both brothers' attention swiveled to the door.

Dom arched a brow above the shaded lens. "A client?"

"No one this late. I was about to close up for the evening when you arrived." Nevertheless, Cael started for the door. "Dom, if you would make yourself scarce." Over his shoulder, he gestured for him to astral away.

"I'm not leaving." Dominic threw a suspicious frown at the shadow lurking in the bottom of the doorframe.

"*Dom.*"

"I said *no*, Cael." A warning note threaded his tone.

"I'm a doctor." Cael insisted.

"Yes, I know," He snapped, "For people touched in the head. Any one of whom could be dangerously unstable-"

"Dominic *please*. My clients are not dangerous, but they are highly sensitive. I have cultivated an air of reassurance and anonymity. *You* of all people should understand that. They will not speak with a witness present. Why else would I have my office so far removed from polite society?"

"Fine." He conceded, with a chaser. "But I will know if something's off."

His brother fingered the knob just as Dominic flickered into his astral self.

TEN

Wind blown and oddly content, Eden strolled along side a woman she grew to like more and more with each passing day. Waning light and a nippy breeze quickened her steps. She did not wish Kathleen to catch a chill, especially in her delicate state. The surrounding trees leveled thick shadows upon the twosome. The end or rather beginning of the path, spilled into a grandiose clearing back of the main house with the dormitory-like servant's quarters set off from the west side a hundred yards or so. Twilight loomed large, playing tricks on the eyes. But Eden could have sworn she glimpsed a figure dart to the right side of the house...where the first floor study opened out onto an enclosed veranda walled with fog-grey cobblestone.

"Kathleen—" Eden could scarcely make out the older woman's frown.

"Aye, I saw." She halted mid-ways the clearing.

"A servant?" Eden went still beside her.

Kathleen was quick to despoil the theory. "They enter and exit through tha west wing, lass. From tha kitchens, leads directly ta tha boarding house there on tha left. Tha grounds-men have likely retired for tha night, and t'would be no need for any maid or footman ta be lurking thereabouts."

"Who then?"

"I fear 'tis some sticky-fingered bandit aiming ta snatch a few trinkets. So rarely Dominic is in town. Could 'no resist."

"Renfred." Alarmed, Eden looked to the servant's quarters, a hand tightening instinctively around the knapsack over her shoulder. "He will know what to do."

"Aye." Kathleen gave a sharp nod. "You fetch Renfred ta do tha talking...and I'll fetch dat brawny groom ta put some steel behind tha words."

Eden struck out for the west wing of the house, thinking to circle back to the front facade, enter and warn the butler. Kathleen followed, and pivoted off to the stables located above the boarding house on the west side.

* * *

This supposedly eccentric nephew, though reclusive, had not been particularly difficult to locate...his estate anyway Matthias thought. Information, on the other hand, was proving difficult to come by. His first approach, pay a loose-lipped local to spill any juicy tidbits, but he'd come up against a conspiracy of silence. The scant smear of servants who weren't sequestered on the estate proper had clamped tighter than a deaf mute. And not a soul in the village and the surrounding area knew heads nor tails of the *blind conte,* who used a falcon as his eyes. No pictures. No portraits. Not even a descent description of the man. He'd had no choice but to sneak onto the grounds and ferret out a stray gardener or disgruntled maid to bribe.

Also...Fausto hadn't mentioned anything about his nephew being blind. Why? Not that he suffered any attack of conscious about falsely committing a blind man...might make his job a touch less troublesome, actually. Blind or naught, the lucky bastard would get no sympathy from him. To his thinking, what good was a weakness if one couldn't exploit it?

"Country gent must be flush wit the Queen's own coffers." Matthias cursed the fates beneath his breath as he shuffled along the palatial country estate.

The woman stumbled into him as he ambled out of the darkness just as she rounded the side of the house. Even in the meager light, Matthias realized his good fortune. Greedy eyes traveled down her person, taking stock of the prey. A live one. Comely enough and fragile to boot. Perfect.

"Pardon me, good woman." A voice gravel deep and razor sharp greeted her. "You be the lady of the house?"

* * *

Face to face with the intruder, Eden tasted panic. Mouth dry, throat poised to scream, she eased away from his person. His outward politeness unnerved her.

She considered her options. If she ran and he decided to give chase, he'd over take her for sure. But if she gathered her wits about her, she could stall the intruder until Kathleen or Renfred came searching for her. Giving him a good once over for the first time, she noted that he hadn't moved to pursue her, nor did he appeared to have a weapon. Of course, should the barrel-chested man attack, she'd be no match for his strength or thickness.

"Eh...sir. I—"

At that moment Kathleen's buxom frame came bounding around the side of the house. She stopped short at the scene and then immediately took up a protective stance beside her. Eden sighed relief. "Sir, 'tis a private estate and tha owner will 'no be pleased at dis intrusion."

"You be da lady of the house, then?"

"Aye, at tha moment." She replied, indignant, her chin nudged upward. Doing her damnedest to trade on intimidation alone Eden realized. "Who are ya?"

"Matthias Montgomery, Ma'am. Formerly of Bow

Street, and I runs the Asylum, St. Ciaran Isis. Been gettin' reports of certain goings-on. Queer sort of 'appenings, strange folks about the place, maybe wot need me services. I come to investigate."

Eden bucked at the mention of madness, helpless to contain the tremor of terror his words induced. Was this why Dominic had departed so abruptly? To summon the *handlers* to come take her away.

"Is dat so?" Kathleen huffed, hands on amble hips. Her flame hair paled in comparison to the venom she spewed. "Is dis how ya investigate then? Lurking about tha bushes, scaring tha blazes out of tha women folk? A pox on ya, sir."

"Loonies lurking about are a public nuisance, Mylady. Danger to themselves and those around 'em." He cast a leering smile over Kathleen's heaving busoms, before shooting a derisive scoff at Eden's softer assets. "They must be dealt wit...one way or another."

"Bah!" She dismissed him. "Get out of 'ere before I summon a footman ta learn ya better manners."

* * *

Eden! Her name was a scream in his mind. Something, some*one* most like, caused her distress. Her suffering pained him like a festering wound or a hungry beast gnawing at his flesh with an insatiable appetite. He hadn't needed to track her. Gossamer violet tinsel still saturated him from being intermingled with her earlier.

Dominic hovered in the timeless black void, infinity's abyss, populated by disembodied souls more numerous than grains of sand on the beach. Mystical, evocative, deceptively alluring, the astral realm was a drug for the mind. While the normal human senses dulled to the point of non-existence, thoughts and emotions were conversely intensified. As if the enhancement of one compensated for the loss of the other. Whatever sentiment a person happened to be experiencing, one's essence experienced a hundredfold.

Dom struggled against a tiny fear exaggerated to nightmarish proportions. His urge to go to her, to protect her...shield her, bodily if necessary, nagged at him. But he would not leave Cael at the mercy of some unrealized threat. Torn, nearly in two, he willed himself calm and steady.

At such a dangerous level of emotional overload, Dominic knew he wouldn't be able to restrain himself for long. He would be forced to either exit the astral and abandon Eden altogether or stay and track both hers and Cael's essence at once. Parallel tracking was draining. He could only take on two people at once and for very short periods of time.

If it were possible to sweat on the astral, his essence would be slick. The first burst of motion alleviated the sensation; giving way to the impression of walking against gale force wind. The twofold effort he extended made astral traveling that much slower. Pausing, he concentrated on Cael's essence alone to give his mind a break. All appeared well with him and the other one. He re-assumed his burden and tracked closer to her. In the eternity of emptiness that seemed to separate him from her, he sensed her anxiety lessen a degree. The apprehension gripping him eased off a little.

Dom paced closer, he could see another nearby. Kathleen. Good, for once she was on her post. Eden's lilac warmth beckoned him, feeding his...attraction? Addiction? Obsession? He knew not what to term the strange emotion that had seized him and continued to intensify. He ached to be with her, near her, touch her, know her.

In his haste to reach her, Dom did not consider what he would do once he had heaven within his grasp. He shied away from disembarking in front of Kathleen. Not because she would be shocked or scared. Dominic knew full well that Ethan had spilled the family secret to his wife. He was mortified at first. The idea of someone he barely knew and trusted even less knowing something so damning about him flung him back in time...to Italy. The threat of being labeled a scourge and cast back in the path of torture and misery up-surged every time he laid eyes on his brother's wife.

Dom avoided her for months after he learned that she knew. Once he'd gotten over the initial horror, he and Kathleen had come to a sort of truce. He'd become familiar with her essence. She possessed a strong life force of dazzling blue-azure...loyal to a fault and filled with a tumult of love. Dominic could not have wished for a more perfect match for Ethan. With time, he found that he could be at ease with his sister-in-law in a causal way, but he wasn't yet comfortable enough with the brass Scottish woman to actually *show* her such an intimate piece of himself. Astral travel was his haven, his secret self, and his soul's savior.

On the other hand, if he exited into invisibility he could avoid Kathleen but Eden would sense him as she had before. He was ill prepared to handle her knowledge of his...uniqueness, as Cael would term it. His essence wobbled, like a scissor-legged drunk. He couldn't delay much longer or he would lose consciousness, which always plopped him from the astral onto the corporeal. He slipped back to monitor only Cael. Ahh, his brother was once again alone and safe and probably annoyed with him for absconding without so much as a by your leave. But Dom would deal with that later. For now, the ethereal blonde reclaimed his full attention.

Dominic paced back a ways, he estimated...spatial arrangements such as depth, foreground, and background meant nothing on the astral. Everything—which was nothing, black space—existed on the same plane. Right blended with left, up blurred into down, front was back and visa versa. Hopeful that he stood a chance of shimmering outside of which ever room they occupied, Dom shed his astral self and his invisible cloak. Legs shaky at first, he leaned heavily against an end table outside one of the lesser-used sitting rooms.

He'd had several extra parlors and sitting rooms and of course bed chambers aired out for Ethan, Kathleen and Eden. The two women must be within one adjacent the portrait gallery. Dom hadn't been in the room in years, keeping to his private suites. Drained, physically and mentally, he slid along the wall to the door, which stood ajar. He could hear Kathleen making soothing cooing noises as if she spoke to a child.

"Eden." He thought only of her as he kicked the door out of his path.

Both women snapped around to stare at him. His spectacles were in place. His clothes were their usual sober eloquence: black coat, silken vest, and trousers, over-starched white shirt, and impeccable cravat. Only his unsteady gait confessed exhaustion. Dom did his best to compose himself, stiffening his spine.

"Dominic." Her voice was a breathy whisper. She drank in his form like a dessert dweller guzzling from a life-saving spring.

"Dom?" Kathleen's crimson brows peaked. "We thought ya in town."

"I was. Now, I'm here." He stated flatly, eyes falling on Eden. She was reclining atop a brocade curb-back chaise, piled high with ridiculous little pillows that spilled out onto the floor. Her shining hair tumbled around her shoulders, attractively disheveled. One hand fluttered near her chest, the other clutched a teacup with white-knuckled fingers. Kathleen stood over her, in full mother-hen stance.

"What the hell happened? Why does she look so…distressed?"

"Why assume somethin' more has happened." Kathleen countered, shifting so that her wide skirts obscured her charge from sight. "'Canna it be delayed reaction from tha numerous other tragedies tha lass has suffered."

"She was perfectly composed when I took my leave." He leveled. "Now she's trembling and white as a sheet."

"'Tis naught a sip of hot tea and a good night's rest canna cure."

He stepped further into the room. To keep his balance, he touched each and every piece of furniture he passed on the precarious trek to the chaise on which Eden sat. "You do not look yourself either." This, he noted with renewed unease. His sister-in-law was not one easily ruffled.

Kathleen humphed. "I think 'tis safe ta say dat no one in dis room is quite themselves tonight."

"Tell me what's happened, Kathleen, or I will track down Ethan and have *him* ring it out of you." An empty threat, of course. He could not have astral-ed across the room, much less brought another person back with him…and he certainly couldn't imagine his peace-keeping brother haranguing information out of anyone, much less his brazen Scottish wife.

"Will ya now?" She challenged.

"I want to know who dared to overset guests in my home?"

Eden poked her head around Kathleen. "It was nothing, really." She declared on the heels of a shaky laugh.

Seeing that he would not be denied, and their head butting, however innocent, caused her charge further anxiety, Kathleen conceded. "Tha wee one and I went for a walk on tha grounds. When we returned, 'twas a man lurking about. Rattled her, 'tis all. Renfred and Booth escorted him off tha estate. He blustered he'd be back with tha district magistrate."

"Not a thief then?"

"Definitely not."

He nodded, with solemn understanding. "A muckraker. My uncle?"

"A muckraker ta be sure, but not yer uncle. Called 'imself Matthias Montgomery. Claimed ta be actin' on official orders."

* * *

Eden trembled anew, not liking the turn events were taking. Preoccupied with a lingering fear, she'd lost the thread of the conversation. There was one thing she had to know, and she couldn't wait a minute longer.

"Dom-inic?"

His shaded gaze shifted downward to meet her hurt-filled hazel eyes. He ached to erase the angst and caress the shivering from her limbs.

"You didn't...send that awful man for me, did you? He—"

"Is *that* what he said? Bloody Hell."

Eden almost chuckled, even in her shaky state. She had never known anyone who cursed quite so matter-of-factly. She watched him come forward, sliding by Kathleen to seat himself in front of her atop the coffee table. Tree-trunk legs crowded her.

"Tell me, Eden." His voice lowered to a beguiling smoothness as he took the tittering cup from her hand. He meant to put her at ease, she imagined. He needn't have bothered. Her name on his lips liquefied her insides. At the moment, she would do anything he asked of her.

"He said he'd been charged to investigate the mental stability of a resident of this estate. I just assumed he meant me."

"No, lass." Kathleen bent to reassure her. "Here now, drink yer tea."

"Forget about him. He won't be bothering either of you again." He set the cup aside out of both her and Kathleen's reach and took Eden's hands in his, pulling her to her feet with him. "Tea can wait until morning. I am taking you up to bed. Kathleen, please wait for me here."

"'Tis 'no proper. Yer accompanying her ta bed."

Dom scoffed testily as he turned them both for the door. "I could have *slept* in her bed for all you know."

A conspirator's smile played on the redhead's lips as she watched them exit. "Aye. Ya haven't yet, but yer thinkin' about it. My Ethan will be pleased."

* * *

They walked to her chamber in silence, though not an awkward silence, as she would have predicted. Eden needed only a moment to realize that Dominic was not himself, or at least, he wasn't himself as she had come to expect. He seemed troubled, vulnerable somehow, his movements slothful and over-prudent. Almost like his hand on the small of her back, the other caressing the tender flesh of her wrist, the entire act of escorting her to her chamber was more for his benefit than hers. What had wrought the change? She wished she'd been paying closer attention in the sitting room. Maybe then she might have gleamed a clue. But it couldn't be helped. She'd been too shaken from her encounter to think clearly.

She reached the chamber door a step ahead of him, and paused, uncertain. Should she open the door, and if so would he follow her inside? Or should she turn and wait for him to bid her goodnight? Neither scenario prepared her for what actually happened.

He never stopped walking until he'd backed her up against the closed door, the hand caressing her palm ventured upwards to lose itself in her hair. The hand at her back inched around to rest on one hip, steadying. The nearness and heat of his body caused her breath to catch...becoming deep and gasping. She felt the brush of his hair, an exhale of breath, the cold metal tip of the spectacles as he dipped, resting his forehead for a moment at the junction of her shoulder....then turned his face to her neck.

"You were alone with him like you are with me now? That's why he frightened you so." He demanded in an urgent whisper, delivered shockingly near her ear. "Answer me, Eden."

Eden's pulse beat staccato, too stunned to do anything but as he commanded. "Yes."

"Did he touch you…hurt you? I have to know. Tell me, or I will strip you naked and search every inch of your body until I'm satisfied you are unharmed."

Something in his manner put her in mind of a child in need of smoothing. "Shhh, Dominic, I am untouched. Kathleen—"

"I will thank God Ethan married her to the day I die." And then his lips were on her. First, worshipping her neck with hot wetness. His hand tilted and guided her head until he could capture her lips in a devouring exploration. His tongued her mercilessly, plundering her mouth at a frantic rhythm born of passion and fury, robbing her of breath. In danger of melting right out of his grasp, Eden wrapped an arm around the scorching mass of trembling muscle pressing into her slender frame. Ahhh, to be cherished again, touched, needed, she came alive…for him. Accepted him with open arms and a tarnished heart. She matched his pace, though she'd never been kissed before, somehow instinct took over.

The fervor eventually cooled. He backed off, his body giving hers room to breathe, his lips slowed to a tantalizing stroke…until at last, he pulled back altogether, his mouth placing a last soft touch to her swollen parted lips.

"Forgive me. I…" He seemed not to know where he was, dropping his hands from her hair and body. Eden watched him began to retreat from her. The air around him thick with shame and regret. "I am not…myself."

"I prefer *this* you." She grasped the lapels of his jacket to keep him within reach. "Don't go."

"I must. Kathleen…" He glanced down the hall from whence they'd come, only turning back to face her when she palmed his cheek in her hand.

"Shhh…you're safe with me." Eden curled her lips into a smile, stroking his cheek. "That's it. See, everything is fine. Stay a moment longer."

He let her urge him a step closer, placidly staring down at her. Their roles somehow reversed. She the caregiver, he the recipient.

"Dominic, I wonder if …" Eden trailed off as her hand inadvertently bumped the rim of his spectacles. He went stiff. She could see the outline of his eyes darting back and forth panicky, behind the tinted lens.

"It's alright." She reassured him, palming his cheek again. "Let me see you…I want to know if *you're* unharmed…and I have to see for myself."

She inched her finger up ever so slightly to grasp one thin metal arm of the spectacles. Slowly, methodically, she slid them forward off his nose, revealing—

"Nooo…" The word came out on a moan of agony.

And then the strangest thing happened. He was gone. Vanished. Her arm still hung in the air caressing empty space.

ELEVEN

Dominic descended the grand staircase decked from heel to crown in pomp and circumstance, spectacles riding rigid on his nose. A livery-ed Renfred met him at the bottom step and fell in beside him.

"Master Ambrosi, sir, your brother arrived some time ago. His became quite agitated at finding his wife absent. I was obliged to direct him to Mrs. Raine, whom Nell discovered asleep in one of the upstairs sitting rooms. He relocated her to their chamber." If Renfred found the events at all peculiar, he did not convey as much in his rendition.

"How is Mrs. Raine this morning?"

"Resting comfortably."

"And Ms. Prescott?"

"Also still abed, sir."

"I am not certain how much longer our guests will be visiting. I hope to have them settled elsewhere soon, but from now until such time as I deem it unnecessary, neither is to leave the house without an escort, Renfred. Is that understood?"

"Certainly, sir."

"Where is my brother now?"

"I believe, helping himself to breakfast in the dinning room."

"Thank you, Renfred, that will be all for now." Dominic strode purposefully for the dinning room as the butler fell back and returned to his post in the foyer. Dominic arrived to find the doctor at the sideboard, piling his plate.

"Ethan. This is a surprise."

"How so?" He arched a brow over his shoulder. "I said I would return."

"I wasn't expecting you this morning, is all." Dominic procured a plate, and began filling it.

"That much is obvious." The doctor shot him a withering glance. "You mind explaining why I arrived to find my wife snoozing in a parlor like a common doxy?"

Dominic managed to adopt a sheepish mien, despite his shaded eyes. "Forgive me, Ethan. I asked her to wait for me, meaning to speak with her about the woman, but eh...I was delayed. There have been some odd goings-on of late—"

"The first of which being your deigning to host a meal with the interlopers. Shocking indeed." Satisfied with his meal choices, the doctor took up a seat at the main dining table that occupied the central space in the room. "Miss Prescott will be joining us, will she not?"

"I have no idea. Renfred informed me that she is presently still abed."

"At brunch time?" A brow shot heavenward.

Plate in hand, Dom strolled to pull back a chair opposite his brother. "As I said, there have been some peculiar happenings recently."

"Such as?" The doctor inquired just before the first forkful passed his lips.

Dom shied away from the topic. "How was London?" He inquired, as if he hadn't been in town just last evening.

The doctor swallowed before he answered. "I wasn't there on holiday, Dom. Now then, what's afoot?"

"I prefer to delay the particulars until Cael is present, so I won't have to repeat myself but you may as well know... a dangerous situation is brewing. We will have to vacate the women of course. And be quick about it, I want her and Kathleen prepared to depart on the morrow. Perhaps the three of you can share a carriage back to town. I'll astral to Cael's later and we can discuss what is to be done then."

"Whoa, Dom. I thought we agreed it was best Miss Prescott remained here, under close supervision."

"Things change."

Breakfast forgotten, Dominic felt his brother's gaze shift to his face and rake over him. "Hmmm...yes, I see they have. But regardless, she is *my* patient. I will decide when she is ready to be moved. She has endured too many sudden upheavals as it is and one more will not help the healing process."

"That is out of your realm of expertise. Cael is the head doctor."

"She may well harm herself." His brother reminded him.

Dom scoffed at this. "Thus far, my estate hasn't lessened the calamities that befall her. She has been here a week. During which time, she nearly drowned in the pond, almost plunged to her death in the library, and been accosted by a hell-bent lecher on the grounds."

"Is *that* what happened while I was gone?"

"Yes." He stated, irked anew. "The woman is prone to disaster. She is no safer here than she would be sheltered with you and Kathleen in London."

"She cannot live with Kathleen and I forever."

"No more than she can reside *here* indefinitely." He reasoned.

The doctor looked as if he wished to argue, but instead said, "Where will she go then? The village? An inn? A rented house in town?"

Anywhere but here! Dom thought. "I was thinking an

obscure relative of some sort." He waved a hand causally as he brought a forkful of eggs to his mouth.

"Relatives will require time to locate." His brother argued. "At least delay until we can arrange for proper relations to see after her. I'll not cast such a fragile creature into the world alone and unprotected."

"Fine. She can stay…for now." He conceded with a long exhale. He ignored the answering arch in Ethan's brow, knowing but beyond caring that his reaction to the girl was obvious to his perceptive brother. "But begin looking into her ancestry immediately. From what she told Kathleen, there is, I believe an English branch of the family."

"You'll have to take care of it." He shrugged off the responsibility like an ill-fitting coat. "I cannot tarry. I just wanted to check in on Kathleen and Ms. Prescott before I made headways to the village. There's a patient of mine there and I promised to look in on how his leg is healing. Bad break."

"Ethan…" His brother's name came out a warning rumble.

Ignoring the menace, the doctor's attention refocused on his food, face as innocent as a newborn babe. "Oh, so tell me, what is this business with Cael?"

The mention diverted his ire. "Do you recall that lecture he and I attended some two months back?"

"Certainly. A shame to have missed it."

"There were some interesting characters in attendance. One in particular, Matthias Montgomery, Cael took an instant disliking to. That Professor Greyson did not like him much either."

"Who is he?"

"A proprietor for one of those paranormal asylums…*and* the intruder that accosted Ms. Prescott last evening. Claimed to be investigating a resident here exhibiting mental instability of a bizarre nature. This comes on the heels of Cael's announcement that Greyson, the paranormal scientist, is interested in Stephan's abilities. I do not frequent society. Cael is neither adept nor insane, and you are…careful. Thus, I believe the someone Montgomery is after is Stephan."

"You think Greyson's interest in Stephan inadvertently tipped off this Montgomery character?"

"That is my theory, yes."

"This could be a problem."

"You've a gift for understatement, Ethan."

The doctor pondered on these facts a moment, gazing unseeing at the floral centerpiece cattycorner. "He could be after you, too…at your uncle's behest. Recall, you recently inherited a title and a fortune. And Nonna warned of this."

"With Montgomery poking around, none of us are safe. It will not take long to scent blood if he learns of Greyson's notice of Stephan. Or for that matter, the reason for the woman's presence here. She is…" He hesitated, trying to personify Eden in one word. "…unusual. That is all the provocation witch-hunters need. Even worse, Cael thinks Stephan is hiding something."

"All the more reason for you to talk to him, Dom."

"Yes, yes." He moved forward impatiently. "I'd already planned to invite him for a visit. But now, with this Montgomery person to contend with…I need to talk to Cael. See what he thinks. Not to mention he's probably a little peeved with me."

"When *isn't* Cael a little peeved with you?" Ethan turned a curious gaze on his brother. "Still, you and he seem chummy these days."

"Cael is not so bad." Dom shrugged. "When he's being my brother and not my doctor."

The doctor chuckled at this, as he pushed back his chair. "Somehow I think I'm included in that comment. Alas, patients await. I must take my leave, but I'll likely be back later in the evening."

"Wait." Dominic stood as well, not used to playing the gracious host, but giving the role a try-on for good measure. "Ahem. Ethan I...congratulations. Please express my regards to your wife."

An uncharacteristic blush stole across the doctor's face. "Yes, I will. Kathleen and I are very happy, but how did you—"

"I knew as soon as she arrived. Souls, they do not change fundamentally nor do they age. There could be only one explanation for the differences I saw in Kathleen's. The child has a beautiful essence, Ethan. Strong and healthy."

TWELVE

Eden awoke to a light tapping. Sleep-dazed, it took several moments to convince herself the noise wasn't another phantom lurking in wait to attack her mind with visions of madness. Her rope-thick plait whipped around to plop on her be-gowned chest as she flipped the covers back and scooped across the counterpane. Nell's mousy mien greeted her at the chamber door.

"Begging your pardon, Miss, but Master Ambrosi wishes to speak with you in the downstairs study at your earliest convenience. Would you like me to fetch water for a bath?"

"Yes, Nell, thank you. And have something light sent up please." Eden hadn't been in the mood for her usual bath after the previous evening's histrionics and now she wished she had. Then, she could have donned a serviceable dress, knotted her hair and been off. As it was, she did not think she'd survive the suspense.

He'd actually *sought* her out. What did he want? To apologize? Or scold? Would he bring up the kiss? Try to marginalize his jaw-dropping vanishing act? Demand she leave? No. She recoiled from the thought. If he were inclined to put her out, he would have done so after the library fray. She bathed, dressed, and ate, her mind aflame with dozens of scenarios.

* * *

Eden entered his study without knocking on the off chance that he had left off his spectacles and she might at last catch a glimpse of the closest guarded secret since Louis the XIV's man-in-the-iron-mask. No such luck. Even from across the room she spied the curved silver spectacles tucked behind his ears. The moody master of the house stood with his back to her, staring out into the gardens abutting the study's window-ed posterior wall. A hand flung carelessly over his shoulder bidding she take a seat, was his only greeting.

Eden surveyed the room as she advanced inside. Should she sit in the hearth-facing couch, or one of two straight-backed interrogation chairs opposite the desk, or the ottoman, standing on wedge legs between the hearth and the couch? She chose the ottoman, anticipating that he would prefer her in one of the desk chairs. Still he did not turn to face her.

Without preamble, he spoke. "Tell me about your early life, your family."

The odd request did not fit any of her scenarios. Nervous and skeptical of his motives, Eden fumbled over her words. "Eh...I...grew up in Boston."

"Yes, that much became obvious the moment Ethan dried you off and your natural voice returned." He cast his face in profile over his shoulder. "What of your English relations?"

"I am not well acquainted with the English branch save for my cousin Millicent and she's..." Eden trailed off, not wishing to re-visit the painful loss. "My grandparents on my father's side are the Lord and Lady Prescott of London. I do not know much about them, having only met them once a very long time ago..."

* * *

Dom relaxed as he listened. Her melodic voice blew like a cool breeze across his skin, making a larger impression on him than the words themselves.

"…And then there are Millie's parents, Uncle Edward and Aunt Margaret I think is her name. I have a clearer picture of them, as they felt obliged to do their "duty" visit to the states once every five years. They always brought my cousin Millie along, and for that I am grateful. She and I were fast friends. We even kept correspondence. Naturally, after mama and papa…eh… I sort her out here in England. Millie has several brothers, but I have never met either of them."

* * *

"Not even at the burial services?" Dominic turned to face her for the first time, staring from behind shaded glass. If Eden didn't know better, she would say that she had shocked him.

"I declined to attend."

"Why?"

"I saw her take her last breath. I did not require further proof that she was dead."

"And yet, you obviously bore your cousin great affection." He seemed to find the information fascinating.

Eden watched him pivot away from the window, coming forward to partially bridge the gulf between them. Seeing her opening, she chanced a question of her own. "Are *your* parents living?"

He stopped mid-stride. Eden feared that she had blind-sided him back into silence. She watched him glide one powerful sinewy hand unhurried along the lacquered tabletop behind the couch, deep in contemplation. Eden swallowed hard as she imagined that same hand roaming down her touch-starved flesh, fingers spread to increase the expansion of skin he caressed. The light caress then evolved into a heavy, demanding stroke, blinding her thought with a frenzy of sensations and...

"No." His voice broke into her thoughts, "My father passed recently. Our...relationship did not reflect what ought to have been between a father and son." He took a step towards her, but then thought better, because he walked in another direction with no great focus of where he was going. "Lucca was weak...ineffectual. He allowed...things he should have prevented. I often worry that I am too much like him."

Eden dogged his meandering steps around the room with sympathetic eyes. His words and manner telegraphed a deep-seated...vulnerability, similar but not as heart wrenching as what she'd witnessed the night before. She longed to enveloped him in a hug, reassure him with words, but truthfully, she did not know him well enough for anything she said to hold much weight. Perhaps it would benefit him to talk about it. So, she did her level best to draw him out into the open.

"What about your mother?"

"There are some women who should not be allowed to procreate. My mother was one such woman. She had strange beliefs—on religion, the Almighty and the other one—beliefs and practices she *inflicted* on us with malicious tenacity."

"But without her you would not exist."

"Perhaps it is better never to be born than to live in suspended agony." He cocked his dark head, supposing she should understand what he meant.

His words alarmed Eden, reminding her of the despair that had prompted her pseudo-suicide, but at the same time his words also wove a tenuous bond between them. Had he, like she, flirted with death? What had he endured to prompt such drastic measures? Abuse? Neglect? A little of both, from what she could gleam.

"Yes. I do see your point." Taking a deep breath, Eden prepared to ask the one question she'd been longing to know since she first laid eyes on his shaded gaze. "Dominic, why do you wear the spectacles?"

He stilled, then straightened...the emotional floodgates dammed. His face was again a stoic mask. Uh-oh. She'd finally driven him a step too far. "Why wear clothes, Miss Prescott?" His tenor clipped and sarcastic.

Familiar with his mood swings, she did not flinch. "Society dictates that one's nakedness be covered."

An inky brow arched above the infamous eyewear. His voice lowered to a velvety rumble. "Society isn't here now, Ms. Prescott. And yet you still conceal your body beneath that dress."

Eden blushed at his outrageous challenge. No doubt, designed to unnerve her. "Mister Ambrosi, I hardly think-"

"Enough." He dismissed any further comment. "Ethan returned this morning. He and I are in agreement. It is time, past time, you re-entered your life. We will send word to The Prescotts. I am sure they will be more than happy to open their home, perhaps even give you a season."

No! Her heart railed against the idea of losing him so soon. "I am not so sure. In fact about it, I have no faith in their willingness to take me in."

He said nothing, but his intense stare demanded an explanation.

"Papa and mama did not feel safe on the same continent with them. Why should I trust them any more than they did? Particularly, now, when I am defenseless. They could very well throw me into the care of that Montgomery character."

He tensed; a tick went to work at his jaw line. "Why do you say that?"

Eden came to a sudden, reckless decision. If what she suspected was true then he wouldn't be altogether horrified. And, she needed a reason...a legitimate reason to avoid being sent away.

"I hear voices." She confessed. "Imagine people…see horrible events that haven't happened." She kept her eyes lowered and her hands clasped. "I feel disembodied hands molesting me, have urges to do abominable things."

Eden allowed her gaze to wonder up to his face, lowering her voice to a mere thread of sound. "You're *different* too, aren't you."

She searched his face for any hint of a reaction: shock, guilt, fear, but found none. Not a twitch. She might just as well have told him she had a bad dream.

He crossed his hands in front. "No. I'm afraid my *differences* must be another of your pesky imaginings." Sarcasm abounded.

Feeling the need for added strength, Eden stood. She approached him with a mind to eradicate his stoic manner once and for all…ready to do battle if necessary. "You disappeared straight from my arms last night. I didn't imagine that, did I?"

"Is that your proof? Do you intend to run to the constable…or better yet…the parish priest? Claiming witchcraft and sacrilege." His cavalier words, dared her to do just that, were as a red flag to a bull. "What will you tell the priest and the constable you were doing at the time, little one? Needle-work?"

Her hands balled into fists at her sides. Damn him! Eden knew she shouldn't let him bait her, but she couldn't seem to control her irritation.

"I am American and I can return there anytime I wish it. Why should I give a hoot if the lot of you English dandies declare me ruined and unmarriageable? Had I any notion of remaining respectable I wouldn't have tarried on *this* estate not one night. Haunted ponds. Scars that aren't there. Voices in the shadows." The accusations slice through the air like flaming darts fired at enemy lines. "Whisperings and frightened servants. A host who hides his fears and inadequacies behind tinted glasses and conceit. I wonder…Just who was Mr. Montgomery really investigating, Dominic, if not me?"

THIRTEEN

Dom stood adjacent his desk, watching her fume. Though logic was on his side, he could tell she wasn't ready to concede the battle. "You, Ms. Prescott, are a woman who has attempted suicide, not once but twice over. Who would believe *you*?"

"Matthias Montgomery for one." She lobbed another stone at his glass house. Despite her delicate feminine appearance, she was far from a shrinking violet. "But even if he did not...what does it matter? It's the implication that damns, not the evidence."

Dominic frowned. She had the right of it, he knew. Hell, he'd echoed the same sentiments to Ethan at breakfast. Having his own argument thrown back in his face worried him. She wasn't a fool either.

He was losing ground...he should retreat, strategize, lest she press her advantage. Instead, he looked down at the cluttered desktop, his fingers toying at the edge of the ink well. He felt her watching him, as the strained silence stretched out over a full minute.

"Would you do that...if I sent you away from here?" He fidgeted with his glasses, waiting for her answer. Was she angling to blackmail him? She could, with the knowledge she had of him.

"No, Dominic. I wouldn't do that to you."

Dom exhaled, lifting his gaze to her. Weary at the moment of fighting the urge to submit to the powerful draw her fragile beauty had on him. He absorbed her graceful stance, the wisps of blonde softness licking her nape. Her pouty rosebud mouth triggered flashes of the night before, when she let him plunder that moist hot cove at his leisure. His groin tightened at the memory.

She'd gained a pound or two, he noticed. The dress she wore today cling to an outlined form beneath...her breast though small, curved hill-like in the bodice while her hips gently made themselves known despite the wealth of under-things insulating them.

"You may remain here while Ethan and I contact your relatives." He heard himself say. His heart filled with a confusing mixture of relief and worry. "If they are as unwelcoming as you claim...then we will make other arrangements."

* * *

That was as much of a reprieve as she was going to get, Eden realized. Still, it bought her hope and a few more days—possibly another week—in the place that held for her a snug fitting rightness. She had a friend in Kathleen, an ally she suspected in the doctor, and a promise of possibilities with the man before her. She felt more at home than she had since she'd fled her home in Boston and all its stifling memories and losses.

He cleared his throat. Eden glanced around to see that Dominic had moved to the door. "If you will excuse me, Ms. Prescott."

"Certainly." She replied, back on her best behavior.

But he paused mid-ways the threshold and turned back.

"Anisocoria. Heterochromia iridium. Unilateral ocular albinism. Take your pick."

Her brow wrinkled at the foreign-sounding words.

Dom tapped the side of his spectacles. "Cael and Ethan are fond of obscure scientific explanations."

"What…does all that mean? Does it affect your sight?"

"Not overmuch."

Eden's gaze followed the Italian enigma as he exited, leaving her with half-an-explanation. Naturally, she spent the rest of the day in his magnificent library, researching the terms. Taking long breaks to nap in front of the hearth, or sketch in the beguiling sunlight beaming in from all directions. She had no qualms about breaking her word to keep clear of his domain…not after that kiss. He obviously had no plans to keep clear of her.

She found herself anticipating rather than dreading their next encounter, and whatever possible delight or shock it may hold. She fed greedily off the provocative sensations, the wayward longings he stirred in her…craving more not less.

FOURTEEN

Rank air hung, chilled, thin, and infused with raw odors, the origins of which were better left unnamed. A sad wooden cot buckled tiredly under the weight of two, one feeble of limb, a second robust and beefy. The mattress, little more than exaggerated straw-stuffed padding, bumped the floor with each new thrust.

Matthias glanced down into bleary unfocused windows to a mind no more aware of what was happening to its body than a tree being chopped for firewood. Disgusted with the slack, drool-smeared mouth, he turned loose one imprisoned wrist to spread-eagle his hand across the nameless female face. He quickened his pace, ready to have his pleasure and be done with the deed…making a silent promise to select a more feisty subject next time, still malleable, but also alive and kicking. Perhaps a fair-skinned blonde like what he'd lucked upon at the Ambrosi estates? Or that red-haired tiger, his cock twitched at the idea of having to tame one for a change. He'd grown tired of the busty brunettes he usually favored.

His current darling, a Baron's illegitimate mongrel, bonnie enough, but she lacked spirit and tended to indulge in stupefying quantities of opium. Sticking his cock in her amounted to little more than necrophilia. He silently reminded himself to make a list in his journal of the new traits he'd require and to have Harry screen the latest batch of inmates for an upgrade as soon as possible.

Breaths shot out in forceful puffs, a guttural moan building deep in his throat as he climaxed strong and lustful. One pivot of his bare backside and he'd disentangled himself and stood next to the sprawled shadow on the cot. The Asylum Keeper finished adjusting himself then retrieved his pants from around hairy ankles.

An abrupt sound of sandpaper against glass announced that someone had shoved the wooden barrier to the peephole back in its sheath. A shaft of hallway light peeped through before a saw-nosed face dominated the opening.

"Mr. Montgomery…" The nervous over-torqued voice belonged to a man living under the gun, unsure if his value outweighed his liabilities.

"I thought I told the lot of ya that I didn't wish to be disturbed."

"But, Boss, we got problems."

Pants secured in place, Matthias cast a final grimace at the blithering simpleton before throwing an age-worn blanket over her gaping nakedness. "Take care." With those parting words, he threw the lock to extricate himself from the depressing cinderblock.

Stepping out into one of many labyrinthine hallways, Matthias felt his chest swell with the power and pride of Napoleon. Here, at St. Ciaran Isis, he reigned. King and keeper, feared and respected alike.

"Boss…"

Matthias, shook prematurely from his post-coital reveling, snapped at the lazy-eyed custodian. "Wot is it, Harry?"

"There's some dandies here—they say from the social reform board—making noise 'bout an inspection." He reported, anxious, as he and the Asylum Keeper walked down the progression of archways leading further into the dark mouth...of madness. "Says they's making the rounds in Southwart. Bedlam, Newgate, Guy's Hospital and wot not. I made 'em wait as long as I could."

They traversed murky shafts of light whenever they passed a door to a common room that had outside windows and natural sunshine.

"Bribe the bastards and be done wit'em. I 'ave more important matters to attend to." Matthias still hadn't found much dirt to work with in the Ambrosi case, little to none, if he were truthful with himself.

"It ain't that simple, Mr. Montgomery, sir. See..." They passed a particularly noisy common room, packed with giggling, screeching, wailing, clawing inmates...unrestrained, many with wild eyes and android movements. Matthias paused to do a peek-a-boo. Hit by the wall of body heat that cooked the crowded space, he quickly counted four cudgel-wielding wardens. Satisfied that there were adequate custodians for the room volume, he moved back into the drafty hallway.

"Go on, Harry, let's 'ave all of it." Matthias prompted, knowing the imbecile had screwed up yet again.

"Dis way, I left 'em at one of the...eh...observation suites." The jittery Harry led the Asylum Keeper down another gloomy hallway.

Imbecile did not begin to describe him. The boy, gangly and just on the right side of twenty, deserved to be locked up in simpleton's prison.

"And just wot the bloody 'ell are they doing outside the observation suites, Harry?" Though Matthias was sickeningly sure he already knew.

"Well, they *tricked* me—"

"Ya 'ave the sense of a bloody imbecile, go on...I'll be wanting to git the 'hole story for yer tombstone."

Matthias took pleasure in the audible gasp his threat evoked from the younger man.

"They said they was 'ere to see the 'Show'. They

seemed real excited-like when I told'em for an extra halfpence they could each 'ave a stick to take a poke at the inactive ones. That shrewd 'un, Greyson, even slipped me a silver piece if I'd give 'em the grand tour."

They came at last to a series of rectangular shaped rooms strung together like connecting cars on a train, with wall-sized windows on one side and open-air prison-bars on the other. Skittish viewers could meander along the window side and laugh or taunt the inmates to their heart's content. Whereas, more bold visitors would in turn walk the iron bar side, and throw rocks or poke sticks at the prisoners within.

Matthias clenched his jaw tight to calm himself, preparing for a dicey situation. The social reform board was once scoffed at as disorganized and ineffective. However, the board had gained power and momentum after successfully lobbying to shut down The Marshaleas Debtor's prison due to the inhumane treatment of its inmates. He cursed the fates for the ill luck to come under their scrutiny.

"Harry, if yer worthless bag of bones 'is still 'ere when I open my eye, ya be a bad smell floatin' up from the Thames before night's fall.".

FIFTEEN

Dominic tapped his foot, patience eroding more and more with each tick of the miniature clock dangling from the silver chain at his vest pocket. Sure, it was rude of him to arrive uninvited…and further presumptuous to declare he would await an audience with the illustrious Lord and Lady…but he possessed no calling card baring his heraldry to announce himself even if he had been so inclined to warn the Prescotts' of an impending visit.

With nothing better to do, Dom observed the room in which he sat. The over-stuffed parlor, all style and no substance, looked as if it were decorated by an extravagant mistress. A hoyden's lair could not have out done the room in senseless excess. He banged his knee twice maneuvering around the clutter of lounging chairs, knickknack-laden tables, and the like. Dominic preferred open spaces free of obstruction. He fidgeted with his watch chain, trying not to think of the precious little room there was for him to move around, but to no avail. Clutter walled him in on all sides. He felt trapped, *cornered…* by encroaching madness. Memories of another time, another place flooded in unbidden.

The slimy chill of the stone caused him to shiver. He lay face-up against the stone alter, but oft-times he lay face down, depending upon who in her coven came up with the most promising new 'technique' to try. No one ever bothered to tie him down. Lillian kept him immobilized atop the solid block of dull grey pewter with a mere thought and wave of her hand. He struggled, sometimes for hours, against impossibly strong psychic shackles, capable of nothing but awaiting what he feared would be his final doom.

He squirmed as the cavern filled with a murky glow of firelight. The low, repetitious chant heralded the beginning of the purification ceremony—as she called them. The words were meaningless to him, they chanted in some ancient tongue no longer used for communication, but for rituals and prayer. Each member of the processional entered the low-ceilinged cavern housing the altar from a different tunnel emptying into it. They emerged from the blackness to encircle him on all sides: the priest, the witch, the druid, and the doctor. Dominic named each based on their appearance and respective approach to curing his 'problem'.

The priest was a bald round man always draped in burlap robes and a nightmare-sized crucifix strangling his non-existent neck. The priest undulated above his fragile seven-year-old body with fervent prayers, doused him in buckets of holy water, and quoted scripture at the top of his lungs.

The witch was an ancient crone of a woman, with hanging skin and wild hair protruding out in some areas and matted to her head in others. She drew ominous symbols on the floor around him, fed him moldy spell-infused concoctions, and riddled his ears with senseless rhyming incantations.

The Druid was completely concealed beneath a black, shroud-like garment, and reminded him of the grim reaper. Together with the "Doctor", the last to join his mother's coven of Spiritualist fanatics, they began the campaign of-"

Dominic jerked forward—into the present—at the sound of his name. The footman before him came into focus.

"The Duke and Duchess will see you now."

The footman led him to another sitting room, which housed the Lord and Lady of the house. It too was mired in senseless pomp and circumstance. Dominic found himself seated opposite two of the oldest, stuffiest, tight-lipped curmudgeons the peerage had to offer. The Prescott's of London were how Dom pictured Mother Nature and Father Time in their dotage...shoehorned into every imaginable finery. Their faces were stoic, unrelenting, and ancient.

The pair of them refused to address him until afternoon tea was served. After five minutes, a nondescript maid appeared with steaming earl grey and crumpets to set out before them on a marble table crouching nearby.

"Forgive the rude manner of my arrival, and my odd eyewear—" He added hastily as he saw the Duchess frowning a glower of disapproval. "—but I have news of an urgent nature regarding your granddaughter, Miss Eden Prescott."

"Lady Prescott." The duchess corrected dourly, as she rested her tea cup. "Despite my son's decision to forsake his legacy and pollute our line with common American stock, any child of his and grandchild of ours will be given the title he or she is due. I will assume by your mentioning only the young lady that she is the sole offspring of his union with that...person?"

"Miss...eh, Lady Prescott has not appraised me of any siblings. No." Dominic cringed, not holding out much hope of their welcoming Eden into the fold. He got the distinct impression that the mere reminder of their ruined pedigree annoyed them. "Lady Prescott's parents, your eldest son and his wife, have both passed on...Mrs. Prescott fairly recently. And of course, you're aware of your other granddaughter's death in childbirth...Lady Millicent St. James—"

The Duke puffed up to twice his minuscule size. "Conte Ambrosi, we do not require an outline of the Prescott family tree. Please do us the courtesy of being brief. What is the exact nature of this...*visit?*"

"Of course. Lady Prescott was most recently residing

with the St. James' on their country estate, which borders my own. In her grief, she suffered a near fatal accident and was rescued by my brother." Dominic rushed on, fearing they would fall asleep or kick him out before he'd gotten to the meat of the matter. "She has since recovered full health, but as I am unmarried and so is she, she cannot continue to reside at my estate. Nor can she reside with St. James, as he too is now unwed. I have come on Lady Prescott's behave as she is not acquainted with either of you and has been in much grief and mourning…so much so that I fear her mind has been affected—"

Dominic broke off at the Duchess' horrified gasp. "Prescott! You mustn't allow it." She seized her husband's arm for comfort.

"There, there, dear." Dominic watched the Duke pat his wife on her stiff, overstuffed shoulder pad, placating, before turning back to address him. "Conte Ambrosi, if you mean to suggest the Duchess and I take in this…addlebrained woman…simply because she is my son's beget, then let me relieve you of any such notion. Did you think to appeal to our sympathies?"

Certainly not, Dom thought, any idiot could see that would be an utter waste of energy. He'd never seen two more indifferent, uncaring individuals.

"Thinking, having lost our beloved son, we would be grateful to play nursemaid to his simpleton brat? Charles was dead to us the moment he stepped off English soil. The fact of his physical death is of little consequence. Since Charles was wise enough to amass a fortune in trade wealth before his death, the girl is hardly destitute. I would suggest that you extend a bit of her funds and apply a place for her at Bedlam. Now then, the Duchess and I find this turn of events most distressing. We must kindly ask you to leave."

Gladly. Dominic did not wait for the footman to see him to the door. Agitated more than he preferred to admit, he hailed a hack instead of shimmering to his brother's

Southwart office front.

* * *

Eden lazed in her nightly steam bath, warm moist haze vaporized off the water in waves and billows, reminding her of a hot spring she'd once visited with her parents. Slippery smooth porcelain squeaked against the wet naked skin of her bottom every time she adjusted her seat. The combined warmth of the water on her partially submerged torso and the steam on her exposed parts settled in her body. She felt boneless and languid, as if she herself had liquefied along with the water in the tub. Eden lay with her head pillowed on the back rim, slim pale neck exposed in the moonlight. Her loose ashen tresses dangled over the back rim and pooled on the floor. She'd had Nellie instruct a manservant to lug the tub nearer the window so she could bath by moonlight instead of lighting the lanterns.

The sweet aroma of peaches and pomegranate bath oils filled her nostrils, drugging her into a sensation-driven semi-conscious state. Lashes fluttered closed, Eden hummed a catchy ditty from her days in the schoolroom. She let the weight of her life's many sorrows sink unnoticed to the bottom of the porcelain-confined ocean, forgotten, if only temporarily.

Her thoughts drifted to another such night that had also found her lounging in the bath...a bath that had ended quite scandalously with an impromptu massage. She re-lived, the sensuous glide of his strong capable hands against the smooth wet skin of her feet, and calves. Eden's thoughts turned to the giver of the forbidden pleasure she enjoyed that not-long-ago evening. Dominic.

Even though she knew his secret, one or two of them anyway—she did not delude herself into thinking she'd solved the complex puzzle that was Dominic Ambrosi— She wondered just what he looked like under the shades? Her research in the library had turned up only general definitions, no pictures or detailed explanation of his...condition. Were they freakish? Scarred? In the visions, his eyes were always shadowed or vaguely lit so that his expression was piercing, but his eyes weren't completely visible. But, since her overactive mind's eye did not appear to be receding in strength or frequency, she'd spent the remainder of the day sketching some of the strange images her mind had conjured up.

A smile spread across Eden's mellowed face when she sensed the presence. It entered the room from the far wall and approached her from behind. She knew she should be outraged, scandalized, swooning from shock or screaming for the maid, but Eden could evoke no such reaction to the approaching entity...other than eager anticipation.

* * *

The crescent moon winked mischievously against a backdrop of star-studded sky by the time Dominic traversed the dusty threshold of Cael's office. His was the only storefront in the square still open for business.

"I thought you never tarried into the evening." Dom spoke as soon as he heard the door shut behind him.

"Just waiting up to hear your explanation for why you disappeared last night."

"How did you-" He turned at his brother's words, his surprise quickly dimmed into muted resignation. "Is there anything you *don't* know?"

"You may find this shocking, Dom, but you're rather predictable." Cael's mouth turned up briefly before he grew serious again. "It's about *her*, of course. So, what is she up to now?"

He exhaled a heavy sigh. "Eden and Kathleen had a visitor yesterday...Matthias Montgomery. He frightened her out of her wits and even set Kathleen on edge. I fear he may have gotten a whiff of Stephan, though Ethan thinks he could just as well be after me. Either way, the situation is volatile and dangerous for the three of us."

"I wouldn't worry over-much about Montgomery. I happen to know that his facility is due to come under scrutiny by the social reform board soon. If nothing else, he'll be too preoccupied to bother us again...if we're lucky, the board will put him out of our hair forever. But wait—" A dark gold brow arched over fascinated amber eyes as if he'd just remembered some scintillating tidbit. "The three of us. You, Stephan and...who's the third?"

"The woman admitted to me that she...sees things, hears voices." Dom knew it hadn't slipped his brother's notice that he'd called her by her Christian name a moment ago. "Which is partially my fault, I suppose. She can somehow sense me when I am invisible...and I...shimmered in front of her."

Dominic heard rather than saw his brother tense at this revelation. He continued on quickly before Cael asked him for details of the occasion. "I had thought to send her packing to her relatives before she becomes too embroiled but one glimpse of the Prescotts has disavowed me of the notion."

Cael arched both brows. "That bad, were they?"

"Worse." He grimaced at the memory. "They suggested I apply for her a place at Bedlam."

"I thought as much." His brother stated, shrugging his shoulders matter-of-factly.

Surprised, Dom frowned at him. "You knew?"

"No, just suspected." He admitted, "If she would rather kill herself, than reach out to them...that alone speaks volumes about their character."

Dom hadn't thought of it quite like that before, however having met them, he conceded. "The pair of them would've driven her around the bend within a week...that is, if they were even willing to accept her into their hollow household."

"If you're being sarcastic, the word is hallowed."

"I wasn't. The place is *hollow*, devoid of emotion. It

reminded me of a mausoleum, for all its warmth and gaiety. She could not be happy there."

"You're worried about her happiness? I thought this was a safety issue."

"It was...*is*." Dominic paced, knowing he'd said too much but beyond caring. He needed a sounding board for his feelings. Ethan, the brother that usually provided the service had voluntarily abandoned him. He would make do with Cael in his absence.

"What else?" He pressed.

"Does there have to be something else?"

"Don't be coy, Dom. What's got you so harassed?"

He felt his brother's hand rest on his shoulder, and stilled. "I'm attracted to her. She is...affecting me."

"And you want my advice about how to counteract the effect."

"Yes, dammit!" He rounded, fiercely. "She's not frightened of me as she should be...as I expected her to be."

Cael's eyes narrowed, as if he were assessing the situation. "Do you truly want my advice?"

"I'm here, aren't I?"

"Well," Cael took a turn about the office, considering, thumb and index finger at his chin. "If she is attracted to you and you to her, I can do nothing about it on either end. And why would I? She is marriageable and so are you. Ethan has Kathleen installed as a chaperon." He came back to stand opposite Dom, gesturing mildly as he spoke. "Why not *court* her? And let things evolve naturally."

"Cael." Dom drew out his name as if he were speaking to a confused child. "Courtly manners are beyond me. I've lived too much in my own company."

"Am I correct in assuming that thus far she's been treated to a thorough display of your...eh proclivities?"

Dom felt his jaw twitch, but he could hardly deny his brutish behavior in respect to his guest.

"That's what I thought." Cael concluded, half-smiling.

"Now, what does it tell you that she hasn't already quit the estate at a run?"

He conceded with a nod but pressed on. "There is still the matter of her sanity to be proved, or disproved. If I am to…" He stumbled to a halt, not sure how to complete the statement. What if he were to become involved with Eden… romantically. What would it be like to invite someone to share his life, ease the perpetual loneliness? Could one small woman fill the deep void in his spirit? What if he truly were broken, unable to be fixed or filled, even by a woman whose essence shone as lovely and giving as Eden's?

Or, what if he and the rest of his mother's offspring did not just inherit their mother's psychic talents, but her mental instability as well? True, he had reached the ripe old age of two and thirty with his wits still intact, but what if the madness did not set in until later? Who knew for sure how many more good years remained to him? Did he dare marry and saddle a wife with a loose-screw husband and children cursed with inevitable madness? And if she too succumbed to mind-rot…what chance did their children have, with two asylum-bound parents?

"Ahem, if I am to consider lifelong companionship, I will not repeat my father's mistake."

"You're being paranoid, but I can plan a trip to the estate in a day or two to access her."

"Bring Stephan." Dom needed a buffer between him and her.

"Certainly. I had planned to."

* * *

"Hmmm, Dom-inic-" Eden purred contentedly at the first touch of invisible hands running through her Repunzel-esque hair. He swept aside her tresses, exposing her neck for his touch. She held her breath, poised for his gentle caress…when suddenly a wintery breeze wafted across the sensitive skin of her nape. Instead of Dominic's warm hands, icy fingertips grasp her throat.

Eden started, upsetting the water in the tub. The clammy, grasping hands couldn't be Dominic's. They were much smaller and thinner than she remembered his being, with knife-point nails. Her shoulders hunched involuntarily as she cringed forward to escape the molesting touch. They followed, grabbing hold of her shoulders, kneading in harsh strokes, inflicting pressure on her upper blades and the junction where her shoulders became her neck. The chilling ministrations grew sharp, pinched, then painful.

Eden flinched as the hands seized her neck, squeezing tightly. Her eyes widened in fear and shock; her first thought to scream...but the hands anticipated her and tightened, strangling off any sound. There would be no yell for help now. Eden began to struggle wildly, madly. She twisted her head from side to side, succeeding in doing nothing but wetting the floor and angering the hands into adding a twisting motion to the vice grip. Blind panic infused her with new strength, the superhuman strength of the desperate. Eden scratched at the unseen claws of death choking the life out of her, legs kicking up into the air. A hoarse thread of sound the only hint of the mortal battle being fought.

Water sloshed over the rim of the tub like tidal waves in the ocean, giving her a last-ditch inspiration. She threw all her weight against one side of the tub, succeeding in knocking it off its clawed feet. Eden tumbled from the capsized porcelain on the heels of the mad rush of water. The unexpected jolt off-balanced the malevolent force by just enough to cause its finger extensions of evil to lose their grip. Able to breathe again after what seemed like eons, Eden sucked in gasps of air post haste. Her breasts, wet and naked, heaved from the effort...a hand clutching instinctively at her heart. She shrank away and scrambled backward awkwardly, as the malevolent force moved in her direction. This time she did scream, a bone-rattling shriek born of sheer terror.

SIXTEEN

Night had fallen. Dominic stood outside his brother's now darkened office, watching as the hack carried him hurriedly away to his London townhouse. Cael's advice laid heavy on his mind, mingling with his old nemesis. The two clashed. Attempts to reconcile his past demons with his present...situation...proved vexing. Weary, Dominic glanced around the gloomy, deserted square, already settling his mind for astral travel.

The second his essence shifted into the void, stark horror impaled him like a million shards of glass. Eden's essence flashed blinding shades of purple and violet...her distress nearly palpable, even on the sense-devoid astral plane.

He sought her out, traveling at instantaneous speed. She was alone, hers the only life force for a good distance. Over the years, he'd taught himself the art of astral-to-corporal spatial estimation, a necessary talent to avoid disembarking in front of witnesses. Without thought, Dominic melted himself with her and exited into the corporeal world.

His senses slammed back into him with painful intensity, a hazard of reckless astral travel. Her ear-splitting scream knocked him further off balance. He fell into a backward slide. His tailbone collided painfully against the far wall of a bedchamber...*her* bedchamber, he realized at the same moment that he also realized he held a flailing, *naked* Eden in his arms.

Wetness seeped into his clothes, and he peeked around her to take in the capsized porcelain and gallons of water sloshing around them in quick shifting waves. Satisfied no imminent danger lurked, his focus shifted back to the hysterical woman fighting desperately to escape his hold. She screamed continuously, pausing only to breathe as she struggled against him. His greater size and strength was the only thing keeping her from disentangling herself. She too was dripping wet he noticed.

"Shhhh...Eden,...EDEN! It's me."

"NOOOOOOO!"

They were face to face, but her eyes were tight closed. She snapped her head from side to side, hands clamped over her ears. Her back arched away from him. "No, NOOOOO!"

"Hush, before you bring the ceiling down. Shhhh, cara, please...do not cry so." He cooed, holding a steady hand at her torso, just under her breast, while the other stroked her hair and back. He tried to stay her even as her feet pushed at the slippery wet floor for leverage to tug herself loose.

"Eden, look at me. Open your eyes. It's Dominic, I've got you."

After a time, the fight seemed to drain out of her. She lapsed forward against him, limp and breathing hard. Her bare legs curled loosely around his hips, arms and hands dead weight. Dom held her close with one arm and shrugged out of his jacket with the other. He shifted her to the opposite side to loose the other sleeve. He slipped the jacket around her tenderly as if dressing a precious little one, taking the time to guide her arms into the too-big garment. Then he gathered her fully into a tight embrace, cupped her head and nestled it against his shoulder. Her small warm form against his body was like holding a little piece of heaven in his arms. He thought her unconscious until he heard her sigh.

"That wasn't you before, Dominic." She accused. Her voice was raw and raspy but calm.

Not wanting to reveal the alarm her statement set off, he did his best to mimic nonchalance. "Before when?"

"I was taking a bath when I sensed it, like before when you came to me. I thought it was you, but…the touch was disturbing, sinister-even. Then, it tried to strangle me."

"Eden, you were alone when I arrived. There was no one here…in the corporeal or the astral world."

She continued as if he hadn't spoken. "It retreated across the room, watching us. It only vanished a moment ago." Eden threw up a limp hand to point to the opposite corner, as if the small movement took all the effort in the world. "Please take me away from here. I know you have odd ways of traveling. *Please.*"

Ahhh…Dominic had wondered that she did not ask what he meant by 'the astral world'. It appeared she'd worked out part of the mystery on her own.

"Hook your arms and legs around me, cara."

Head still pillowed on his shoulder, she wrapped her legs around his back while her hands slid into his vest to clutch at the thin silk shirt beneath. Dom nearly forgot himself. He breathed slow and even. By the third long breath, he was steadier. Piggy-backing required a certain amount of expertise and concentration. Eden's enticing body wrapped around him like a hug unsettled his usual calm but he wouldn't have traded the experience for anything in the world. He rubbed her back and rested his cheek against her still-damp hair, breathing in the fruity scent lingering there. A tremor ran threw her, reminding him of their wetness. He'd have to dry them off…and soon or risk them both catching a chill.

"Relax, cara, I won't let anything more frighten you

tonight." With that, he shimmered them onto the astral, orienting himself by the two familiar souls on the estate…Kathleen's and Renfred's, noting that Ethan had arrived. He angled away from all three toward the essence-less space. Dominic kept his suites emptied of servants, for two main reasons: so his domain was easier for him to pinpoint on the directionless plane and so he wouldn't have to worry about someone stumbling upon him as he rematerialized.

They stepped back onto the corporeal in his bedchamber. Dom stood beside the bed, with Eden still in his arms. He was undecided, knowing the danger that lurked within himself. He wanted her. She beckoned to him on so many levels. Her essence was so alluring, calming and beautiful: her body, warm, welcoming, fine, but gently curved…her eyes, those beautiful hazel windows he loved to stare into. Her bruised spirit called out to his broken one. They were alone, with her naked and clinging to his affection-starved body. Dom did not know if he could stop himself from sinking into the abyss of passion her body promised.

"This is your room." Her sweet voice fluttered near his ear like the wings of a hummingbird.

"Yes."

"Your…bed."

He nodded. "Yes."

"Who is 'Cara'?"

"Not a person…an endearment."

"Oh."

She lifted her head up from his shoulder, pulling back to look into his face. "Why the circles, Dom? The bed, the music room, your library, all with a cyclic design."

He smiled unabashed, amused at the guileless curiosity in her expression. He also noted that his nickname had spread…like gossip in the ton. By society's standards, it was, ruinously inappropriate for her to refer to him by his Christian name, much less anything as intimate as 'Dom'.

He frowned, at the thought, and tilted a little out of her space. He shouldn't be so free with her either.

"I've said something wrong, haven't I?"

"No." He took the two steps to the bed, and bent to deposit her on its soft counterpane, careful to pull together the lapels of his jacket around her. "We need to dry off. Stay. I'll find some towels."

* * *

Eden watched her enigmatic host exit through a side door. Instinctively she curled her wet, chilled feet under her. She snuggled, inhaling the woodsy scent of him permeating all around her. His jacket sleeves dangled overlong as she toyed with the brocade pattern of blue-black bedding. She shoved the sleeves back several times before finally giving up. What would he do with her now?

She knew he did not believe her about the evil thing. She shook her head. Why couldn't he feel it too? It did not make sense. If he traveled by the same conventions as the evil thing, then wouldn't they—pass each other on the street, so to speak? The evil had seen *him*. It defied logic that he was so completely oblivious. Her brow furrowed on a sobering thought. Why could *she* see it...and *him*? To her knowledge, she couldn't travel as they did, so why would she be able to sense them 'on the astral'?

Dominic reappeared through the same door, jarring her from her thoughts. Eden appraised him openly. He'd changed his pants, removed the vest and shoes...and now walked purposefully toward her on bare feet with an armful of towels and a white garment of some sort.

"Come." He dumped the load on the bed and beckoned for her to scoop nearer the edge.

Holding his jacket closed with one hand, she complied; dangled her bare legs off the bed just next to where he knelt. He took up one of the towels and started to rub the chill from her foot with vigorous efficiency. Enjoying his taking care of her, she braced herself on her free hand, and watched his dark half-bowed head, looking for any tiny change in the lines around his mouth or the tension in his jaw. If she observed him diligently enough she could gleam subtle changes in his moods, despite the disadvantage of never seeing his eyes.

"Tell me how it works then. This astral/corporeal travel." She longed to hear his voice...deep, unintentionally sensuous, thick sometimes with emotions he chose to either hide or deny. Surprising her, he complied, though he never lifted his bespectacled eyes from his task.

"The corporeal is this world...any mode of normal travel, me walking across the room or you traversing the ocean in a three-month sea voyage. The astral is more undefined. It affects the same surreal, ethereal quality of a dream." He switched feet and again rubbed vigorously to extinguish the bluish twinge from her shivering toes.

"It's timeless, directionless, airless space. There are no landmarks. All the normal senses are dulled, replaced by mindsight, a psychic perception of sorts."

"Then how do you find your way around?"

"Practice. I navigate using human touchstones. Emotions run wild there. That's how I always find you, know when you're overset. People exist in elemental form...all spirit. Everyone's is unique. They have their own soul or essence on the astral. So I learn certain souls of people who are close or familiar to me. People whose habits I know, and they help me know where I am in respect to them and visa versa."

He finished up on her feet, tossed the towel aside and reached for a fresh one from the pile beside her. "Lean forward a bit."

He slung the towel over her hair and began blotting dampened chunks of blonde with circular massages and horizontal propagating rubs between his toweled hands. Her scalp tinkled deliciously. Eden's eyes drifted closed, savoring the soothing sensations, leaning even further into the circle of his arms and resting her head on his shoulder as he pulled the towel the length of her hair, blotting the still dripping ends especially.

"Hmmm...and you can see everyone, their souls I mean."

"Yes, but mostly they are random strangers I do not recognize."

"Why can I sense you there?"

"You can't. You've only ever sensed me when I step off the astral into invisibility."

"Oh." Eden frowned into his shirt, confused. This was something new. "What's the difference?"

"When I am invisible, I am as I am now, except you cannot see me...but if I were to touch you, it would be as I'm touching you now. If I made a sound, you would hear me, as you hear me talking now. On the astral, there is no sound, no sense of touch, no corporal form to touch even if touch existed there. You see the difference."

"I think so." She nodded against him, lingering absently to butt her head against him like an affectionate kitten.

Eden felt him give her hair a final wringing twist with the towel before it plopped on the floor several feet away. With a sigh, she straightened. He too moved back from her.

"Give me your hand."

She hadn't realized they were bluish and shaking until he said the words, and she noticed the concerned crinkle on his forehead as he eyed the one she rubbed unconsciously against her thigh for warmth. Lulled, and eager for more of his tender loving care, she thrust both of her hands at him...forgetting that the one hand acted as a button holding the slack, knee-length garment closed around her. The jacket dropped open, an innocent instigator of passion.

Frozen in the act of reaching for a third towel, his breath split the air, audibly sharp, as he caught her reckless

127

hands in his. "Eden...I—"

The rest of what he said was a mystery to her as he spoke sharply...in some foreign language she assumed to be Italian.

* * *

He was having a hard enough time trying to ignore the tiny glimpses of her body. Now, privy to a long, thorough view of the gentle curves of her taunt pink-tipped breasts, expanding and contracting with each hitching breath she took, as if teasing him...begging him to pleasure them. He did not dare let his eyes drift down, knowing what he would see there.

Dominic knew he'd never win the battle with his desires, much less the war with his conscience. Slowly, he clamped a hand at her waist. Sliding his thumb in a caressing arch across her stomach, he hissed out a breath at the silky smooth texture of her skin. He was lost. His other, outstretched hand shook as it shifted direction, inching toward her exposed loveliness.

Their gazes collided for a moment, his smoldering, hopeful, and lost behind the shaded barrier, hers open, giving, longing even...he noted with mild surprise. Further lured by enticing mother-of-pearl skin and rosebud nipples, his hand closed over her left breast. Her eyes registered shock and silent wonder. He loved how her hazel eyes burned hot at even his lightest touch. Her lids drifted half closed when he brushed her budded nipple with his thumb, testing its sensitivity.

* * *

"Ahhh..." Eden's back arched forward a little. Her breast seeking out his caress. She'd been worried at first that he'd be disappointed in her barely-there endowments. She trembled anew, but not from cold.

"Beautiful...cara." She heard him murmur, a moment later she felt the flutter of his other hand wander up her torso to cover her other breast with warm engulfing fingers. Eden, unable to hold herself still under the collective onslaught, dropped back landing with her elbows braced against the bed. The jacket spread even wider until it fell off her shoulders altogether and pooled on the bed around her.

Pausing, he slid an arm under her slight frame, lifted her, and shifted them further onto the bed. He eased his weigh onto his side and propped himself up on his elbow to one side of her.

"Lie flat, cara...for me, please." Eden smiled at the pleading in his voice. She turned her face to see him again reach a tentative hand across to her breast. A deep furrow marred his forehead and Eden couldn't stop herself turning toward him to place a soft kiss there. The gesture brought her breast into contact with his seeking palm. She let him ease her back flat with a gentle nudge...and then his hand was caressing her breast again. Eden let her eyes drift closed. Unbidden, her hand wondered over to lose itself in his thick black locks. She felt him tense; his hand froze mid-caress.

"Shhh, Dom, let me touch you." She whispered soothing promises, and words of encouragement to him and was rewarded when he relaxed into her light ruffling of his hair. "I won't hurt you, I promise. Please. You can trust me."

His fingers switched back into a light caress over her chest, traveling from stroking her breast to touching the tender skin of her throat and then palming her cheek. It was like he was getting used to the feel of her, allowing himself to relax and enjoy another's touch, presence, and proximity.

"Eden." He said her name in a husky yearning voice that made her sigh. A fresh surge of protectiveness and righteous anger whelmed up inside Eden at the thought of what some sadistic person could have done to create such a fragile vulnerability in a man his size and strength. At that moment, she felt quite certain that she could murder them.

"Dominic." She opened her hazel gaze on him, still toying with his hair. "Close your eyes."

He did not respond. She waited a beat before letting her fingers drift out of his hair on to his cheek and come to rest at the edge of his specs. She paused there, cautious.

His hand on her cheek stilled, his breath now a quiet pant.

"May I?" She whispered.

His lips parted. Eden watched him. He hesitated, seemed caught in a web of anxiety and indecision.

"I...can't." The words tore from him, tortured. Then, like before, he simply wasn't there anymore...except, he was.

"Dom?"

"Yes."

She could still feel his hand against her cheek. The heat of his body poised a scant foot from her naked form. She could see the indentation on the counterpane and hear tiny puffs of air going in and out of his lungs as he breathed. He's invisible! The oddness and delight left her disconcerted, excited, and aroused all at once. He did not protest when she slid the spectacles off his nose and set them aside.

"Does it...bother you? My being...here, but not here." His deep voice asked near her ear.

"No, Dom." And to show him just how very little she minded, Eden, slid her hands back in his hair and exerted pressure to propel him forward. She'd seen him do something to her in one of her ever-intruding visions that had intrigued her enough to want to test it out in the real world. "Kiss me where your hand was before."

Her arm curled around his head as he followed her urging and leaned in to close his hot moist mouth over her jutted nipple. Her back jackknifed off the bed. Her arm, free of the cumbersome sleeves, tightened, clasping him to her breast. She lapsed easily into a sensuous daze, created by his disembodied lips and hot, moist tongue waxing erotic over her skin. Foreign yet addictive sensations spread throughout her body, a tidal wave of heat and undulating pulsations gripped her. A deep burning settled at the pit of her stomach. She hungered for something she could not name.

"Ummm…" Her fingers snaked in his hair.

Warm hands grasped her hips and lifted her to sit astride him, as he rose so that he too sat up. This he did without breaking the delicious hold he had on her breast. She was wickedly naked, while he still wore pants, shirt and an open waistcoat. Eden scooped forward, the textured material of his trousers wreaking havoc on the sensitive folds of her most intimate place. She shuddered.

Dominic left off, pulling slightly away.

"I'm not cold." Eden cut off his concern…but got no further, as his hands found her hair and pulled her to him in a deep, bottomless kiss. Her heart exploded, pounding hard against her rib cage…growing louder and more intense by the second.

Knock! Knock! Knock! A firm succession of raps snapped Eden back into her right mind.

"Dominic?" The sound of Kathleen's voice so close was like a bucket of cold water. "Is tha wee one in there with you? I'll no' have any slap-n-tickle on my watch. Open dis door, I tell ya!"

SEVENTEEN

Blushing from head to toe, Eden just did yank a thick cotton towel over her pink-skinned nudity before Kathleen came bounding through the door. Eden turned what she prayed could pass for an innocent expression on the irate Scottish woman. Kathleen's keen, knowing eyes scanned her face, then trailed down her hastily-covered, still-twitching frame. Unsatisfied, the determined redhead turned to scan the room. Her blunt mien lingered in particular on the abandoned spectacles and the second dent in the counterpane. No, Eden thought, she wasn't fooled.

"Where is dat shady-eyed scoundrel?"

"Dominic isn't here."

"Aye, *now*." She corrected, her manner as blunt as the business end of a battering ram. "Tell me, lass, tis' ya virtue still intact?"

Eden blushed from tip to toes, dropping her head in a faint, humble nod. "Yes, Kathleen."

"Come, we must 'ave a chat, you and I. 'Tis a conversation reserved for mothers and daughters. Most lassies are no' privy ta it until a weddin' is pendin', but there is naught ta be done for it. Aye, ya need a good talkin' ta, and weddin' or no', you're goin' get it!"

* * ×

Instinct had propelled Dom out of her arms and onto the astral. A sharp pang throbbed in his chest. He cherished her tender lulling warmth, missing it at once. Even his essence suffered, wanting very much to exit the astral realm and be reunited with Eden's seductive corporeal body. Dominic suppressed the enticing compulsion and instead sought out Ethan's essence.

He disembarked just outside the dramatic moon-kissed stage at the center of his music room. "Your wife is on the rampage."

From the shadows, Dom watched his brother pivot to face his general direction. "Yes, I know. When Ms. Prescott failed to turn up at the dinner table, Kathleen grew concerned. I gather she found her charge in your company."

"You know me better than that, Ethan. I left before being discovered." He prowled at the edge of the light streaming down from the glass Cyclops aloft, and wondered at the mixed expression flitting across the other man's features, features so like his own until he wondered if he were staring at another version of himself. Ethan was the man he could have been, no, *would* have been, had fate not chosen to kick him in the teeth.

He could feel his brother's eyes groping for him. "Dom, have you, eh—"

"Debauched her?"

"Not quite the sentiment I was aiming at, but a relevant question nevertheless." His let out a heavy sigh, shoulders slumped. "Aren't we beyond this?"

Dom stepped out at once, breaking the perfect circle of light. "You could just as easily step into the shadows with me." His gaze shifted constantly, as to avoid colliding with his brother's.

"I have spent a lifetime escaping from *my* shadows. Walking into yours would be suicide. I'm surprised *you've* survived this long."

He sensed Ethan had a specific agenda even as he relaxed against the black lacquered grand. "Now, you sound like Cael."

"Cael makes a lot of sense. Maybe you should take a closer listen sometimes."

"If I took Cael's advice…" Dominic trailed off, casting his gaze downward to tickle the ivories at the high end.

Exasperated, Ethan shook his head. "Enough, Dom. I'll not chase you around the room. Please put on the bloody spectacles so we can have a normal conversation."

"I don't have them."

"Well, where are they then?"

"Where do you think?" He lifted his lashes over fraternal twins and inclined his head thereabouts. "With her."

"Kathleen?"

"Eden."

His brother's gaze stilled, seeming to almost dissect him. "Dominic, *have* you debauched her?"

"Nearly, Kathleen interrupted." He could admit it. He wasn't proud but he was honest. "I *want* her. And I've never wanted…*that*…before. She did not even pretend to stop me." He sensed in the other man a subtle…dissatisfaction, frustration almost, at his answer.

"Perhaps it would not be so bad if—"

"If what? If I court her as Cael suggested? Or if I married her, an idea you so obviously esteem." He dismissed both notions with a wave of his hand, unbreakable steel back in his voice. "She is unstable, and I am done pretending otherwise. Would you have me tied to a woman destined to descend into madness? I'll not damn myself or innocent children to suffer my tragedy."

"Eden is *not* Lillian, Dom. You do her a disservice to even make such an unflattering comparison. She is fragile at the moment, yes, but she's not dangerous or off-balanced. I have glimpsed a strength in her, I am certain."

"Oh really?" Brows ascended to mock his brother's conviction. "When I astraled home, I found her writhing naked and hysterical on the bedchamber floor, dripping wet next to a capsized tub. She was screaming her lungs out. After I calmed her down enough to explain, she swore there was a presence of some sort there. She claimed that it attacked, bent on strangling her to death."

"What is Cael's opinion?"

He exhaled deep and long. "I don't know. He's to come assess her in two days time. But after tonight, there is little doubt that *something* is amiss with her. There was no one else, evil or otherwise; she was alone. I would know. How long do you think, before she starts to…hurt herself?"

"Do me a favor, and don't leap to any conclusions…leastwise not until after Cael makes his analysis."

"Wishful thinking will never do."

"As a favor to me then."

A familiar tune trilled from his fingers as Dominic considered the request. If there were a hidden truth, no one better to uncover it than Cael. His younger brother's keen sense of people and discerning eye for details served him well.

"We'll wait." He decided.

"Ahem… in the meantime, I suggest no more, eh, boundary-crossing social behaviors, unless of course you don't mind a stinging slap on the wrist." A haphazard smile spread across the doctor's features. "Kathleen's become a bit overzealous with the pregnancy."

"I will consider myself warned."

* * *

Two days. Therein lay the full measure of his self-control…before he cast common sense aside and pursued his baser instincts. The memory of her passion-daze eyes, soft feminine sighs, and inviting arms open for him and inviting his touch dogged him. The promise of unspeakable pleasures plagued him, a virus in his mind, a carnal itch, eroding his resolve. What did it say about his character, his future sanity to which he clung so desperately, that he remained stimulated, against even his own judgment, to seek solace in the arms of a would-be madwoman? That he knew without a doubt despite the wrongness of it, that reassurance and calm could be found in such an unlikely place.

* * *

Eden sat in front of the vanity, Kathleen's none-too-gentle set down still ringing in her ears from days before. She wondered if Dominic had endured a cutting lecture from Dr. Raine? Or mayhap from Kathleen herself? Eden wouldn't put it pass the brass Scottish woman to rake him across the coals just as she had done to her.

She ran a soft-bristled brush over her hair, more concern with concealing the deep blue and purple contusions blinking back at her from the mirror. The milky pearl of her skin at her shoulders and throat were marred with evidence of the entity's attack. She tried to obscure them with a bit of excess lace strategically looped behind her neck and tucked into the cleavage of her dress. But the bruising outshone the flimsy fabric, calling for a conspicuous shawl. Eyeing herself, Eden knew the odd ensemble would not go unnoticed at the breakfast table. Even now that they'd ascended to a poignant, if erratic closeness, Dominic only sporadically appeared at meals so she was less concerned in that corner. Of course with his unique talents, he might have already seen the bruises.

Exasperated, Eden shrugged her shoulders and shifted her attention to her hair. The dark strands she'd noticed several days before were still there. They seemed more numerous, although no more noticeable than before...to anyone but her, that is. She shifted a handful of blonde and finger-combing it. Yes, there were definitely new strands of brunette. It troubled her. People grayed with age, not the other way around.

Just then, an infinitesimal disturbance in the room captured her attention. She grew still. A moment of silent apprehension later, something like the flutter of a moth wing touched her hand. She jumped. The brush clattered to the floor.

"Shhhh. Do not be alarmed." The deep, familiar voice soothed her fears. "I'll not hurt you."

He must have bent to pick up the brush because the next she knew, a hand slid into her hair, while another pulled the soft bristles through the thick masses. He brushed in long, lingering strokes, massaging her scalp lightly with his other hand. Eden rested her eyes and relaxed into the tingling rightness of his ministrations.

"Better?"

"Yessss." The word came out a hiss of feminine satisfaction. She purred like a cat being petted. For he had slowly lowered his free hand to her breast, where he began massaging it through the fabric of her dress. Eden's lips parted, luminous hazel eyes stared upward at nothing, but she felt his gaze on her. She strained her neck, seeking, silently inviting his kiss. The soft tentative touch of his mouth branded her a moment later. The warm, moist tongue slipped between her parted lips like a thief in the night.

"Hmmm..." Eden moaned deep in her throat, as she heard the brush once again clash unceremoniously against the floor. His now-free hand entwined itself in her hair, and guided her head back so he could explore her at his leisure. His other hand was still a caressing menace at her gowned breast. Pleasure spiked. And soon, she longed to feel his hand against her bared breast, though now, thanks to Kathleen, she knew it wanton to give in to the desire.

Her hands which had been erratically gripping the knobs of the armrests under the onslaught of dizzying sensations, stirred into action. She reached around the hand that was caressed her throbbing breast to awkwardly shove the top of her bodice loose and guide his willing fingers to close over her tender naked flesh. So responsive was the wee nub until she could feel the tiny corrugations of his fingertips, raking an enticing friction back and forth, creating a wonderful answering throb, which sent shockwaves tingling through her body.

"Ohhh." Her other hand cupped the back of his head, as she continued to take his tongue eagerly into her mouth.

Restless, and fast succumbing to a more far-reaching appetite, Eden shifted in the seat. Her legs, she did not quite know what to do with them. More and more, the junction between them burned with some gnawing emptiness, that yearned to be filled. It felt as if her core were salivating, starved for a specific fulfillment, only she did not quite know what. She twisted and turned, the dress with its endless undergarments were as so many cloying blankets smothering off her oxygen, the shawl suddenly over-warm around her neck. Though she'd asked, Kathleen had left many details out of her explanation of what went on between married men and women. She'd only say that the illusive *it* was forbidden and led to sinful indulgence…an apt description, indeed Eden thought.

* * *

Dominic felt her twitch and jerk beneath his hand, and his lips. He was perversely aroused by the fact that he could reduce her to a quivering heap of raw needs just as completely as she could him. He recognized the peculiar new, yet somehow familiar stirring in his groin. He also knew he'd have to do something definitive about it eventually, but for now, he relished the heightened sensations. Loved the throb of awareness touching her set off in him.

He finally broke off the never-ending kiss. Her panting breaths matched his own. Her hand was still lost in his hair. She curled it around to cup his cheek. He knew the instant she noticed he hadn't donned his usual eyewear. Her hand stilled then grappled around in search.

"You aren't wearing your spectacles?" She asked, voice thick and throaty, yet bewildered.

"I find immense pleasure in gazing upon your body unhindered by obstruction."

"You've seen all of me and yet you refused me a glimpse of your eyes."

"Eden..." He frowned beneath her fingertips.

"Another time, Dom. For now, *this* is enough." And with that she urged his head forward to arch over her. He took the cue, with flawless execution, retracting his hand from her bodice only to fling aside the shawl and bits of lace, and shove the dress low enough so that her small pert breasts popped completely free. the one already rigid and winking at him. He dipped to capture a pink-tipped crest between nibbling lips...stopping short. Her lush, tempting hilltops no longer garnered his attention, instead he was riveted by the ugly, bluish purple ruin on her otherwise smooth alabaster skin. All else paled in importance.

"Eden?"

"Hmmm..." She answered, passion-dazed.

"Where did these bruises come from?" Dominic pulled out of her reach, walked around to face her and get a better look at them.

Incandescent hazel eyes blinked, confused, shifting around in restless search of him. His form remained cloaked.

"The entity from the other night made them." She aimed her voice in his general direction.

"There was no one. I would have seen a second essence when I approached you."

She shook her head vehement. "For some reason, I have yet to work out, you cannot sense it. I can. It attacked me."

Dom recoiled from her words. They were damning evidence of her declining mental state. He tried to steady his shaking hands, glad that she could not see the horror on his face. He reached out and touched the damaged skin at her throat.

"Eden, please." The entreaty surfaced from a deep grave of fears, long buried but never forgotten. "I want you to meet my brother, Cael. He will visit the estate before the week is out, and I would like you to speak with him."

"The other doctor?"

"Yes, Cael is a doctor for the mind."

"Why is it imperative that *I* meet him?" She asked. Stark pain swam in her eyes.

"I fear you are not well, and I—"

"—don't want to become involved with a lunatic?" She finished the sentence for him.

He winched at her candor, and retracted his hand as if bitten. A knock at the door saved them both from an awkward moment. Eden immediately tugged her sagging bodice up to cover her breasts.

"That's just Nell with breakfast." He informed her.

She stared from his invisible form to the closed chamber door, with an awe-struck expression. "You can see through walls when you're like this?"

"No."

"Then, how…"

"I told her to bring a tray up to your chamber." He explained.

"Why?" She asked, curious. "Did you think I wouldn't come down to breakfast?"

"I needed her to interrupt us, so I'd have a reason to stop."

"Oh."

Dominic watched the frown form, a childish confusion clouding her features. "Must we stop, then?"

"We're not married. It's improper."

"Are you that much concerned with propriety, Dominic?" She shot the empty space where he was a dubious glance.

"No." He admitted on a woeful sigh. His insides twisted, turning, this way and that, his heart constipated by frustration, indecision, and doubt.

"Then, it's my supposed insanity that you find so vexing and un-bedable? Is that right?" This she said with angry sarcasm.

"Miss?" The maid called through the door. "Are you awake?"

"Yes, Nell, one moment." She refocused her attention. "Can she see you? Sense you as I do."

"My brothers and you are the only persons I've come into contact with that are able to call me out."

"In that case, be silent." Before he could know her intention, she called through the door. "You may enter now. I am...decent."

Despite her wish to stay him, Eden knew the instant the door opened and she felt the soft touch of his lips at her temple that in the next instant he would be gone. And he was.

EIGHTEEN

Eden was surprised when not two but three of Dominic's brothers turned up at the noon meal, along with herself and Kathleen. Even Dom made one of his rare appearances in the dining hall. Despite the crowd the conversation often limped to a halt and consisted mostly of the weather and mishmash about Ethan and Kathleen's future bundle-of-joy. The newcomers, introduced to her as Cael and Stephan Atherton, were not what she expected. They resembled one another greatly, barring a few scattered details, but neither looked even the tiniest bit like either Dominic or Dr. Raine.

The one called Stephan ate very little and spoke even less, choosing instead to brood over each course before waving a hand to order it away. Intrigued, Eden angled to catch his eye only to have him unsettle her with a fathomless scrutiny until she reddened and broke contact. Cael, the one she'd agreed to meet, possessed a pleasing deportment. He chatted, smiled and joked when appropriate and seemed to aim at easing the awkward burden of several unacknowledged elephants lumbering about the room. Eden was glad of his presence. Otherwise, the prickly atmosphere, writhing with tensions and secrets, would have choked her just as surely as a noose around her neck. When, at last, the ax dropped and the captives scattered to freedom, Eden found herself on the nervous end of a liquid smile.

"Miss Prescott."

"Dr. Atherton." She twinned her curtsey with a nod. "I understand it's you I have to thank for my life."

"Oh please, I don't stand upon formal manners. And, I'd like to think that we all have a little hero in us." He chuckled at the thought, as he took her arm into the crook of his. "Might I be so bold as to invite you on a stroll to the portrait library. Have you seen it?"

"No. I didn't even know there was one."

"Well, my brother is an abominable host, so I cannot say as I'm surprised. He probably left off showing the wine vault as well." He lowered his voice to conspiracy level. "Sour grapes."

Eden fought with a smile, but it won. She did not want to like him because he'd been forced on her. As his steered her up two flights and down a succession of ubiquitous hallways she had a feeling she was being finessed out of her dislike, with a natural sort of grace, but finessed all the same.

"He tells me you're an artist."

"Yes, I sketch."

"Would you mind terribly if I begged a peek at your work?"

"You have an interest in the arts?" She kept her tone light and her face forward. "Dom painted you as strictly a man of science."

"My work consists of the mind's science, thus I crave more artistic pastimes. A man cannot live by bread alone."

She conceded with a nod, as he stopped them in front of a camouflaged door, with only a knob to distinguish it from the wall's wainscoting. "Is there a bell-pull in the portrait gallery, do you know?"

"Not unless Dom had one installed recently."

"Oh. I was going to have one of the maids fetch my sketches."

"I'll wait. It's no bother."

"I'm afraid I haven't been paying much attention to how we arrived here." Eden confessed. She was too caught up in trying to puzzle him out. He did not treat her like a mental case, but Dominic must have discussed her peculiarities with him.

"Ahhh. I'll walk you back to the stairs."

From there, Eden ran down to retrieve her sketches, not dreading the meeting so much anymore. Truth be told, Atherton presented a challenge. She found herself anxious for his opinion of her works. Perhaps if she were shrewd, she could finagle some information out of him.

* * *

The first sketch was of Kathleen in the gazebo. Eden watched as recognition dawned, but he made no overt comment on the quality of her talent.

"Did you know, Ms Prescott, that the brain is the most complex organ in the body?"

"It seems logical that it would be." She agreed, as she shuffled along past a much-mounted wall in the portrait gallery.

Framed portraits in varying size and shape adorned every conceivable inch of the mile-long walls, as many of landscapes as of persons. The central space housed free-standing room-dividers covered with still more oils of people and places. The towering faux walls left off in certain spots to make room for an odd divan or two. Atherton rested upon one such luxury. Eden estimated it would probably take several hours to view each and every rendering in the gallery, so rest areas were a clever idea.

Next, he flipped to a dodgy scribbling of Dr. Raine. Eden squirmed.

"The chin is all wrong." He proclaimed. "An admirable effort, but obviously done without benefit of a sitting."

"The doctor never tarries here long enough to pose for a portrait."

"He is absent a lot then."

"Almost constantly, returning more to check on his wife than Dominic or I."

"Does that bother you?"

"Not particularly, but you asked."

He lowered the sketches to his lap, and tilted her his first personal inquiry of the day. "Tell me, do you still consider yourself in need of a doctor...or would you say you're completely healed."

"I require neither yours, nor your brother's services, Dr. Atherton. I do, however, want to allay Dominic's concerns. He specifically asked me to see you in this capacity. I wouldn't have otherwise, even were I as mad as King George."

Atherton chuckled. And Eden got the distinct impression the head doctor approved of her. "I did wonder if he appraised you of my true reason for coming here, speaking to you. Forgive me for being circumspect, but it took me a while to ascertain that you were indeed aware and in compliance with my assessing your...eh, "

"Mental prowess?"

"Yes, I like that." He nodded and went back to the sketchbook.

Eden saw the chance to sneak in a question of her own. "Outside of height, you don't look anything like Dominic or the other doctor."

"Dominic and Ethan resemble our mother. Stephan and I do not."

"What about the other two? Kathleen said there were six."

"Gideon and Gabriel. Actually, there's an oil of them in this gallery somewhere. Perhaps we'll come across it."

Intrigued, she followed with a second question. "Were

the six of you not reared together?"

"Miss Prescott, this meeting is about you. If you wish to know more about Dominic's childhood, why not just ask him."

"He won't even show me his face, and you think he'd discuss his childhood with me." Eden scoffed. "You've seen them, haven't you?"

"His eyes, yes, but I'd known him for two years before he allowed me the privilege. He's known Kathleen four and she still thinks they're sensitive to the sun or some such nonsense. I wouldn't back him into a corner about it if I were you." Cael flipped to the next page in the sketches. Eden could tell by his sudden stillness and the new look of interest that he'd come to the series of sketches she'd done on Dominic. He turned another page, Dominic without his specs, another, again Dominic without his specs, her colored speculations.

"I see you have been curious."

"He told me the condition is trifold."

"That is correct."

"Why is he so phobic about it?"

"That is a question even I would like the answer to." He glanced up at her then, by now she hovered next to him to gauge his reactions to her work, all pretense of viewing the gallery forgotten. His gaze, the same liquid amber as the sphinx-like Stephan, blazed into her, burning away the superficial to get at her inner most thoughts.

She broke off first as she had with his brother. "I don't believe you know much more about Dominic than I do, Dr. Atherton." Eden couldn't help making her words a half-accusation.

"Since you seem bent on discussing him, I'll make you a deal."

She conveyed her interest with an arched brow.

"You answer my questions, and I'll answer yours."

* * *

Dominic wasn't sure what approach he should take. He'd never really ceased thinking of Stephan as a child. Now seemed an appropriate time to promote him to adulthood; he'd made two and twenty his birthday. With his recent manifestation—of what, Dom didn't know— Stephan would have to brazen out a new path. Whether he cared to accept it or not a conventional life lay beyond his reach.

They strolled in the stone garden at the back of the house. Winter had not yet relinquished its bitter hold, so many of the flowering plants weren't in bloom.

Dom tilted his gaze. His slightly taller height and copper hair were Stephan's main distinction from Cael.

"Please don't stare as if I am some stranger who just happens to resemble your brother. Even though I have maimed and nearly killed, I'm still me."

"My apologies."

"Cael suggested this?"

Dom noticed that his words were a statement.

"Ethan. I actually think it shocked Cael. But I wouldn't have extended the invitation unless your being here suited me."

"What's wrong?"

Dom frowned. The younger man should have already been apprised of the situation, particularly since a good deal of it concerned him. "Cael hasn't spoken about Gabriel? Montgomery's threats? Greyson?"

"He may have." His shrug belied the seriousness of his next words. "My *ability* is quiet only when I am passive, numb almost, so I have taken to avoiding stimulus...of any kind. Cael is frustrating, and I don't wish to hurt him. But existing in a stupor grows old, and tiring. Even that I worry about. Could fatigue light the fuse again and consume those around me? Or anxiety, if I worry overmuch?"

Ahhh, Cael had spoken of Stephan's remoteness.

Though he hardly needed the memory to register his youngest brother's much-altered demeanor. "But you are comfortable talking to me."

"Yes."

"No twinges or volatile emotion?"

"None."

Dom nodded. "Excellent. A coping strategy."

For the first time, Stephan, turned to eye him head-on. "Is that why *she's* still here? The woman, I mean. She helps you cope."

Dom bristled, but the reaction only sparked more scrutiny from amber eyes burning with curiosity. "Her name is Eden."

He nodded. "When Ethan introduced us, I remember thinking the name apt. Her presence, it calmed the thing within me. It took me a while to realize it was *her*. A serene wind, that's the only way to describe it. I wished I had been seated adjacent her instead of across, perhaps then I could have participated in the conversation."

"She is affecting me as well." Dominic marveled, suddenly keen for Cael's assessment and desperate for it to be optimistic news.

Just then, the clack of footsteps against cobblestone echoed. Both brothers turned to receive the slow-gaited Renfred around a weed-choked flowerbed.

"Master Ambrosi, message just arrived, sir."

Dom accepted the square-fold communiqué hesitantly. "How was it delivery?"

"By special carrier."

"Will he wait for a response?"

"No, sir. The barer departed almost immediately."

"Thank you, Renfred."

"Gideon?" Stephan supposed after the butler had departed.

Dom eyed the small parcel in his hands as if he were afraid it would bite him. "I have never received a written message from Gideon in my life. Have you?"

He shrugged. "I've never received a written message from you either."

* * *

Eden paced away, giddy. She had stored up a wealth of questions during her two-week sojourn, and hardly knew which one to pose first. Pivoting around, she came to stand in front of him.

"Anything? You'll tell me *anything* I want to know?"

A thought flashed in his eyes before his unreadable facade returned. "Anything that doesn't violate a confidence."

"Fair enough. I agree." She posed the first question, not sure how long her good fortune would last, she decided on the most controversial. "Does Dominic have a network of scars marring his torso, either in front or at his back?"

Atherton had returned his attention to the makeshift sketchbook, only to freeze amidst flipping to the next page. "No. What would prompt such a question?"

"I…" Eden hesitated. She wasn't supposed to have seen him without his shirt, now she'd have to admit to it or risk his thinking her a loon. "An accident. I tumbled from the ladder in the library and Dom caught me. In the midst of untangling ourselves, I saw the scars…But when I asked how he got them, he denied it."

Eden did not like the focused amber pinning her in place. The scrutiny reminded her of the Sphinx. "So, you do see things. I wondered."

She sagged, that was a 'no'. At least now she knew, the scars truly were her own imaginings. She'd been so sure that he was somehow hiding them from her. Maybe she needed Atherton's services after all.

"What kinds of things have you seen?"

"People, strange happenings. Distortions of reality."

"Be more specific, Ms. Prescott."

149

Eden inhaled deep, and dropped down beside him on the divan, suddenly weary. "On the day that you found me half-drown in the marsh. Whilst I stood on the brink, desperate for a reason, any random inclination not to succumb to my grief, an image formed just under the surface of the water...a woman and her infant called to me. My first thought was that they were drowning and I ought to save them. I don't know what happened then, but the next thing I knew the water had me. And then later I awoke here, with Dr. Raine attending at my bedside."

"Hmmm. Were the faces familiar at all?"

"No."

"Are the...visions...frequent?"

"Very."

"Tell me about this vision the other night."

She felt her spine toughen up. So, Dom had enlightened his brother about a good many things. "That was not a vision, and I have the bruises to prove it." She snatched the shawl from her shoulders, indignantly. The doctor gave the discolored skin at her neck the briefest glance, but exhibited no discernable reaction. Strange. She had expected him to gasp or interrogate her about the bruising. When he continued on without incident, she re-adjusted her cover-up.

"My brother insists there was no attack." The doctor's focus shifted back to his lap as he flipped the page. "That you caused the bruises yourself."

"I am aware of his opinion." She knew she sounded waspish, but blast the man for coloring the doctor against her. "But, I wonder...If Dominic can travel as he does, why assume no one else can? Perhaps there is another with equal talents, and fewer scruples. By the by, I'd like to know. Are you...different...like Dom or is it just him?"

As Eden piqued an ire brow at him, she noticed Atherton's attentions lay elsewhere. His vague, "Define different." seemed spoken as an afterthought, so absorbed was he with the chalk visages staring out from the page.

"Dominic travels in another realm. He can cloak himself and skulk about unnoticed. Do *you* do that? *Would you* spy on me, if I refuse to spill all my dirty little secrets?"

Still he only had amber eyes for her artistic renderings. "The two of you had a spat recently, I see. But to answer your question, no, I am not adept. Tell me, what was the impetus for these last few drawings?"

"The visions, what else." Exasperated by Atherton's odd fascination, Eden snapped out her next inquiry. "What the devil is so interesting about that one anyway?" He couldn't even be bothered to notice her annoyance. The quiet answer she received startled her.

"I know them. And I must say you've captured the likeness and the differences rather brilliantly. One would almost think…"

"Who…are they?" The pair of them had greeted her in the vanity mirror one morning, blinking back at her just as they did from the sketch the vision had inspired. Alluring, yet eerie…almost like a blurring of one image into two. Both with midnight hair and tan-olive skin, rather like Dominic's she realized suddenly…but his face was fleshy, rounded, less angular than the two in her vision.

"Come."

That broke the spell. Eden followed him as he laid her sketches aside on the divan, stood and held a hand out for her. Atherton drew her along the back wall of the L-shaped gallery, until they stood before a wide rectangular oil of the same two in her sketch. Identical visages, bust-only, posed shoulder-to-shoulder.

"That's Gideon there on the right and Gabriel on the left." He gestured. "Are you sure you've never been in this room before?"

"No. Never."

"How interesting."

NINETEEN

Matthias twitched. He sweated it out alone in a room with the size and appeal of a privy. The voices of the Social Reform Board in the adjacent meeting hall carried just enough for him to discern who spoke but not enough to make out what was being said.

He called in a few favors from the contacts he still claimed on Bow Street and squeezed a handful of inmates' relatives—influential peers—to apply pressure to the board. Blackmailed a half dozen of his off-the-books clientele into endorsing St. Ciaran Isis as a godsend and offering funds to help refurbish his establishment and modernize any archaic practices.

Still, he worried. Harry had, as predicted, rolled over and played snitch like a yellow-tailed pig. Enlightening the board about the Asylum Keeper's more unsavory practices with a select number of female inmates. Most of the ones he'd had a turn with recently were too blissed out on opiates to bare witness. But the implication alone was damning, particularly on top of the other deficiencies leveled against St. Ciaran Isis.

The door creaked open and a bookish-type ushered him back before the full-paneled board of Social Reform.

Matthias teamed with an underlying frenzy. Nobody came into St. Ciaran Isis and superseded his authority. No matter how the cards fell, Greyson would suffer for the privilege.

Poking the top-drawer bastard in the eye with a heated promise, Matthias squared himself for the verdict. He'd let Greyson win this round, damn the fates, but he'd make sure his was the last word. Yeah, he liked that. The very last word.

TWENTY

Dom watched his brother from behind the desk in his study as he mulled. Stephan advanced on the flickering blaze in the hearth. Firelight sparked off a dance of mahogany highlights in his hair.

"What are you going to do about Greyson's request?" Even as the younger man posed the question, his eyes had yet to break free of the crackle of scarlet-yellow flame and occasional indigo hiss that chewed up the kindling with burning passion.

"I am inclined to disallow it. I don't trust these scientific spiritualist types. Science and religion, an unholy union if ever there was one."

"And the warning?" Stephan fingered the coiled iron poker standing sentry, and sank into a low squat at the edge of the fire's reach. The writhing flames licked mere inches from his rapt expression, throwing off bold shadows and tiny glowing sparks which landing on his jacket-ed shoulders. His interest bordered on fixation.

"I'll speak with Cael first. It is wise to consider another's opinion." Dominic frowned at the backlit profile, again noting the oddness in his brother's actions. "Stephan?"

"Hmmm."

"Are you sure you're alright? This thing…don't allow it to mar the rest of your days."

Just as his fingers reached out into the licking flames, he paused and lowered his arm. "I don't know if I will ever be as I was before it happened. That person is no more."

Dominic nodded. "Your life will be different, no doubt, but not without hope. Ethan lives quite content with his gift-"

"There is no comparison. Ethan's gift is not dangerous to those around him, neither is yours for that matter." He head snapped around to flash horror-stricken eyes. "I live at the mercy of an evil, seething within, turbulent and deadly, poised to lash out at the slightest provocation. The tiniest lapse of control and I'd be responsible for…" He trailed off. "Mine is not a gift, it's a curse."

Dom opened his mouth to protest, but could not think of a single point to make.

"I had thought at first to…" He paused, eyeing Dom with an odd, almost un-nerving expression. "I even acquired a pistol…but I could not. Cael."

Alarmed, Dominic lurched from behind the desk to come to his brother's side. Now, he'd have to watch Stephan as he did Eden. "Don't do anything drastic, please. We will find a solution to this. If it is easier for you here, then stay, indefinitely. Cael will understand."

His brother straightened, amber orbs blazed with disbelief. "But you dislike unnecessary people loitering about."

"I will adjust." He insisted. "I've had Ms. Prescott, Kathleen, and Ethan lurking around a fortnight. Even Nonna managed to force a visit. And I haven't gone 'round the bend yet."

"Nonna?" Though he did not smile, Dom could see some of the anxiety ease from his face. "I suppose if you withstood the devil herself, I cannot do much harm."

Dom smiled, in relief as much as amusement.

* * *

Long after Stephan had departed the study, Dominic mused behind his desk. Alone, he rested his specs on the stained cider desk in front of him. He fiddled with the message, folding and unfolding it along the original lines. The contents of the letter replayed in his mind. Greyson wanted an audience with him, for what reason the letter did not specify. He had most likely omitted the impetus for his request hoping curiosity would lure Dom into granting a meeting. Dom reached back to what he knew of the man. Greyson delved into psionics, the science of adepts and mental instability. Maybe he could help Stephan, or maybe…Dom remember another such scientist, from long ago who claimed to want to *help*.

"Check his eyes." She directed.

Lillian always kept a safe distance away, preferring to observe from the shadows of the room's many archways that spilled into the underground torture chamber.

The doctor was tall and reed thin, with a whip of a mustache and a hallow face with skin stretched tight over the skull. He pried Dominic's lids back with jabbing fingers and shined a candle at him. Mind-shackled to the pewter stone, all he could manage was to squirm against the invasion.

"Still he stares out with the devil's gaze." The doctor's voice was the last judgment.

"Purify him." His mother's dulcet tone echoed across the wet, musty chamber, mocking her condemning words. "I'll have my son back. My flesh and blood, not this atrocity hiding behind sweet little Dominic's face."

"Come, let us prepare."

Lillian's coven of spiritualists filed out through various archways: the druid, the witch, the priest, and finally the doctor, leaving him isolated on the island dais surrounded by chill and misery. The mingled sound of dripping water and scurrying rodents punctuated the nightmarish darkness.

He often wondered why none of them had ever thought to simply gouge out his eyes. Attack the demon at its source. Dominic weighed the alternative: the broken bones, bleedings, stench of scorched hair and flesh. His throat still screamed from retching up the foul concoctions the witch routinely forced into him. All that would cease, if they simply plucked out the mismatched orbs dirtying the windows to his mind. Blindness. It was acceptable to have the ceremonies stop, and the horror of knowing his soul damned to hell fade. His mother might even love him again.

He couldn't do it himself. He was always restrained either by his mother's mind or the grated pit. Suggesting the solution to his tormentors was also out of the question. Lillian and her spiritualist cronies were a keen and radical bunch, but he doubted even they would allow the possessed to direct the manner of his own exorcism.

A faint scrambling shattered the silence. His dread spiked, thinking they'd returned sooner than usual to begin the next effort to drive the demon out.

"Dominic?" The thin shaky squeak alleviated his fear. "Dominic, please, I can't see! Tell me where I'm going."

He couldn't shout because his voice just barely worked. "Shhh, don't let them hear you."

The scrambling grew louder and more confident.

"Dominic?" His brother's murmur wafted from a few feet away.

"Here, Ethan."

"What's wrong with your voice?" He asked, as he climbed atop the stone platform.

"Nothing, just the chill." He lied. Though Dominic was younger by a couple of years, his brother Ethan had only recently fallen into the care of their mother. He felt obligated to shield Ethan as much as possible, lest Lillian take it in her mind that he too needed 'curing'. "You shouldn't be here."

Dominic closed his eyes when his brother's warm gentle fingers closed around his neck. The rawness and the ache faded like liquid through a sieve. "How did you do that?" His voice carried strong and deep.

"I don't know." He shrugged. "I've always been able to."

"Can you fix my wrist? I think one of em's broken."

"I'll try." Warm, nervous fingers trailed down both his arms until they found the useless flopping hand.

"Don't worry about hurting me. They're both numb." As with his throat, the feeling and strength flowed back into his hands in a matter of moments. "Never let her know, ever, what you can do. Ever! Promise me."

"I promise." The small voice agreed.

"Where are Gideon and Gabriel?"

"Confined in the cellar most of the time. Are they my brothers too?"

"Yeah." If she'd started in on the twins, she'd eventually turn on Ethan as well. He'd been foolish to hope. "She lets you see them?"

"Sure, whenever I ask. Dominic, how come mama does this to you?"

He stiffened. "It's mostly the others."

"Only because she allows it. I know. Gabriel told me. He dreams things, things about you and our mother. He's how I knew where to come."

Ahhh, Gabriel. Dominic had wondered about that.

"He wanted me to find out if you were…alive. I did not know what he meant at first. I called him a liar."

"Ethan." A plan formed in his mind.

"Yes."

"Would you do me a favor?" If he could get Ethan to comply, maybe he could trick her.

"Sure."

"It will be hard. And painful. I would rather not have you involved, but there is no one else." Once he convinced his mother he was cured, they could devise a plan. His blindness would be a handicap, but it could work. As long as Ethan knew where the twins were and still had access to them.

"What is it?"

Dominic took a deep breath. "The next time you come, bring a metal rod, sharpened to a point and hot. The poker from one of the fireplaces, that'll do."

"Do for what?" His brother's voice shook, seeming to not want the answer to his own question.

158

"You will gouge out my eyes." Dominic spoke as commanding as he could. "Then use your fingers to heal up the empty sockets. Make it look like a miracle from Heaven."

The answering wobble was not encouraging. "But you'll be blind."

"Once my eyes are gone, she'll think I'm normal again and let me out of here."

"No, Dominic. I...can't."

"Yes, you can. It's the only way. We have to save Gideon and Gabriel before they end up like me."

"She doesn't hurt them."

"She didn't hurt me at first either."

"We can find another way."

"In the meantime they'll torture me. Do you want that?"

"What if I just keep coming back to heal what they do."

"That's not a good plan, Ethan. They'll notice if I heal too quickly. Or worse, what if mama catches you? And do you want Gabriel to dream about what they do to me? I bet he hasn't admitted the worse of it."

"I...I have to go."

"No, Ethan, wait. Please. Ethan?" But he could already hear the retreating scramble.

"I'll think of something else." He called back.

"Ethan!" He strained against the invisible hold.

"Dom." Cael's quiet, rational voice answered instead.

"ETHAN!" He snapped back in the chair and shot up to his feet, upending the desk in the process. It flipped over onto its side in a deafening crash with fly-away papers, fallen books, and much scattering of knickknacks.

"Dominic?"

"I want to see him!" Wild-eyed, he raked over the room, but saw nothing but reflections of his own blurred panic. "Where is he? I have to make him understand."

"Dom, calm down. Whatever was happening to you a moment ago is over now. Ethan is fine; he's upstairs with Kathleen and Stephan."

Sweaty and panting, his first sane thought was that he'd

crushed the letter. He held its crumpled remains to his forehead, sopping the wetness there. "Oh, Gawd."

"Are you alright?" He heard Cael's concerned voice from somewhere close.

"No, I'm not." He felt the tears coming, but couldn't stop them. He blinked furiously, trying to bring Cael's face into focus.

"I'm not alright, Cael. She'll start in on Gideon next." Gentle, guiding hands propelled him around the cedar titan and he followed, grateful for their support. "He's different, too. I couldn't stop her...I begged Ethan to help me stop her but he wouldn't...Gideon, Gabriel, then Ethan. Now Stephan. I'm going to kill her!"

"Dom, you're not making any sense. Come from behind the desk. Come on, come over here and sit down. That's right, step over the mess."

"Its my fault." He should have been able to stop her before she'd gotten to Stephan.

"Dom?" She stepped forward.

His ears perked up at the small female voice. "Eden."

"Yes." Her stomach did summersaults when his naked eyes clapped on her face for the first time. They were...haunting. She'd never forget the sight even if this were the only time she had the privilege. His left eye was a striking shade of blue, bright, almost luminescent sky blue. The right one was slate gray, with a lighter pewter variation towards the center. The anguish she saw in their depths was a palpable thing. She wanted to go to him immediately, but Cael stayed her just inside the door with a firm gesture.

"Miss Prescott, I think it would be best if you left us alone."

Eden frowned at Atherton's suggestion, but her eyes never left Dominic's frayed expression. "Dom?"

He seemed confused, caught somewhere between past and present. Atherton led his docile bulk over to the sofa facing the hearth. Still, he did not speak to her, merely shifted his gaze from her face to his brother's hovering concern. Perhaps the mind doctor was right. Dominic would not want her to see him thus and even though it went against her instincts to leave, she believed Atherton would treat him with care.

"You'll call me if he asks-"

"I promise."

TWENTY ONE

Eden ought to be rejoicing. She wasn't a lunatic. Atherton had proclaimed it so and he was a head doctor. His opinion held weight. But happiness wasn't on the menu as long as Dominic suffered. She wished that she were the one with him right now. She wanted him to trust and accept comfort from her. She yearned to be the woman he confided in, leaned on, loved. *Loved?* Where had that word come from? No, he didn't love her. Desired, sure…but loved? Not likely.

She wandered down the hallway, no particular destination in mine. Her footsteps were muted by the narrow paisley rug that ran across the cherrywood. End tables lurked in alcoves, primed to launch out at her as she ambled past them. The afternoon sun shone through bay windows that resembled giant eyes peering through curtained lashes. She hitched up her shawl, turned right at the familiar fork that led to Dominic's domain. Despite her host's warning, Eden spit in the eye of the Goliath door writhing with bas-relief satyrs and winged dragons. She bypassed the sun-bathed pianoforte and crossed into the cozy seclusion of the library. Only, today, she found it wasn't so secluded.

She did not notice him at first, but suffered a twinge of unease and surveyed her surroundings for the source. When her eyes fell upon the Sphinx, poised in the action of extracting a book from the shelf, she walked out of her shoe.

Sunlight played over his wine-red hair teasing out mahogany highlights. Eden couldn't be sure. His expression did not emote any specific sentiment, but he seemed just as surprised to find her rattling about Dom's lair, as she was to find him.

She slipped her stocking clad foot back where it belonged. "I did not expect anyone would be in here."

Seconds ticked by. Still, warm amber eyes melted over her without a word. His presence was a silent roar in her ears. For a moment she tensed. Was he really there?

She stepped forward. "Mr. Atherton?"

"Stephan." He corrected.

Eden exhaled. He was real, at least. "And you may call me, Eden."

Silence reigned again as he pulled the book from the shelf, and took up a seat on the brocaded sofa. She strained to identify the leather-bound volume in his lap. When she again met his face, she found him reading her instead of the book he'd chosen. Eden shifted her weight from one foot to the other. Was he waiting for her to leave or to sit down?

When he finally did speak again, his voice was refined and educated. He held out the volume for her inspection. "*The Modern Prometheus.* Have you read it?"

Eden stumbled again, this time knocking her shawl askew. She recovered and ambled forward to the olive branch he offered. Somehow she managed to make it to the ottoman without twisting an ankle. "No. I prefer poetry to prose: Byron, Keats, and the like."

She rolled the volume around in her hands, flipping through the gold-edge pages with vague interest. "What is it about?"

"A man who creates a monster, and then refuses to love it. The monster does not respond well to rejection."

"A horror novel, then." Her hands stilled, and she held the book out to him.

Amber glistened on her face, ignoring her outstretched hand. "Will you read a passage?"

Subtle challenge or polite request? His inflectionless voice didn't convey. Eden retracted the book, and flipped to the front page. She felt his eyes stalking her like a shadow.

"You don't trust me."

"Why do you say that?"

His expression would reveal nothing, so Eden did not bother looking up. "The way you stare, I feel like I should make off with the silver so as not to disappoint."

"Curiosity, not mistrust."

When she did chance a glimpse, he was leaning back, amber cloaked, with his head resting partially on the table back of the sofa. An elegant enigma. If nothing else, she found him a distraction from her own thoughts.

"Read."

So, she did.

* * *

Dominic reclined on the settee, not relaxed, but striving to appear so. Cael hovered at the mantle, toying with the crumpled parchment. Dominic had rarely seen his self-possessed brother fidget.

"Is this what triggered it?" He held up Greyson's message, not quite looking at him.

"In a way. Ethan is upstairs, you say?"

"Yes, shall I summon him?" Cael pivoted toward the study door.

Alarmed at the prospect of being alone with his thoughts, Dom halted him. "Don't leave."

"Eh, that makes it rather difficult."

"I will see him later then." He caught Cael observing him askance a third time. "Wha's on your mind Cael?"

"Just wondering when you're going to realize you're not wearing your spectacles."

He blinked twice before the words soaked through. "She saw me."

Cael nodded. "Funny, how the mind works, protecting us from things we aren't quite ready to know."

Dominic remembered vividly seeing her, being overcome by her calming spirit. But no thoughts existed of her specific expression as she stared at him. "How did she react? Was she...repulsed?"

"Hardly." His brother scoffed with a half-smile. "Just the opposite. I practically had to muscle her out the door."

Dom pretended interest in the hearthrug, whilst the fist gripping his heart slackened. She'd seen him and still did not shy away. "You know, I once begged Ethan to gouge them out." Dom felt Cael's flinch at his revelation. "But he wouldn't."

"It was Lillian, then, not Lucca. I always thought..."

Dom raised his asymmetrical gaze to collide with his brother's concerned eyes. His strength swelled with the knowledge that Eden could still want him even after witnessing his deformity. "My father never laid a finger on me...but stood by and did nothing."

A beat passed before either man spoke again, worried amber searched for something in the pewter-blue irises.

"Dominic, please tell me what happened. This isn't healthy. It's poisoning you."

He looked away. "I haven't hidden it completely. Ethan knows and so do Gideon and Gabriel."

"They know only because they were victims of the same woman's abuse. Have you ever voluntarily unburdened yourself to anyone?"

He hesitated, but deep down, he knew it was time. Time to let it all out, and perhaps finally heal from the festering wound of his childhood. Stephan needed him whole. Eden deserved a true mate, not a stigmatic man-child with an Oedipal complex. "Talk to me about Eden first."

"Alright." Cael's fidgeting ceased, and he abandoned the message on the mantle. "I find Miss Prescott to be lucid and quick-witted, with a healthy buoyancy. I haven't the slightest doubt of her sanity."

"What about the hallucinations? The bruises. That cannot be normal."

He tilted a hand to punctuate as he spoke. "I agree there is something different about her, but she isn't mad nor is she likely to be in the foreseeable future. The ordered manner of her thoughts, the subjects she chooses to draw, the details on her sketches, her response to the world around her, yes, even her visions, none are the workings of a madwoman."

Dominic met his brother's optimism with caution. "No more riddles, Cael. How do you explain the things she sees, if not—"

"Everything without explanation is not madness, Dominic. Remember, she also *sees* you."

Dominic sensed Cael was working up to something. He walked over to retrieve some forgotten item from across the room.

"Here, let me show you something that may better illustrate my point."

Poised for revelation, Dominic frowned at the unremarkable drawing Cael placed in front of him. "The Duchess and her infant. I don't understand."

"Miss Prescott rendered the portrait. When I asked her what led her to sketch those particular faces, she admitted she'd seen them recently."

His brow crinkled. "How? They're dead."

"Dominic, *this* is the woman and infant Miss Prescott claims she leapt into the marsh to save…the very same marsh where they drowned if memory serves."

Dom opened his mouth to say…nothing. He couldn't

think of a single coherent word.

"Flip to the next one."

When he did, he saw yet another sketch. His breath caught. "Eden drew this?" His fingers flitted over the images on the page, tentative, awed. "Gideon...Gabriel..."

"I think it's time you face the possibility that there's something else at work here."

* * *

The light had grown dim. Even in a hexagonal room with panoramic windows, the sun must set some time. Eden folded the corner of the page and closed the book as quietly as she could, lest she awaken a sleeping Stephan. He looked especially defenseless in slumber, his fallen angel face half-masked in twilight.

From the time she'd read the first word to the whisper of the last one, he hadn't spoken. He seemed content to listen, quieted. Occasionally he'd pierced her with amber orbs. She assumed, to gleam her reaction to a certain scene in the novel.

If pressed she'd acknowledge that Mrs. Shelley's *Prometheus* had its merits, but she found the man stretched out lengthwise before her a more compelling read. So unlike Dominic in manner and appearance, Eden marveled at the similar vulnerability she sensed in him. She couldn't dismiss it. Neither Atherton nor Dr. Raine had called forth her sympathies. But somehow, their brother Stephan did.

The thought of Atherton led her back to worries over Dominic. She rose from the ottoman amid protesting joints and stiff muscles. She wouldn't solve the mystery of Stephan tonight. With a thought to let Dr. Raine know of his brother's whereabouts, Eden gathered up her shoes and shawl and tiptoed out of the library.

She halted inside Dominic's music room, struck by night's transformation of it into a backdrop from one of Byron's poems. The full moon clouded the eye overhead, illuminating the stage in a perfect spotlight. Eden emerged from the pitch shadows outside the circle to pay homage to the lacquered black lady. She sat down at the keys, let her lids rest and hoped she remembered all the notes.

Midways through the requiem, the hairs at her nape bristled. Still she played, swaying as her almond-shaped nails flitting over the ivory. The lingering bass chords echoed off the walls and seemed to close in on its maker, even as she brought the solemn melody to a finish.

"I warned you never to come here."

His voice emanated from the opaque edges of the room, its familiarity a relief to her.

"As long as you visit my chamber, I'll go where I please." She closed the top down over the ivory, and stood. "Do you play?"

"Music is curative. I find solace in it."

The resonance and direction of his baritone changed subtly every few seconds, orbiting just inside the rim of darkness. Was he tracking her? Eden shuffled her feet, and pulled the shawl tighter around her shoulders. She knew the edgy fright of deer facing a hunting party. But this was worse, much worse. She couldn't pinpoint her stalker's angle of ...approach? Attack? What would he do when he finally decided to strike? Her bravado vanished so completely until she wondered where she'd mustered the courage to taunt him only moments ago. Trembling lips voiced the first thought that popped into her mind.

"I left Stephan in the library."

A pause. She sensed a hitch in his step. "He is...alright?"

"Yes, he's asleep." Why wouldn't he be alright? But she bit back the question. Time enough to get into that later. A little more to the left, yes, his voice had come from there. Confidence rebounding, Eden pivoted around the pianoforte's bench to extend a hand in his direction. The loose fringes of the shawl fluttered with her movements.

"Have you ever noticed that shadows exaggerate even

the tiniest fears? Come."

An eon passed. He wouldn't expose himself. Her arm ached, but the pain in her chest was an all-consuming agony that cut right to her soul. Defeated, she let her hand fall and turned to grant him his solitude. Sooner or later she would have to admit that he would never...

The thought dissipated as the touch of warm skin slipped into her palm. She spun so quickly that her slipper's heel tilted at an awkward angle. The shawl tumbled, forgotten, to the floor. Bracing herself for a fall, Eden grappled for the nearest support. Him.

His arms enveloped her in a safety-hug, fitting her petite frame into his chiseled stone torso...clothed only by a cotton, dress shirt she realized. The material seemed blindingly white so near her eye. She stood silent. Cheek pillowed against chest, his gentle fingers massaged into her hair just above her ears. Willfully disassembling her bun, she suspected. Eden remained content to soak up the intoxicating heat of his embrace, until her disjointed heaving breaths righted to a mild pant, and finally a sigh.

"They're beautiful, Dom."

"They are grotesque. I didn't imagine you'd like them."

She smiled, loving the deep rumble the words produced against her cheek. "Why ever not?"

"My eyes have been the single most damning pall over my life. Every awful thing that's happened to me has been because of them."

"Well, I've seen them, and nothing dire has happened." His body went stiff against hers, as if he did not quite agree or perhaps he feared she tempted fate by saying so. She let her hands migrate upward. One to rest atop his shoulder; the other encircled his back. She trailed soothing caresses down his chest and at the small of his back

"Are you wearing the spectacles now? I'll wager you aren't."

"How did you and Cael get on?"

She aimed to talk until she got him to relax again.

"Fabulously, once the battle lines were drawn. He is very different from Dr. Raine, but I rather liked him. He did not treat me like a madwoman, though he must have thought me one."

Eden exerted a small pressure against their embrace. When he let her pull back, she chanced a glance up. He gazed down at her, unabashed, naked eyes bathed in radiance and shadow. They were as mismatched jewels twinkling in the moonlight, fringed by ink-dirtied bristle lashes.

"What are you so afraid of?"

His gaze shifted, infinitesimal. The hand that had been lost in her ruined bun dropped down to curl around her throat, in a dangerous and possessive caress. "That you'll hurt me...like she did. Or that I'll hurt you...like she did."

Eden couldn't keep the tremor from her voice. "She who?"

"My mother."

His thumb, flitting back and forth over her bare skin, stroked her breathing up to hitch and skip rhythm. She closed her eyes to savor his touch, her fingers restless to rob him of the shirt so they could roam his chest. The memory of his artist-rendered torso sent another quiver of anticipation down her spine, even as he seized her face in both his hands, tilting her expression to collide with his.

Desire soared in the face of his frown and the strange emotion swimming in the depths of his eyes.

"Dammit. Haven't you any sense of self-preservation?"

She softened her lips with a smile, her fingers already plucking at the buttons of his shirt. "No, I haven't."

TWENTY TWO

Gawd! She didn't know what she did to him with those adoring hazel eyes that seemed an open window to her soul. A soul he'd seen and embraced many times and knew to be just as pure and perfect as the delicate beauty of her face. He could spill himself just from that expression, gazing upon her and having her see *them* and not shrink away, but shine back at him with passion dipped in green-gold. Passion for him. He couldn't resist.

Ahhh...but touching her, thinking about her beneath his body, lips parted, eyes shining. There was a time when he'd contemplated which was worse...the years spent alone, devoid of all human contact, or those endured in hell when every touch was one of pain and torture...but not now. Now he knew the truth: her touch was the sweetest pain of all.

The moment his lips closed over hers, some primal instinct seized control of him. Denied warmth and affection for so long, he was like a ravenous beast, desperate to satisfy the craving lest the prey somehow free itself and he lose the opportunity forever. He devoured her mouth, taking from her the sweetly-offered gift of her innocence. Her hands, light and tentative, caressed his chest...she must have finished with the buttons some time ago, because her fingers set fire to his skin. He relinquished his hold on her just long enough to divest himself of the cotton barrier and fling it to parts unknown.

She killed him, her mouth just like her hands, so accepting, so open, hot...moist heat that he sank his tongue into, sucking, tasting, lavishing with an urgent gentleness. He felt her groan into his mouth, echoing his own growing need. Wait...

Abruptly, he broke off. Her breathing was as erratic as his. Her stare, confused. His body throbbed from loss; his nether regions protested most of all. "Eden, not...here. My room."

He searched her upturned face, needing to be sure she knew what she was letting herself into. "Do you know what I'm asking? What'll happen if I take us there now?"

Her voice hitched, he noticed. She had to swallow several times to get the words out. "Yes, Dom, I know. I want to."

And he was too weak to say no. "Climb up and hold on to me like before."

Waves of desire shot threw him as she hooked her arms around his neck. He helped her shove the heavy skirts aside so she could twin her legs around his waist. Her inner thighs hugging him, her face turned into his throat...his groin spiked when she touched a light kiss just shy of his Adam's apple.

"That's right, cara. I've got you."

After adjusting his hands so that one supported her gown-ed bottom and the other steadied her head against his shoulder, he took several deep breaths to calm himself enough to shimmer. When he did, he wasn't prepared for the tenfold boost to an already blazing need. He hoped she didn't change her mind when he exited the astral, because the after burn alone would leave him hard for hours, semi-hard for days. He'd deny himself if he had to, but that would mean avoiding her while he battled his overwrought desire. And not seeing Eden had become a torture all by itself; her half-smile, the white-blonde wisps tickling her nape. No, none of that. He forced himself to concentrate on their destination.

He stepped off the astral and shattered into a million prickling shards of desire, screaming throughout his body, jagged and shrill. They touched down adjacent the bed, and flopped in a messy heap on the counterpane. He rolled over so that she clung shivering atop his body. Her hair curtained over both their heads.

"Eden?"

Dominic ran gentling hands through her hair, smoothing it back so he could pry her face away from his neck.

"Eden, what's wrong?"

"I...I feel hot...all over, tingly. My breasts, they ache." Her gaze was flushed, excited. "And the mouth between my legs, it's...hungry."

Hell. The astral had affected her. Of course, he should have realized it would. She, for reasons he'd yet to discover, seemed touched by otherworldly things. Her sensitivity to his presence, her hallucinations—or visions as Cael wanted to call them—were proof enough.

He strained up and kissed her forehead. "Do not fear, cara. It's an effect of the way I travel. Normally, it does not extend to...passengers."

"But I never felt this...effect before."

"Whatever emotion you're feeling at the time is magnified. The day Cael rescued you we piggybacked, but you were unconscious. After the incident the other night, you were calm, so you only became more so. This time was different. Your emotions were wild."

"Will it...abate?"

He let his hands slide down her sleeved arms, hoping to help calm her. "In time. But if you're feeling like I feel now, it will take a hour or two before the heightened awareness is gone."

"Dom, are we still going to…"

He closed his eyes to lock out the pulsating throb her words caused. Gawd, he hurt for her. "Yes, cara, I would like to so very much."

"Me too."

She was so slight in his arms, so trusting. He needed to be careful with her, that much he knew. But knowing and doing were two separate demons.

The mechanics he could handle. He'd seen it done. He'd read books, overheard gossip, but they were racy books, experienced hoydens in the gossip. Nothing learned from those sources would help him please an innocent like Eden. And he ached to please her.

But, he existed mostly on the outskirts of love, looking in. After all, what gentlewoman would lay with a man who hid his face like a bandit? And no woman, gentle or otherwise, would want him after she'd witnessed his shame. He wished now he'd discussed the matter with Cael or Ethan. Hell, even *Stephan* probably could have provided some direction.

"Dom?"

He opened his eyes on her, and brought his hands up to hold her face. She laid her hands atop his. The contrast of fine porcelain to his olive ruggedness appalled him. Had his hands always been so large and fearsome-looking? He'd have to take things slow. Gauge her reactions, and see what she liked…what she disliked. Make certain he did everything right. Take care not to harm her.

When her hands fell away to light once again on his chest, Dominic let his migrate into her hair. He applied a light pressure to close the distance between them in a kiss that started off sweet and grew spicy with the melting of tongues. She shifted her position further up his torso, probably to accommodate his blossoming affection.

He liked the weight of her on top of him. But soon just that and kissing her wasn't enough. He needed more. His fingers combed the length of her ashen mane, spraying it out around their bodies. He strayed down her cheek and nibbled like an adoring pet at her earlobe. His hands found the back of her dress. There seemed to be a million slippery buttons encasing her in the garment. She chuckled softly at his troubles.

"Here, why don't you leave that to me."

She moved to sit up but he couldn't bear to let her go, so he followed her up in a seated position. She slid into his lap. He continued to lavish first her bruised neck then the creamy skin of her shoulder with butterfly kisses and nips. Her intoxicating taste, her bottom wiggling against his most sensitive organ...it was sweet torture.

"Uhhhn...cara, please." His voice came out thick and tight.

Amazing, Eden managed to reach behind her back and finish undoing her gown. With much angling and shifting, he managed to pull it over her head. The skirts were next. She stood on the bed, dropped the thick layers down, and stepped out of the pool at her ankles for him to fling aside.

Clothed in only her chemise and ruffled drawers, she lowered herself back on him, stocking-ed legs folded under at the knee and straddling his thighs. She nestled in his lap, with a wicked expression, surprising him. She knew just what effect the movement had on him. Before he knew her intent, she was teasing at his nipple with a fingernail, playful...eyeing him.

"Is this bothering you?"

"No, cara." A jolt of dizzying awareness shot through him, as if tiny fibers connected the bronze plug to his lower regions. His groin bulged against his trousers, throbbing and painful until he could ignore it no longer. He covered either side of her hips with his hands, repositioned her so her heat pressed down on him, rocking her back and forth against his erection...stroking it higher while alleviating some of his need.

The little hitch in her breath told him she enjoyed the effect as much as he. Her hips kicked in, undulating to the example he set. She left off teasing him and went for the full-armored attack, lowering her mouth to the erect plug. He jerked when her wet heat latched on to him, and caged her head, encouraging her, eager for her tongue's suckling and teeth nibbling at his skin. He fell back on the bed, her, the pleasure giver at the moment.

She set him on fire, a soaring inferno. His eyes must be wild again, because when she pulled back and looked down at him, her smile turned to a gasp.

"Dom, your eyes…the left one is-."

"Yes, I know." He panted. "They get like this under bright lights or when I am…emotional."

* * *

Eden stared, mesmerized by the smoldering starburst grey and eerie blue trained on her. His eyes were more than excited. They were greedy, for her…almost predatory. If it were possible, the place between her legs burned even hotter, wetter. The dampened cotton drawers grew uncomfortable against her feverish desire to be rid of them, to rid him of the blasted trousers so she could be skin to skin with the seeking bulge wedged at her thigh's apex.

He pushed back cascading tresses, and devoured her with another deep kiss, rolling her onto her back in the process. Eden v-ed her legs at the knee to accommodate his girth. She suffered his weight but a moment before he braced himself on an elbow.

A delicious thrill went through her when his other hand migrated down to cover her breast, kneading it, worrying the sensitive peak with his thumb until she panted, arching her back. Her own hands clawed the offending chemise denying her his full touch.

"Shhhh, patience cara. Let me please you." His voice was a guttural whisper, near the lip of the garment.

Scorching breath wafted across her skin at the place

where her neck dipped into cleavage. She felt his lips touch her there briefly, and let her hands fall away to her sides, gripping the counterpane maniacally. Her head shifted to and fro, as he trailed kisses in a path to her heaving breasts, closing his mouth over chemise and all. Unable to stop herself, Eden caged his head against her…one leg coming over the back of him to rub impatiently at his taunt thigh and buttocks.

His tongue lapped at her incessantly, soaking the material, molesting her nipple to a pain-edged pleasure. Her hands got lost in his coal-black waves.

"Ohhhh…" A sigh escaped her when he loosed the satin ribbon securing the garment and drew the satin from the eyelets. Bagging cotton drawn down, the room's cool air wafted across her buds just before his tongue's coarse wetness raked maddeningly across it.

Eyes closed, head arched back, panting through her mouth, Eden abandoned herself to the bombardment of sensations and shivers. Her hips began to undulate upward. Her wayward leg pressured his hips, trying to grind the pulsating bulge into her core. Some place in the corner of her mind suspected that he'd deliberately agitated her into a writhing frenzy.

"Dom…" She exhaled his name.

That's when she felt it, a hand, his hand, inching over her drawers. Her hips jumped as his fingers slipped beneath the waistband, twined in her nether hair and finally sprayed over dew-moistened lips.

"For me, cara?" He lifted from her breast.

She lulled her head to the side. Her passion-fogged mind was slow to react…what had he said? Why had he stopped? Forcing laden eyes to work, she glanced at the ruby pebble he'd abandoned and then turned up to collide with his face. Eyes brimming with awe stared back at her.

His palm, warm and seeking, moved against the delicate flesh between her legs. When his fingers fondled over an especially sensitive nub, she nearly screamed at the burning ache that resounded throughout her entire body. Her hands clutched at his shoulders when he kept up the movement, worrying her flesh. The minuscule corrugations on his thumb wrecked havoc, feeding her throbbing need. Her legs widened, seeking more. Her hips moved in time with his hand, rising to beg for fulfillment.

"Please..." The roar in her ears nearly drowned out her own strangled plea.

Even when he retreated away, her hips kept up their vigil...she heard a rustling and moments later her dew-soaked drawers were sliding down her legs, his hands pausing just long enough to strip the stockings away as well. The forgotten chemise went next. At last, she lay naked and spread before him. Ripe for pleasure.

He, too, was naked, Eden noted. His magnificent form loomed over her, an olive-skinned Adonis. Taunt rippled chest and stomach muscles shifted just under his skin as he moved over her. His broad torso tapered to sturdy hips. Her eyes wandered lower to the curious appendage that poked out, stiff and ominous, from a hairy place between his tree-trunk thighs. She knew a moment of panic. Is that what had been pulsating inside his trousers? How had she not noticed the monstrous thing before?

The instant his hands were back on her, the fear and the reason for it fled her mind. All she felt was clawing desire for more of him in however form that fulfillment took. He settled between her legs, weight shifted to one elbow...leaving one hand free to part the lips of her hungry mouth.

"Ahh..."

Wicked was the only word she could think to describe what he did next, wedging one of his sausage thick fingers inside her tight mouth.

"Soon, cara, I promise."

His voice sounded strained, painful almost...a pain mirrored in the tight expression on his face.

"Now..." She moaned, able to stand it no longer. "Do

whatever it is, *now*."

He eased fully over her pliant body, unsheathed his finger and nudged her entrance with…the thing she'd seen before. Time slowed as their eyes met, his tortured by some nameless anxiety she struggled to identify. Not fear exactly. His expression said that they were crossing over to a new place and once passed no bridge existed to cross back.

Eden's breath hitched and then she felt it, the thing pushing slow but relentless into her tight moist mouth. A veil of scarlet clouded her vision and her head jerked back against the bed…fingers tore at the counterpane. She felt a sharp, tearing pain at the core of her body and froze, afraid that if she moved, the damage would be worse.

"Dom, it hurts." Her voice, small, high-pitched.

"I know, cara, and I'm sorry." She felt a tender touch to her cheek…then her forehead, next her breast. He was kissing her, apologizing with actions as well as words. "Forgive me, please. I would not harm you for the world."

When the thing in her began to retreat, instinct overtook her and she collapsed her legs around his hips. Her hands shot up to lock in his hair.

"No, please. It will hurt worse if you leave me."

"Shhh…" His soft lips touched hers, soothing.

She hadn't realized she was crying until she felt his tongue licking at her temple to catch a falling tear. The weight of his body sank into hers and she felt the thing nudging into her again…this time with less effort and a burning friction that spread deliciously to overtake the pain. Eden relaxed into the evolving pleasure.

His kisses too evolved, from soothing to sensual. His tongue slid unbidden into her mouth just as his appendage slid home a third time, filling her with an edgy bliss that radiated out from her core like ripples in a pond…leaking into her entire consciousness.

The thing inside her was over-large, feverish and quivering. It felt like he had shoehorned a sizzling, straight-from-the-skillet bratwurst fully into her. Nevertheless, the rawness of the act, heat, pulse, and jolt of sensations it set off had her ready for another thrust.

Again and again his came into her, the pleasure building higher, climbing towards frenzy. His hips grinding on hers, his weight a decadent delight. Eden tangled her fingers in his hair and down his back, urging him to continue. She felt as though they were careening towards the edge of a precipice, neither willing to break before they tumbled over the side.

Dominic groaned his pleasure into her mouth, his forceful thrusts quickening with urgency. The same urgency she sensed in herself. Her inner muscles gripped him with rhythm to match her run-away heartbeat. Racked by a sensation so overwhelming that her skin couldn't contain, her body writhed and twitched, the hot acid-burn of something spewing inside her drove her over the edge...

She splintered into mindless ecstasy, the whole spectrum of fulfillment running its course in the space of a few moment's bliss. A hail of colorful spangles fluttered above. In her disconnected world filled only with sensations and feelings, it took Eden a second to realize the starburst she saw were Dominic's eyes...lost in the same wondrous place with her.

TWENTY THREE

Her body felt weak, boneless and only semi-conscious beneath a pressing weight. Hot breath at her neck, she realized that Dominic lay on top of her...and inside of her. The thing that had given her so much pleasure lay dormant now, its presence warm and filling. She liked the feel of him, hot and heavy, his luscious black hair tickling her throat and shoulder as he turned his face and placed a light kiss against her bruised skin.

His breath grazed her throat when he spoke. "I want Ethan to heal these. I never want to see them again."

She chuckled at his childish faith in his brother's medical skills, and laid a hand atop his head to play in the soft waves. "Dom, no doctor can heal a bruise. They will fade with time."

"Ethan will heal them if I ask him to."

He spoke with a certainty that struck her as sincere. As if he had some knowledge she did not.

"How?"

When he did not immediately answer, she assumed he wouldn't. Content, Eden did not press. He took her by surprise when he propped himself up on his elbows and then shifted off her, dislodging himself from her body.

Eden sighed at the loss. She didn't have long to feel abandoned. He was gone from her no more than the time it took for him to pull back the blue-black bedspread and sheets.

"Come, before you catch a chill."

She scrambled over to burrow beneath the sheets. He joined her there and pulled her flush against the side of his torso. Only when they were propped on a nest of pillows and settled into a snug cocoon, did he speak again.

"There are more bruises than before. Why?"

He must have noticed the lighter bruises marring her hip and thigh. "When I fell from the tub, I banged against the floor. At the time, it didn't hurt, but later..." She let the words trailed off.

"Hmm."

She looked up at him, curious, but he eyes stared out over her head, possessed by some unexpressed thought. He didn't turn his gaze down to her, even at his next words.

"Do you remember that first day you awoke in this room? You had a sore throat and a developing lung congestion."

She nodded against him. "You were over there sitting in the window sill. I did not notice at first."

"Ethan healed you then."

Her rational mind protested. "The doctor gave me a fast-acting elixir to sooth the ache and ease my airways."

"The liquid you drank was spiced tea imported from the Indies. An exotic expense, but necessary. Ethan is a practiced hand at healing partially, subtly, so as not to draw undue attention to his gift. You assumed the tea to be an elixir because it was strong and spicy and he was a doctor administering it in a healing setting. It helped that he did not clarify the grave nature of your condition. The truth is, Ethan saw the progression of the illness. You wouldn't have lasted the week. Do you still think an elixir fixed it...in the space of five minutes?"

She wasn't sure how to react. Her mind writhed first with awe, before settling at last on gratitude. At the time, all she wanted was the peace that death could provide, but now, reminded how sweet life could be she thanked the heavens Dominic and his brothers saved her. Though, the way Dom explained the doctor's ruse made her feel like a gullible idiot. Why hadn't she thought to question her sudden recovery?

He seemed to read her mind without even looking at her. "There is no need to feel foolish. Most folks want to believe that because Ethan is a doctor he has a miracle cure for their ailments. Even those few who don't, seem content instead to attribute their recovery to the Almighty above. Perhaps they are right to do so, who but God could give such a gift."

Some of her embarrassment eased knowing she wasn't the first—and certainly not the last—to be duped. "So, he can heal anything. Your eyes?"

"He's grown strong over the years, but, no. His ability is limited to injuries and simple illnesses. Complex problems such as inherited conditions, mental illness and age-related degeneration are beyond his scope."

Fascinated, she could not help but ask, "Consumption?"

"Yes. He is especially good with lung infections and broken bones."

"What about heart ailments?"

"If it were mechanical in nature, an injury or the result of a physical malady, yes, but a heart that is rotting from age, no. He could sooth the pain if necessary, like in cases of rheumatism, but not fix the problem because aging is not an illness."

"If he can do all that then why not wipe out influenza, malaria, and all manner of deadly diseases?"

He shifted so that he could look down into her face. The humor lurking in his asymmetrical gaze caused her heart to flip over. "You know, Cael asked me the same question not so long ago. Ethan could no more wipe out influenza than he could the common cold. His healing ability is like my astral travel. It is draining. The more complex the problem, the more energy is required. The more patients he heals, the more he is depleted. Not to mention, the very idea of him having such an ability is sacrilege. He must be careful and discrete. Even if he could transcend all that, he cannot be everywhere at once. Influenza passes from person to person rapidly. He would have to heal everyone simultaneously to eradicate it."

"Oh." She felt silly again and knew the instant the blush gave her away. "Yes, I see what you mean."

"Sleep now, cara, I feel I have robbed you of enough for one evening."

"Not yet." She did not want the moment to end. This time with him was precious to her, a rare gift. Dominic had never been so relaxed and forthcoming around her, carefree almost. They were chatting like...lovers, true lovers who held a genuine long-term affection for one another. She frowned at the thought, her affection was genuine, but what of his? The question begged to be asked, but she held back not sure if it was proper for a lady of gentle breeding to demand declarations from a gentleman. Of course, having surrendered her virtue to a man she wasn't married to, she could hardly claim a close acquaintance with propriety. Still, the question would not dislodge from her mouth. Instead, she heard herself asking him more about his family.

"Are all your brothers...blessed with gifts such as you and he?"

"Blessed is not the word I would use in Stephan and Gabriel's circumstance but yes, all except for Cael."

"Tell me more about your eyes. I thought there was just a color difference, but before, the blue one appeared...bigger."

He nodded. "According to Ethan and Cael, my left eye lacks proper pigmentation, which is why it is an unnatural shade of blue when it should be grey like the right one. My left eye also has a slow-closing pupil. Under bright light, the additive disparity of both size and color is...freakish."

"They're odd, yes." She agreed, guessing her best course of action would not be to placate him with false assurances but to tell him what she really thought. "But not grotesque or freakish as you assume. Honestly, I think it all depends on you...your expressions. When you were upset before, they made you look vulnerable, younger. I wanted to hug you. And then while we were...eh, ahem...they were fascinating...the way you looked at me was flattering. But, if you were angry or shouting, I imagine it would be a bit off-putting to look you in the eye."

When she opened her mouth to saying something else, he shushed her with an index finger against her lips. "May I ask you something?"

Her brow shot up in surprise, but she smiled letting him know she didn't mind.

"Why did they name you 'Eden'? Its lovely, but uncommon."

His was an easy question to answer, and one of her favorite stories. She remembered her parents fondly whenever she told the miracle of her birth, particularly now when memories were all she had left of them. "Mama and Papa always planned to have a brood of children. Years passed, and they weren't blessed with even one child. Papa consulted with doctor after doctor, but they could find no obvious impediment. When both mama and papa passed out of their fourth decade they gave up hope, content in their love for each other."

Eden paused and looked up from toying with his nipple to gauge his reaction, both to the story and her playfulness. He'd closed his eyes and rested his head on the pillows as he listened, much like Stephan had done when she read to him. His hand continued to stroke her cheek.

"Go on."

"Until, the summer of mama's fifty-sixth year. She fell low with a strange malady; mama described it as a moody illness. Papa said the doctor examined her three times to ensure he had the diagnosis correct. When he finally came from the sick room to 'confront the husband', Papa feared the worse. The doctor said he'd never seen anything like it in all his born days, but that mama was with child and quite healthily so. Mama was seven and fifty when I was born. They named me 'Eden' because they said that I couldn't have been anything less than a blessing from God."

As she brought the anecdote to a close she couldn't stifle her yawn.

"Your parents were wise people." He cradled her against his chest. "Go to sleep now, Eden."

TWENTY FOUR

"You lied."

He came awake to the sound of her voice, as well as an exploring hand flitting over his hip. Even half-conscious he felt himself swelling in anticipation. That was only until the tone and content of her words sank in. She sounded... angry.

"You lied to me, Dominic."

He opened his eyes; curious and confused why she should be cross with him. What he saw snapped him up, all thoughts of passion forgotten. Eden hovered over his naked body, the covers flipped back so that he lay exposed in all his nightmarish glory. His disfigurement lay visible for her inspection. Every scar, slice, gouge, and burn he'd endure before Ethan came to live in Italy and meticulously healed him after each "purification" ceremony. The layer upon layer of rough-healed slits over each wrist, the textured mesh of ruined skin on his chest, and the discolored series of parallel slivers at the sides of his stomach. He even felt the presence of the deep, ugly groves of gouged out flesh in his back.

When she tried to pull the sheets and counterpane even lower, he assumed to inspect his legs, he jerked away so abruptly that he fell backwards off the bed. Landing with little grace on his bare bottom. Eden followed him over the edge to pierce his heart with an expression of mingled anger, horror...and something else. Could it be...betrayal?

He panicked. Bloody Hell! He'd let his guard down, but how? She'd seen them...gotten a good long look. There'd be no convincing her that they weren't really there this time. DAMMIT! He wasn't prepared for this. Telling Cael was one thing, but having Eden know. He couldn't bear it, exposing his shame, the years of torture and abuse, the demented things Lillian had subjected him to. Enduring her pity, revulsion...the shudder that would undoubtedly go through her at having a disfigured monster in her bed, lusting for her body. Now she would detest him, never allow him to touch her again. Worse, never want to see him again.

When she reached down a hand to help him up, he recoiled, scrambling backwards until his back slammed none-too-gently into the cider wardrobe. Seeing a method of escaping, hiding, he stumbled up from the floor and pivoted around to fling open the doors of the wardrobe. They rebounded hard and swung back to whack either side of his body.

She called across the room. "Where are you going?"

He snatched the first garment his fingers fell on and draped the shirt around his shoulders, then snatched at a pair of trousers with equal vehement and shove his legs into them.

Suddenly she was there, not touching him but in close enough proximity behind him so that he stiffened. "Tell me how you got the scars, Dominic. And how you've managed to hide them all this time."

"Don't ask me that. Don't, I can't..."

"Why not?!" Her voice snapped at his back, angrily, like a forgotten child demanding her due. "What is it? What! Just *what* the devil did you think I'd do, anyway... Run? Scream? Faint? Call for a priest? Dom...look around, I haven't done any of that. Don't you understand? I've *seen* you and I'm still here."

She touched him then, even as he jabbed, frantic, at the buttons of the shirt to get the infernal thing closed...hide his shame once again from the world. Her light fingers tested the waters at his shoulders, putting a whisper of pressure on them to make him turn.

He gave up on the buttons. His fumbling hands shook too badly, competing only with the panting breaths shooting in and out of his lungs like ricocheted bullets. He didn't turn around, couldn't. Not yet. He needed a few more moments to compose himself. To let the impossible soak into his heart, and warm the chill of fear beating there. Did he dare believe her?

Her arms inched around him, like crawling vines encroaching upon a trellis. He watched as her delicate bird-boned hands came up to rest palm-side against his chest, deliberately casting aside the gapping shirt. She moved closer to him, pressed her front against his back, burrowing in like she was home after a long holiday. He could tell from the heat of her body that she wore nothing.

It moved him to speak, her obvious desire to be this close to him even with what she'd seen. "It did not occur to me that they would be visible when I slept."

"But, eh, how did you hide them before?" She hesitated, seemed reluctant, but she rushed on anyway. "I mean, with other...*women*."

"There were no others, cara. Only you." He would have liked to see her face to gauge what she thought of knowing she was his only lover.

"What about your brothers, how did-"

"Ethan already knew. I told Cael yesterday. He cast up his accounts when I showed him what our mother let them do."

He felt her body tense against him. "*Them?*"

"Long story." It came out a faint whisper.

"It's barely dawn." She rubbed the skin of his chest

gently, speaking into his shirt. He felt the effects of her voice all the way down to his toes. "There is an eternity of time before anyone comes asking after either of us. Will you come back to bed, then, before I catch my death."

Just then, he caught a flutter at the corner of his vision. The falcon alit the roost adjacent the window, and made a show of settling his impressive plumage around his small powerful body. The bird trained a black, pupil-less eye on him. Dominic's heart sank. That could only mean one thing. Gideon needed him in Italy. He supposed he would have to face his demons sooner or later.

"Dom?"

He cocked his head over his shoulder. Eden would not take the news well. And he didn't like the idea either, but bringing her along was out of the question. They weren't married. Both had sinned and would likely continue to do so, but the brunt of society's disapproval would rest on her. He would not have her subjected to ridicule. Nonna and the aunts could be malicious about family obligations and propriety.

"Are you coming back to bed?"

"No."

"You're not going to tell me." Her hands fell from him. Her words were a statement, dripping with defeat.

"I need to walk around a bit. Go back to bed or cover yourself so you don't catch a chill." He walked out of her arms and over to the falcon's roost. The falcon accepted his invitation, alit his forearm, and then transferred to his shoulder when he lifted his wrist to a height level to it. Dominic pivoted on the rustling noise behind him.

"Eden?"

No answer.

She struggled into her multitude of undergarments, her movements stiff and angry, sleep-messed tresses haloed around her. He hadn't quite worked out how to start his tale. Should he pretty it up from what he'd told Cael? As long as she understood the gist, what did it matter. Either way, he'd have to say something soon because she looked about ready to bolt…and then he'd be leaving for Italy before the day's end. He might not have the nerve to revisit the subject upon his return.

"It started when I was five, perhaps six years old."

She stilled, the petticoat drifted from her hand forgotten. He watched her, as realization dawned. His angel.

"If I looked at her too long or smiled a certain way, she'd become annoyed, agitated even. It went on like that for a few months, half a year. I tried to avert my eyes, but I'd forget. Or the babies would do something funny and I'd laugh wrong."

"The babies?" She plopped down on the bed, face turned on his, rapt.

"Gideon and Gabriel were just learning to walk then." She looked so right, nestled in his bed on her stomach, palms propped under her chin.

"Where was your brother Ethan?"

"With his father in England. She'd had a…relationship…with an English dandy, which produced Ethan. When Ethan's father discovered that she was already married, he took the baby and returned home. Ethan only came to live with us in Italy after his father died. Later, there would be the American who fathered Cael and Stephan."

She looked very serious, his cara, a furrow marring her gentle features. Despite the dire tale he recounted, a brief smile touched his lips. He wanted to kiss away the frown from her brow.

"She took to locking me in the cellar when I was seven, as punishment. Sometimes for days."

"Where was your father during all of this?"

"He chose not to involve himself with us: Gideon, Gabriel and I. Their marriage was arranged, quite brilliantly. Mama possessed a striking beauty both in looks and manners. I imagine that is the only reason her family was able to conceal her… peculiarities. Lucca did not play the fool for long. Though he forgave her after Ethan, he never forgot. Never truly believed any of us were his true children. For months, sometimes a year at a time, he would not darken the same wing of the house as us. It was as if we did not exist. I went to him for help once or twice at the beginning but he looked right through me, almost disconnected. Claiming that Mama knew what was best and that if I obeyed her like a good little boy, I'd fair better. I tried, but she'd fly into rages at the sight of me, saying that I was an evil spirit sent to torment her. Asking where her sweet little Dominic was, what had I done with him. After a while, I longed for the serenity of the wine cellar."

He began to pace, averting his gaze from hers, knowing what he would find there: dismay, pity, and finally sadness. All emotions he had once felt about himself and his situation, only his sadness was more akin to despair. No. He had to keep the emotions at bay if he had a prayer of surviving the retelling.

"She called in a mystic of sorts. He was the first; I called him 'The Priest'. He declared me to be possessed by one of Lucifer's soldiers, and took the religious approach to exorcism. My eyes, he said, were the mark of the beast. You'd think someone had sentenced her to death. She tore at her clothes; clawed herself until she bled…in penance, she said, to atone for her sins. For she must have done something wrong to be cursed with a demon-possessed son who stared back at her with the devil in his eyes. For the most part the purification ceremonies the two of them conducted were more frightening than painful. You see, since I'd been declared evil incarnate, the wine cellar just wouldn't do. They kept me in a square pit in the dungeons, and held the ceremonies among the vacant tombs below ground. Castello di Ambrosi is more of a citadel than anything else, dating back to the 1500s, complete with turrets, portcullis, dungeons…and catacombs."

"Oh, Dom—"

He cut off her small anguished voice. "Don't. Let me finish."

"But couldn't you escape? The way you travel, it should have been easy."

He laughed, a short bitter sound that upset the falcon from his shoulder. Dom waited for him to settle his wings before he spoke again. "My ability did not manifest until my twelfth year. And mama was not without her own *talents*. She could…move things with her mind, restrain me physically with just a thought. They never even bothered to tie me down."

He dared a glance at her then. She sat up in the bed with her knees folded beneath her, hazel eyes wild, shaky hands covering what could only be a mouth gaped in shock. She was as much affected by the harrowing events as he. Somehow that knowledge warmed him.

"After the priest was unsuccessful, the witch, the druid and finally the doctor appeared. The witch and the druid were gruesome and the things they did unpleasant, but again not particularly harmful. With the doctor came a new régime, purification by pain. I lost count of the bleedings, trials by fire, broken bones, whippings and the like…but they never touched my face. Always afterward they would check to see if my eyes had changed, because that would mean the demon had fled. I began to wish they would gouge the damned things out and be done with it. Or kill me.

That's when Ethan came. For some reason—a fine thread of sanity left in her, the new baby—I don't know but the ceremonies stopped for a while. She even allowed me back into my old room. I took care not to look at her though. Even still, things slowly went back to the way they were. I was around ten or eleven. Ethan would always come…to heal what they had done…sooth the pain. I was so afraid, despite Gabriel's guiding him, that he'd get caught or mama would somehow find out about his ability and do to him what they'd done to me. By then, you see she'd begun locking Gabriel and Gideon in the cellar so I knew she was capable of it. Gideon is phobic about enclosed places to this day."

"How did you-" Her voice cracked. "-finally escape?"

Dom collided with her tender expression, and he longed to wipe away the tears streaming unchecked down her face.

"When I manifest my traveling ability, I gained a decisive advantage. It took me a few months to exercise a higher level of control, but I was proficient enough to evade mama and her coven of exorcists. We plotted, Ethan, the twins and I, but by then we had a new complication. Cael...and Stephan, who was just born. We all agreed that they shouldn't be left with her, but we could not think of a way to escape with them. Ethan brought up the fact that she'd only begun to act weirdly toward us once we were five or six years old, so maybe Cael and the new baby would be safe until then. That bought us two years. We went to England, to Ethan's uncle who took us in. I was unwilling to share what was done to me so it took us a while to convince Ethan's uncle of what kind of woman our mother truly was."

"Didn't you have any family in Italy besides your parents?"

"My grandmother, several aunts still in the schoolroom and Uncle Fausto. Uncle did not endear himself to us so we would not have sought refuge with him in any case. And the women....You need to understand. The rights of women are severely limited, even more so than in England. Even if they'd known, they could not have interfered unless Lucca, Conte Ambrosi, allowed it. Ethan's uncle was a man of rank and wealth and he backed our claims.

When we arrived to save Cael and Stephan—almost exactly two years later—we found that Mama had absconded with them and married their father. At the time, we knew little about him. Lucca was a bitter drunk by then and could tell us nothing. Several months later, we tracked down mama in Bedlam…a raving madwoman. We did not see Cael again for another ten years. All I remembered of him was a little blonde boy with a crooked smile. Back then we still called him 'Michael'. Stephan, we wouldn't meet until he was twelve."

* * *

"What happened to…the others, the ones who helped your mother?" Eden knew she shouldn't ask, but she had to know. Perhaps if those monsters had gotten their comeuppance, the anger boiling in her gut would dissipate. However, she was careful to keep her expression passive, tender.

"I imagine they met fates similar to hers. I have never returned to Italy, so I cannot say for certain. It must seem selfish of me, but I did not wish for justice. I was content merely to be safe from them. Ethan's Uncle Quinn raised us. He has since retired to his Scottish lands."

A silence fell, during which she watched him meander back to the window. He stood facing the wide square aperture, as the new day broke, his shirt billowing around him in the chilly breeze. Eden was glad of the covers around her and licking warmth of the fireplace. The falcon at his shoulder fussed and fluttered until he turned and whispered in that direction. She wondered. Did he really have so much to say to the bird or was he avoiding her. Dreading her reaction. Embarrassed, even.

"I love you." The words came without thought, but she knew they were true the instant they left her mouth. "I'd love you even if you had a third eye and webbed feet. It's the way you touch me, that lofty arrogance you use to hide your fears, the awe and longing I see in your eyes when you look at me. Its those things that drew me to you, and no one else."

He sat the falcon aside on the perch and came back to

her, eyes brimming with an emotion she'd ached to see reflected back at her. Hope. As he drew to a stop at the side of the bed, new tears swelled at the site. His scars were visible, beautiful and heartbreaking at once. She scooted to the curved edge of the bed.

"I hide them using my ability. It's a complex illusion that radiates off my body like heat, creating a fine layer around my skin. I've done so for so long, it's like breathing. I've tried, but the illusion does not work on my eyes."

Eden felt a tremor run through him at her first touch to the side of his stomach, she bent to kiss the series of parallel slash marks running from taunt muscles to the sides of his torso.

"Eden…"

"Come back to bed now, Dom." She stood on her knees to push the shirt off his shoulders.

"We don't have to…do that again, if you'd rather not."

"What makes you think I'd rather not?" She kissed her way up his chest, stopping only to pay tender loving attention to an especially jagged patch of skin below his nipple.

"I hurt you before."

"Not much."

He grasped her and pulled her against his body, cradling her close. She kissed her way up his throat until she reached the tempting lobe of his ear. She soon found herself swept up in his arms.

He moved onto the bed, and laid her down amid the rumbled sheets. A moment later he joined her, naked and scarred. Her arms twined around him when he lay half atop her, pillowing his head on her chemise-d bosom. She fingered the variety of textures and puckers dotting his back.

"Didn't you…like it?" Her face colored pink waiting for his answer.

"I was unprepared for the bliss of being with you. It

was heaven…and hell. But yes, cara, I liked it." He propped himself on his elbows to gaze at her with mix-matched jewels. "I would like to enjoy such feelings again."

"I would like to as well…" She smiled, quite certain she was beet red. All embarrassment abated when his lips touched hers.

TWENTY FIVE

Eden tried to ignore Kathleen's shrewd gaze as she tore into the breakfast feast Dominic had no doubt instructed the maid to bring to her room. The hot porridge, sticky bun, and heavenly cup of chocolate melted in her mouth. In her greed, she choked on a warm bite of the honey-sweetened bun when the older woman aired her thoughts.

"Aye, so ya waited until tha babe had brought me low and ya let' im have his way wit ya." Kathleen halted any reply with a quelling hand, and a shake of her head. "No use denying it, lass. You've a glow dat would send St. Mary to tha gallows."

Eden forced the morsel down the wrong leg of her throat, just to be able to breath again.

"What 'ave ya ta say for yourself, then?"

With a churlish sigh, she sat the tray aside and stood to face the stanch chaperon whom she'd come to regard as more of a friend. Nevertheless, she needed to set the Scotswoman straight about the previous evening's activities. She was, after all, a grown woman, responsible for herself and her own small fortune…though admittedly she'd neglected both dreadfully.

"I don't know that there is anything to say…or do for

that matter. The deed cannot be undone and what's more I wouldn't wish it reversed even if I could. There now, I have said my peace. Are you...very disappointed in me?" She knew a moment of unease.

"Heavens no. Dominic would've had ya sooner or later. I would rather it were later...say, after tha wedding. Ethan, I do no' think he cares dis way or dat. He's been over tha moon ever since Cael fished ya water-logged bones out of tha bog. Hush, now, ya mustn't cry."

Oh! She felt the tears burst forth. Kathleen pulled her into a tight hug she didn't realize she needed. Much as she'd been prepared to go toe to toe, she was glad a battle hadn't been necessary. Kathleen's good opinion meant the world to her.

"Now, ya mustn't let him dawdle too long in gettin' ya to tha alter."

"Certainly." Eden nodded, sniffling into her shoulder. "But, he hasn't mentioned marriage. I must wait until he asks me."

"Goodness, who told ya *dat*?" Kathleen pulled back and trained an eagle's eye on her. "'Member what I warned tha marriage bed leads ta, lass...Has he spilled himself inside ya?"

Wiping at a wayward tear, she nodded. "Yes, I dare say I cherish it, the tiny part of him that he's left with me."

"Aye, if it takes root, he *or she* will no' remain tiny."

Try as she might, Eden could not drudge up an inkling of worry or regret. If a child resulted from being with Dominic...the thought alone warmed her, filling her with visions of a raven-haired boy with haunted eyes and a serious mien she would love to tease a giggle from.

"Where is Dominic?" She asked, suddenly longing to see him.

"He an' tha brothers have gathered in tha library. Can no' be good news. Whenever dat many men come together ta discuss anythin', there are ill tidings afoot. Rest assured."

* * *

Dominic shuffled his feet, the urge to bolt nagging at him. Without his spectacles in place, he suffered anxiety being the focus of so many faces at once…that they were those of his brothers eased him some. Cael's expression dogged him, a constant source of reassurance and support. For now his brother truly knew the reason for his solitary existence, realized the difficulty of enduring strangers and their staring eyes.

Stephan languished on the sofa, a wrinkled mess from the previous night spent atop the cushy three-seater. The relaxed pose belied the keen interest leveled from him. Dom noted that his youngest brother looked more himself, still quiet but no longer a dispirited shell. He probably had Eden to thank for that as well. A few steps away Ethan stood, a booted foot resting on the cornered edge of the ottoman. He hummed with approval.

Dom endeavored to concentrate, ease his nerves with the one image capable of gentling his anxiety…Eden. Her visage came easily to his mind, assuaging his uncertainties. He conjured her voice…'They're beautiful, Dom'. With her by his side, even in thought only, he stood straighter, cleared his throat and looked each of his three brothers square in the face. Dom had their undivided attention.

"Ahem. Last evening, I received a message from Davide Greyson requesting an audience with me. For what, the letter does not specify. It does, however, also inform me that during an inspection of St. Ciaran Isis Asylum, owned by one Matthias Montgomery, a suspected blackmail log was discovered. According to Greyson, the newest entry reads Conte Dominic Ambrosi. So, I think it safe to say that our Mr. Montgomery is well informed."

"I don't suppose there was any mention of the blackmail material to be used against you." Ethan asked.

"None, but I think we can all guess what advantage Montgomery intends to press. Here, read for yourself."

Dominic extracted the crumpled communiqué from his lapel pocket, and handed it off to Ethan.

"Do you plan to receive Greyson?"

"I would rather not." Dominic saw in Cael that he did not agree with the decision but he seemed to both expect and accept it. "This warning of blackmail could be a ruse on Greyson's part to press a meeting with me. He obviously knows something of Stephan's ability. Perhaps he suspects that all of us are equally endowed. How he discovered we are related is another concern. I take it you did not inform him of our connection."

Cael shook his head, a frown formed over troubled amber at the thought.

"Would you care for my opinion, big brother?"

All three brothers eyed the youngest. Stephan's attention never left Dominic. "It isn't me he's after. If Greyson really wants to see me, he need only ask. I would not refuse, even if Cael forbade it. He has never asked."

"That is true." Cael confirmed. "I met with Greyson on several occasions. He spoke of it, alluded that he would be interested in helping Stephan, but he has never issued a specific request."

"Perhaps he has some passing interest in me, but what he really wants is an audience with you, Dom. He approached Cael about me as an incentive for you to initiate a conversation with him."

"But that would mean that he's known our family background for some time." Cael pointed out.

"Perhaps he has, and is choosing to use it now out of desperation." Stephan shrugged. "But, he's not lying about the blackmail."

"How do you know?" Dom inquired.

"I received a note demanding a large sum from an unspecified person." Stephan's eyes sparkled but his tone he kept flat and informative, as if he were relaying his agenda for the day. "Any student at the university would be too wealthy to bother with blackmail, and possibly too frightened of me to do so even were they poor enough to warrant it. Also, the person is not educated, so that rules out Greyson. In any case, the handwriting on Greyson's message is not the same as the one I received. It only occurred to me last evening that Montgomery is the most-likely culprit, though I doubt he knows of our kinship, otherwise you'd have already received a similar request for funds upon threat of his doing some harm to me."

Cael immediately came to his brother's side, an agitated hand lost in dark gold hair. "And you don't tell me this?"

"I am of age, and I prefer to handle my own affairs."

"How have you handled it?" Dom was disturbed. He'd been right to worry about Montgomery targeting Stephan.

"I burned the note." He shrugged, his continence not wavering from his eerie calm. "Montgomery cannot harm me. More like, his provoking me would result in my accidentally killing him. The fact that he does not realize this is why I believe his threat to expose me is a bluff."

"A lesser man would have panicked." Dom admired such clarity of thought.

"Something more will need to be done about him." Ethan, who had thus far been a mere observer, asserted himself into the conversation.

"Let's wait and see what the reform board will do with him first." Dominic could tell by his tone that Cael had become uneasy. "With each new incident, the picture we are painting of Montgomery grows more alarming. He is shrewd and that makes him dangerous. We should avoid a direct battle with him if at all possible."

Ethan and Stephan deferred.

"Agreed, then." Why borrow trouble, Dom concluded, when they already had enough to go around. "In the meantime, Gideon requires my presence in Italy. Gabriel's condition has not improved and Uncle Fausto continues to make a nuisance of himself. I will be leaving at sunset. Also, I have invited Stephan to be my permanent houseguest and he has agreed. Cael, I realize this may come as a shock, but he is no longer a child. Stephan, I would ask that you look after Eden in my absence. You must promise me to safeguard her."

"She will not accompany you to Italy then?" To Dom's surprise, Stephan showed more emotion than Cael. He sat up, then stood, an enigmatic expression on his face.

Cael merely nodded.

"No. I wish it, but Nonna and the donnas will not be kind to her. The situation with Gideon and Gabriel does not permit them to entertain guests. Plus, I may not be able to astral the whole way if I bring Eden along, and Gideon is impatient. Under the circumstances, there is no choice but for her to remain here. But if I know that she is protected I will rest easy."

"Rest easy then. I would be honored to protect what is yours." He came forward, and offered a hand. Dominic used it to pull his brother into a brief embrace. He noted that Stephan seemed flushed...over-warm. Afterward, he watched him ambled back to the sofa, shaken.

He directed his next statement to Ethan and Cael. "Ethan, you and Cael, stay close at hand if at all possible. Eden is not the only woman here in need of protection. There is Kathleen and the servants to think of. Montgomery is not above targeting the maids and whatnot. I'll have none of that here. Ethan if you feel strongly enough I will understand if you extract Kathleen and protect her from you own home in town."

"I will stay close." Ethan promised. "With the three of us keeping diligent watch, I believe everyone will be safe."

"I do not have to return immediately to town." Cael stated.

"That's settled then. I have one last request. Cael, if you and Stephan would excuse us, I must speak with Ethan."

When they were alone, Ethan was the first to speak. "You told Cael."

"Yes." He frowned. "I wouldn't think he'd run to you and discuss it."

"He didn't. Nevertheless, it is obvious he knows. Another of his headaches struck last night. Between his and Kathleen's malaise, I scarcely slept a wink."

"I should have known. When I let him see...he retched."

Ethan returned his frown. "But that's usually the sign of an abating migraine."

"This is one of the reasons I resisted telling him. He feels too much."

"Yes, empathy. It's what makes him so effective with his patients. By the way, what was it you wanted to ask of me?"

He hesitated, not sure his request wasn't a selfish one. If Ethan had been awake the entire night attending to illness he was tired and his ability, weakened. "Never mind. You need to rest."

"I'm fine. The migraine was easily remedied. Kathleen, I could scarcely help except to hold her hair back. I spent most of the night standing vigil. What is it?"

Ethan wore concern like a favorite suit. Dominic almost smiled. He'd been doing a lot of that lately...resisting the urge to smile, *having* the urge to begin with.

"Eden. I would like you to take away the bruises on her throat and at her..." He did not avert his eyes, knowing what his was about to reveal. Ethan would surely guess. "...left hip and thigh."

Concern drained, replaced by pleasant surprise. "So that's it, then. You de-flowered her."

It was as blunt a statement as he'd ever heard grace the lips of his pristine brother. Perhaps Kathleen had managed to curdle Ethan's flawless manners at last.

"We deflowered each other."

"What are you going to do?"

"Nothing, everything...I don't know. The feelings rage in one direction and then the next. They don't allow for common sense. I know I cannot let her go." Just the thought of losing her caused a pang. He looked down to find his hand rubbed at the place over his heart. "She is mine now, a part of me. It...it hurts to think of being without her."

"Are you in love with her?" With his question, hope sprang.

He let his hand fall to his side, trying to get control of rioting insides. "Love is not a familiar emotion. Is this how it was for you...with Kathleen?"

"Yes, at first. The feelings were confusing and powerful." He paused. Dominic waited as he searched for his next words. "Kathleen was alluring, addictive. I had to have her, always. The want is still there, but it has tempered with time. Do not worry. If you love her, when you fall completely, you'll know."

TWENTY SIX

"But why must it be you?" She stamped her slipper-clad foot against the be-rugged floor, hazel orbs ablaze. "You aren't a doctor, you can do naught but sympathize. Send Atherton or Dr. Raine."

"Gabriel is not sick, nor is he insane."

"Then what the devil is the matter with him that only you can fix?!"

"Cara, please. He suffers. Do not force me to choose between the two of you."

He was beside himself. She saw the conflict raging in him. If she continued on, she could probably break him. He'd delay, at least long enough to placate her, convince her that the trip could not be avoided. But is that what she wanted? To nag at him like a shrew until he surrendered. Somehow, it did not seem a wise precedent to set for a marriage-minded lady, but she couldn't help herself. In her head she knew her demands were bratty, unreasonable, ruthless even…her woman's heart, however, railed against his leaving. Had she a sibling to teach her the concept of sharing, perhaps she could have resisted. At the moment, there was but room for one person in her heart and he wanted to leave her.

"Take me with you."

"No." The word slapped her in the face. He wouldn't bend on that point, so she'd have to work on keeping him here.

"Then, you have already chosen."

"That is not true. I could not."

She rounded on him, stalking forward, narrowing her focus to just his bejeweled orbs. "You don't want to leave, I can see it in your eyes. You're dreading it...being back in the very place where those vile people hurt you. Stay here with me, where you'll be safe from the memories. Tell the one called Gideon to bring Gabriel to England. They are cruel to make you go back there."

"Ethan and Cael will be close at hand. And I have also asked Stephan to watch over you. Please do not be frightened of him. Stephan is—"

"The Sphinx does not scare me. He's a lamb in wolf's clothing." She snapped, again stalking to and fro. "Odd to be sure, but not frightening. It's..."

Panic seized her, stopped her dead in her tracks. Her fears must have showed because he was at her side in an instant, pulling her flush with his hard, masculine strength. "What? Tell me, Eden."

She lifted her face to his. "Dom, what if *it* comes back? The evil thing. Or the visions."

He exhaled. "The visions are of real people, real events. Cael showed me your drawings. The woman and her infant are dead now, but they lived on this estate before I acquired it from her widower. She drowned trying to save her child who had fallen in the marsh."

She gestured the issue aside. "Yes, yes, Atherton explained all that. But the entity, do you still think I imagined it?"

Anguished, he stared down at her. "I...I...Cael seems to think there is an explanation other than insanity and I am happy to embrace his theory over mine."

"That does not answer my question, Dominic."

"We will confront this issue when I return." He tightened his hold on her when she tried to recoil out of his hold. She glared up to find pewter-sapphire sparks exploding with intensity. "No. Hear me, cara, and heed my words. I will attend to Gabriel for as long as he requires me. Do not assume that means that you can escape me. Why do you believe I can be without you so easily? That I'd choose to leave when there was any other option. I want to have you right now, beneath me, here on the floor of your chamber without preamble. Do you require proof, then? Shall I strip your clothes off, spread your legs and sink myself into your body to ease the ache I feel. Does the image frighten you, cara? It does me. I wonder…would you let me take you that way?"

"Yes, Dom…" She tilted heavily against him. The curious dampness plagued her drawers once again. Was it depraved to be aroused by such rough talk…to give herself to him in whatever way he wished despite Kathleen's warning, and the inevitable outcome?

Her breath hitched when his hand snaked out to grasp hers and brought it to his trouser front. He hissed through his teeth when she closed her fingers around him. His other hand cupped the nape of her neck. "You will sleep in my bed until I return. At night, I will come to you as often as I can. If I don't find you there, I will shimmer to wherever you are and the devil take who sees me. Do you understand me, Eden?"

She could do nothing but nod and accept the searing kiss he blazed on her mouth an instant later.

TWENTY SEVEN

His brother's essence shone strong, but the sharpness of the edges and the over-bright current swirling in the center denoted no small amount of distress. Not only that, Dom saw a minute difference in Gabriel's essence. Impossible, yet undeniable. A new element existed.

As he suspected, Gideon hovered nearby, his distress less obvious. Dominic stepped from the astral and into the corporeal world. He knew immediately that the room in which he stood belonged to one of the over fifty boasted by his childhood home, an unwanted legacy his by birthright, the Castello di Ambrosi.

The exaggerated surroundings reminded him of scenery in a stage drama. Simple paintings wouldn't do, the walls writhed with gilt murals of great and tragic events. The mile-high ceiling was cluttered with mosaic frescos. Gideon, at six-four, leaned against the lip of the fireplace that stood tall enough for him to walk into without stooping. Windows stretched from floor to ceiling. His twin Gabriel lay in a canopied bed fit for the Almighty himself, complete with wine-red drapery of the finest textured satin. The Prescotts of London, who took gaudy elegance to new heights, would be jealous. The only thing out of place was the makeshift cot in the opposite corner of the room.

"It's good to see you, Dominic…*all* of you." The taller man inclined a brow at him.

"Likewise." He turned from Gideon and approached the bed. "How is he? Any change?"

"No." Gideon came around to the opposite side of the bed. "At night he sleeps in the normal way, except for the nightmare. The same one repeats every night. Always, at dawn he becomes like this. Trapped in a waking dream. Eyes open, but sightless, lifeless. His chest moves, but that is the only proof that he lives. Feeding him is a chore. I can manage to get him to swallow only if I pinch off his nose."

"Aww, Muse, I should have known I would find you here." Dominic spared the Himalayan feline a brief smile as he bent to stroke the opulent silver-grey fur where it lay flush with his brother's corded olive skin. Muse trilled, and then redirected soulful azures back to nuzzle her head beneath her master's limp hand. "How long?"

"A fortnight." Gideon was the worse for wear. Chaotic blue-black locks much like his own, shadowy jaw, and a suit that looked more slept on than the over-plush bedcovers that lay sprayed out over his comatose mirror image.

"Have you tried to arouse him?"

"With every technique I can think of. Buckets of water, hot wax, smelling salts. I've even been at him with a needle. Nothing."

"The dreams have always disturbed him, but this…" Dom trailed off, lifting his eyes to catch the troubled expression across the great divide of the bed. "Has *this*…happened before?"

"A few times, but it only lasted an hour or so, and only after an especially vivid dream…most had to do with violent events."

"He is distressed for sure." Dominic nodded. "His

essence practically vibrates. But what do you think he's seeing? What could put him in such a state?"

"I have thought about it." Gideon glanced down at his twin's sightless stare. "The only event that comes to mind is...my death."

"No." He recoiled from the idea, even as the word shot from his mouth. When his brother looked back up at him, Dominic backed away from what he saw. Gideon's intense slate grey gaze held neither fear nor defiance, no preference for life over death...only concern for his twin. "No, Gideon."

"That is the real reason I summoned you here. If I am right, you'll need to take care of Gabriel...after." Gideon followed him. "I have already begun to put my affairs in order. We, by we I mean you, the true Conte Ambrosi, must also be prepared to take your place as the head of the family. I realize that it will be difficult and I would have been more than willing to take on the burden instead, but—"

The sight of his brother's expressionless acceptance fueled an increasing panic in Dom. "I don't want to hear this. I won't have it!" He shook his head, and pivoted to take full strides for the window. Gideon followed. "Gabriel is wrong this time."

"When has Gabriel ever been wrong? Was he wrong about our mother?"

The rawness of the words chafed his heart.

"Tell me, Dom, was he wrong about Stephan?"

His head snapped around. "He saw..."

"Stephan's ability is quite extraordinary. Would you like to know the nature of it? By the by, you should talk to Cael. His headaches are worsening and more frequent than he's let on." Gideon continued, bearing down on him, driving a knife through his heart. His eyes like cold marcasite crystals, glittering in the sunlight that leached through the grand cathedral windows. He didn't walk, no, his looming form glided across the floor with predatory elegance. "Oh, congratulate Ethan for us. Tell him he can stop worrying, Kathleen will make it through the birth just fine. Would you like to know the gender of the child?"

For a moment, a split second, anxiety played havoc with his mind. He saw Lillian stalking towards him, relentless, remorseless...her dark beauty more frightening than death itself. The twins resembled their mother the most. Particularly Gideon when he bowed to fatalism and macabre tactics. His short, coiffed locks morphed into Rapunzel-length vines. His grey orbs darkened to soulless black holes. The angular planes of his face softened to creamy cheeks, a serpentine smile slithered across her lips...

"Stop it!"

Even his voice somehow lifted from bass to contralto. "Your woman. She is exquisite, Dominic, if a bit reedy. Both Gabriel and I were pleasantly surprised."

"Gideon, please, no more...do you want me lying on that bed beside Gabriel?"

At last he stopped, coming to stand behind him, compassion melted he stony gaze to a warm smoky gray. "Forgive me, but I do not fear it and neither should you. Death is a natural part of life. Come, if talking about my passing makes you this uncomfortable we can put it off a day or so, but I warn you, we'll have to discuss it soon. Tell me about *her*. Surely it is she who has wrought the changes I see in you. I had thought you would bring her along."

The vice around his throat loosened when Gideon clapped him on the back and propelled him towards a matched pair of throne-esque chairs separated by a claw-foot marble table.

"Bring Eden here? And have Nonna and the aunts rake her across the coals while the servants use her for gossip fodder? Hell no."

* * *

Hundreds of miles away, Eden gazed unseeing out the drawing room window at a day so dreary it almost rivaled the gloom hanging over her heart. Fat raindrops splattered like tears against the glass. The menacing billows overhead emptied their contents on the land in a mad rage, obscuring the landscape but for the occasional dagger of lightening. After an hour, she ceased to start at the crackles of thunder that preceded each flash bolt.

"Do you intend to mope around for the whole of his absence?"

She abandoned her vigil at the window to find the Sphinx, awaiting an answer to his riddle. Her mood did not make for good conversation but she didn't have the heart to request to be left alone. He'd come looking for her. Perhaps wishing to continue with the book they'd begun, though she did not spy it in his hand.

"Maybe." She shrugged, an edgy apathy to her words. "I only recently gave up suicide, you know."

Warm amber crinkled at the corners as they would if he'd smile, only his lips remained uncurved. "Death would not become you."

She hardly needed reminding that her skin shone pale as a corpse. With her natural thinness and white-blonde hair, if she skipped even one meal she tended to resemble just that. "Have you come to suggest a diverting occupation, then?"

"If you like."

He came forward to sit across from her on a silly-looking chaise, made even more ridiculous by the intense gentleman adorning it. The carved wood feet seemed to shrink in shame at being upstaged in both import and interest.

"What shall it be then…The pianoforte? Reading in the library? Surely not brandy over a game of whist?"

"In a mood, I see." His expression said that he could relate. She even detected a note of enjoyment in his voice.

"I am at your service."

"I played twenty questions with your brother." She challenged, determined to provoke a glimpse beneath the old world gentleman persona he choose to don.

"Dominic? Playing a game? Not likely."

"Atherton." She corrected. "You first."

He leaned forward, an assessing look in his eyes. "Why are you so phobic about my brother's absence?"

She sighed at the question. Not surprising. "I miss him." She admitted, which was true enough.

"This melancholy of yours goes beyond yearning for a lover."

Eden's eyes bucked. Her first thought was that Dominic had told him, but she quickly discarded that notion. "Can you read minds? Is that your gift?"

"Dominic is very forthcoming, I see." No gasp or owlish look of surprise from the Sphinx. He merely acknowledged a fact. "Mine is a curse, not a gift."

"But did you read my mind?" She persisted.

"No. You did not answer *my* question, Eden. Dominic's absence, why does it affect you so?"

She shrugged, allowing her eyes to wonder around the room before they came to rest again on him. "I should think it rather obvious. You're his brother. Your place in his life and his affection is secure. Me, I could be tossed out with the garbage at the slightest provocation. What if this Gideon character does not approve? Dominic holds him and the other one in great esteem…certainly greater than whatever he feels for me."

"You have nothing to fear."

Her expression became incredulous. "You say that with such finality. Dominic and Dr. Raine both think I am a Bedlamite-in-the-making."

"If Ethan gave you that impression it was accidental, I'm sure. He favors you for a sister-in-law and he would not be above matchmaking to accomplish it. A blind man could see that Dominic wants you…and has clearly had you. He would not take a madwoman to bed."

"But how do you know." She insisted, desperate to believe him.

"Because before he left he charged me with the duty of protecting his woman. He said nothing of his house, his lands, his accounts; he merely wanted *you* to be safe. It was not difficult to see that his attachment is profound. Dominic wouldn't have spilled the family secret unless he already considered you to be part of the family. Trust me, there is nothing to fear."

Some of her anxiety abated. With its loss came more curiosity about the man before her. She tilted her head to the side, and studied him. "I want to see what haunts you."

His eyes shuttered at the request, and he leaned away from her. "I don't know if I can limit it to a small display, even with you here."

Confusion swelled. "What does my being here have to do with anything?"

He was no longer an old world gentleman; the enigmatic sphinx stared back at her. This time she did not flinch or avoid the burning-amber scrutiny.

"Try not to blink your eyes." He inclined his head at her answering frown. "Go on, try."

She took a deep breath and met his, determined hazel focused and ready. Ten seconds later, she blinked. But he never wavered, holding her in a blink-less trance for what seemed like days. When graceful mahogany lashes at last swooped elegantly downward, she exhaled a sigh she didn't realize she was holding.

"Not as easy as it seems, is it? You have to concentrate every second because the instant your mind wanders impulse takes over. And you blink. Or suppose you don't forget. Eventually the impulse to blink becomes so strong that it overrides your willpower to resist it." He reached out, took her hand and deftly arranged her fingers to resemble a revolver pointed at him.

"Now, imagine you have a pistol in your hand, finger

twitching at the trigger. And every time you forget or succumb to the impulse to blink, it fires…hitting any luckless soul who happens to be in your line of sight. Bam!"

She jumped when a particularly loud clap of thunder punctuated his last word. The shawl slipped from her shoulders, and she dropped the 'pistol' in her hand. His eyes immediately focused on her exposed throat and remained there a beat longer than she was comfortable with. It took her a moment to regain her composure, even after he spoke and broke the spell.

"That is what my gift is like. I'm not sure why, or even how, but your presence has a dampening effect. Makes it less of an effort to deaden the impulse." He paused, amber glistening. "Still want to witness my curse, Eden?"

"Yes." The word came out a breathless murmur. He'd meant to frighten her she suspected, but his little demonstration intrigued her all the more.

TWENTY EIGHT

Dom exited from invisibility as soon as the door closed behind the chambermaid who came to change the dingy linens.

"How long are you staying?" Gideon inquired.

"Had circumstances permitted, I would have *arrived* with all the necessary pomp and circumstance of a carriage, rumpled traveling clothes, and miles of luggage to occupy a multitude of fawning footman."

"All acquired in the village after you'd shimmered, no doubt."

He'd had to alter his original plans. Eden could not endure a long absence and Dom found neither could he. "It will be a strain, but my visit needs to be kept covert. I cannot tarry long and I'll need to astral in and out. If Nonna and the aunts get a whiff, I'll be trapped in the castle for a fortnight or more…and they'll be no opportunity to astral."

Gideon motioned toward the still figure on the bed. "Gabriel is no different today than yesterday."

"Yes." He drawled out. "I've been thinking of…taking him into the astral realm. The shock of having whatever he's feeling intensified tenfold may jolt him awake. It's drastic, I admit."

"Could work."

"You'll have to restrain Muse." Dom eyed the clingy feline atop his brother's chest. Her furry head rested on her paws as if she too were holding a vigil.

"Of course." Gideon bent to retrieve the cat. Muse moaned her displeasure and attempted to burrow even closer. He had to dislodge each claw from both the counterpane and the linen nightshirt. She wailed an almost human cry at the separation, and seemed to Dom to cling to Gideon as would a ship captain's wife at the docks on the day of her husband's maiden voyage.

Dominic shook his head, "That cat is over-indulged."

"Gabriel denies her nothing." He cradled the anxious feline in the crook of his elbow and stroked the silver-grey mane, all the while cooing reassurance and soft endearments.

"Just Gabriel?" Dominic quipped, even as he flipped back the covers and hoisted his brother's inert body off the bed. Though the twins had a good two inches on him, Dominic's frame was the studier and boasted greater muscle mass. It took a bit of maneuvering, but he achieved a serviceable grasp to support the dead weight. A moment later, he shimmered.

The essence intermingled with his was all shakes and shudders, with jagged edges that flashed blinding lights and shades. Emotions magnified to nightmarish intensity. The anomaly Dominic had noticed before was no longer visible…in Gabriel's essence. But an identical anomaly now existed in Gideon's. The shock of seeing the appendage-like glitch transferred from one twin to the other distracted him. He'd meant to flash in and out on the same breath. But his loss of focus stayed him an extra second or two.

He stepped off into the physical world with his burden, more shaken than his brother's essence. Gideon immediately relinquished Muse to help him reposition his clammy twin in the bed.

"What the devil happened? His pallor is worse than before."

"I stayed a few moments longer than intended. He's pale, but at least his eyes are closed."

Dominic pulled the covers over him as far as Muse's renewed position on his chest would allow. "Gideon, is there something you're not telling me."

Sharp slate eyes snapped to his face. "Explain yourself."

He didn't quite know how. No logical explanation existed. Souls simply did not change, beyond intensity of color and sharpened edges during heightened emotion or distress. In the case of women, a pregnancy yielded an overflow of essence easily identifiable as fusion and eventual fission of two souls.

"His essence is different. Or rather *was* different yesterday when I first located the two of you. Today, just now when I shimmered, his essence was normal and yours held an identical anomaly. Souls do not change Gideon. For yours and Gabriel's to be transferring the same aberration back and forth is…peculiar. I need to know if you've left out something. Anything."

His gaze, anguished apparent, lingered on his twin. "No. I told you everything."

"Did anything happen just now when I shimmered?"

"No." He looked up then. "I stood here and didn't move until you reappeared."

"What about yesterday when I shimmered in, had anything unusual happened just then?"

Slate-grey eyes glassed over momentarily, in thought. "No."

"And you have no idea what he could be dreaming about?" He pressed, desperate for even a scrap of a clue.

"Outside of the theory I already shared, no. Since he began having this particular dream, he hasn't been lucid enough to speak about it."

219

"This is strange." Dom frowned. "I've never seen it before. How do you feel?"

"Fine. I assume my death will result from either an accident or a murder since I am not ill nor do I plan to commit suicide."

Too bemused by the paradox to be alarmed by his casual talk of death, Dominic only nodded and continued to shift through the short list of possibilities. Looking down at Gabriel, a radical thought flashed in his mind.

"Gideon, wait here. Don't move or do anything. Just stand there."

"Where are you going?"

"Astraling. Something's occurred to me and I dare not air it until I'm sure." He did not give his brother the chance to argue or question him further, but shimmered out. The anomaly was again attached to Gabriel's essence. In the mere minutes since his last shimmer, Gabriel's essence had relaxed some, appeared less distressed. Dominic exited to an anxious Gideon waiting in the exact same spot as when he'd left.

"Well?"

"The anomaly is not an anomaly...at least not one that belongs to either of you."

"Am I supposed to know what that means?"

Dominic found his brother observing him with frayed patience. "Muse. How did Gabriel acquire her?"

"Dom if you don't tell me what the hell is wrong with—"

"It isn't him or you, it's Muse. When I arrived yesterday and noticed the change in Gabriel's essence, Muse lay against his side. When I shimmered and noticed the change in your essence, you held Muse in your arms. Just now when I shimmered and again saw the change, Muse lay on Gabriel's chest."

"So what you're telling me is Muse has an essence?"

"Yes and no. I've shimmered in her presence a dozen times and never seen her on the astral so she couldn't have a separate essence of her own. She only pops up as an appendage of you or Gabriel. That, in itself, is strange. Animals cannot inhabit the astral for the simple reason that they do not possess a soul. Unless I were shielding it, any normal cat I tried to shimmer with would not survive the trip."

"And Muse?"

He sighed. "I don't know. Maybe. I'm loath to try. If I'm wrong..."

The taller man shook his head. "The last thing we need is to kill Gabriel's cat. He'd never forgive me...and certainly not if I have to tell him that we experimented with her."

"Is she unusual in any other way?"

"She's polydactyl, but it does not appear to impede her agility."

* * *

Stephan stood facing her, halfway across the drawing room, one arm held out in front of him. But he wasn't looking at her. He'd divested himself of the coat and rolled up the sleeve of his outstretched arm. He twisted and rotated his elbow so that his fisted palm faced down and then up, all the while eyeing his arm as if it were a snake about to bite him. Eden waited by the window, a pail of water sat close at hand as he'd instructed. She watched poised on the edge of her chair, afraid to blink not because of his warning but because she did not want to miss even the tiniest glimpse.

She saw it then. A crawling plume of scarlet gold poof-ed into being and darted along his forearm towards the fisted palm. When it reached his wrist he unfurled his hand and let the hypnotic flame collect in his palm, a cauldron of sorts. She sat, riveted, as the caged inferno writhed and spit behind the restraining bars of his fingers.

"Is it safe to come closer now?"

At his nod, Eden abandoned the shawl and crossed the room. She shuffled around to stand beside him so she wouldn't be in-the-line-of-fire, so to speak. Warmth emanated from not just his hand but his entire body. But no charred smell or smoke rose from the bristled sprigs of hair dotting his arm.

Tentative, not wishing to break his obvious concentration on keeping the blaze contained, she reached to skim her fingertips along the taunt sinewy length where the flame had traveled. His tan-gold skin threatened to singe the pads of her fingers but was itself neither scorched nor burned. She snatched her hand back and blew cool air on it.

Stephan tracked the movement with his sphinx eyes, and did the oddest thing. He smiled down at her. It was the crooked smile of a naughty two-year old.

"Sorry."

Fascinated, she asked, "What would happen if I were not here?"

The smile died and he returned his gaze to the ball of fire licking upward his palm. "The whole room would be ablaze. Bring the pail, please."

She returned just in time to see him slowly close his fingers around the flame to snuff it out. Then he pivoted and dove his fisted arm into the proffered bucket. The water sizzled and hissed against his skin, tossing up billows of steam.

"What a remarkable gift. I wish I were blessed with some noteworthy talent."

"No, you don't." He pulled free of the bucket, and loosed the snowy cotton down over his arm.

Eden noticed that no moisture dampened his shirt's sleeve. Also noting the negligible weight of the bucket, she peered over the rim to find it as dry as a desert.

"Stephan—" She tracked him back to the window.

"I believe it's my turn to ask a question."

"Yes of course." She conceded and took up her

previous seat.

"The bruises at your throat the other night, how did you come by them?"

Eden's shoulders slumped. He would have to ask her *that*. Obviously, he'd noticed them at some point during their 'reading' or the sight of her smooth unblemished neck wouldn't have drawn such interest earlier. Did she dare tell him that an unseen entity had attacked her in the bath? The explanation sounded ludicrous enough in her head, heaven knew what his reaction would be if she aired it.

"An accident." She heard herself saying.

He was immediately stiff and alert. Her half-truth only begged more questions. "When? Under what circumstances?"

"In the bath, and I don't think we should discuss it."

Suspicion darkened his brow. "After what I have shared, you owe me the truth Eden."

She inhaled a fortifying breath. "Alright."

To her amazement, he cracked neither a smile nor a frown, merely listened with his usual silent intensity. Speaking only when she'd finished.

"Have there been similar incidents before?"

She found herself unleashing all her horrors upon him, the incident at the Hen party, and her peculiar visions, even her 'dip' in the pond. His mien showed no revulsion, pity or disbelief. Instead he seemed absorbed, soaking up the information in an almost scholarly manner.

"Nothing you've told me suggests that you are a madwoman."

"I am not sure Dominic would agree." She scoffed.

"He is not an impartial party, Eden." He informed her in a cautionary tone. "Our mother was a raving lunatic who died in an insane asylum. The stigma affects Dom much more so than the rest of us. Remember that."

Before she could ask him another question, he stood and bowed. "Forgive me, but I must excuse myself.

"We'll speak again?" She wished it very much. Confiding in the Sphinx had quite lightened her worries.

"Of course." Enigmatic amber sparkled, and Eden could have sworn she saw flames flicker in their depths. Then, he turned and exited the room.

TWENTY NINE

Stephan did not appear at the dinner table that evening. Disappointment mingled with worry. But, since neither doctor seemed concerned by his absence Eden soon relaxed and slipped into easy conversation with them and Kathleen. Afterward, she retired to the library hoping to come across the prodigal brother. No such luck.

Not willing to give up, she shuffled along the third floor hallway. Perhaps he'd closeted himself off in the portrait gallery. When she passed under a familiar stretch of hallway, she began trolling along patterned wainscoting in search of the knob. It did not take long to find.

The gallery was more looming than she remembered. A multitude of unsmiling faces, and flat lifeless eyes followed her. Silence as loud as death put haste in her steps as she made a quick sweep of the L-shaped room. Finding it empty, she pivoted with every intention of escaping, but a glimpse of one portrait in particular stilled her. It drew her until she stood enthralled before the last two of Dominic's brothers she'd yet to meet.

She wondered how the one called Gabriel fared. When would his condition, whatever it was, improve enough so that Dominic could return to her? How many endless days *and nights* would she be forced to endure without him? Five? Ten? Twenty? Perhaps his brother's suffering had worsened and that was why he hadn't come to visit her as he'd promised.

Bored and restless without Stephan or Kathleen to distract her, Eden quit the gallery and went in pursuit of a new pastime. The nasty weather had slackened some, but did not permit her to take the must-needed stroll on the outdoors. So she took it indoors instead. Her aimless wandering led her to the sub-floor below the first, housing the kitchens and servant's work areas. She passed the pressing room, butler's pantry, and food preparation room, startling two scullery maids, and a very harassed-looking footman. It was as many servants as she'd seen the whole of her stay on the estate.

She came to a massive door, re-enforced with sheets of dull bronze nailed over hardwood. Curious what the sentry door could be protecting, she slid back the bar holding the locking mechanism in place. It took all her weight thrown backward to budge the three-inch thick metal monstrosity.

A damp musty odor assailed her nostrils. Stone and mortar steps led down into hazy darkness, where large mounds were distinguishable beyond the bottom tier. Something reckless flared in her and she strode forward, into the bowls of the mouth-like threshold. A voice from the hidden alcove of her mind compelled her. *Come to me.*

The second she was beyond the safety of the hallway, a familiar chill seized her…the sudden awareness that she was no longer alone. For an instant she panicked, froze. That second of indecision and fear doomed her. A sharp shove at her back plummeted her down the stone steps. Her body sprawled in a painful heap, chin-first on the packed dirt floor. The cackle of malevolent laughter echoed off the walls of her mind. Through slit lids she watched the curious wedge of light projected from the threshold grow thinner, too dazed to realize the significance.

Horror dawned as total darkness engulfed her. The fatal boom of the locking mechanism sliding back into place from outside jarred her to life. Her breathing went erratic in the aftermath. She screamed. Her eyes darted back and forth, seeing nothing. Anxiety beat at her chest, buzzed in her ears. Her mind screamed. The high-pitched fear more a product of the entity's possible return than her entrapment. She went absolutely still, combing the darkness for any sign of movement or presence. Precious moments ticked by, nothing. She relaxed in degrees, grateful, despite her predicament, to be alone.

Common sense told her that she was in no real danger. The brothers or Kathleen would miss her. They would search the house and, not finding her in any of her usual havens, would eventually question the servants. She had caused too big a stir on the lower levels to be forgotten. They'd find her. She just had to be patient until then.

Soon, curiosity encroached. The entity had locked her inside…but inside what? She flexed all her muscles, stiff from maintaining the rigid stillness too long, and pushed up into a kneeling seat on the dirt floor. Her eyes began to adjust to the darkness. She noticed after a more composed inspection of her surroundings that she could make out a repeating row of fat barrel-like objects lining either side of the floor. But if the room lay in pitch-blackness how was she able to distinguish even these murky forms? There must be a faint source of illumination somewhere.

Cautious, she moved down what seemed to be an aisle, hugged close on either side by successive rows of barrels. She paused to run her hand along one of the massive shapes, tapping the ground around it with her foot. Wooden, rough-hewed, definitely a barrel…supported by a low-lying frame of some sort. Continuing down the aisle, the barrels became distinct. Even before she reached the skull-grey wall, she'd identified her prison as the wine vault Atherton had joked her about.

Tiny morsels of light streamed in from two age-dulled

windows. They were cut into the stone at ground level and looked up to a half cloudy sky, which had begun to wane into night. Lined up against the rear wall she found a smaller racking system, housing wine bottles instead of wine barrels. She rested a hand on the cool glass neck of one of the top-shelf wines and after only a moment's hesitation pulled it out. The label read: Ambrosia, 1801.

* * *

Eden had no idea how long she'd been trapped in the vault when she heard the locking mechanism slide out from its sheath. She stumbled up from the floor, one hand clawing at the cedar wine rack to steady herself. The empty bottle that had rested in her lap plunked against her thigh. She looked down at the forgotten weight still clutched in her free hand.

"Eden."

Her head snapped up at the sound of her name.

"Wee one?"

"Miss Prescott. Are you there?"

"Yes…" The word sounded strange, drug out too long. Her head swam when she stepped away from her support and toward the approaching voices. They overtook her wobbling form midways the aisle.

"Stee-fen. I found you. Hell-o Dr…Dr." Her mind wandered in the middle of her thought and she shook her head to clear it. "Oh, eh, which one are you again?"

"Why she's—" Ethan left off.

"Drunk." Cael finished succinctly.

"Aye, cocked out of her head, she is."

"*Foxed*, I believe is the more appropriate term." Ethan corrected his wife.

"What's dat streaked in ya hair, lass?"

"Dust and grime most like. Take a look around."

"Oh." Eden swayed. Their prattle made her head swim. Stephan uttered not a sound, merely swung her up into his arms and strode out. Eden allowed her head to lull against his shoulder. Arms curled around his neck with the wine bottle dangling from her fingers.

"Hmmm...tired." She closed her eyes against the whirling faces and bright seeming lights, content to be carried up to bed.

Only when the movement stopped and she felt herself being lowered onto a soft surface did she stir. "No....Dom said his chamber. Stee-fen." Lazy eyes pled with him.

"Why dat blimey rascal—"

"Ahem." Cael cleared his throat stopping his sister-in-law mid-rant.

A cough penetrated Eden's fogged mind. There they went prattling again.

"She'll have quite a headache in the morning." Ethan declared.

"Serves her right." Kathleen humphed. "Did she have ta finish tha entire bottle?"

* * *

Dominic shimmered into his chamber expecting to find her waiting up for him. Instead, she was already abed, a fire blazing in the hearth. He stood, knees flush with the curved edge of the bed, and exhaled a sigh, debating whether or not to wake her. The journey home had been draining. The clandestine nature of his visit to Italy necessitated excessive astraling, and he didn't know if he'd be able to continue consuming energy at such an exhaustive rate. If he did not see her tonight, most likely he wouldn't see her again until he returned home for good.

She slept on her stomach, facing away from him. Her hair unbound and cascading over the pillow in a shadowy river of light. Over-warm flames played on the milky skin where the sheets had slipped down to reveal her slender back. She embodied perfection and radiance. Her soft femininity and gentle spirit called to him.

As if she could somehow sense his scrutiny or feel his yearning, she shifted in her sleep...flopping her head over. Eyes slitted and groggy.

He crouched before her, whispering a kiss on her cheek. "Wake for me, cara."

"Hmmm, Dom?" She cocked her head, sleep-messed and lovely. Bewildered hazel fixed on him.

"I've missed you." His hand slid easily into her silken mane and massaged her scalp as he tugged her closer.

She flew at him with gale force, burying her face in his neck and wrapped her shockingly naked body around him in a full-body hug. She felt like heaven in his arms. He relaxed backward so that he sat on the floor with her atop him.

"How is your brother Gabriel?" She murmured, twisting her fingers in the thick cotton nightshirt at his chest, her other arm at his back.

Had he heard her correctly? 'How is Gabriel?', not 'when are you coming home?' or 'why haven't you visited before now?' Her concern surprised him. Before, she'd seemed almost antagonistic towards his brother. "Better, I think, but not altogether himself yet. I'm actually more worried about Gideon."

"What is the matter with him?" With the question, she hummed a contented note.

"He's convinced Gabriel's catatonia is somehow related to his...imminent death." He held her to his heart, soothing her hair, caressing her cheek, running his hands down the smooth skin of her back.

"Is he ill, then?"

"No. He thinks a vision of his death is what's causing Gabriel's distress. The possibility is distressing for me as well. But how are things with you? Any new *encounters*." She trembled in his embrace. The pulse so fleeting that he wasn't sure he'd actually felt it.

"All is well. I've been getting acquainted with the Athertons. I...I like Stephan. He's what I'd want for a brother if I had one."

It pleased him, he realized. Some feral, possessive side of him liked that she seemed to be ingratiating herself into his life, his family...cementing a permanent place. Courting friendship with Kathleen, gaining approval from Ethan and Cael, showing concern for Gabriel and now a bond with his youngest brother. His already heated desire for her flared.

Unable to resist the lure of her lush body pressed so wickedly against him, his hands wandered lower to cup her bottom...grind her tantalizing heat into his budding affection.

"Did you miss me, cara? Hmmm."

"Oh...yes, Dom." She moaned into his ear, than began nibbling at the rim. The hot rush of breath grew his erection all the more.

Gawd, he couldn't get enough of her...the sweet, peaches and pomegranate scent he recognized from his bath visits. The enthralling heat of her body sheathing him like a glove, the quick little breaths she took...each rise and fall of small plumb breasts were a teasing torture.

"I must...taste you, cara." He stood with her, grateful the bed was only a few steps away. A longer distance would have been unmanageable at his advanced state of arousal.

Her soft butterfly kisses trailed down his throat, only halted when he laid her out on the bed and slid down her body. Kissing and nipping at her collar bone, breasts, and several points on her delectable flat stomach along the descent.

She made a disapproving sound. Her hands converged on his head. Tugging at his hair, trying to halt his progress. "No, Eden, you'll take pleasure in this. I promise."

He paused just long enough to give her his eyes, knowing she liked them and it would quiet her...reassure her of his affection and that the trust now ran both ways. His hands restlessly kneading the skin at her hips, slipping lower to cap over each thigh. She lifted her head off the pillows meeting his gaze over the mound of her nether hairs.

"Open for me." And when she did, he nearly came right then and there from the sweet perfume of her arousal. A quiver troubled his hands as he lowered his mouth to her threshold, holding her jittery gaze until the very last moment.

* * *

Eden trembled inwardly at the erotic sight of Dominic's midnight head hovering between her V-ed thighs. Pewter-sapphire orbs glistened with his excitement. She nearly knifed off the bed when she felt his mouth, delicately kiss her folds, one, twice, the third time with a slight parting of his lips...then, his tongue peeked out to lick at her, molest the very sensitive nub there. Her head felt back.

"Dom...." She tunneled her hands in his hair, this time to encourage him forward, to do more, and be bolder.

His mouth closed over her most sensitive areas, the hot wet sucking of his tongue built up a tension in her, a beat of wanting that pounded through her body demanding to be satisfied. She couldn't keep still under the achingly sweet assault. When he used a thumb to tweak the nub, whilst his tongue's tip edged slightly into her, she knew a moment of madness. Her breathing staccatoed, hips writhed in sync with his rhythm, mind screaming in ecstasy. The mini thrust of his tongue mimicked those of his man's appendage, driving her ever wilder. She was Icarus, flying too close to the sun, in grave danger of bursting into flames...

Just as she felt herself about to explode, he withdrew his lavish tongue and mounded her. She had but a moment to wait for him to dissolve himself of the pants he wore. Then, his center aligned with hers, the pulsating heat of his arousal lay at her entrance. Without preamble, he surged forward, at the same time closing his mouth over hers in an open-mouth kiss hotter than the bowels of hell. She took both with a greed abandon, her body more his than hers. His weight pressing into her, the heat, the texture of the cotton nightshirt he still wore sliding luxurious against her skin. The wondrous friction, and spicy fullness of him pumping endlessly inside her. Pleasure blossomed like a rare flower until it ignited into a thousand pinpricks of sensation ravishing her body. She broke the endless kiss in a scream of release.

Afterward, Dom lay with his head on her stomach and his body to the side of her. He toyed with her pink-tipped nipples, fascinated. He wore the nightshirt still, but didn't seem at all bothered by her slipping her hands underneath it to caress the flawed skin at his back.

"You're going to leave again." He hadn't said, but she knew.

"There is still business to attend to there. Gideon is insisting that I be prepared to take over the family lands and legacy in the event of his untimely death."

"How long will you be gone?" She frowned. Her head seemed fuzzy all of a sudden, but what he spoke of sounded like a lengthy process.

He raised up then to look her straight in the eye. "Hopefully no more than a few days…just so he can give me the grand tour and take care of some legal matters."

She nodded, trying to beat back the fear he would never return from Italy…that death would take him from her like it had so many others she loved.

"But you'll visit again."

"I'm…not sure."

She withdrew from the apology she saw in his eyes.

"No, cara, don't." She tried to shift away from him, but he wasn't having it. He simply grasped her despite the struggle and re-deposited her onto his lap. "Shhh. I won't go until you fall asleep."

Amid his soothing hands, soft whispers, and butterfly kisses, Eden relaxed. He slipped back inside her and showed her how to ride him...sweet and slow. Afterwards, she fell asleep cocooned in his embrace, head pillowed on his shoulder.

* * *

She stirred, jarred by an arctic draft grazing across her naked skin. The next thing she felt was the pounding in her head...the pain refused to be ignored. Ugh! The caressed of icy fingers at her breasts shocked her into full consciousness. It wasn't Dominic's gentle palm molesting her nor was it his presence in bed with her. Her eyes popped open, her splintered head snapped around, a familiar dread setting in as she realized just whose hand had ahold of her.

"DOM!" She called for him even though her rational mind knew that he was gone, far away in Italy and would not be back for who knew how long.

Pure anguish poured forth from her lungs as she snatched the sheet around her and stumbled from the bed. Blind, grappling along the floor in the blackness that rivaled the darkest pit, she screamed again. Where was Stephan's fire? He promised to keep it burning all night.

A maniacal sound crackled inside her head; a frigid claw seethed around her body, the chill creeping into her soul. The invasion bordered on a rape. A mental rape, where her own consciousness was shoved aside. For one horrifying moment her world shifted from one of participant to observer. Chill and ice replaced her life's blood. Death filled her heart. Wild panic thoughts, alive with hatred and distorted images overtook her mind.

"Eden!" Somewhere to her right a new fire roared to life, dazzling and violent, licking out of the hearth like arms trying to save a drowning man. The flames illuminated the chamber to the intensity of midday.

The icy grip loosened, and burned away like frost at sunrise. Her mind was hers again. "Stephan…" a collapsed heap on the floor, she managed to croak out his name.

He brought with him a wall of heat, stopping just short of where she lay. She thought his hesitation due to some concern that he would inadvertently harm her, but his expression reflected confusion and then a predatory menace when he shifted on the balls of his feet. He eagle-eyed the room.

Could he sense it too? No, impossible… Because if Stephan sensed the entity, that meant she wasn't a lunatic. Dominic would have to believe her now.

"Eden?" He looked down at her then, questioning, "What did that *thing* do to you?"

"Do? I…don't know." She stammered. The growing queasiness in her stomach and pounding in her head made any high level of thought difficult for her battle-scarred mind. She wrapped the sheet more securely around herself.

He seemed to realize a proper answer was not forthcoming, and shoveled her into his arms.

"Where are we going?" was all she could manage.

"Anywhere but here."

THIRTY

"Tell me good news." Matthias willed under his breath and beckoned Egan into his office. The dinky little hovel was the only private space afforded him by the Reform Board. Their sentry lurked up and down the halls, supervising the procedural changes mandated by the Board as a condition of allowing Ciaran Isis Asylum to remain open and operating. In the wake, half the inmates were temporarily relocated to other facilities, including the delectable morsel he'd slated to be his next conquest.

His new custodian, Egan, was a definite trade-up from the traitorous Harry. Matthias had taken a different approach in the acquisition process. With Harry, he'd prized obedience over intelligence. The second go 'round, he'd gone into the slums of Southwart seeking reliability and cunning and found a god sent in Egan. An Irish lad, pale as death with a panoramic gaze in perpetual tracking mode, and lithe cheetah's grace...a combination Matthias himself found a touch unsettling.

"Well?"

"Target has some interest in a recluse. Foreign noble. The name Ambrosi mean anything to you?"

Matthias' ear peaked like a pointer on the trail of

downed game. "The blind Conte."

"Aye, that's him but he ain't blind, lest not in the regular way. Target sent a message requesting an audience. Request was denied. Target exhibited frustration."

This was too good to be true. He already had a line on the reticent Conte. He hadn't heard from the client since his initial visit, and given his precarious circumstances, he'd decided to put the investigation on hold. Perhaps now was the time to re-open his dig into the Ambrosi closet of secrets. If nothing else his involvement would irritate Greyson and probably jeopardize any ambitions he had of gaining Ambrosi's cooperation in whatever it was he wanted from the Conte.

Always suspicious of any good fortune that was not hard won, Matthias narrowed his focus to the lad before him. "How did ya come by dis information?"

"Tumbled one of the maids a couple of times."

"Any chance you can plow'er for more information?"

His cruel twist of a mouth turned up in a smile. "Anything in particular you want to know?"

Therein lay his weakness. He was stumbling around in the dark when he came to specifics. "Anything on Greyson." In the mean time, he'd just have to work with what he had. "An' whose tha blonde livin' at Ambrosi's. Bony, middling height, genteel. I wanna know her purpose there."

THIRTY ONE

Daybreak found Dominic in the most unlikely place...the dungeons beneath the heart of Castello di Ambrosi. Flickering candelabrum in hand, he paced towards the edge of the granite pit, the very one from his tormented childhood. He had expected to be paralyzed by memories, dread his constant companion, reliving the nightmare with each panting breath. When first he stepped off the astral into his ancestral home he was prepared to be laid low by aftershocks of past wounds he'd bandaged over but never healed from. But his breathing remained even, as it was now. He came to the lip of the pit. The memories of the torture he'd endure in this place did not overwhelm him. Instead, they seemed muted, so far removed that even when he made a concentrated effort to call forth the horror only faded images appeared to him. Where pain should have surfaced, a dulling ache pricked at his heart.

He squatted, setting the brass candelabrum on the stone floor. Where the pit had once been, lay a slab of grey-green limestone.

"My first official business as the acting Conte Ambrosi was to fill in this pit. I had plans to wall off the whole of the dungeons and lower tombs but that was before

Gabriel..." The words hung.

Dominic straightened to find his brother Gideon walking up behind him.

"I knew I'd find you here."

Nonplused, he gestured to the limestone. "Returning isn't as I thought it would be. The past does not affect me overmuch. I am finally free of *Her*."

The taller man inclined his shadowed brow at Dom's upper torso, pensive. "There is a school of thought that says: two women cannot occupy the same house. Perhaps the saying is also true for the same heart."

Dominic looked down at himself to find a hand rubbed at the place over his heart. "Perhaps." He dropped the hand and shed his thoughts of the past. The time had come for him to come out of hiding. "Gideon. I would prefer not to think on your death, but I will admit that I can no longer shirk my familial responsibilities. If this trip to Italy has taught me one lesson it is that I am not that wounded little boy anymore. It's time I conduct myself appropriately. If you would, please re-acquaint me with the Ambrosi estates. In the event of...for when I take my place as the reigning Conte Ambrosi."

His brother nodded, slate grey eyes twinkling. "Certainly. I shall have Valentina to sit with Gabriel in our absence."

Dominic bent to retrieve the candelabrum, then straightened to meet his brother's gaze in the gentle candle glow.

"It's good to have you back, Dominic."

* * *

"*This* is the Chateau Ambrosia?" The infamous Chateau 'Aphrodisia', where their mother had conducted numerous illicit relationships. Dominic did not bother to disguise his bemusement.

"What is left of it, yes. The front façade hinges at the

cliff's edge overlooking the vineyard proper and adjoining winery. Ambrosia has somehow managed a modest profit even under Lucca's neglect but nothing resembling the golden days when Nonno was Conte Ambrosi. The Ambrosia label graced every aristocrat's table here and abroad..."

Dom scarcely heard Gideon's financial report. Being denied the chance to own and presumably restore *this* crumbling ruin had sparked his uncle Fausto's wrath and subsequent swath of mischief. Impossible. Nonna must have exaggerated her younger son's motives. No noble in his right mind would want the hassle and expense of owning such a worthless monstrosity...which according to Gideon was only marginally profitable.

Perhaps, if one were a business-minded person and had an interest in the vinification process, there would be some personal satisfaction in rebuilding the adjoining winery to its former magnificence. But he knew Fausto well enough to rule out that possibility. His uncle was not an intellectual nor was he a man of business. His forethought did not extend beyond immediate self-indulgence and the bolstering of his own image. Neither of which were boosted by inheriting a rotting heap villa and mediocre winery.

Gideon continued his status report as they strolled along the grounds of the skeletal masonry remains. Glass-less windows abounded, as did crumbling spires and turrets of eroded sandstone. The sight put Dom in mind of a beggar's smile filled with shattered teeth, tooth-shaped gaps and blacken gums.

"Lucca let it sink to ruin, but the foundation is surprisingly strong. Gabriel and I have...*had* plans drawn up to restore it." He waxed eloquent and matter-of-factly, flourishing a hand in the chateau's direction. "...Perhaps, as a second residence, a dowry for a future niece or if Stephan should ever wish to become an active part of the legacy I think he would enjoy the business aspects of the

Chateau."

"Enough, Gideon." Dominic halted him with a sharp gesture when they reached the cliff's face. "Why do you think Uncle Fausto would be in such a lather to preside over these ruins?"

Grandiose did not come close to an adequate description of the vineyard below. The lush green patchwork of alternating crop squares started halfway down the face of the cliff and extended onto the valley floor. A fat ribbon of blue zigzagged through the valley cutting Ambrosia in half. The vines of the opposite bank continued, running up the face of the next hillside and ended just short of its crest. The winery proper nestled into the hill's base.

"It's a beautiful property to be sure, but the annual income from the Castello and adjacent lands is worth a multitude both in monies and prestige. Even some of the lesser holdings, Ambrosi Shipping or Ambrose Manor with it's sizable trade wealth and I believe a hereditary seat as the local magistrate should present more of a lure than this place."

"The nearest Gabriel and I could figure is that he had or rather *has* some hope of searching for the legacy's origin and finding the famed Ambrosia treasure."

"That's a myth. Nothing more."

"Uncle does not concur."

"Do you?" He tore his gaze from the splendor below and pinned the man beside him.

"Truthfully, Dominic..." After an age, his brother returned a resigned expression. "The rumors have endured too long to be completely baseless. I believe there is a mystery to be solved. Whether or not the answer to the fourth century riddle is a pot of gold at the end of the rainbow is arguable."

THIRTY TWO

Her head throbbed to the rhythm of a waltz. Her throat felt like someone had shoved a wad of mildewed cotton into her mouth and forced her to swallow. Eden stretched a hand for the vat of ice chips positioned on the nightstand. When Nell had first banged on the chamber door and then promptly dropped the tray upon nearing the bed, she'd wanted to strangle the mousey nuisance. But now cursed with dry mouth, thirst, *and* nausea, she could kiss her for her thoughtfulness.

"Drat."

Her senses reeled with even the minimal movement needed to grasp a handful of ice and bring it to her mouth. She relaxed back against the pillows, repositioned the cold compress atop her temple and suckled…letting her lids drift closed.

She'd scarcely gotten comfortable when the chamber's adjoining door opened. Ugh! Not more visitors.

"Canna say as I like her hair dat-a-way. As if she's graying, only in reverse."

"*Kathleen.*"

"Alright, I'm on me best behavior."

Eden opened her eyes to find husband and wife

ambling into the room, Dr. Raine with his medical bag in tow.

"Ahh, you're awake." The doctor smiled at her.

"Yes." She moved the compress off to the side with a grimace. Putting a hand to the braid pinned atop her head, she struggled to sit up properly. Sometime during the night the gown Stephan had given her had become twisted around her legs. "What…did you mean, before, about my hair?"

They exchanged a glance.

Kathleen crossed the room quickly, made a seat next to her and put an arm around her shoulders. "'Tis nothing, lass. No need ta worry. Never seen a more luxurious mane in all me days."

Eden frowned. It was not like her friend to lie. "Nell dropped the tray when she first saw me."

"Nervous Nellie?" Kathleen dismissed the issue. "Tha lass probably faints at her own shadow."

"How are we feeling, Eden?" The doctor bumped aside the pail of ice with his medical bag on the opposite side of the bed, pivoting to train his discerning eye on her.

"Dreadful." No point in lying, she probably looked every bit as vile as she felt.

"Well, let's see what we can do about that." Dr. Raine leaned in and placed his palm to her temple. "First the headache."

Relief was not immediate, but rather a gradual seeping of ease, as if his skin were a balm transferring its healing influence to her. The once pounding beat in her head lessened to an occasional twinge of discomfort. Her nausea winkled out of existence altogether.

"The thirst I cannot lessen, I'm afraid." He blessed her with a rueful smile.

Just then a knock sounded from the outside door of the bedchamber. Her bedchamber, she noted for the first time. Stephan must have brought her here last night, after…The evening's events were a tad fuzzy. She distinctly remembered being cast into the wine vault, rescued by Kathleen and the brothers…But then that was when things started to go hazy. Had she dreamed the wonderful visit from Dominic? And had that dream then turned into a nightmare when the entity materialized?

"Morning Eden, Kathleen." Stephan's greeting wrenched her from her thoughts. She focused on his face and found him his usual subdued self.

Ethan straightened. "If you've come to inquire after the patient, I can assure you she is resting comfortably."

"I need to speak with *you*." His warm honey eyes crystallized to hard, faceted amber.

The doctor gave them a departing gesture and slipped out with the Sphinx.

Kathleen turned an arched brow on her. "What do ya suppose dat is about?"

"Me." She said with absolute certainty, flinging the covers aside. It was time she saw just why everyone kept gawking at her. No longer hampered by pain and nausea, she had her plait half-unbound by the time she stepped within view of the vanity mirror. Her hands stilled above the braid half-cascaded over her left shoulder. Hair, that had all her life been a pale, ash blond was now threaded liberally with ebony. The scattering of dark strands she'd noticed before seemed to have coalesced and produced a wide ebony stripe just off the center of her head.

Eden scarcely recognized the peculiar visage staring at her through the looking glass. She resembled a character from one of Poe's horrids. What was happening to her? Frantic eyes collided with Kathleen over the shoulder of her reflection.

"Now, lass, 'tis not as bad as all dat." The older woman came forward to lay a calming hand to the shock of ebony.

"I'll have to powder it. Otherwise people will gawk." She inclined her head to the chamber door. "That's what they are out there discussing right now, isn't it? What's to be done with me…now that I look the madwoman they all expect I am."

"No, I'd wager they're trying ta figure out what did happen an' how ta prevent it 'appening again. Tha boys like ya...if for no other reason than tha positive changes you've wrought in their brother."

She cringed as a new thought occurred to her. "What will Dominic think when he sees me?"

Kathleen scoffed. "Dominic would no' care if ya hair were streaked wit violet."

"How the devil would you know?!" She snapped the words out, but she had not idea where they'd came from. The voice sounded harsh...and not wholly her own. Frightened, her eyes jerked back around to the looking glass. Instead of her own bizarre reflection, she spied a raven-haired goddess snarling at her, with the vehemence of a jilted mistress. Eden recoiled from the venom those black eyes spewed, stumbling out of the vanity chair and bumbled into the Scotswoman.

"Oh, pardon...I don't know what's come over me."

Kathleen frowned at her. "Aye, you're overwrought."

She snatched at the explanation, desperate for a rational basis for her own erratic behavior. "Yes, yes, that must be it." She needed help. The fact could no longer be denied. Her first thought was Dominic, but she dismissed him. He still had lingering doubts about her sanity and she'd give him no new cause for worry. Though she liked both the doctors, they were men of science, and by virtue, more willing to accept a simple medical diagnosis...insanity. But the Sphinx. He was free-thinking and open-minded as well as sympathetic to her plight. He would not condemn her outright. She'd tell him and see what he thought of her new reflection.

"Stephan, I wish to speak with him." Her request paused Kathleen in the chamber's threshold. "Could you let him know please?"

"Aye." And she was gone. Leaving Eden alone...with the scowling reflection.

"He's mine! You cannot have him."

Scared to face the vanity, knowing what she would see there, Eden turned her back on the looking glass and stalked for the bed. She just needed to rest, like Kathleen said, and then the voice would go away. The image in the mirror would once again be her own.

"It was his choice to leave. He could have sent one of the others, but he left anyway. Abandoned you to me."

Eyes squeezed tight shut, Eden curled up on the bed with her knees to her chest and hands plastered flat over her ears.

"Shut up, damn you!"

The voice, sinister, sensual, and serpentine, reverberated within the walls of her mind, eating away her confidence, her hope, her rationale. Until soon, the words were all she heard. Fear all she felt. Dread and torment, plagued her to no end.

"Dominic doesn't love you. He's never coming back."

She had to get away from that voice, to some place safe. Eden bounded up and off the bed, the drafty floor felt cold against her bare feet despite a toasty fire in the hearth. She crossed the room, not bothering to don her dressing gown.

The vanity loomed from the corner. A dark force within compelled her forth to it. Wielding a pull so strong she could not break from its thrall. Though she'd risen in haste intending to quit the room, she found herself trembling before the cursed looking glass. Eyes squeezed tight shut. Did she dare?

"Eden...come with me. I miss you."

The voice differed. Softer, less menacing and...familiar. Her eyes popped open, and there trapped in the vanity, smiling and beckoning was a vision of Millie. Without realizing, she stepped forward. Reached out. Wait, her quivering hand stilled a fraction of an inch from the glass...how could she be seeing her cousin Millie?...her *very dead* cousin Millie.

"It's lovely here...no pain, no worries, no death."

"No life either." Eden countered, instinctively knowing that something was off about her cousin. Millie was gone. "There's no life where you are, and no death because everyone there is already dead."

Her cousin's image flashed and writhing as if in pain, and then gave way to her raven-haired tormentor. She snatched her hand back. Even if she hadn't been staring at her, she'd recognized that malevolent cackle and the chilling crawl of her voice every time she encountered it. This was the thing, the evil entity that plagued her. It finally had a face. And it was time, pastime she faced her demon.

"I don't know what you want with me, but leave my cousin out of it." She put steel behind the words and planted her feet, more to brace her nerves than anything else.

"Ahh, the kitten grows claws..."

The sharp voice slashed across the delicate fabric of her mind, cutting deep gashes in her subconscious. Eden tried to stitch up the holes, but she could not keep up with the entity's destructive power. Soon, the grotesque thing pounded at the door of her conscious mind. Whisperings and hushed suggestions bombarded her.

"Get out of my head."

The raven beauty let her head dropped back in full-scale malice. Her too-sharp teeth gleamed sinister. Her tongue somehow seemed pointy and over-long. Serpent-like.

When she finished the creepy excuse for a laugh, she impaled Eden with white-less eyes, an eerie speckled black...and bottomless, like the astral realm Dominic had once described to her.

"Give me back what's mine."

"Stop it!" Eden went a little crazy then. Panic from the creeping possession of her mind rallied her and she struck a physical blow at the evil in the silvery surface. The glass splintered on impact. She flinched from the sharp slice of pain that screamed at her wrist even as her head snapped sideways to avoid the flying shards.

Standing amid a sea of glass, the ruined mirror a wooden hull before her, crimson leaking in a steady dribble from her palm and wrist...Eden felt her head turn, saw herself surveying the chamber as if she were seeing it for the first time. Disjointed images, not her own, flitted through her mind, of a remote residence and foreign-speaking people she did not recognize. She had the sensation of being an observer instead of a participant in the events. The same stifling fog overtook her, like at Lady Haversdale's disastrous table turn.

That's when she knew she had lost the battle. The evil thing had control of her. Had somehow possessed her like that lost spirit she helped conjure nearly two months ago. Her legs moved, stepping around the glass and she wondered where the thing was taking her. Or rather *them*. Her mind and body was now occupied by two warring beings. The entity had the upper hand at the moment.

Eden felt her body sway. The evil-thing felt it too because their head glanced down at the bloody mess and shifted direction to the nightstand. Dr. Raine's medical bag. At least she was logical.

Logical, but incompetent, Eden surmised a time later. The evil-thing's attempt at bandaging veered just left of useless. She did not apply pressure to stop the bleeding, nor did she make any effort to clean or close the wound. But merely looped a wad of gauze over the end of the arm and mixed a concoction from powder-packets Eden surmised were laudanum. Blood continued to ooze through the loose wrapping leaving a macabre trail as the entity exited them from the room.

* * *

"I must return today. At dust." Dominic forsook the

pedestrian view from his brother's windows. After the magnificence of Château Ambrosia's panoramic valley, all other scenery paled.

"Gabriel has not yet awakened." His brother made the statement in a bald voice Dominic recognized as disapproval. Gideon did not like leaving things unfinished, he knew.

"He's improved. His essence is more at peace." Dominic gestured across the room to where the man in question lay still as stone, the ever-present feline sleeping at his side. "I don't believe he's dreaming anymore, merely asleep. You know yourself it is not odd for Gabriel to recover for extended periods after a disturbing premonition."

"What of Muse?"

"Send for me when he awakens and I'll speak with him about the cat."

"And if I am dead by then?"

"Then I shall attend the services and speak with Gabriel after!" His rarely-seen temper flared at his brother's flippant macabre attitude. Only Gideon could accept death with such a serene affect, not even bested by Cael. Cael's extraordinary poise, while unnerving at times, could also be calm and reassuring, but Gideon's fatalistic indifference evoked a chilling sort of unease that Dominic had never gotten used to. If not for Gabriel, Dom worried at the person Gideon would become.

"Gideon, something has happened. When we astraled back, I sought out Eden. She was disturbed. I would not cut my visit short otherwise."

"This woman is that important to you?" Standing with his back to the wall of windows, the taller man twined his fingers behind him. The question echoed curiosity more than resentment.

"Gabriel is out of danger and he has you to oversee the remainder of his recovery. And she is not the only reason." He sighed, as he thought of the myriad of troubles that awaited him back home. "Stephan did not look altogether calm. If he too is disturbed then it is imperative that I return. His ability is volatile and he is not in full control of it. We cannot afford another incident. The talk will not be so easily quelled outside the University walls. Gossip travels fast, especially damning gossip."

"Very well, then. I shall speak with the solicitor about your 'change of heart' concerning the management of the legacy." His brother shot him a sardonic smile. "Nonna will be ecstatic."

Dominic groaned. One thing about Gideon, he did have a sense of humor, albeit macabre. "Please endeavor to contain her euphoria within the Italian borders. The estate is full-up at the moment."

* * *

The lacquered grand pitched sideways, throwing an already unsteady gait into further peril. The influx of alien memories and distorted perceptions assailing her caged mind did not help the situation. She careened through decayed settings and murky hallways with rank odors. Witnessed bizarre scenes of screaming and crying. In one particularly disturbing visualization she watched a woman being held down by pawing men on crisp sheets...which seemed more like freakish love-play, than a forced act. Flashes of the same woman slashing her forearm and thighs with a knife came at her, sickening her.

Strange figures, some shroud in hooded capes, paraded around intoning words that she couldn't make sense of, that seemed somehow sinister in their repetition. She wished she could shut her eyes tight to somehow close them out, or raise her hands and pound the visions from her head with the heels of her palms. When she made the effort, only a flailing uncoordinated movement resulted.

"They think you're a lunatic, you and I both."

She could scarcely keep her thoughts clear of the

bombardment of images. Horror played in her mind like a phonograph on infinite loop. The thoughts and events she saw must belong to the evil thing taking over her body. If this was what the entity's mental process looked like, then Eden agreed...the evil-thing was mad, and herself too by virtue of housing the spirit of a madwoman inside her mind. She must get free somehow, and this time, retain control of her facilities. It took a great deal of mental fortitude, but she was able to shove the ceaseless visions to an alcove at the back of her mind. Only then was she at liberty to try her hand at dislodging the intruder. Flexing all her inner energies and her will, she pushed against the presence.

"Worrisome bitch!"

One realization encouraged her. The entity could not sustain absolute control of her body. Instead of a steady walking movement, against Eden's concentrated mental resistance the thing could only maneuver an undulating shuffle much like a crippled or a hunchback. Or, she considered bitterly, it could be that the wound at her wrist bled too profusely for her to hold a proper stance. By then, the wad of gauze was soaked through with crimson.

Bobbing and weaving on scissored legs and a twisted psyche, the entity brought them to a chamber door. Dominic's chamber door. Her hand slipped in smeared blood as the entity fumbled with the metal knob. After six successive tries she was successful.

"There is more amiss than Dominic knows..."

This time the voices did not originate from inside her head. They drifted in from the adjoining room, the door of which lay ajar.

"It must be dealt with, any threat to..."

She only caught snatches of the conversation, not able to summon further strength to ambled past the bedpost. The entity coiled her good arm around the carved cedar armoire and slumped over. Blood lost, the strain of keeping her thoughts clear of the mental garbage, and the energy she extended trying to evict her unwanted visitor finally toppled them both. Her consciousness blurred. The fine line between them, Eden's psyche and the entity's also blurred. Unwanted feelings and remembrances attacked her like so many vampire bats in a feeding frenzy. Her last rational thought was of Dominic and how grateful she felt that he was still in Italy so that at least he wouldn't be the one to find her bloody, stripe-haired corpse.

THIRTY THREE

If he could breathe on the astral, he would have sighed. But what he observed in his household left him more confused than relieved. Eden's essence hummed in a state of profound calm, a striking contrast from the near palpable anxiety evident in Kathleen and all three of his brothers. Forced by Nell's presence, he rematerialized a distance away, and found himself in the deserted hallway outside his bedchamber door.

The vinegary scent of cleaning soap rent the air. Dom frowned. This stretch of floor wasn't scheduled to be swabbed for another two weeks. And Nell should have been retired to the boarding house for the night.

The servants were told nothing of his absence so he had no need to make a show of his arrival home. He often absented himself for days at a time so not seeing him would not strike anyone as odd.

He slipped the spectacles from his lapel pocket. After days of viewing the world free of their dimming pall, donning them seemed wrong somehow. But no matter, he had bigger concerns with which to occupy his mind. Dominic fingered the knob, noticing it too had recently come under a polishing rag. What would he find behind the door?

His brothers and Kathleen ringed the bed like pallbearers surrounding a coffin, with solemn expressions and slumped shoulders. Wash bucket within arm's reach, Nell scrubbed hard at the floor. The unholy scent of blood and cleaning soap cloyed at his nostrils whilst fear seized his heart.

No one seemed to notice his arrival. Except for the quiet squish of Nell's monotonous swabbing, the room was still. He advanced, dreading what he would find yet knowing all the same. *She is alive.* He repeated the words in his head, over and over, fortifying himself. Were she not, then her essence would no longer dwell on the astral. He believed that after death, souls sojourn to either heaven or hell, but even if they did not, he knew that they left the astral realm.

"Cara?" Her wan visage stood out against the dark bedding, almost as white as the thick wrapping of gauze and bandages bound to her wrist with tight-drawn surgeon's tape. He almost didn't recognize her, his Eden. Her hair fanned the pillow in interlocking ribbons of ink and ash. The contrast was starker than the dark circles against her porcelain complexion. Dominic turned his horror on the one person he knew should have been able to prevent it.

"Ethan?"

His brother met the silent question with confusion as profound as his own.

"She attempted to harm herself again, did in fact, within an inch of her life. Took an overdose of laudanum and then slit her wrist."

He looked to the taller man at Ethan's right. "Stephan…"

The Sphinx spoke with solemn calm. His jaw set in stone. "I have come to know Eden, and I do not believe that is what happened."

"And Cael, what is your opinion?

"I haven't formulated a precise scenario, but I agree with Stephan. A second suicide attempt is not consistent with my assessment of Miss Prescott. She was not despondent in the least, much less desperate enough to…"

"Ahem. Kathleen?"

Her head snapped around. Dominic knew he caught the Scottswoman off-guard. He generally made a point of excluding her in matters he considered family business. Over the years he had become lax, but never comfortable enough to solicit an opinion. Of late, her constant presence allowed a certain level of familiarity even he found surprising.

"I would like to know your mind on the subject."

She gave a stiff nod. "Aye, tis' something amiss. I donna what, but tha wee one was no' herself. She asked ta see Stephan before I left her alone ta rest. Was insistent about it, 'twas as if she had something especially urgent she wished ta discuss with him. I canna say for sure, but it strikes me false dat tha lass would knock herself off before she'd done so."

"Perhaps, she sent you on a fool's errand, fetching Stephan." Ethan suggested. "So she could get at the laudanum in my bag."

"Naw. I was half out tha door anyways. 'Twas my idea dat she should be alone ta rest, 'specially after dat ordeal. Tha wee one asked ta see him because she had somethin' on her mind. I'm sure of it."

"Ordeal?" Dominic glanced from face to face, settling at last on the kneeling maid. "Nell, the floor is clean enough. Please take yourself off to bed."

"Yes, sir." The jittery maid managed to exit without sloshing too much water over the edge of the swabbing bucket.

"Now then. Stephan, what's happened?"

He didn't hesitate. "She spent several hours locked in the wine vault last evening. There was no harm done, but she emerged a bit—"

255

"Tilted ta tha wind." Kathleen finished colorfully.

Dominic tensed, seized by long ago memories of his own imprisonment. On some level he knew his reaction was more to his own experiences but he couldn't seem to call back the words or the angry frustration behind them. "She is precious to me. I entrusted her to your care, how on earth did she manage to get herself foxed in the cellar."

His younger brother did not flinch nor shirk the accusation. "I protected her as best I could, but you neglected to mention that we were up against an otherworldly threat."

Ahhh, now he understood. The imagined entity again. "She told you about this thing she claims plagues her."

"You sound as if you doubt of its existence."

"I…" Did he? Was he willing to subscribe to the inane theory of otherworldly evil bent on mischief just to avoid the realization that he'd willfully gotten involved with a woman no more stable than his long dead mother?

"I sensed it for myself, Dominic. Last night, after you'd gone she cried out. When I entered the room…" he paused, as if trying to find the words to explain what he'd witnessed.

"What did you see?" Cael prompted.

By now, all eyes were on Stephan.

"I didn't *see* anything. I sensed it, a residual awareness that comes along with my…gift. A coldness inhabited the room. The cold shrank away from me as if it were almost…alive."

"The fireplace was blazing when I left."

"Yes. I know. The fire was my doing. But later the hearth was barren, although the room itself did not feel chilled. Only when I neared her did the cold hit me. It pricked my skin. I have not your ability to see human souls or sense spirits in the otherworld, but on my *life*… Eden was not alone in this room and the thing with her wished her ill. Her hair had turned thus, as you see it now."

An awkward silence settled over the foursome.

Dominic took that opportunity to bend and take Eden's bandaged hand lovingly in his. Pain slashed at him.

"What did you mean, the fire was your doing?" Cael inquired.

Stephan faced him across the bed, and gestured eloquently in the direction of the hearth. Crimson-orange flames roared to life.

"Heavens!" Kathleen's eyes grew round.

"The fire at the university that razed the dormitory…" Cael trailed off.

"I thought you couldn't control it." Ethan mused.

"I usually can't. For whatever reason, I have it more in hand when Eden is in close proximity."

"Fascinating." Cael stared at Stephan whilst Ethan's and Kathleen's faces lingered on the hypnotic flames dancing behind the grate.

"Ahem, Ethan." Dominic cleared his throat and lay Eden's limp arm back down on the bed. "You healed her wrist."

He snapped back to his patient. "Of course, but the effects of the laudanum I could not counteract. Either she will come out of it or she won't. There is no way to know, but I can tell you this: from my estimation she downed enough of the stuff to fell a person twice her size. She lay unconscious there where the maid scrubbed, in a pool of her own blood. I don't even see how she was able to walk from her chamber to yours in her condition. By rights she should be dead twice over."

Dominic reached down to stroke her two-tone hair, reverently. "She mustn't be left alone. I want someone sitting with her until she recovers and is able to provide an explanation…for this as well." He let the tresses drift through his fingers.

"You don't believe me then."

Dominic eyed Stephan askance. "I am not willing to take a chance either way. She must be protected, both from herself and this mysterious entity until such time as we are able to find a permanent solution."

Ethan chimed in, speaking to no one in particular. "Which ever of us is sitting with her in the morning hours will have to make a show of changing the bandage. I am amply supplied with pig's blood for authenticity's sake."

"And if the entity *does* truly exist?" Stephan probed Dominic.

He cringed from the very idea, but he could no longer ignore the mounting evidence. Eden's problems went beyond merely the possibility of mental instability.

"I'll take first watch." Kathleen offered. "Since me mornings are spent hunched over tha chamber pot with Ethan rubbing me back."

"Dear, mightn't you be a touch more delicate in describing certain matters."

THIRTY FOUR

The full board did not convene. Matthias had expected as much when he made the decision to seek out an audience with the pompous head of social reform. No matter. All he required were one or two witnesses to legitimize his claim. He would have rather dealt with Greyson individually, but anything less than a formal accusation of misconduct and Greyson would know the grievance for what it was, a personal swipe at him.

His charge must be irreproachable. A citizen doing his duty towards his fellow man...or rather in this case, his fellow lady.

He waited in the board's meeting hall with Egan by his side prepared to back up his claims. Finally, the clanging of a chime signaled the period of consideration for citizen's concerns and complaints. Matthias heaved his stocky bulk from the squat rows of chairs in the public area of the hall. The hall was divided into two areas by a waist-high gate with a swinging door. The raised panel behind the swinging door housed seats reserved for board members. Centered in front of the panel was a speaker's podium. The five members present were scattered among the empty spaces along the semicircular panel that spanned the entire far wall of the meeting hall.

Gleeful at striking his first blow at the man he deemed the cause of his recent misfortune, Matthias squared his shoulders and ambled to the podium with purpose. He scanned the panel, bringing his gaze to rest on the straight-nosed, scholarly mien of Davide Greyson.

"Ahem, Matthias Montgomery wit a citizen's concern."

"What is the nature of your concern?" Greyson inquired formally.

"I knows of a lady wot's being held against 'er will by a nobleman. Touch in tha head, most like. Dat's tha reason tha gent was able ta cart her off from polite society so discreet-like. 'Tis often tha case when madness strikes an aristocratic family." Matthias puffed out his chest. "'Tis tha general way of things, among tha genteel crowd dat such blights in lineage must be kept quiet by any means, ya understand? If I had me a nickel for every nervous, after-hours visit I've received from Lords seeking ta whisk away a cousin or uncle a bit touched in tha head—"

Greyson held up his palm. "Mr. Montgomery, if you will please focus on the matter at hand. Now then, tell us, who is this young woman and on what estate is she being held."

He had him right where he wanted him. "Don't rightly know tha lady's name, but I say someone ought ta inquire immediate-like into tha goings-on at dat estate of 'is…Conte Dominic Ambrosi."

He watched the furrow in the haughty Davide Greyson's brow deepen. The self-righteous ass. Let him squirm. Matthias struggled to contain his triumphant smile. Greyson would be forced to institute some sort of action against Ambrosi or risk alienating the other board members. Matthias scanned the faces of the four. A bloody disapproving lot, they were. The chorus of resolved nods and murmurs coalesced into a final consensus that something would have to be done. Yes, his own board would help Matthias paint their leader into a corner.

Just to be on the safe side, he stroked their passion for justice by throwing another log on the fire. "Has her housed in his private suites, he does, and uses her most abominably." His voice boomed like a rector working up his sermon. "He must be confronted and stopped, tha bastard, for exploitin' tha young miss, featherhead dat she is."

Greyson narrowed his eyes on him. "Prey, tell us, Mr. Montgomery, how did the Lady's precarious position become known to you?"

The Asylum Keeper gestured to his most trusted custodian. "My man Egan 'ere, he keeps company wit one of tha maids. She told him tha way of things at tha Ambrosi 'ouse, knowing Egan ta be connected ta those who would help folks in need."

Egan stood from his seat, a ways behind the podium. Shoulders slumped in deference, and crushing his hat in his hand he spoke low and reverent. "I passed my gal's concerns for the young miss's welfare along to Mr. Montgomery, see."

Matthias could have kissed Egan. Instead he followed the prompt. "And I passed 'is concerns on ta ya. I would 'ave intervened myself, but wot wit Ambrosi being a high-ranking noble an' all. Thought it best left up ta tha Board."

"You did right." One of the other members returned, with a sharp decisive nod.

THIRTY FIVE

Three days had passed since Dominic returned to find Eden in the grip of death. He'd scarcely left her side. Though the five of them agreed to share the burden of sitting with her, he couldn't tear himself away for fear some unseen evil would swoop down and take her from him. Even as Ethan slipped quietly into the chamber to relieve him, he resisted.

"Dominic you need to rest. If she wakes up and catches a glimpse of your sleep-weary eyes and three-day beard it will likely startle her back into unconsciousness."

He gently laid her limp hand back down. His gaze lingered on the soft rise and fall of her chest to reassure himself of her continued safety. "Her coloring is better today. I think she looks more...alive."

"Yes..." Ethan lifted the same wrist with careful fingers whilst he laid his other palm against her brow to take her temperature. Next, he clapped his hands just inches above her stoic face, poked and prodded her with a rubber tipped hammer-like instrument. Dominic watched him perform the same cursory exam for the past three days.

"How is she?" He demanded the second the doctor

had finished his tasks.

"I believe she will awaken soon. She is responsive to stimuli. According to Kathleen, her sleep has become increasingly restless."

Dominic took his first easy breath in days. He would soon have his heart back.

"Now, will you rest?" The doctor turned his concern on his brother.

"No, I want to be here when she awakens." He missed her luminous hazel eyes and soft welcoming expression, the warm seduction of her body curled around him beneath the very sheets upon which she now lay. He even missed the silky feel of her hair twined between his fingers...remembering its natural texture and color. His eyes roamed to her current style. He winced at the striped mess.

"Promise me you will rest once she is conscious."

He raised his gaze, odd eyes twinkling mischievously. "You may tie me to the bed if you like, Ethan."

Dominic nearly smiled at his brother's pained expression. "I fear Kathleen is not a good influence on your already atrocious lack of etiquette."

Just then, an especially forceful exhale of breath drew their attention back to the patient. Dominic was at her side in an instant, caressing her uninjured hand against his cheek.

"Cara?"

Her head lulled to the side, seeming to seek out his voice. Her lips parted.

* * *

Eden struggled mightily to rise above the lethargic haze that gripped her body like a vice. Her lids were as lead, her mind a blur...filled with blank spots and indistinct thoughts. She must focus.

"Dom?" Her voice sounded weak, confused even to

her ears.

"Yes, cara. I'm here."

Her foggy mind became aware of her hand caressing someone's stubble-roughened skin. Had the entity taken over again? At the moment, she possessed neither the strength nor the coordination in either of her limbs to navigate such a pleasing stroke.

The spicy scent of male wafted up her nostrils drugging her with languid pleasure, making her forget her thought. What had she been concerned about?

"Is it really you this time?"

"You are welcome to open your eyes and see for yourself."

His voice sounded urgent, anxious.

"Don't rush her, Dom. Let her acclimate."

Dr. Raine. She recognized him. Again she tried to peel back her lids. This time she succeeded in slitting them just enough to glimpse a visage looming large over her.

"I'm thirsty."

The face moved away and then she heard the splash of water being poured into a glass. Nell must have taken to leaving a pitcher by the bed since she so frequently spent time recovering from various follies. And almost always woke up craving a refreshing drink.

In the next moment, her hand abruptly stopped stroking his face. Two strong arms half lifted her into a sitting position and held her there while a cool surface touched her lips. She parted them on instinct and was rewarded with a steady trickled of water poured carefully into her mouth. The coolness on her parched tongue was like manna from heaven. She drank greedily, somehow finding the strength to bring one hand up to tilt the glass at a steeper angle. When it was empty, the arms allowed her to collapse gently back onto the pillows.

She fought the lethargy to pry her lids further open. Ahhh, she loved his eyes. Those mix-matched wonders of his were so expressive.

"Thank you, Dom."

"Are you hungry? You've taken only broth and minimal sips of water for the past three days."

Not until he posed the question did she realize just how ravenous she was. She parted her lips to answer in the affirmative, when her stomach howled quite embarrassingly.

"Ethan—" Dom began.

"Yes, of course, I'll alert someone from the kitchens about having a tray up for her."

Eden watched Dominic through tired eyes, turning the corners of her mouth to try for a smile. He must have enjoyed the effort, because as soon as she heard the doctor close the door behind him, Dominic was on the bed with her cradled in his loving arms.

"Ahhh, cara, you gave us all quite a scare. I ought to throttle you."

"Are you back? From Italy, I mean."

"Yes." His answer sounded tentative, as if he had more to say on the subject. "But that can wait."

Eden slid her cheek along his shirted chest, tilted her head back so that it rested on the crook of his elbow. The sluggishness was slowly receding. Her eyes blinked more readily, her vision clearer. For the first time she noticed the strain around his mouth, the worry lines marring the usually smooth olive of his forehead, his anxious gaze searching her face for any sign of distress or pain.

"I am well now, Dominic. You can tell me."

His expression changed subtly, a vague sadness enveloping him. "No, cara...I don't believe you are. I cannot ignore the truth any longer."

She frowned, but before she could ask what he meant, a firm knock came at the chamber door. Dominic's body went rigid when Renfred popped his head around the door and begged their pardon. Sans his spectacles, Eden noted that Dom inclined his ear to the butler, but angled his face in profile.

"Master Ambrosi, sir, there is a gentleman claiming to be here to investigate." He hesitated, his distaste of the coming words apparent. "A rather rough-hewed lad with him insists that he has second-hand knowledge of certain 'goings-on'."

Eden saw that Renfred's watery eyes strayed to her for an instant. Surely, he could not mean…that she was the victim of some supposed cruelty? Depravity?

Jaw set in granite; Dominic put her aside and was on his feet before Renfred finished speaking.

"Your brothers are downstairs, sir, they sent me to fetch you."

"Where'd you leave them?"

"In the foyer."

"Find a maid to sit with Miss Prescott. I don't want her left alone."

Eden followed his movements with nervous eyes as he stalked to the pine wardrobe with purpose, yanked a dress jacket over the crumpled linen shirt and slept-in trousers. She'd turned her head without her vision swimming. But when she tried to sit up, every muscle in her body protested.

"Sir, Master Ethan sent Nell to request a tray be sent up. I shall instruct her to come up directly and wait until she is relieved."

"Very good, Renfred. Is Ethan in the foyer as well?"

"Yes, sir. There is some difference of opinion as to what is to be done with the gentleman and his companion."

"I would imagine so."

Eden became increasingly alarmed at the bend the conversation took. She recognized the name Montgomery as belonging to the fellow who'd turned up on the grounds and frightened her. Was he back to cart her off to Bedlam then? Now that she lay helpless in bed, unable to put up even the tiniest fight. A desperate sort of fear seized her.

"Dom?"

He motioned for Renfred to carry on and came back over to sit beside her on the bed.

"Do not worry, cara, I will not let them take you from here." His hand rested on her cheek as he spoke.

"But he's come back…with reinforcements just as he threatened to. How do you mean to stop him if he has the law on his side? You yourself do not think I am sane." She snatched a fistful of her zebra-esque hair. "Now, I *look* the part of a lunatic."

He tilted his head, studying her appearance gravely. "Is there anything that can be done about your hair? I will try to avoid it, but it may be necessary for them to see for themselves that you are unharmed, and properly chaperoned."

"I meant to powder it before you returned, but it will be a laborious endeavor. Someone needs to fetch the vanity case from my chamber and—"

"Have Nell assist you with whatever. And make haste." He leaned in to plant a lingering kiss on her mouth before he stood to leave.

* * *

Dominic arrived at the bottom of the main staircase eyes shaded, freshly-shaven and coifed to face a bickering horde, Kathleen neck-deep in the fray. The foursome parted as he approached.

"Kathleen, Eden has need of you upstairs."

"Oh, no ya don't. I'll not be sent ta tha tower rooms like a weak-willed ninny. Tha wee one—"

Dominic scoffed. Kathleen…weak? He would have howled with laughter had the present situation not been so serious. "Madam, I do not now, nor have I *ever* considered you weak-willed or a ninny. At the moment though, Ms. Prescott is in need of a proper chaperon, as she is *allegedly* at the mercy of several lecherous noblemen. I do not mean to belittle, but please go to your charge. After our guests have departed, you may impugn me with whatever profanities fancy you."

"Humph!" The wisdom of his words must have penetrated her ire because she murmured something abrasive in her native tongue and stalked off up the stairs.

Cael arched a brow akin to a salute.

Ethan stared in awe at his retreating wife. "You know, Dom, for a recluse, you handle people very efficiently."

Stephan inclined his head in the direction of the study. "Have you a mind to send the pair on their way."

Though he delivered the words in a devil-may-care tone, Dominic sensed that his youngest brother championed unceremonious eviction as a solution to the two muckrakers.

Dominic directed his gaze to the hallway struck off from the foyer, leading to the study. "I would like nothing more than to evict them, Montgomery especially, but we cannot afford to alienate Greyson. The man has an agenda or he would not be this determined to have an audience with me. What's more, he is in a position to make life very difficult for all of us."

"A defensive move implies we have something to hide." Cael stated.

"We *do*." Stephan countered, his liquid amber clashing with his brother's warm amber.

"True, but I have found the best place to hide is in plain sight."

"How do you aim to handle them?" Ethan aimed at Dominic.

"I'll talk to Greyson, see if I can discern what he really wants. This nasty business with Eden is obviously a ruse."

"Maybe not." Cael suggested with a thoughtful expression. "What I mean to say is, maybe coming here wasn't Greyson's idea. Until now, his bid for your attention has been non-threatening. Why would he switch tactics and throw in with a brute like Montgomery? Casting a murky light on an innocent woman's virtue as well as her sanity in the bargain...Unlikely, and a conflict of interest."

"Wasn't Montgomery recently under investigation by Greyson's own board?" Ethan fell in line with his reasoning, turning to address Dominic and then Cael. "Cael, didn't you say that Greyson took a dislike to Montgomery that night at the lecture, 'gave him the cut direct' was your exact description of their parting exchange."

"Yes..." Dominic mused on this himself. "No matter. I won't know what either's ultimate goals are until I field them myself. Stephan will accompany me. Ethan, you and Cael assist Kathleen upstairs. If it becomes necessary to prove to the gentleman that she is not a captive victim, I want it to appear as if she is in bed recovering from her ordeal in the wine vault, which occurred *last* night. There will be no mention of entities and visions."

THIRTY SIX

Dominic hesitated, his palm poised to depress the elegant brass door handle, knowing he had a daunting task ahead of him. Here he was, a hermetic eccentric who had always shrank away from scrutiny, strangers and confrontations. Yet, he was attempting to play the part...no, not just play the part, but to assume his rightful role as patriarch of the Atherton-Raine-Ambrosi brood. Strange, how the brothers had naturally deferred to him, even Kathleen seemed to acknowledge his authority.

At the moment though, having the respect of his family wasn't sufficient. He needed to establish his authority with Greyson and Montgomery, convince them that he ran a wholesome household, and put them on edge enough to gain and maintain control of the situation. He needed a strategy, an approach...then, he remembered something Eden said. That people's reaction to him would all depend on him, his expression and demeanor.

A radical idea struck him. It would test his resolve and truth be told he wasn't sure he had the polish to carry it off. He turned to Stephan who nodded his readiness.

They entered the study, where a pair of near identical footman stood as stoic centuries on either side of the door's threshold. Dominic checked his insecurities at the door, along with his spectacles. The persona he wished to emulate would not hide behind tinted glass.

Ducking his head, he slid them deftly off his nose and stowed them in his breast pocket. Intimidation was the key, he reminded himself. Show no fear, no nervousness, no hesitation. With Stephan by his side, he stiffened his spine and summoned all the forgotten rules of protocol and etiquette he'd thwarted over the years.

The stout figure of Matthias Montgomery turned to face them from his stance just beyond the barren fireplace. His already sour face grew sharp and predatory at the sight of Stephan. Interesting.

At his host's arrival, Greyson rose to a stately height from the sofa. His intelligent expression remained blank.

"Gentleman, forgive me for keeping you waiting." Dom executed a posh bow, for no other reason than to afford the two men a generous glimpse of his unusual eyes. "I do not believe we have been properly introduced. I am Conte Dominic Alessandro Giovanni Ambrosi di Castello, the 26th Earl of the region. And this is my brother Stephan."

Stephan inclined his head, keeping his hands twinned behind his back.

"Davide Greyson." Greyson strolled forth and took the hand he offered. His grip was firm and straight forward. Dominic knew the moment Greyson noticed his uniqueness. His mud brown eyes shifted back and forth over Dominic's in an accessing manner.

"I am loathe to make your acquaintance under such circumstances, but I am here in an official capacity on behalf of the social reform board at the urgings of...a concern citizen—"

Montgomery chose that moment to clear his throat, demanding an introduction Dominic knew. The area around Greysons' eyes tightened infinitesimally. It spoke volumes of Greyson's opinion of the shorter man.

Montgomery reminded Dominic of a greedy child as he wedged his squat frame between Greyson and himself to proffer his own hand. "Matthias Montgomery, at yer service."

As Dominic came away from the ham-fisted troll, he wished he had taken the forethought to steal a glance at each man's essence. Of course, such a feat would have been impossible with both them and the two footmen in the same room. Not being familiar with either's appearance on the astral he wouldn't have been able to tell which essence belonged to whom, much less gleam any useful tidbits.

Greyson stepped forward once more, offering an apologetic mien. "Again, forgive us this abrupt intrusion. I'm only glad I was able to dissuade the board from a full-scale stopover."

Dominic caught the asylum keeper's glower out of the corner of his eye. He waved a solicitous hand urging the twosome to make themselves comfortable on the sofa. "Now, then, what moral turpitude is it you suspect me of exactly? Renfred's idea of tact is to be vague beyond comprehension."

"Ahem, there has been talk of a gently bred young woman with a less than steady mind, being held on the estate against her wishes and subjected to...nefarious crimes against her virtue."

"How...theatrical." Dominic shot the two of them a winsome smile, the picture of a carefree country gent. "You believe I have kidnapped a noblewoman and chained her up in my secret pleasure chamber, or rather in this case not so secret. Stephan, does it not sound like the plot of some insipid horror novel."

"A poorly written one, at that." He concurred with a bored air.

"Do ya deny then dat tha Lady Prescott is at dis very moment 'oused in yer bed chamber an' used a'bominably for yer pleasure?"

"That is a distortion of the truth." Dom let the words roll off his tongue like melted butter. "Miss Prescott is here on a visit and closely chaperoned by my brother Ethan's wife. Her presence in my suites while irregular is temporary and due entirely to an unfortunate mishap that led to her spending a very frightening hour locked in the wine vault. Ethan and our other brother Cael are both physicians. They have been looking after her. My chamber is nearer to theirs and more isolated than the guest chamber that she normally occupies and thus more suitable as a sickroom. She is there merely for convenience sake. "

"Why 'is chamber?" Montgomery persisted, in a tone that rang with accusation.

"I was away until recently."

"And how come she's 'ere at all instead of 'aving herself a season in tha bosom of them rich grandparents of 'ers. "

Greyson obviously didn't care for Montgomery's crass inquires, but his resigned silence said that he needed a reasonable explanation all the same.

"If you know her background, then you are also familiar with her circumstances. I sought an audience with the Duke and Duchess, and informed them of their Granddaughter's plight. They suggested I apply for her a place at Bedlam. But by all means, speak with them yourself if you have any doubt of their indifference." He invited generously. "Pray, mention having her to stay with them if you wish to see the full measure of their repugnance."

Dominic did not miss the quelling glance the taller man shot the asylum keeper before turning to ask, "How did your brother and sister-in-law become acquainted with the young lady?"

He strolled about the room as he strung together a plausible story from fragments and half-truths. "One of his colleagues attended the birthing and subsequent death of her cousin, a Lady Millicent St. James. This colleague relayed the sad tale to Ethan, and well, Ethan and Cael both have rather tender hearts...cultivated by their profession. When he learned that her cousin's widower along with the Duke and Duchess had spurned her, he offered refuge with he and his wife Kathleen. My sister-in-law is increasing and much favors female companionship."

"So ya struck while tha young miss was vulnerable, alone, out of 'er head wit grief—"

"She is as sane as you or I." Stephan corrected Montgomery, a hint of something lethal edged into his voice.

"What my brother says is true. Outside of some lingering malaise over the sudden loss of her parents, aunts and most recently her cousin, the young woman is quite rational. One can hardly fault her for needing a period of adjustment. All that she knew and held dear is gone. She's had to assimilate into a whole new society."

"An' I suppose, we're ta take ya word for dat...as a *gentleman*." Montgomery openly mocked his credibility.

"Give your oath that you'll do or say nothing to upset her, and I will allow a short visit with Miss Prescott. You may form your own opinion as to the state of her well-being." Dominic made the offer as graciously as possible considering the idea of Eden being within a mile of either man raised a tumult of dread and protectiveness.

* * *

Cael surveyed her from the window. "That will have to do. I can't imagine Dom can stall them much longer. Montgomery is not the sort to be reasoned with."

"Thank you, Nell. That will be all." Ethan excused the maid, who scurried away as was her custom.

Eden stared at the reflection in the silver-handled mirror Kathleen had given her. The layer of powder had leeched the two striped plaits to an impossibly pale white blonde. Thankfully she was supposed to be recovering from a terrible shock, because little else could account for her hollow cheeks and death-pallor. Her eyes seemed different, darker, more almond-shaped. Or, was her mind playing tricks on her again.

Looking away from the ghost woman she'd become, she handed the mirror back to Kathleen without comment. She was dying by degrees, but at least she'd regained a measure of mobility in the last twenty or so minutes. When the faint knock came at the chamber door, she was sitting up on her own, tense fingers gripping the counterpane.

Kathleen laid a quelling hand atop hers. "Easy, lass. Remember ta keep ya bandaged hand beneath tha counterpane."

Eden nodded and did her best to calm her rioting fears.

Stephan entered first, ushering in a tall, scholarly-looking gentleman and the stout balding Montgomery. Her jaw nearly dropped in shock when next Dominic strolled forth...sans his spectacles. Her slack gaze did not leave his face until the taller gentlemen addressed her directly.

"May I present Drs. Ethan Raine and Cael Atherton. My sister-in-law Mrs. Kathleen Raine, and of course, Miss Prescott." Dom gestured lastly to her.

"Gentleman. Mrs. Raine." The tall one inclined his head. "Lady Prescott."

"I much prefer *Miss* Prescott. I am American at heart." She met his apologetic expression, and relaxed a bit more at the non-threatening manner.

"Tha sight of *her* is supposed ta prove dat there's been no breech of morals 'ere?" Montgomery stalked closer to the bed, curling his lip at her. "Tha chit couldn't pass for a week-old corpse. People 'ould swear she'd been dead a fortnight at least."

Eden flinched.

"Miss Prescott does not care for your tone...and neither do I."

Montgomery ignored Dom's polite reproach. "Gads,

275

Ambrosi, 'ave the decency ta feed tha gel.'" A note of relish crept in his voice like a secret lover. "Or, is dat how ya control'er, huh? Deny' er food until she denies ya nothin'? Though why anyone 'ould bother ta spread dat bag of bones, I'd—"

The Asylum Keeper never got to finish his thought. Stephan had him by the throat in a grip that put pressure enough on his spine to cause a yelp of pain.

"I don't care for your tone either, Mr. Montgomery." Stephan delivered the words with quiet menace. "Either conduct your inquiries in a seemly manner or I shall relocate your jaw and let the other one ask the questions."

Face etched in fear, Montgomery managed to choke out a plea despite the strangle hold. "Pull 'im off me, Ambrosi."

Tension griped the room. A bead of sweat rolled down her temple. Eden had suspected the Sphinx possessed a dark side, but never in her wildest imaginings did she glimpse even a shadow of the contained fury she saw lurking in the depths of his eyes. She found herself breathing hard, pulling at the collar of her gown. Suddenly, she felt uncomfortably warm. The room itself seemed…realization hit hard. Her eyes flew to the grate in the fireplace, still a small flame, but it shone white-hot.

Both doctors made a move to defuse the situation, while panic sparked her into action.

"No." She stayed them with a word, knowing she alone could pull him back from the brink. "Let me." Out of instinct, she looked to Dom, but he wasn't where he had been just seconds before.

"Stephan." His grip tightened at the sound of her voice. "Stephan, please, I cannot reach the pitcher and I've grown thirsty."

His head tilted toward her. "We can't have that." He dropped his hold on the Asylum Keeper with the nonchalance of a youngster tossing aside a toy that had cease to amuse him.

As he neared, Eden heard the sizzle of the water and hoped that it wouldn't throw off steam.

"Ya address an unmarried gent by 'is Christian name? How odd." Montgomery massaged his throat, brows draw together in thunderous hatred. If he had wanted to cause mischief before, he would most likely be out for blood now... judging from his expression. Eden saw him glance around the room, pinning each occupant, including his companion with a look that promised they would all pay for his humiliation and pay dearly.

"Better to leave well-enough alone." Greyson murmured the words, but Eden heard them still. He turned to Dominic, who had reappeared right where she'd last seen him. "Conte Ambrosi, I can see that all is well with the young miss. The citizen who made the report was obviously misinformed. Have no doubt, I shall relay as much to the board. I will trouble you no longer then. Montgomery, let us go."

"Not just yet. 'Tis somethin' going on 'ere. I can smell it. Where does he sleep, then? If dat one's in 'is bed. And 'ow tha devil did she get locked in tha wine cellar anyway?"

Greyson's elegant shoulders slumped, as if he himself had suffered a personal disappointment. "Mr. Montgomery let me remind you." He eyed his companion pointedly. "We agreed that you were not to speak unless I or Conte Ambrosi addressed you directly and gave you leave to do so. That was the condition of your accompanying me."

"Its alright." Dominic gestured. "You may as well know—I want no repeat of *this*—Miss Prescott and I are hand-fasted. She uses a familiar address because she and I will be wed before All Hallows. We have agreed on a six-months handfast instead of the traditional year, you see. I prefer a proper engagement, but the rules of mourning forbid it. And, too, the sad state of affairs with her English relations. I was unwilling to subject her or myself to the publicity of town, a season, bans and all that nonsense. I need hardly add that my privacy is of extreme importance to me."

"Is that true?" The taller man questioned.

Eden felt color rise under the weight of Greyson's scrutiny, and the scorn of Montgomery's skepticism. She deliberately avoided catching anyone else's eye lest her blush deepen.

"Yes, we are... betrothed." Greyson seemed to accept her answer and returned his attention to Dominic.

"Might have done better to inform the household at least."

"I value my privacy, Professor, and I did not think it decent to expose Ms. Prescott to any further social difficulties. My household is very fond of the young lady and I do not believe one numbered among them requested *this inquisition*...eh, or, whatever it is." Dominic turned to his companion. "This was, no doubt your handiwork. There is no use denying it, Mr. Montgomery. You have been on the estate previously, then too as an unwelcomed guest. Isn't that so, Kathleen?"

"Aye, 'tis him...frightened tha wits out of myself and tha wee lass, here."

Dominic cleared his throat. "Professor Greyson, I have been as gracious as it is within me to be under the circumstances, but my patience is at an end, I'm afraid. Stephan, you will please see the gentleman and his... *acquaintance* out. Now."

Stephan spoke, darkly sarcastic, as he gestured for them to precede him to the door. "Always a pleasure."

THIRTY SEVEN

"Where the devil did you go? Do you have any idea how reckless that was?"

"Aye, one of 'em could've noticed." Kathleen agreed, though she put a quelling hand on her brother-in-law's shoulder. "Cael-"

"For a man who's spent a lifetime protecting himself and his secrets from the world you certainly chose an odd moment to become adventurous."

"Stephan had everyone's attention. There was no danger. I glanced at their souls. The opportunity might not have arisen again." Dominic watched Cael morph from annoyed to intrigued.

"Well...What did you see?"

"Montgomery's life force was a tumult of ill feelings."

"That's nothing we didn't already know." Stephan injected from his perch by the windows. "The man is not subtle."

"It's more than that. His essence was not under stress. It appeared as though his natural state of being is a frenzy of rage and hatred. I would not be surprised if he had a history of violent deeds. Greyson, unfortunately, proved more difficult to read. No overt emotion. Nothing unique

279

or identifiable about his essence."

"Enough about Greyson an' dat misanthrope." Kathleen waved them away, and squared her eyes on Dom. "'Tis high time we speak of practical matters. I did no' care for tha way dat one carried on but he makes a point. What of dis engagement? Do ya intend ta honor it?"

"I admit I merely provided a convenient excuse to waylay more speculation with regards to her virtue. Moreover, Miss Prescott and I have not yet discussed marriage."

A chortle came from the doorway. Dominic glanced to find Ethan crossing the study's threshold. "I believe you mean to say her *lack* of virtue."

"Aye." Kathleen seconded her husband's sentiment with a sharp nod. "And I wanna know what ya intentions are towards my charge? You've let it be known dat Ethan and I are responsible for tha wee one. So, it'll be our hides when the lass' middle starts ta spread before tha vows."

Dominic cleared his throat, as he looked down the barrel of a cocked shotgun. "Yes, that thought has occurred to me. I am a man of dignity and honor, if indeed a deplorable lack of propriety. We *will* be married, once she is physically and mentally fit. In the meanwhile, I suggest we have a cleric of some sort for a visit to make this hara-kiri hand-fasting a documented fact."

"Do not forget to ask her first, Dominic." Stephan said. "Eden deserves a measure of consideration in her own future."

"And donna make tha proposal as though ya are duty-bound ta do so." Kathleen injected. "A woman likes a 'lil romance, ya know."

"But it is imperative that you convey to her the necessity for a wedding in the very near future." Cael cautioned.

Dom's head swam at the myriad of advice. He looked to Ethan. "How is she?"

"Resting. Nell is sitting with her now."

"Good. Cael, as soon as she is able I would like you to have another interview with her. Stephan and I will look into the possibility of a spiritual disturbance and if need be, an exorcism."

* * *

The instant the door had closed behind Dr. Raine the evil-thing started pounding on the walls of her mind. She tried to concentrate amid the assault, rebuild the numerous cracks in her foundation. Instead they broke open wider, letting the disturbing presence leak in. NO! Her mind screamed. She felt as if someone was slowly strangling off her air supply.

"Did you think you could control me forever?"

Ignoring the taunt, she redoubled her efforts. But she knew she was fighting a losing battle. The evil was too strong. It was only a matter of time before the evil would again possess her mind.

"Nell." Frantic eyes sought the jittery housemaid, fussing with the bed linens. "You must help me."

"Would you like a spot to eat now that all the excitement is over, then?" She quit twittering at the foot of the bed, and came to place the forgotten food tray before her.

"Stephan, I must… speak with him." Eden followed the girl's movement, trying to catch her eye. But it seemed as if Nell deliberately avoided looking at her. She didn't half blame the maid for being frightened of her. She probably would be too if the shoes were on her feet.

"Mr. Atherton and the others are downstairs in the study having a chat. I was told not to leave you alone. Relax miss, one of 'em will be up to check on you soon." With that, she spooned up a steaming heap of something from the bowl. "Shall I?"

Eden backhanded her hard across the cheek. The food spilled in a grotesque slash of chunks across the counterpane and over the side of the bed. "Bothersome chit! Quit hovering and let me be."

Eden gave the evil thing a hard mental strove to dislodge it...with little success. She was a prisoner in her own consciousness, a passenger in a carriage being driven by a malevolent force. Nell trembled on the floor, clutching her struck cheek. The thing sneered into that shocked expression.

"*Get gone*, do you hear me!" Try as she might, Eden could not stop her features from contorting in hatred as more cruel words left her mouth. The shrill command held a note of warning, which threatened retribution if not obeyed.

"Y-y-y-yes, Miss." The maid stammered. "I w-w-won't disturb you again."

Poor Nell. Eden made a mental note to make it up to the girl once she had better control of herself. For now, it looked as if the entity was about to get her way. Nell, scrambled off the floor, giving the bed a wide girth, as she made tracks to the opposite end of the room. To Eden's surprise, the maid sidestepped the chamber door and instead positioned herself in the furthest corner from the bed and set knees to her chest on the floor.

"I said, get out."

Eden felt the thing's intentions and wanted to cry. It wasn't done with Nell yet. It wanted her gone from the room. The entity flipped back the ruined covers, flinging a spray of loose food across the other side of the counterpane. Rising on wobbly feet, she felt herself stalk towards the frightened maid. Eden saw images of her own fist pounding into the young maid's back and a hand snatching painfully at her hair. She knew Nell. The meek girl would make no struggle, raise not a finger to her betters.

"*No, please, don't do this.*" Eden begged. "*Let her alone! If you truly want her to go, allow me to talk to her. I'll convince her.*"

"*My way works best.*"

"Let us leave the room then. You can say that you've gone to seek another's company. She won't follow."

Undeterred, the entity was nearly upon her when a soft knock came at the chamber door. Without waiting for an answer the door opened to admit Dominic.

Dom!" Eden wanted to run to him, throw her arms around him and stay cocooned in his gentle warmth forever. The evil thing though, staggered like a toddler just learning to walk. Though at least it did not sneer at him as it had Nell. It seemed to Eden to be eager to see him. Even trying for a smile.

"Dominic, is it really you?" The awe and familiarity the entity put into her voice puzzled Eden. Did it know Dom outside of its knowledge of him through her memories? Up until now, she assumed the thing plaguing her was a pointless evil that chose to victimize her because she was feeble-minded. Could it be possible the evil had a premeditated agenda...that somehow involved Dominic?

"Eden. What are you doing out of bed?" His eyes widen.

Eden couldn't tell if he was more surprised or worried. He was upon her in an instant, and would have lifted her into his arms...when the thing within her cringed away. Preferring to fall backward on her bottom than be touched by Dominic.

"Eden?"

"Keep away from me you odd-eyed fiend." Just as quickly as the outburst sprang forth, she cut herself off. Her next words were spoken in soft dulcet tones. Eden felt a swell of hate overtake her thoughts belying the sweetness she proffered.

"Forgive me, Dom. I don't know what has come over me lately."

Blast! The evil thing had just undone weeks of careful prodding, gentle words and trust-building. Now, he had that shell-shocked expression again. Frantic to sooth the hurt and explain that the words had not come from her, but the evil thing possessing her, Eden struck out at the thing in the only manner left to her.

"Hurt him again and I'll make sure you regret it." Just to prove the threat wasn't empty, she garnered all her mental efforts to bombard the evil with images from her own memories. Much like the entity had done to her. She chose the most painful and debilitating points in her life, the deaths of her parents, the time in youth when she'd broken her ankle. Images and feelings flooded the foreign consciousness squatting in her mind. Eden smiled with satisfaction when the entity writhed under the onslaught.

"Cara, are you hurt? You've a queer sort of smile." Dom was at her side, lifting her into his arms. "I am happy to see that you're improving, but for my sake please take it slow. Where the devil is Nell?"

He could see her smile? Was she free of the entity's thrall then? She tested the boundaries, probing her consciousness. No. The dark cloud in her mind still hovered, encroaching once again on her freewill. She must warn him before it overshadowed her completely.

"Don't trust anything I say." She clutched at his collar pleading with her eyes.

He frowned. "Eden?"

By the time he had walked them to the edge of the bed, the evil had recovered.

"What happened here?" He looked from the ruined tray to the bedding abandoned on the floor and spotted the maid hovering in the corner. "Nell?"

"Oh, it's nothing." Evil Eden explained, waving a dismissive hand. "Nell accidentally upset the tray in my lap and then retreated in fear of being scolded. I was trying to reassure her that it was no harm done when you came. Run along dear and fetch someone to change the bedding."

* * *

All frightened eyes and stammering voice, Nell rushed forward to clear away the tray and its fallen contents.

"Have a fresh tray sent up as well." Dominic called after her.

"Yes, Master Ambrosi." She dropped a curtsey and fled.

Nell returned a short time later with a new tray and a younger even more skittish protégé burdened with a stack of bedding that threatened to topple with her every step. The maid deposited the new tray on the night table and the two of them made quick work of the bed.

"Will that be all, then."

"Yes, you may go about your normal business." Dom excused the two and gazed down at the bundle still in his arms. Wondering how best to begin.

How did one propose a handfast? He hadn't any idea how one even proposed a marriage. He tried to recall the advice that the others had given him. Kathleen had said not to treat the proposal as an obligation. Therefore, he must affect spontaneity and romance.

Then he thought of Cael. His brother had reminded him that the need for a wedding was imminent. Yes, indeed, now more than ever. His expression softened at the memory of the life force he'd witnessed mingled with hers. His child, their child, at this moment grew inside the slight woman he now held within his arms. He felt her stiffen.

"Dominic, you may put me down."

He complied, setting next to her at the bed's edge. "Eden, I've been thinking…about what I said earlier."

"You said many things earlier."

"I refer specifically to my mention of a hand-fasting." He eyed her askance, wanting to gauge her reaction. "We have not discussed marriage, I know, but the incident earlier has made me see just how precarious our current…eh…arrangement is. I…that is, I mean to say that, I've come to realize that I wish you to be a…permanent figure on the estate. Not only that, but in my life as well. So, I wanted to ask, would you perhaps consider making our pretend hand-fast a real one?"

"Why hand-fast? Why not a formal betrothal and marriage?"

"For the same reasons I relayed to Greyson." His shoulders drooped. She was not eager to enter into it as he had hoped. He loathed telling her of her condition. It seemed an underhanded means of persuasion. Of course she would say yes faced with the social ridicule that came with unwed pregnancy. He wanted her to say yes because she wanted him as her husband, not because she had no other option.

"Recall, there is the possibility of a child to be considered." He broached the topic feigning an indifference he did not feel. "What I propose is a two-month hand-fast. During which time, we can search for a solution to this entity business. Afterward we will be married in a traditional ceremony before God and church. Cara, will you look at me at least?"

He caught her under the chin with his thumb and second finger. Lower lip trembling, her eyes watered with tears. "Is this arrangement so abhorrent to you?"

"Yes."

Thoughtless cad! He scolded himself for being such an unfeeling fool. Even if she had not been privileged to the full measure of deference her title and status afforded her by the peerage, she was raised a lady of some import in Boston. A woman like Eden would not leap into a pagan marriage ritual not even recognized by the Church of England. If he were truthful with himself, he too preferred a traditional sort of betrothal and marriage. Particularly when the mother of his unborn child was concerned. So what was holding him back? Why not offer her what she deserved, what they both wanted…

Lucca. The horror of repeating the past. But really, what did that matter anymore? Cael had pronounced that she was sane. Stephan and ever Kathleen seemed more than ready to believe her problems steamed from some external threat. So why shouldn't he be free to marry the woman he loved?

Love. A new experience for him, and like making love...it held a multitude of promise and yet an equal measure of uncertainty. Love could ignite a towering inferno of both passion and pain. Perhaps that was the natural order of things. Nothing good came without a counterbalance of evil. There could be no heaven, without a hell.

Though conflicted about taking their relationship to the next level, there was one solid fact etched in his mind and his heart: he would never love another the way he adored the woman sitting before him now.

"Marry me, then." He said the words in a rush, afraid if he did not get them all out at once, he'd lose his nerve. He fell to one knee, grasping her pale delicate hands in his. "With all the trappings. Before God and all who care to attend, marry me, cara."

He knew a moment of panic. Her eyes did not touch his face...she seemed to be avoiding looking at him. Her hands were limp in his. She didn't leap into his arms, burst into tears of joy, or gasp with delight. In fact, he could sense no outward reaction at all. She just sat there...then she turned her face slowly, serene. Her mouth curved upward.

"Yes, Dominic. I'll marry you."

He sighed. The thrill and satisfaction of knowing that she would soon be his warmed his heart, swelled his pride, *and* fired his loins.

* * *

Eden could only watch the scene play out before her, no more than an on-looker at a spectacle. She'd longed for this moment. Imagined a dozen different ways he would finally ask her to be his, only to miss out now. She writhed in frustration and displeasure at having to share Dominic's proposal. At least the crazy bitch had the sense enough to say 'yes'. She had worried for a moment, being bombarded by the thing's blaring hostility. A 'yes' had not seemed likely and certainly wasn't sincere, not with the swirl of antagonistic images the sight of Dominic provoked.

At present, his eyes sparkled with excitement. A boyish giddiness that melted her heart...and enraged the entity. His hands dropped from her face to the hem of her gown...toying with the ticklish bottoms of her feet. The entity did not recoil from his touch, but let Eden enjoy the wonderful sensations. She felt the giggle bubbling forth. Not a peep of protest as his warm palms slid at a leisurely and seductive pace up her calves, taking the nightshift along with them.

"Oh..." Having a sensation all her own was intoxicating, overwhelmed her thoughts. "Dom, make love to me."

The thoughts, the feelings were hers and hers alone. The evil had retreated to the outskirts of her mind, disgusted with the pleasure she found in his kisses...running up the hallow of her throat and nibbling at her tender flesh. She must not lose her head. She needed to keep her wits about her, seize control now that the entity seemed less dominant. Not to mention, the idea of sharing their intimate moments with an interloper was abhorrent to her.

His hand pushed gently at the insides of her knees, coaxing her legs astride. "Dominic, no, we must talk."

The heat rose in a haze of lust. She felt over warm and fidgety. Her skin begged to be caressed, all over. Desire for him flared to undeniable intensity. It swamped her senses and scattered her thoughts, thwarting her very will. She had to have him, now, inside her, stroking her, kissing her, pleasuring the hungry mouth between her legs. She spread her thighs, ripping the garment in her haste. Drawers damp with arousal, her hips writhed upward, seeking, begging for gratification.

The entity must be manipulating her again. Using her arousal against her. Distorting it, exaggerating it to frantic propositions. Her breasts were unbearably heavy and sensitive to even the cotton of her gown. She couldn't stand the texture of it against her skin and began tearing her under-things and the remains of the gown off her body. The action made her appear wanton and perhaps crazed, but she could not seem to stop herself.

"Dominic!" She heard her panicked voice as her body gyrated wildly, her hands clawing at his clothes once she'd relieved herself of her own. "Now. I need you…"

"Patience. There is no rush." He joined her on the bed, poised on one knee bracing himself over her.

She succeeded in ripping the shirt from his body. Buttons shot like bullets around them. Blood roared in her ears. The only sound she heard was the beating of her own heart.

"Eden—"

She pressed her mouth into his, plunging her tongue inside, groaning. Her hands found the waist of his trousers, gripping his man's appendage. Massaging it, for some reason she found pleasure in the act and longed to feel it's slick heat pulsating in her palm as she tightened her fingers around it's girth and squeezed, stroked, teased…and not just with her palm, with her mouth as well. The thought of the wicked deed provoked a white-hot image of her doing just that. She couldn't stop herself unbuckling the trousers to loose the object of her desires.

Somehow, she flipped them so that she straddled him. In some corner of her mind that was still sane she acknowledged that the feat should have been impossible. He outweighed her by some pounds. He must have realized it at the same instant she did because an incredulous looked marred his features. But she was too deeply snared in the entity's thrall to stop. Her nails raked down the sides of his torso. A hiss of pleasure followed...or was it pain?

He let out a string of Italian words Eden could not understand. Guided by the image in her head, she shimmied down his body until she was upon his engorged appendage. It beckoned her with the wicked lure of gratification...

For the most part, Dominic kept up with the vigorous pace of their lovemaking to its lusty orgasmic climax. Ending with her scream of release.

She was panting like an animal with him still sheathed inside, her nails embedded in his back. The sweet aroma of satisfaction wafted between them, both slick with sweat and their mingled juices. Spent and feeling the first twinge of embarrassment she could do nothing save for turn her head from his bewildered expression and bury her face in the counterpane.

"Forgive me, Dom. I don't know what's come over me."

Dominic withdrew himself from her body altogether. Ashamed and disgusted no doubt. She could feel him staring at her from where he stood beside the bed.

"You're saying that a lot lately." The words were an accusation.

She felt his hands halt her as she tried to curl her trembling body into a ball.

"See what you've done...to yourself and to me." His voice sounded urgent. "Look, dammit! Now, do you want to tell me the entity made these as well?!"

He caught her chin in a firm grip and forced her to see the evidence of her haste in removing their clothes. Thin red welts marred both his torso and her own.

THIRTY EIGHT

He never expected to have to face his fears. He planned to avoid all that…love, loss, sorrow, pain…by avoiding people in general. Instead, here he was, embroiled in a love affair, betrothed, and seeking the advice of a clergyman. Three things he swore he'd never do.

"You're cagey."

Dominic paused, undecided, spectacles clasped in one hand. His brother's guileless expression confused him for a moment. Of course…Cael wouldn't have told Stephan.

"I don't trust the clergy." It was why he never attended Sunday service, preferring instead to commune with the Almighty on his own terms. Cut out the middleman, so to speak.

"Why not?"

It must seem odd to mistrust a servant of God. But all who claimed religion were not righteous men. He remembered another sort of religious group. Spiritualists. They believed in communing with spirits, incantations, mediums, séances and all manner of sacrilegious practices.

"I've known one too many priests." He left it at that and turned back to begin pacing again. Where the bloody hell was the cleric anyway? They'd been squatting in the rectory for nearly an hour. Supposing he'd come with the notion to confess his sins? He would certainly have given up and returned to his wicked ways by now.

"You know, Dom, we could forget the cleric in favor of a ship's captain or perhaps—"

"Gentlemen. I am Reverend Martin." The cleric came bounding through at set of double doors behind them. He quickly waived their attempts to stand. "Oh, no, no please stay seated."

Dominic half-expected a sinister old codger with gnarled fingers and a dodgy manner. The reverend was neither. The man who emerged from the parlor's entranceway was of middling age and only average height. He greeted them with a genuine smile and a firm handshake, shifting the leather-bound bible to the opposite hand to do so. If he noticed Dominic's odd eyes he did not give away as much.

"I am Dominic Ambrosi and this is my brother Stephan."

The robed and collared cleric took a seat opposite them on a once stylish divan just starting to show its age. "Ah, yes, Conte Ambrosi, you reside at the Duke and Duchess's old estate."

"That I do. Rev. Martin, we've come to seek your counsel and to beg a favor."

"Forgive me for saying, but I did not think you a religious man, as I've never seen you at services."

"I am a believer but I prefer to commune with God on my own terms. That being said, I find that my latest endeavor will require your…Eh, input."

"Certainly, if it is in my power to help, I will. What is it you require me to do?"

"Marry me."

"Oh…". The reverend's eyes grew wide, as he smiled. "I did not realize you were affianced."

"Yes, well, I have only recently become betrothed to a certain lady and would like you to perform the nuptials.

My bride-to-be wants a traditional sort of ceremony, and I am dedicated to her happiness."

"I usually require a counseling session before marrying couples that I am not previously acquainted with." He cleared his throat, and Dom found himself on the business end of a stern Father-son expression. "Just for the purposes of relaying the seriousness of the marriage vows and evaluating the couple's maturity and commitment to a lifelong bond. God has appointed me as spiritual guide over a portion of his flock. I would be remiss if I did not take some responsibility for their future happiness in such an important step. If you are in agreement and I find no obvious nor grievous impediment to the match then I would be most delighted to put the two of you together. When did you wish the ceremony to take place, next spring?"

"As soon as possible, in fact, as soon as it can be arranged. I will be leaving directly to obtain a special license." Dom cringed inwardly. He knew his coming words were presumptive and condescending, but there was no polite way to say it. He might as well clear the air as to his intentions. "Understand me, I would prefer your cooperation, but we will be married whether you deem us appropriate or not. There has been some...hint of impropriety on my part. I am a private man by nature, which has made me the target of idle chatter. Though, the rumors are not altogether untrue...I have over-stepped. Nevertheless, I want the allegations hushed before general gossip begins to circulate and her reputation ends in shreds. She is...precious to me...my Eden. I'll not have her branded as a tarnished Lady dragging the cad responsible for her ruin to the altar kicking and screaming."

The reverend was all smiles. "Well said, Conte Ambrosi. And I believe, under the circumstances, you have the right of it. A speedy ceremony is best. Barring our counseling session, is two weeks ample time to complete the preparations?"

Dominic relaxed, vastly relieved. "Yes."

"Now then, what's this other matter on which you seek my counsel?"

Stephan cleared his throat. "I have a friend who is considering marriage…to a woman who is not altogether suitable in the eyes of his family. There is some question of her mental facilities being unsound. You see, the young woman claims to be the victim of an evil spirit of some sort. From my observation, she does not appear unsound. In short, I believe her claim. My friend is skeptical. He asked my opinion. Now, I am asking yours. Do you think it is possible she is telling the truth?"

Rev. Martin reached for the bible he'd sat to the side, flipping to various scriptures. "There are many documented instances of spirits with the ability to possess unwitting folks. Luke six, seventeen through nineteen speaks of Jesus healing demon-possessed persons. Matthew chapter twenty-eight, Jesus sends a herd of demons from two men into a herd of pigs. In the gospel of Mark, Jesus heals a lunatic by driving out a demon from him." He closed the book with a slap. "Can I tell you definitely whether the young lady is afflicted by a demonic spirit, no. But, the possibility *does* exist. It would be a mistake for your friend to dismiss it out of hand. I would offer my direct assistance, but I sense the situation is such that extreme discretion is preferred?"

Stephan nodded.

"In that case, let me acquaint you with some relevant scriptures, in addition to the ones I have already mentioned that would help you to identify a probable demonic possession." The reverend shifted the bible over in favor of his quill and ink well, situated on the table behind the divan on which he sat. When he'd finished writing, he turned back around and handed the brothers the list.

"Tell your friend to watch the young lady carefully. If

she exhibits behaviors akin to what is described in the scriptures, then, I would say you have a problem on your hands."

THIRTY NINE

Eden twisted her hand this way and that, still mesmerized by the size and splendor of the glinting topaz affixed on her ring finger. She thought he would take back his proposal, given her strange behavior. Instead he'd surprised her with the beautiful ring and expressed his wish to wed her as soon as possible. He was being so particular about the ceremony. Instructing Kathleen to procure her a special dress from the village, purchasing rings and even demanding that the entire household attend.

They were watching her, of course. Always one of the brothers, Kathleen or Nell hovered about, monitoring everything she did. She felt like a sideshow freak. The fact that neither Dominic nor Stephan brought up the matter of the entity made her even more nervous. She tried to bring up the subject, to explain what the entity had caused her to do. No one refuted her. In fact, Dom continually assured her that she was safe, that everything was fine, and no one was plotting to have her committed.

So then, why, two days later, did she find herself closed off in the library with his mind-bending brother, anxious to pick her apart? She dropped her hand in her lap to tangle within the folds of her skirt. Obviously he was back to thinking her crazy. Damn him for making her love him so much that even the tiniest lack of faith on his part could pain her so.

She'd have to be more careful. Guard her mind, make certain her thoughts were a fortress the entity could not penetrate. She could ill afford to let the thing rule her again or every tiny bit of trust she managed to cultivate would be lost. She was safe for the time being…but Dominic would not go ahead with the marriage if he believed her to be insane.

"Eden…that is, may I call you 'Eden'?"

The masculine voice jolted her out of her thoughts. "Yes, please."

"And you must call me 'Cael'." He stretched his legs out cattycorner her in one of the library's high-backed chairs. "Now then, first, I want to put your mind at ease. I do not think that you're insane. However, I do believe there is a puzzle to be solved."

"Is that what Dominic thinks too?"

"As a matter of fact it is. He and Stephan are on a fact-finding expedition to discover an alternative explanation for whatever it is that's troubling you."

Relief came fast and strong. She'd been plagued with a sense of dread…like something was brewing ever since the morning she'd awoken and Dominic had declared flat out that she wasn't well. She worried that perhaps the "marriage" was just a sham to keep her placated whilst they made…other "arrangements" for her.

"That's what this session is about? I thought…" She let the words trail off.

"No, my dear."

"But what other explanation could there possibly be?"

"That's what I aim to discover. What I need from you is a detailed recount of every incident beginning with the day I rescued you from the pond. Leave nothing out, anything you can remember. Oh, and I must also ask you to surrender any sketches that you made which might be of interest."

She lowered her eyes to her lap, staring fixedly at the shimmering topaz once again. "Has Stephan already mentioned the incident at the table turning and the images in the mirror?" Eden imagined Atherton's amber gaze was transfixed and glowing with curiosity. His eyes, like Stephan's, took on a certain sparkle when his interest was stirred. "No, he hasn't. Let us start there, shall we."

* * *

Dominic stepped off the astral and into the downstairs study with Stephan in tow. The added strain of piggybacking had him lowering himself into the nearest chair. Stephan took up his usual vigil at the hearth, amber fixed on the licking flames.

"Yours is an amazing gift, Dominic." He continued to stare at the fire as he spoke. "Tell me, have you ever seen anything other than human souls? Assuming you could sense something unnatural."

The question hovered in the air between them, triggering his memory. He thought of his recent time in Italy, and the odd appendage-like protrusion he'd observed in both Gideon and Gabriel's essence. The anomaly did not have a human counterpart. Muse was not human, possessed no soul and yet...no. The idea was too farfetched. "I...No."

"What about the essence of a dead person?"

"After a body dies, their essence no longer inhabits the astral plane." He admitted, knowing where the conversation was headed. "I know what you're thinking. I *still* should have sensed *something*."

"That's your heart talking not your head." Stephan swiveled around to bore into him with amber eyes. "Consider, if the entity is demonic or the spirit of a dead person then it follows that you would not have seen it. The only reason I could was because it disrupted the normal pattern of heat in the room. Sometimes, particularly now that Eden dampens the wilder aspects of my ability, I can sense you, and everyone around me, as a vision of heat. It is like souls in the astral realm only I am sensing the heat contained by each person in *this* realm. That night, there was a pattern of heat in the room or rather an abnormal pattern, devoid of heat. It couldn't have been a person...not any living person, anyway."

Dominic absorbed the logic in his brother's words with a heavy heart. Stephan was right of course. "We need Cael's input." He should have completed his follow-up interview by now. Dom was about to quit the room when Stephan halted him.

"I'll go."

Dom ducked his head on the astral for the briefest instant. "They're in the library." He called as his brother reached the study's door.

* * *

"Will you stay with her while I speak with Dominic?" Cael whispered.

"That was my intention." Stephan returned his hushed tone.

Eden reclined against the spongy cushions. With arms spread out on the back lip of the couch, she watched the two from across the hexagonal room. They probably thought they were being discreet. She could hear them as if they were shouting. Even if she hadn't been able too, she might just as easily have guessed what was said.

Ever the polite dandy, the mind doctor excused himself, leaving her alone with the other one. The Dangerous One. The sniveling twit she presently inhabited had rightfully christened him 'the Sphinx'. This one was perceptive, with a cold shrewdness that made him the most difficult to read. One thing she knew, he was not to be trifled with, not with that ability of his. She'd have to get rid of him, discredit him somehow.

He approached her with a volume in his hand. "Shall we continue our reading, then?"

She waited until he stood just in front of where she'd poised the girl's alluring body. "Books are for bluestockings who are too dull to keep up their end of a conversation. I never bother with them, having found a much more pleasurable pursuit for my eyes…" Raking him over with a predatory gaze, stopping deliberately at the junction of his thighs. "…and my mouth. Would you like to join?"

His hard amber stare said he didn't. She sensed from that look that she wouldn't have an easy time with him.

He shifted his towering frame and sat on the upholstered stool opposite the couch, as far from her as possible.

"What have you done with Eden?" His voice was deadly calm, his mien a wall of menace.

"*I* am the new, improved Eden." She purred in a soft seductive voice, pulling a slow hand through the once blond tresses. Since the initial appearance of the wide raven band at her temple, increasing strands had encroached, threading the blonde with lustrous black.

"Know this. If you harm her again you will suffer… a great deal. Dominic is not a violent man. I am."

She let her hand fall from her hair to the modest neckline of the gown, tugging recklessly at the delicate lacing there. "What do you think he'll do when he learns his trusted and beloved brother attacked his helpless betrothed? Forcing himself on her mercilessly."

"Knowing Dom, he wouldn't believe you but he'd disown me anyway to save her from disgrace. Then, he'd spend the rest of his life torturing himself with guilt and regrets."

The fabric tore loose, exposing a creamy swell of breast and the crisp white corset beneath. Next, she kicked free of one slipper, and viciously scratched and banged the second one against the wood floor until the heel broke from its base.

"Care to wager?"

"Do not underestimate him. He will not be fooled."

"We shall see."

FORTY

The door opened and in strolled Cael. His solemn manner spoke volumes.

"Bad news?" Dominic predicted.

"I'm afraid so."

"Same here."

"Well, let's have yours first then."

Cael listened, his face intense and thoughtful as Dominic relayed the particulars of his and Stephan's meeting with the Reverend Martin ending with his previous conversation with Stephan.

Cael remained silent at the end of his spiel. Dom scanned him for a reaction, finding nothing but a rueful expression, "Well?"

"Hmm...I'm not sure which is worse, your news...or mine."

"The interview?" Dom prompted again.

He sighed a long, telling breath. "It differs...vastly, from my previous assessment. Her mood was erratic: one minute hostile, the next aloof, and at times overly affectionate. She would not answer direct questions, and I caught her in several unsolicited lies."

"What does all that mean?" He cringed, dreading the

answer to his own question.

Cael ran a hand through his hair, rucking up the dark gold tuffs. "Dominic, if I had read a transcript of the two sessions instead of conducting the assessments myself, there would be no convincing me that they were describing the same patient. This new Eden—" He paused, massaging his temples. "She is indeed showing signs of mental distress as well as a significant dissociation from reality."

"Is she...?"

"There *are* several cognitive disorders which could explain *some* of her behaviors."

"So it is as I thought. Insanity."

To Dominic's utter surprise. .and relief, Cael shook his head. "Then, too, there is still the matter of the visions, her affect on Stephan, and her ability to sense *you*. No, insanity is not my final consensus. It does not fit her case. I have what I believe to be an answer to your question, which ironically is not a solution to her problem."

Dom exhaled the longest breath he'd ever held in his life. Dread turned to hope. "What is it, then?! If not insanity, what else could be causing—"

"Dominic, have you considered the possibility that Eden is *adept?*" Cael posed the question in a quiet, scientific voice. "That these strange happenings are the manifestation of a gift she has not yet realized and the nature of which is volatile...perhaps even dangerous. I think it is *that* stress on her psyche causing the instability and not some inherent mental weakness. There is documented evidence that certain psychic abilities put extra strains on the mind. I've...seen it myself, with one of my patients...suspected it in several others."

Dominic reeled at his brother's words. The thought had not occurred to him...so simple, so logical. The more he considered it; the more it made sense. Her sensitivity to astral travel, her uncanny ability to sense him when he was invisible, her affinity for Stephan, the visions, not prophetic like Gabriel's, but certainly of a psychic nature.

"Cael, you're a genius. Stephan thinks she is possessed by an evil spirit of some sort."

"I think my theory more likely...and possibly more hopeful than the alternative." He held up the forgotten list. "Spirit possession has no basis in scientific or medical fact...and thus, no literature, no treatment options. We *know* that adepts exist. Plus, she has displayed signs of an ability of some sort."

"Say, you're right...what do you suggest?"

"First, I recommend postponing the wedding-"

"No. Out of the question." The wedding was non-negotiable. "She is with child. I've seen a second essence mingled with hers."

Cael conceded without a fight. "Well, in that case, I would recommend calling in someone with more expertise on the subject. We don't even know the nature of her gift. We need someone who can help us figure out exactly what we're dealing with...as well as help her exercise some level of control over whatever talent she has."

Dominic knew of whom he spoke. "Greyson?"

Cael nodded. "We are out of options and I think we can both agree her condition is worsening. Will you at least consider it?"

"Yes. I'll consider it." What other choice did he have?

* * *

"You won't find a letter opener or any other sharp or harmful object in that desk or any other room on this floor. I suggested to Dominic after your last 'accident' that it would be prudent to remove the apple from the Garden."

"High and mighty bastard!" She sent the drawer skidding across the floor, sending paper, and various knick knacks flying in its wake. Her hair was deliberately messed, dress torn to shreds, and her face splashed with water from the vase that now lay upturned and cracked in a puddle of expanding liquid.

Seizing upon a leg of the desk, she snapped it from its socket with little effort. The desk tittered precariously like a spider trying to starve off the throws of death. Her eyes narrowed upon the jagged trio of nails protruding from the deep mahogany wood.

"I'm curious, what you plan to do with that." He impaled her with that prying gaze of his.

She threw him a serpent's smile, flipping the wood so the dangerous end aimed at the flat curve of her stomach exposed by the torn corset and ruined dress. Let the Sphinx try to explain fresh wounds on the demon's whore. With that delicious thought, she struck downward, anticipating the pain that always came with victory. But it never was. The three nails plopped to the floor. White-grey ash from incinerated wood floated away on air, some landing on her person.

"No matter." She snatched up the nails only to fling them down just as quickly, shrieking in pain.

"I will not allow you to harm my brother's fiancée." He aimed his gaze at the scorching hot nails, melting them down to a silvery viscous liquid.

The evil was enraged. Eden could feel its anger and hatred rushing through her quivering frame like a runaway locomotive, engines dangerously close to overload. It began shrieking, spitting out what sounded like angry curses in a tongue she herself neither spoke nor understood. She launched them up from the floor and across the room in a fantastic leap that rattled Eden's nerves. A minute or so passed before she regained any awareness of the surroundings and the entity's actions.

Since having the interloper's will imposed on her mind and body, she'd been having a progressively more difficult time maintaining her own consciousness. At times her essence seemed to be displaced to another realm. A dark, hollow place where she saw nothing, heard only echoes of silence, and was completely cut off from her physical self. The realm rendered her unable even to listen in or observe the entity's actions. Minutes sometimes hours passed before she returned to her body. She knew because there were holes in her memory that signified a 'loss of time'.

She was just coming out of one such blackout, trying to reorient herself when the smarting pains along her torso hit her. She, or rather the entity was struggling, writhing and shrieking beneath a great weight. Her wrists shackled wide apart by that same weight pinning her squirming body to a cushioned surface.

Stephan. He had a hold of her, restraining her clawing hands, trying to still her as she thrashed about. Although he was a sizeable man and physically strong, if not overtly burly, it seemed to be a struggle for him to maintain his hold on her.

That was how Dominic and Atherton found them: tussling atop the ottoman.

"Stephan!"

The entity hyper-extended their neck in the direction of the voice. Eden caught a distorted glimpse of Dom and Atherton's shocked expressions. She screamed anew, a fearful note injected deliberately by the entity. Likewise tears sprang to her eyes.

"Dom…" A pitiful whine.

Stephan relinquished his hold on her, owning to her cease struggle. "Do not be deceived. She was attempting to injure herself."

Free of his hold, the entity staggered them over to fling herself in Dominic's waiting arms. "He-e-e-e…attacked me. I couldn't get away."

"She attacked herself."

"And that necessitated such force holding her down?" Dominic couldn't help but be skeptical. It was ludicrous to think the slight woman trembling in his arms would require such maneuvers to restrain. But he was reminded of her relative ease in flipping him over not two days before.

"I was not wholly successful in protecting her." Still breathing heavily, Stephan gestured to her person.

"Liar!" She spewed at Stephan before turning pleading hazel eyes up to his face. "He fell on me with the intent to rape, thinking I would be too ashamed and frightened afterward to tell of it. He even went so far as to brag that even if I attempted to expose him, no one would believe it. Dominic, you believe me don't you?"

* * *

Dom hesitated, glancing from his brother's flush face and the ransacked library to Eden's sincere mien. His brother could be rash, impulsive even, though his recent behavior was anything but. Stephan *had* shown a certain predilection for Eden. Could it be possible? His heart railed against the idea. He would have to think on it logically, and at a less emotionally charged moment. Seeing his pregnant fiancée, whom he loved dearly, penned beneath his brother was not an image he wanted fresh in his mind when trying to decide who to believe.

"Cael...I-"

"Tread carefully." Came his brother's warning. "Stephan is out-of-sorts."

For the first time since he'd arrived on the estate his brother looked like his old self: hair messed, eyes ablaze with defiance and passion. Before the incident at the university, evenings had often found Stephan engaging in a philanthropic tête-à-tête. He loved politics and a spirited debate.

"If I *had* attacked her in a fit of lust and rage, this estate would be a smothering pile of cinders. Think on that."

Dominic swung a disheveled Eden up in his arms and turned to exit the library. "You said it yourself. Her presence helps keep your gift in check."

"That thing in your arms is not Eden." Stephan

countered. "Can't you feel the coldness, Dominic? The evil?"

Cael stepped forward, between the two brothers. Dominic felt the heat of disapproval trained on him. Heat?…come to think of it. The room had grown hot. With this realization, Dominic dropped a protesting Eden out of his arms and pivoted.

Cael put a hand to his chest to stop him. "This conversation is dangerous. Go. Have Ethan look her over. I'll speak with Stephan."

Dominic ignored the warning, brotherly concern winning out over his better judgment. "Stephan…"

His breathing was pronounced, erratic. Amber eyes alit with a luminous glow were peeled and wild…darting about, frantic almost. "Get out of here…Now!"

No sooner had the words left his mouth, the hearth erupted. Intense blue and white shards of heat shot out of the opening, blowing the grate with such force that it sliced through the air and clattered to the floor on the opposite side of the library.

Heat hit him in intense waves. His lungs felt like they were on fire with each arid intake. A cough overtook him. He snapped his eyes shut but not before they'd begun to sting and burn. The only sounds louder than the roar of flames and his own desperate attempts to breathe were Eden's hysterical shrieks. Eden. He must protect her.

"Cara, shhhh, you must calm down. The heat, it is intense but not unbearable."

She lay huddled on the floor, too panicked for his words to register. He collected his wits about him as best he could under the onslaught and took a deep scorching breath. It took some doing to get a secure enough grip to lift her writhing body. "Cael! Where are you?"

"Here." The answer was muffled but close.

"Where's Stephan?"

"Behind me somewhere. I cannot see."

"Try to calm him down."

He piggybacked her to Ethan and Kathleen. Normally, he would have looked before he leaped. He hoped that he wouldn't interrupt them in flagrante delecto.

As luck would have it, they were sitting alone in one of the parlors having afternoon tea. When he materialized with his burden, Kathleen upset the teapot...or so he thought from the reddish blur and swirl of fabric he could make out. Likewise, he heard crockery breaking. And he could smell the rich cinnamon-y aroma of Ethan's favorite chai.

"Dominic, what's happened? Is she injured?"

His ears still rang. It took him a few seconds to make out the words. He inhaled several gulps of cool refreshing air. Blinking maniacally to clear his bone-dry eyes, he succumbed to a fit of coughs. Ethan caught him as he stumbled.

Eden must have fainted. Her shrieks and struggles had ceased. He shoved her into Ethan's arms. "Take her, I haven't the time to explain. Kathleen, help Ethan. And keep away from the library until you hear from me. Is that clear?"

"Yes, of course, but...wait-"

He was back in the library an instant later, purposefully astraling adjacent to his younger brother. The heat was still intense, but not so much as before. The air scorched his nasal passages and throat, but he seemed able to keep his eyes open. Blinking often to keep them lubricated, he stepped forward.

"Stephan..." Though his vision was still blurry he was able to follow the tall figure with the shock of dark mahogany hair. It moved to and fro, near visible emissions coming off his body.

"Dom, no, you mustn't touch him." Cael's warning froze his movement. "He's lucid but for some reason he hasn't spoken. The effort may be too much."

"How can you tell?"

"When you left the heat crescendo-ed. He seemed to

notice my distress and blew out some of the windows so I could breathe. Plus, if you'll look to the hearth, the flames have subsided some. I think my voice, even just our being here helps him focus. He's easing down but it's going to take some time."

"Talking helps then." Dominic nodded. "We'll talk to him."

FORTY ONE

Ethan left the bedside and met him before he could set a full three feet into his chamber. "How is Stephan?"

Dom ran a frustrated hand through his hair. Singed bits disintegrated in his fingers and floated away. "He stalks about like an animal. He can't sit down, stand still, or even cover himself. Anything put against his skin is reduced to ash in a matter of seconds…including the floorboards, if he stops pacing." Dom closed his eyes, gesturing as a testament to his own uselessness. "I don't know, Ethan…he claims its normal. We've put him in the still room below levels as a precaution."

"What's so special about the still room?"

"It has a stone floor that he cannot burn through. After an hour Cael suggested we just let him walk it off. The room remains cool, so he must have his talent under *some* control."

Dom watched Ethan's thoughtful expression as he processed the information. "I'll take a look at him in the morning. What did you tell the servants about what happened in the library?"

"That Miss Prescott stumbled near the hearth with an oil lantern in her hand."

311

"Do you think that explanation will hold? This estate is equipped with gaslight. Why would anyone be using a portable oil lamp?"

Dominic shot him a caustic look. "No one is likely to question the eccentric Conte Ambrosi. Half the staff thinks I'm blind."

"True." The doctor turned his attention back to his patient. "She rests well."

Dominic followed his brother's gaze to the bed. The expression was anything but reassuring. "What is it?" He demanded, anxious.

Dominic watched Kathleen carefully arranging the sheet up to cover a dosing Eden. Ethan then pulled him over by the window, further out of earshot.

"I am unable to heal the newer wounds: the scorch marks on her palm and wrists, the scratches and bruising along her torso."

"How is that possible…" The doctor's worry mirrored his own.

"I don't know, but Dom, that's not even the strangest part. There are more scars than before, as from long-ago healed gashes. This is the first of my seeing them and I examined her not one week ago. The wound signature is completely different."

"Wound signature?"

"I determine a history of past diseases and injuries by touch. For instance, by touching a patient's foot, I can ascertain if that person had ever broken a bone in that area. By touching a scar I am able to ascertain the type and cause of the wound that resulted. As of right now Eden's wound signature is different. The Eden that I examined just now has never suffered a skeletal injury in her life. The Eden that I examined on all previous occasions dislocated her shoulder when she was five or six years old, and fractured her ankle in her early teen years."

"So what are you saying, that she is not Eden?"

"I am saying that her wound signature does not match

Eden's. Beyond that, I don't know."

"What of the child? Is it unharmed?"

Ethan gaped at him. "What child?"

"She is with child. Surely, you must have recognized her condition." When Ethan's expression conveyed no such knowledge, his fear doubled. "You can ascertain that she broke her foot a decade ago but you cannot sense the life growing inside her. Don't look at me like that, dammit! I have seen a change in her life force...something else intermingled with hers, like with Kathleen."

"Dominic, I don't know what you're seeing, but *that* woman lying on the bed over there is NOT with child. If you do not believe me, you have only a few days to wait before her monthly visitor arrives to confirm her lack of pregnancy. Although..." He hesitated. "There is evidence that she has given birth before...numerous times."

"That is a lie!"

"It is preposterous, I know." He agreed, hunching up his shoulders. "I'm at a loss to explain it. Her...ahem, hymen was quite firmly in place when she arrived on the estate. A broken hymen leaves a wound signature."

"English Ethan." He snapped.

"Her maidenhead was still in tact a month ago when I first examined her. It is quite impossible that she bore seven children since then, but nevertheless that is the echo I get from her signature."

"Will she...heal normally without your help?" Dominic's eyes tracked back to the sleeping form across the room, a frown marring his features.

The doctor waved away his concern. "Yes, yes, most certainly. There is nothing to be worried about on that front. I've put a salve on the burns, plus given her a sedative to alleviate her nerves and help her rest."

"Have someone alert me when she awakens."

"Of course." The doctor answered automatically even as he made his way back to his patient's bedside. "Oh, one other thing."

Dominic shrugged, indifferent to any further upset.

"I don't know if you've noticed but her hair is steadily darkening. I don't know how or why. But in conjunction with the other changes and it's almost as if she is... transforming into a different person."

* * *

Evening found Dominic swirling a snifter of much-needed after-dinner brandy. He dug his free hand through freshly cropped hair. He'd had Renfred snip off the ruined bits after he showered and donned fresh clothes. He watched as his brother Cael slipped into the study with a quiet calm that Dominic had come to appreciate. He, too, had bathed and changed.

"Renfred?" Dominic inclined a brow to his brother's shorter hair.

"Kathleen."

"Ahh." He nodded and went back to swirling his drink. Dom gestured for him to pour himself a snifter, and waited until he did before he asked, "What is it?"

"Stephan's asleep. Kathleen is beside herself with worry that he will catch a chill sleeping unclothed on the stone floor. I tried to explain to her that that was not likely."

Dom humph-ed and raised the glass to his lips. "Ethan informed you about Eden?"

"Yes."

He felt his brother's eyes following him, discreetly, of course. Cael was the master of covert observation. "I'm fine, Cael. There is no need to hover like a wet-nurse."

"I wasn't aware that's what I was doing." He countered as he took a sip of his brandy. "I thought we were having an evening drink. You are my brother. Is it so odd that I should seek your company?"

Dom sighed. The brandy had a rich flavor, almost florid, but he hardly noticed. "You were right, of course. This situation with Eden, and Stephan as well, is beyond us. I intend to seek Greyson's expertise. Since you are already familiar with the man and he with you, I would ask you to accompany me."

The mind doctor's only reaction was a lift of his brow. "When?"

His snifter resounded against the shiny metallic tray as he sat it down. "Tonight. And we will not have the luxury of being discreet...or polite."

"Very well, then."

Dominic watched him take another leisurely sip of brandy. "You don't seem surprised."

"You've shocked me so much of late until I have become adept at not reacting." He confessed with a half-smile.

Of late, he'd been surprising even himself. "I will need several hours of rest first. Please awaken me at midnight."

FORTY TWO

Tonight was the night she would free him of his demons. Once the doctor and his red-haired harpy had given up their bedside vigil, she'd been able to sneak down to the kitchens and collect the last tool. It wasn't a proper ceremonial dagger but it would have to do. She was also forced to substitute a porridge bowl for a chalice, mismatched dinner candles as incenses, pilfered ribbons and cravats for binding cord, and a woolen dressing gown as the ritual robe.

She crept into the darkened bedchamber draped in the hooded dressing gown, using stray shafts of moonlight to navigate. When she reached the bed on which he slumbered, knife clutched in one hand, she crotched. As silent as a shadow, she scurried about the floor drawing a pentagram with the bed as its center. The bed's circular shape would enhance the ritual's effectiveness. She would have liked to perform the séance in the music room, with the added power of the full moon beaming down from the skylight, the ceremonial circle set up where the pianoforte stood. The space, its architecture, the raised circle, the direct connection with celestial bodies all exuded ambient energy.

"Soon, my love."

When she was done, a flickering candle rested at each of the five points in the pentagram. Binding him was pointless, but for compliance with ritualistic tradition. Since she had already deviated from protocol she decided to adhere to as many of the sworn ways as possible. She waved a hand over his prone form. The counterpane and the sheet beneath levitated off the bed and floated noiselessly away. He squirmed under the chilly night air, twisting himself up in his nightclothes. An arm reached out as if seeking something but he did not awaken. She alit the bed, levitated his right ankle just enough to encircle it with a strip of cloth…likewise his left wrist, which hung off the edge. The circular bed was without posts so she connected each ankle with the opposite wrist by a connecting strip that crisscrossed his back.

She concocted a potion in the 'chalice' and placed it in the approximate center of the bed. His nose twitched, followed by a muffled grunt. The smoke emanating from the candles and the concoction's sharp aroma threatened to rouse him. If she delayed any longer she'd waste her advantage, and she meant to keep the upper hand long enough to accomplish her goal. She flipped the hood of the dressing gown over her head and arranged herself so that she levitated, seated Indian-style, over the exact center of the circle within the pentagram.

She began the harmonious vocalization, a string of mystical prayers and phrases murmured over and over, specifically to raise and channel psychic and spiritual energies alike. The power she would need to trap the spirit inside the body long enough to cast out the demon inside him once and for all. Her voice deep and throaty and touched with the fervor of madness rose with the power of the incantation, climbing ominously towards its zenith. Almost there. The power surged within and with it she shook off the last remnants of the sniveling one. She had complete physical and mental control over her conduit...her old abilities were not just restored but magnified. Doubled, no tripled, and still growing.

* * *

Dominic awakened to a chill crawling along his skin. Odd. It had been years since he'd had a nightmare. He shook his head to clear away the dream's thrall. His recent trip to Italy and the business with Gabriel had trudged up more than just memories. He could almost hear the humming in his ear from the...wait, not humming, chanting and this time it was no dream. Someone was chanting. But who would be in his room besides...

"Eden?"

Blinking and disoriented, he tried to turn but found his hands and feet were bound together. When he tugged with wrist or ankle he was at war with the other and doing so only served to tighten the cords holding him. The droning above him continued in a deep accented voice. He recognized the invocation as one the Witch used on him years ago. There was something in the air, a heavy scent that reeked of candles...or perhaps incense. He caught sight of a lit taper on the floor at the point of a triangle and a second one a yard or so away. A pentagram. Panic arose.

"Who is there?!" His voice trembled.

"Don't worry my darling, it will be over soon." A woman's voice, familiar.

His breathing grew rapid and shallow as the horrors of his childhood swallowed him.

He longed to wipe his eyes. They were beginning to water and burned. The chanting started up again. He had to get a'hold of himself, his fears, push them aside long enough to free himself and deal with the woman. Logic dictated it must be Eden, probably in the thrall of another of her visions...or at the mercy of some unseen force. Panicky, he flashed into the astral, disintegrating the bonds at his wrists and ankles. Nothing but souls survived a trip to the astral realm.

Trepidation beat at his brow like the heat of midday. The essence nearest to his was not Eden's. The second essence he had noticed before had grown considerably. It eclipsed Eden, reducing her to a mere appendage...not unlike the anomaly he'd observed in the twins. Trepidation turned to fear. The dominating essence was a monstrous thing, opaque and foreboding; with a flurry of crazed colors and distorted spheres that continuously elongated until they tore in two and converged on other disquieting globules. It was an essence he hadn't seen in years, one he'd recognize anywhere, his worse nightmare...come true.

Dominic returned to the corporal world, face up on the bed with a woman hovering mid-air over his chest like a djinni from Scheherazade's thousand and one nights. He just did make out her features in the eerie flicker of light.

"Mama?"

The chanting ceased. She shrieked and hissed away from his visage, flying backward in a nimble maneuver to land in a defensive stance. The hood of the dressing gown slipped from her head. Her raven-hair and night eyes were much the same as he remembered. The telltale streak of white-blond at her temple and the tiny hazel flecks embedded in her irises, the only proof that the body she inhabited was not her own. Stephan had been right. Eden was possessed by something evil.

"There is no escape this time. I will send you to hell where you belong!"

She lunged forward. He caught the silver glint of a blade as she sliced it towards him. Pinned to the bed by an invisible force, he did the only thing he could...he astraled. But that was as far as he got. She must have erected a psychic barrier of some sort. He could not travel beyond a certain distance, the outer edge of the pentagram's points his suspected.

The one thing she was never able to do in her lifetime was capture him after the onset of his astraling ability. She must have grown stronger in death…or perhaps she was using some unrealized talent of Eden's, which would explain why his mother had chosen to possess her. Or, perhaps, it had nothing to do with Eden at all, maybe she just needed someone close to him, who had access to his person, someone he trusted, someone he loved…

In either case, she'd trapped him. He couldn't move about on the astral to warn his brothers or to escape. Neither could he reappear on the corporal or she would maim him with the blade. She'd dipped it in poison, no doubt. He supposed he could try to overpower her, a ludicrous idea given her telekinetic abilities. He abandoned the thought. Perhaps if he shimmered directly behind her and caught her by surprise… The problem was, shimmering wasn't that precise. He had no way to discern which direction she faced from the featureless canvas of the astral. She could be constantly shifting her position, anticipating such a move. No, that would never do.

He was safe for now, but he'd have to come up with a viable plan soon. He couldn't remain on the astral too long; what would become of Eden in the meantime? Having her essence displaced by his mother's did not bode well for her continued health he suspected. Then, there was Cael to consider. One of his brothers would come to check on him soon. Stephan could handle himself if necessary. Ethan, though no match for Lillian, at least had self-healing capability. But Cael was defenseless against a psychic threat.

Cael! As if the very thought of him conjured his essence, Dominic noticed that his most vulnerable brother approached them. Dom had anticipated having more time to strategize, although he supposed several hours could have passed in the waking world. Hell and damnation! He'd have to shimmer in to warn him. With any luck maybe Lillian would be more willing to take a stab at him rather than Cael.

He waited until he saw a simultaneous shift in emotion of both Cael and his mother's essence, predicting that to be the exact moment that his brother entered the room and the one took notice of the other. He shimmered, landing on his feet beside the bed, behind and to the right of where Lillian hovered.

"Run, Cael! She will immobilize you with her mind. It's useless to combat her."

The younger man appeared not to hear him. His amber gaze fixed on the woman above the bed.

"Cael, are you listening to me? I cannot move beyond the chalk outline even on the astral plane. If you can still move, leave now before she——"

"Michael, my precious little love." She called to him in a sweet voice, cream put out to bait a kitten. "Don't be frightened. It's mama. Come to me."

"Mama..." Cael took a step forward, horror and disbelief streaked across his face. He turned to Dominic, confused. "Dom, I don't...understand."

For the first time since their childhood, Cael seemed to desperately need him. A memory hit him square in the face of a white blond Cael, two years old staring up at him teary-eyed after scraping his knee, a similar expression on his face. It was a humbling experience.

"Michael...Mama needs your help."

"Cael! Don't you *dare*!" Dominic spat. "Turn around and get the hell out of here."

Dom would have ripped off his nightclothes to remind him of exactly the sort of monster Lillian was, but she had frozen him again. Cael, however, appeared in complete control of his movement. He couldn't understand it. Why didn't she simply seize him with her mind? Unless...she wasn't able to. Perhaps by confining him to the inside of the pentagram, she'd confined herself as well.

"Remember what she did to me, Cael."

He could only watch and hope as his brother shook

himself and stumbled backward. "Dom, astral out of there. She's got a knife!"

"I cannot astral beyond the pentagram." Yes, that had to be it, he thought. By limiting him she limited herself as well. "I don't think her ability extends outside it either, otherwise you'd already be at her mercy."

She laughed, a brittle humorless sound. "Very well then, I'll have to save him myself."

Dom felt a ghastly sharp pain in his right eye before she allowed him to collapse out of her control onto the floor. The triangular tip of the knife cracked the delicate bones of his eye-socket. He screamed in agony as his vision died in that eye, tasting the blood that ran down the side of his face and over his lips.

"DOM!" Cael started for him.

"Don't. You cannot help me."

Cael halted at his words. "Tell me what to do then."

The blade dislodged a short distance preparing to strike again. His mother hadn't moved from her position.

"Find...Grey...son." He shimmered back to the astral, narrowing escaping a second jab. The stabbing pain magnified to nightmarish intensity, skewing his mind into a silent scream. Eons pasted before his thoughts could coalesce and block out the agony. When he was able to bear it with some level of finesse, the first thing he noticed was Cael once again approaching...with Stephan and Ethan in tow. Bloody Hell, what did they aim to do? Cael and Stephan didn't realize what they were up against, but dammit Ethan should know better!

He could not let her hurt them. He shimmered in but did not uncloak himself. The haze of pain cleared, and his thoughts sharpened. Invisibility would make him a more difficult target. She might get in a few good jabs, but if she couldn't locate him she wouldn't be able to immobilize him again. Anything to keep her focus away from his brothers.

The knife hovered mid-air between the ceiling and

floor, along with its mistress, keen and ready to strike. Lillian stalked with the cold, predatory stance of a cobra. Her eyes were black pits with no iris. Her elegant neck moved in trance-like undulations.

Ethan's gaze riveted to the spill of crimson below her on the floor. "You said it wasn't that serious."

"I said it was *fixable*." Cael tossed over his shoulder, before addressing Stephan. "Are you sure you can handle this?"

"Why ask questions you already know the answer to." He replied.

Cael turned back to his older brother. "Ethan-"

"If we don't do something, she'll kill him." Ethan pointed out. "With *that* wound, how long do you think he can stay in the astral realm? If he passes out—"

"Ethan's right." The blade stabbed out into the air missing his good eye, but slicing the lid open. More pain, so much pain... Dominic dipped and dodged, the bloody mess making it difficult to see even out of his good eye.

"Dom, are you all right?" Ethan aimed at him.

"Fine." The tip of the blade nicked his shoulder that time.

"Keep still you fiend!"

Stephan stepped forward wordlessly, brandishing a hand out front.

"Be ready." Cael advised.

A wave of heat rolled over the room. The candles adorning the Pentagram liquefied into five puddles of gooey wax. The next instant flames burst forth, sending trails sprawling in all directions. Most so weak and aimless that they winkled out within seconds. The strongest strain, a scarlet-yellow plume, ran across the floor like a swift-fleeing rodent and connected the empty space between the pentagram's points, creating a circular wall of flames.

Lillian toppled off her throne of air. The knife, too, clattered to the floor. Dom wiped the veil of blood from his eye and watched with half-vision while his mother shrieked and writhed. She darted this way and that. The blazing heat swayed whichever way she went, a taunting shadow licking at her flesh. She screamed an inhuman howl of madness, clawing at herself in a frenzy to elude the flames.

"Astral now!" Ethan ordered. "We think it's the chanting that strengthens the pentagram, creating the barrier."

Self-preservation propelled him back onto the astral plane. Agony dogged him even the short time required to close the distance between him and his brothers. He materialized only semi-conscious behind Ethan, just short of the chamber door.

"Leave...now. Circle broken." One hand over his ruined eye, he fumbled for the doorknob, his free hand slick with blood from his good eye. It took him several tries before Cael reached around him.

Cael caught him under his shoulders, steadying him. "Stephan, we're leaving."

"Go!"

"Remember, she has to breathe." Ethan emphasized. "For all we know if she dies, so does Miss Prescott."

"Be quick. Without Eden, I cannot keep it level for very long."

FORTY THREE

The library still lay in chaos. A charred pile of bricks where the fireplace once stood, blackened half-melted glass shards littered the floor on one side of the room. Someone had covered the hole where the window had been with a tarp.

"Stop. Ethan, do it now." Weak but determined, Dom shook off Cael's steadying arm and stumbled to the ash-covered sofa and sat. "Who's idea was it anyway to pit Stephan against her?"

"His, and for what it's worth, we don't like it anymore than you do." Cael stated as he moved aside to let Ethan by. "We couldn't think of another way. Stephan's the only one of us with an aggressive gift."

Dom dropped his hand and let Ethan exam the damage. He rested his head against the back rim of the couch and breathed easier as the soothing waves of Ethan's gift swept over his injuries. "Let us hope she doesn't gather her wits enough to thwart him before we return with Greyson." A blurry image began to flicker in his injured eye. He tried to raise his head only to be pushed back down. "Ethan?"

"Almost done, lie still."

"You cannot be serious." Cael stared at Dominic incredulously. "You're too weak to shimmer two and then shimmer back three. Plus, how do we even know Greyson can help?"

"I don't bloody know!" Dom snapped back. "You're the one who's been extolling his praises as the foremost expert on adeptness and psychological science."

"That was before our deranged mother possessed your fiancée's body and started knife-wielding from beyond the grave." Cael returned dryly.

Just then there came a discreet knock on the crumbling shards of wood still passing for a door.

"What?!" Dom called out.

He heard several planks fall to the floor. "Ahem, Master Ambrosi forgive me for disturbing you. A guest has just arrived. I was obliged to-"

"Get rid of whoever it is." Dominic waved a hand, the torn bloody sleeve of his nightshirt dangling off his forearm.

"That was my first inclination sir, but-"

"Hell and damnation, Renfred!" His head snapped up despite Ethan's protest. The butler had stuck his ancient face just within the threshold. He could make out enough to know that Renfred was his usual portrait of refined dignity. Dominic cringed at the thought of his own appearance. "Do I look like I can spare a moment to entertain just now?"

"Of course not, sir, and I do hope the injury is nothing serious, but your brother insisted." He stood aside to reveal someone standing behind him.

"My——what?!" A towering blur appeared where Renfred had been. "Ethan, my eyes——"

"Should clear in just a moment."

"Where are his spectacles?"

That voice.

"Gabriel?" The next instant he found himself staring at Muse resting in the crook of his brother's elbow, and the falcon perched over his right shoulder. "What the devil are you doing here? You're supposed to be comatose in Italy."

"Nice to see you, too, Dominic." Gabriel quipped as he let the cat down and tilted his head to the bird. The falcon gave a quarrelsome squawk. "Gideon is being difficult. I am not at all certain he will grace us with his presence. But then, you know how he is about carriages."

"Lillian's back." Dominic stated baldly.

"Yes, I know." The taller man did not flinch. "I am relieved that her attempt on your life was unsuccessful. We had hoped to arrive in time to prevent it, but no matter, all is well."

"Not quite. Didn't you see—"

"I saw nothing beyond your death. It was a nightmare I could not shake off until recently. By the by, where is Stephan? I had thought to see him while we were here."

"They will have to fill you in. Enough Ethan." Dominic batted the doctor away, stood and held his arm for the falcon. The bird alit his shoulder instead. "Gideon will accompany me. That way I'll only have to shimmer two back. Is that an acceptable alternative, Cael?"

"I suppose it'll have to be."

"For propriety's sake, at least don a dressing gown before you go."

Only Ethan would be concerned with decorum at such a moment. Dominic accepted the gown the doctor removed from his own shoulders, delaying just long enough to shove his arms in the sleeves. The falcon protested being upset.

"Simmer down, we're going."

* * *

Greyson's essence wasn't difficult to locate. He remembered it well from his one glimpse. Thankfully, the essence seemed fairly isolated, although Dom noted that there was an unusual density of souls in the not-so-immediate vicinity…more than could be explained away as servants. No one man, living alone, would require so numerous a staff as this.

He slid off the astral in what appeared to be a gentleman's dressing room. Light shone in from the partially opened door. The falcon vacated his shoulder. Dom felt rather than saw his brother's transformation.

"Nice of you to join me, Gideon."

"Dom, this room is the size of a coffin."

"We will not be here long." He inclined his head to the neatly hung rack of shirts and trousers to their right. "It might make our convincing him to come back with us easier if you were wearing more than a fig leaf."

"Why do we need him?" The rustle of clothing mingled with his words.

"We have to evict Lillian from Eden's body before she does irreparable damage. Cael thinks he could help." Dominic took the opportunity to creep closer to the adjoining door while he waited for the rustling to stop.

"Are you suggesting an… *exorcism?*"

Being reminded of the countless tortures he endured in the name of the process, he too flinched away from the idea. "If Greyson cannot offer an enlightened approach I don't see any alternative."

The gentleman in question did not react in the shocked manner Dominic had expect at being confronted with two uninvited guests breaching the sanity of his private chambers.

Greyson sat propped up in a massive four-poster bed of dyed-black wood. He calmly put aside the volume in his lap and stood. "Conte Ambrosi, this is a surprise." The professor took in the second man with a cursory glance. "I don't believe we have met."

"Uh, this is Gideon–" Dominic supposed he ought to at least solicit his willingness before he sank to kidnapping. "My brother. Forgive me, but we haven't the time for pleasantries. There is a situation that requires your assistance. Help me and I will grant you the audience you requested."

"And if I choose not to?"

"I'll have to insist." Gideon stepped forward. The floor-skirting grey robe he'd chosen only heightened his sinister hint of violence.

The professor seemed to take the threat in stride. "Let me just get dressed and we'll take my carriage."

"No time for carriages and fancy dress. As my brother explained, time is in limited supply. You will accompany us, *now*."

Dom did not miss Gideon's shudder at the mention of a carriage.

"Very well then. Just let me collect my journals and we'll be off." The professor waved away Gideon's protest with an impatient hand, and strolled forth. "They are imperative if your problem is of a psychic nature. It's where I document the whole of my knowledge and research. An encyclopedia of psychic phenomena, if you will."

Much too easy. Dominic had to wonder at his willingness. "You're not even curious how we plan to transport you or how we managed to elude your vast staff to gain entry to your bedchamber. "

"I won't be coy. I know that you are adept...and I suspect that it runs in the family." He eyed Gideon warily, as he came to a small writing desk situated in the corner. "That is why I wished to speak with you. I have committed to a great task, part of which includes identifying and classifying psychic abilities and their associated cognitive abnormalities. When I'm done, there will be a taxonomic and nomenclature system for the science of psionics, a factual guide to the—"

Dominic looked to the three leather-bound tomes Greyson collected from the desktop. "Is that them?"

"Yes."

"Good. Let's go."

* * *

It was a testament to his stubbornness that he did not collapse when the threesome materialized, to his surprise, outside his bedchamber door. Gideon didn't need to be shielded because unlike other animals, he possessed a soul even as the falcon, so piggybacking him was effortless. It was the energy he'd extended masking Greyson's books that had drained him. Shielding inanimate objects always proved difficult.

Cael and Ethan rushed at him. The falcon squawked testily and flew to join Muse at Gabriel's side.

"That's it. No more astraling tonight." Ethan declared.

"Where is Gideon?" Greyson looked around, tensing at the site of Gabriel several yards away. He fumbled with the books in his hands, trying to open one whilst holding on to the other two. "How did he...Yes, of course, I have documented several cases-"

"Gideon's mood has not improved." Gabriel lifted a hand to accommodate the bird, before acknowledging the newcomer. "I am *Gabriel*. Though we are identical, people do not often confuse us. Since we have only just met I will overlook it."

"I am Professor Greyson." Greyson returned, bewildered and still battling to keep hold of all three books. "Uh, forgive me. I did not realize there were two of you...that you were twins, I mean. I meant no offense."

The door just beyond them bulged out, rending the air with a sharp popping noise.

"What is that?" The professor stumbled away from the buckling wood, loosing his grip on two of the volumes.

"We're out of time." Cael's pleading gaze alternated from Dominic to the professor. "We have to get him out of there."

"Who's in there?" Greyson asked no one in particular.

"Stephan. He has manifested the ability to manipulate

fire with his mind."

"Pyrokenesis." Greyson's face lit up like a child at Christmastime as he turned to eye the rending shards flaking off the doorjamb. "Firestarters are extremely rare...and very volatile. Pyrokenesis is one of several emotion-linked abilities. Emotion-linked abilities are much less psychologically damaging and less draining. Most pyrokinetics do not even—"

Dominic brought him up short. "That's all very interesting, Professor Greyson, but how do we help him control it?"

"Right, yes." He redirected his attentions to the remaining tome in his hands. "Well, it has been my observation that the older a person is at manifestation, the more difficult the ability is to direct. Well-adjusted adepts manifest at or even before puberty. At what age would you say your brother Stephan manifest?"

"Two and twenty."

"Oh dear...I had not thought it so late as that." He dropped the volume he held and instead picked up one from the floor, flipping through it. "Having met only one firestarter in this lifetime, I must confess my knowledge is limited on the subject. Let's see, according to the notes I made, he shouldn't restrain the impulse. In this case, it caused a dangerous build-up of pressure...to explosive proportions. The key element to her control was balance. She described it as 'a boomerang cast at just the right angle so that it returns to it's bearer with a neat catch'...if that makes any sense to you."

"No," Cael stepped nearer the chamber door. "But, Stephan will probably know what you mean. Stephen! Can you hear me?! Dom..."

"I'll astral." He did not wait for the inevitable protest from Ethan.

The scene mimicked the one in the library the day before. Both windows were reduced to charred holes with bits of shattered glass strewn on the sill and beyond. The flames were no longer confided to the ring imprisoning their mother, but engulfed the room entirely. He couldn't see what had become of Lillian, couldn't see anything with the intense heat crawling along his skin, burning his lashes and brows, drying out his eyes. Only blind luck or perhaps Stephan's quick instincts drew him to a flame-retardant spot on the warm stone floor. He closed his eyes against the heat, and breathed the dragon's breath through his mouth to spare his nasal passage a certain scorching.

"Stephan, don't fight it! Greyson says the more you restrain your ability the more it slips beyond your control. Let go and it will peak and snap back to you." He swiveled this way and that, not sure of his brother's exact location in the room. His voice grew more hoarse with each syllable.

"Stephan!" A deep-throated cough mangled his next words. He wondered if Stephan could even comprehend him. "Don't fight...Can't yooo...feel...growing wilder? Meant to be thrown...like fishing... reeled back in..."

A blinding flash of heat walloped him like a boxer's fist, knocking him backward. His legs buckled as Dante's inferno blazed around him, a teeming mob on the verge of violence.

FORTY FOUR

"Are you alright?" Cael asked, while the twins hovered, Gideon shirtless.

Ethan answered for him. "He's fine. The brows and lashes will grow back."

Stephan, bare-assed and sheepish, apologized as he melted back into the darkness. "Sorry, Dom."

He sat up to find himself covered with a blanket atop the pianoforte in the music room. The moon beamed down soft shadowy light, which partially illuminated the room in a broad central circle, leaving the corners steeped in darkness. Greyson stood on the opposite end of the pianoforte thumbing through one of his volumes.

"Good, you're awake." The professor did not look up as he spoke. "We'll need the six of you if this is going to work."

"If *what* is going to work?" He asked.

"The exorcism. We have to expel your mother as soon as possible. Due to the nature of their ability, necromantics are extremely vulnerable to possession...*and* unfortunately prone to suicide, but we'll save that for later."

"Necromantics?" His eyes sought Cael.

"Dominic...Eden is adept. Her gift has to do with

calling forth and communicating with disembodied spirits."

"Our psychopathic mother's, for instance." Gideon injected a bit of the macabre.

Greyson looked up from his journal. "Uh, no, I don't actually think it is that simple." He explained. "The souls of the departed are confined to either Heaven or Hell. The evil that we are dealing with has to have a demonic component as well. What I believe is that-"

"Now, isn't really the ideal time to flesh out your theory, is it?" Ethan looked askance, shifting his weight from one foot to the other.

Gideon pinned Ethan with a wooden stare. "Perhaps it's more appropriately discussed next week, at the celebratory dinner…or rather the funeral services, depending, of course, on the outcome of tonight's…*festivities*."

Ethan winced. Cael exhaled a long-suffering sigh. Greyson glanced from one brother to the other, undecidedly.

"Gideon, please, don't be flippant." Gabriel reproached his twin in a quiet beseeching tone. "A woman's life is at stake here."

"Yes, and we could be helping her along to the netherworld with this profane witchery. Tampering with her soul is blasphemous."

"Enough." Dominic ended the discussion with blunt authority that no one dared question. "I will decide what is best. Cael?"

Cael ran his hand through frustration-mangled hair, "Dom, if we don't evict Lillian and whatever demon spawn she is in league with…He, she or *it* could permanently displace Eden's essence."

Greyson concurred, "And you should know, the process is fatal. Her body will die without its rightful soul."

"How much time?"

"Exact stipulations are difficult to—" Greyson began.

Dominic cut him off. "Cael, how long?"

"We don't know. It could be happening already."

"Then what are we waiting for, where is Eden?"

Ethan pointed downward. "Beneath you on the floor. Luckily, she fainted when the heat intensified." He said, then added guiltily. "I chloroformed her just to make sure; we could not risk her coming to before we were ready."

Gideon stood in silence, an unfathomable expression masking his thoughts.

"The pianoforte will need to be moved." Gabriel, ever the practical twin, stated matter-of-factly.

"Allow me." Dom blinked to the astral, disintegrating the massive instrument the same way he'd dispensed with his mother's bindings.

"We could have moved it the normal way." Ethan chided when Dominic collapsed back on the empty circular platform beside an unconscious Eden. "You'll do her no good by pushing yourself to the brink of exhaustion."

"Don't astral again." Cael ordered with a hint of foreboding. "We need you lucid and your ability in tact. Once she comes to, it will take all of you to keep Lillian's ability at bay long enough to exorcise her."

A harried Greyson lay sprawled at the fringe of the platform clutching his journal and eyeing Dom. "You might have warned me."

But Dominic's mind was riveted to Eden. Her slim, be-robed figure lay facedown, the mass of blonde hair skewing his view. Her dainty arm once a clean and translucent pale reached out, limp and dirtied with soot. He ached to hold her, comfort her, and confess to her how much she meant to him. He'd never gotten the chance and now, perhaps he never would.

Just then, his mind seized on her hair. Blonde. "Her hair..." Maybe the exorcism wouldn't be necessary. He turned pleading eyes on the professor. "Doesn't that mean she is normal again?"

"In my experience, uninvited guests do not leave voluntarily."

Dom's face fell. "Tell me what to do to get her back."

FORTY FIVE

Eden's limp unconscious form lay upon the center of the circular platform, with Ethan and Dominic kneeling beside her. Gideon and Gabriel stood like sentries, each stationed as points of a human triangle at the outer edge of the platform...while Cael backed away from the third point. "It'll have to be Ethan or Stephan. I am not adept."

Stephan spoke from a shadowy corner of the room. "If Lillian breaks loose I have to be able to contain her. My control is dubious at best; it will require my complete focus. It's the only way we have of combating her mental abilities."

"And we need Dr. Raine poised to attend to any injuries that might arise." Greyson explained. "Any one of us might be in dire need of medical attention if anything...unexpected, happens. I need hardly add that we've no idea what condition the young lady will be in once we've evicted her uninvited guest."

"Yes, I appreciate all that, but we may not be able to evict Lillian at all unless she is surrounded by forces as powerful as she... *adepts*." Cael warned. "I would be a weak link in the chain."

"Not necessarily." Greyson posed. "I have done

337

extensive research on heredity, insanity and adeptness. All five of your siblings are adept which means more likely than not, you are a strong latent. There is a school of thought that suggests *all* non-adepts are merely latents who have yet to manifest, but that's neither here nor there. For *our* purpose a strong latent is a workable substitution for a manifest adept. It's a risk, yes, but a calculated one."

Dominic forced himself to pull his gaze away from Eden's lifeless form. He was half afraid she would fade away from him if he averted his attention even for a moment. The fear was crippling almost. All his will and his energies were focused on keeping her alive even as he looked to his worried brother. "Cael, I suggest we trust him. Like you said, we are out of our depth."

"*Dominic?*" Gideon addressed his brother, with a pointed look.

A charged silence hung between them, before he answered. "I *know*, Gideon, but I have to try."

"Hurry, she's coming to." Ethan rose.

Resigned, Cael ambled into position as the third point in the triangle. Greyson nodded for the remaining three to take their positions around the room. Stephan remained out of sight, obscured in the murky depths of one of the corners, where he could keep a watchful eye. Ethan stepped just outside the triangle, off the platform. Greyson, too, stood just outside the circle, but was a ways from the doctor. Dom positioned himself in the eye of the triangle and carefully scooped Eden's wan form into his arms. The flowing silk of her hair tickling the skin of his chest and shoulders where her head rested. He glanced down at the gentle moan from her to see her eyes twitch beneath her lids.

"She's coming to."

"Start the verse." Greyson directed immediately.

And they did, but instead of the sinister mumble of foreign syllables he had awoken to earlier, the four of them, Dom, Cael and the twins, recited a clear and resonant rendition of the twenty-third Psalms. Dom chose a scripture that had always brought him peace. He prayed that it would provide a powerful force of good, born of God's Holy Spirit that would protect and strengthen them as they fought to expel the evil spirit threatening to devour his Eden.

Her lids fluttered open in the middle of the second recitation. Dom willed himself to stay focused, continuing to repeat the verse along with his brothers.

"Yea, though I walk through the valley of the shadow of death. I will fear no evil…"

For a moment, Dom relaxed as Eden's warm hazel eyes blinked back at him. He let his arm under her knee slide down until her feet touched the floor. He kept both arms around her to make certain she had the strength to stand on her own.

He broke off the recitation, as she stood by herself, serene, blinking up at him, both of her pale slender hands rested lightly on his bare chest. "Eden…"

"NO! Don't stop. You must keep repeating–"

Greyson never finished his sentence. In a split second, the pupils of her eyes pooled outward, a spreading blackness that engulfed the irises. Her lips curled back to reveal teeth poised to bite. She unleashed a vampire's hiss at the same instant she clawed at his chest with hands that had just moments before been almost caressing. Dominic stumbled backward at the suddenness and strength of the attack.

Inky black, rope-like hair flew wildly about as they wrestled, her a seething harpy, all claws and biting teeth. She came at him kicking, and screeching, with unnatural strength, while he strove to contain her without harming her person. Within minutes, his chest and upper arms were regaled with swollen bite marks, and long welt-like scratches oozing blood…most in various stages of healing. Ethan, powerful enough that he did not need direct skin contact, effected immediate repairs as new injuries appeared.

"The Lord is my shepherd; I shall not want..."

Cael, Gideon and Gabriel continued to recite. The three of them were stationed around the struggling pair like sentries protecting the king.

"Keep it up! Don't break the trinity!" Greyson barked out. "It's the only hope we have of keeping her confined."

Ethan watched the tussling twosome, worried. "He will not be able to control her forever...not without hurting her." He said, looking to Greyson.

Stephan spoke for the first time. "Something is off. Why isn't she using her telekinetic abilities like before?"

"Eden's fighting it." Ethan concluded aloud. "Look, the hair, there are streaks of blonde threading through it. There must be some sort of power struggle going on."

Greyson frowned as he acknowledged the brothers' astute observations. "In order for this to work, Lillian has to surface...completely. Otherwise, it might kill them both."

Dom caught the grain of the conversation. "Greyson?!"

At the seventh recitation of the twenty-third psalms, a current rippled through the room. Dom could feel it surrounding them. A wall of pure psi energy, invisible, intangible but as real as any brick and mortar barricade...impenetrable. Its emanations resonated with his own as well as his brothers' psychic ability, creating a pyramid of both protection and imprisonment around the four brothers and Eden.

"I can't heal him anymore." Ethan announced. "Something is blocking me. Greyson?"

"It's working."

Dominic managed to encase both her wrists in a semi-quelling grip...pausing the onslaught temporarily. "The wall is up...I can feel it. Tell me when?!"

"Not yet." Greyson stayed him. "Your mother's essence has to take full possession...to maximize exposure."

"Eden!" Dom shook the she-thing, on the off-chance that Eden had even the tiniest level of awareness of what was happening to her. "You have to let go. Don't fight it. Let her take over, Cara."

* * *

She felt...faint, weightless. Her consciousness ripped away from her body with a violent, disorienting tear. The darkness, a spreading evil, seeped into her mind like blood soaking a crisp white cloth. She clawed for a lifeline, an anchor, some thread of reality to which to cling...even as her thoughts began to fade away like dreams forgotten in the morning, her emotions deadened, her sight dimmed. Her very breath hitched, the darkness was so suffocating.

You have to let go. Don't fight it. Let her take over, Cara...

Her last vestige of hope died...She, the soul called Eden, was lost. No use fighting anymore. Perhaps she would find peace in death. The void seeped in, unbidden. Everything around her deadened...her hold on life was so slight. Colors paled to grey, voices faded to silence, the pain and pleasures of life numbed to nothing. No landscape...no time... Her mind screamed at the horror of knowing she would soon be no more.

* * *

The next instant, Eden stilled...struggling no more. Dom doubled over from a telekinetic knee to the stomach.

"Now, Dominic! Do it, NOW!"

He vanished into invisibility, temporarily pre-empting any further telekinetic strikes. In the close space inside the triangle, there were few places to hide, even invisible as he was. Lillian shrieked and struck out blindly with telekinetic probes, one of which glazed his hip as he dropped down to the floor and rolled left to avoid her. He'd only have one, maybe two attempts before she located him...

"He restoreth my soul: he leadeth me in the paths of righteousness for his name's sake..."

Dom inhaled deep, gathering all his psi energies, and focused them on Eden. He'd never tried to send anyone to the astral realm unaccompanied before. Centered, calm and focused, he felt the simultaneous waver in both his hearing and vision that signal the beginnings of Astral travel. He reached out his hand, grasped her ankle, projecting her onto the astral while keeping a thin psychic 'rope' around her ankle so he could pull her back. Amazing...He felt a violent psychic ripple wash over him, and reverse ricochet back over him like river rapids crashing against rock. The force knocked him forward. His energy flickered dangerously close to winkling out. He concentrated his efforts into one final surge, to jerk the rope...just before he collapsed in a dead faint.

FORTY SIX

"Dom? Dom, can you hear me?"

Consciousness prodded at him. The first thing he became aware of were someone's fingers poking him in the throat, just beneath his jawline...Ethan checking for a pulse, no doubt. Then palming his forehead, peeling back an eyelid, and finally tapping his wrist. "Hmm...his pupils are non-responsive."

He kept his eyes closed.

"I *know* I saw him move. His eyes shifted under the lids." He recognized Eden's worried voice. "This cannot be normal. He's been unconscious for three days."

"Asleep, not unconscious—" Dom heard Greyson's airy tone launch into a scholarly explanation of the differential between the two states. He was further from the bed, judging by his voice. Egads! The man was exhausting. Did he always speak with such...encyclopedic depth, as if he must give every last detail of his knowledge to even the most mundane of topics. "Do not worry, Ms. Prescott. I can assure you, it is quite common among adepts. He is not just recovering from a physical exhaustion, but a psychic burnout as well. He needs rest, mind and body. I have seen adepts on overload sleep for a full week."

"Is that true?" The angle of her voice changed, she must have turned to speak in another direction, Dom thought, possibly taking a step in that direction.

"I don't... *tired*, easily." Ahh, Stephan was present...holding up the wall in a corner as usual. "I have never required sleep beyond a normal night's rest."

"It is different for everyone, Ms. Prescott." Greyson again, speaking from further away.

"If that's true then how do you know this is normal for Dominic?"

"Eden, what Professor Greyson means, is that it's too early to panic. He has seen cases where this amount of sleep is not harmful." Cael, and he was to the left somewhere close. Dom inclined his head to get a better angle.

"Dom?" Cael's voice redirected, closer still. Of course, Cael would be the first to notice he was awake.

"Cael." His voice was hoarse from non-use. He slit his eyes open. "E-than... everyone well?"

Again, he felt a shift in the voices, their locations. Someone moved closer to him. He couldn't see who...couldn't see anything but shadowy blurs.

"Dom?" Cael hovered, the blur on the left.

"Dominic?" Ethan sounded worried, confused. "Dom—"

"Too bright." He closed his eyes deliberately, hoping Ethan would get the hint. "Light is too bright. Stephan, dim it please."

He had no idea if Stephan dimmed the lights or not; the only thing he could make out was blurred lateral movements. Damn, he wished they would stop playing ring-around-the-rosy.

"Better?" Stephan spoke a moment latter from the same position. "Ethan has your spectacles, would you like them?"

"Yes, and yes."

Thankfully, he felt Ethan put the specs in place on the

bridge of his nose. The rest of his body seemed to be in perfect working order, he noted as he sat up in the bed. "Ethan, I'm hungry. Have Nell send something up."

"Of course." And then footsteps. So far, so good. He'd be willing to bet that Kathleen was not present. Nothing would have kept her silent this long. That left Cael, Stephan, Greyson, Eden…and possibly the twins. Neither twin was chatty so their lack of conversation did not necessarily mean they weren't present. He'd have to get rid of Greyson before he addressed Gideon or Gabriel just in case.

"Dom, are you alright? You've been out for three days."

"Yes, cara, I am well." He reassured her, smiling, lulling his head. "Just tired. Stephan, I trust you have been attending to my affairs during my convalescence?"

"Yes, shall I catch you up?"

"Later, after I eat. Also, can you let Kathleen know that she is needed here, please." Dom angled towards where he last heard Greyson's voice. "Professor, I trust you will not report Ms. Prescott's momentary lack of chaperon to the social reformers? I would hate to have a repeat of your previous visit."

A chuckle followed his good-natured jibe. "I didn't see anything…compromising."

"All joking aside…Thank you." He did not like being beholden to anyone, particularly a man whom he knew so little about. "I have not forgotten our gentleman's agreement. You may have an audience with me at a later date. I will receive you, on the estate, whenever you like, with a day's notice. Is that agreeable to you?"

"Certainly, Conte Ambrosi."

"There is no need for pomp and circumstance. Call me, Dominic."

Just then he heard someone enter the room.

"Aye, tha rascal is awake, is he?"

"Ahh, Kathleen. Forgive me, but I promised my sister-in-law she could have a go at me and I think she has decided to collect." He smiled despite himself. "Cael, would you see Professor Greyson out?"

"Certainly. After you, Professor."

"Ms. Prescott, Mrs. Raine." Dom imagined the professor genuflected before following Cael out of the room. No Gideon, no Gabriel.

Once he heard the click of the door and Kathleen's rustling skirts, he exhaled. "Who is here?"

"Just me and Kathleen. Dom, you can't see, can you?"

"No, Cara. My vision is tied to my ability. Once I am fully recovered my sight will return. It is not a weakness that I wish exposed."

"Then why tha devil admit as much in front of me?" Kathleen's snappish reply amused him.

"I dare say that Ethan has figured it out by now and I doubt there is one secret between the two of you."

"Aye, my Ethan tells me all."

"Out. I want to be alone with my fiancée..." He held up his hand, knowing the Scottswoman's proclivities. "She is quite thoroughly compromised and a wedding is eminent so please spare me the matronly protests."

"Impudent bastard, dat ya are...Procreating and such before tha banns-"

"OUT!"

Dom waited for the still-murmuring Kathleen to exit before he spoke again.

"Eden...Come, sit." He patted the bed next to him, and smiled when he felt the bed depress to his left. "Are you...alright?"

"You mean, am I *me* again? Yes, Dom. The other one is gone. My hair is back to normal. Dr. Raine...eh, Ethan, says my wound signature looks good, whatever that means. And Atherton was all smiles after my last interview. Even without the 'Dr.' it sounds priggish, but 'Cael' just seems too familiar. You were still out so....eh, Dom?"

"Hmm?" He sighed. He wasn't so much listening to

her words as he was soaking in her presence…the soft lilting voice, her delicate scent from the perfumed baths she took at night.

"The spectacles…do you mind?" He felt her nervous fingertips at his temple even as she spoke. "I have grown to prefer you without them."

He nodded, closing his eyes to savor the gentle touch of her as she slid the wire-rims off. Unable to stop himself, he caught her in his arms and pulled her further onto the bed, half in his lap.

She yelped at the unexpected movement. "Dom…*Kathleen—*"

"—is not here to protest." He cut off the rest of whatever she was going to say. "And I doubt she'll be back, if Ethan has anything to do with it. I missed you. Lillian was a grotesque substitution." He caught hold of a handful of fabric, and pulled her forward for a kiss…and he came up with all nose.

"Your aim is off." She snickered against his cheek.

"Are you still going to marry me?" He murmured, nuzzling his nose against the soft skin of her cheek. "Now that you've seen the worse of us…the Ambrosi'…Oh Bloody hell, there is still Nonna in Italy."

"Yes, Dom."

He kissed her cheek briefly, the smile dying a little as he contemplated just what he was asking of her. "Even though, there is no guarantee that our children won't be…like me."

"What? An Italian Adonis with odd eyes and a massive inferiority complex?"

"I am serious, Eden."

"I know, Dom. That is what makes this conversation so ridiculous." She shifted back from him and he felt her hands on either side of his face. "Now you listen to me. I am no picnic either. I channel demons and dead people into the living world…and I clearly have no control over it. Because of this I have suicidal tendencies. Plus, I'm an only child and wretchedly spoiled. Can you live with *that*?"

"Yes." He answered with no hesitation.

He felt her kiss his forehead. "Well, if you are willing to take a chance on me...then I am willing to take my chances with you."

"I love you, Eden."

"Good...Show me."

READER'S DISCUSSION GUIDE

1. Reaction to the book as a whole:
   - Was reading the book a positive experience?
   - Were you engaged immediately, or did it take you a while to "get into the story?"

2. Is this a plot-driven book: a fast-paced page-turner? Or does the story unfold slowly with a focus on character development?

3. Were you surprised by the plot's complications? Or did you find it predictable, even formulaic?

4. Do the flashbacks enhance or take away from the story? Why or why not?

5. In most traditional romance novels, the story is told almost exclusively from the female/heroine's point of view. In Dominic's Nemesis, the author spends a significant amount of time in the Hero's voice. What did you think? How does this make you feel? Does it contribute to or take away from the romance?

6. Do you think Lillian was truly possessed by a demon spirit or just criminally insane?

7. Were the hero and heroine developed sufficiently? Were they likeable? Was their romance believable?

8. Who was your favorite 2ndary character and why?

9. What main ideas—**themes**—does the author explore?

10. Who/What do you think the "Nemesis" in the book's title refers to? Give examples to support your theory.

11. Is the **ending** satisfying? If so, why? If not, why not...and how would you change it?

12. What do you suppose is going on with Gabriel's cat, Muse? Theories? Did the author leave it hanging on purpose? Will it be explored in a follow-up book?

13. The book is fairly genre-bending. If you had to force it into one romantic subcategory, which would it be? Paranormal? Gothic? Historical? Provide support for your answer.

14. If there were to be a sequel to Dominic's Nemesis...who's story would you want told next? Which character would you want to know more about? What loose end would you most want to see explained?

15. If you could ask the author of Dominic's Nemesis a question, what would it be? Would you read another book by this author?

OTHER BOOKS BY THIS AUTHOR

When Lucifer Met Calamity
(Available Spring/2016)

Preview of Untitled Sequel to Dominic's Nemesis

EXCERPT

He had never been troubled with dreams before.

He writhed in his sleep, seeking an escape from his mutinous subconscious. His dark cap of wavy hair chaotic from tossing his head back and forth against the pillow. The dream's thrall crawled into his mind like a poisonous snake slithering along the ground to catch its unsuspecting prey. It was strange in its reality. The in-dream boy lay on his own bed, with his brother sleeping beside him blissfully unaware...just as his waking self and his brother slept most nights. Except, in the dream his small form was wracked by spasms of blinding pain. His very bones felt as if they were being pulled apart.

The boy shifted his shoulder to try to shake off the pain, and felt something snap out of place. He screamed at the horror of the sound more than the pain of the bone's dislocation. The pop of his other shoulder followed suit, but somehow he was still able to move his arms. Sweat glistened off his face, his breaths came in audible gasps. He held up his hands out in front of him. They looked wrong. The skin of his forearms rippled...normally smooth skin bristled with cactus spines...growing, protruding grotesquely from his arms, spreading like a rash to cover the entire surface so that all he saw were spines...elongating...now less like cactus...morphing into porcupine's quills…that blended and weaved together, the quill ends softening into feathers. His arms were no longer discernable, transformed into flapping, wing-like appendages.

Crack. His hip bone crumbled inward, with horrifying suddenness. His legs…he caught sight of them. The boy could see the online of his bones beneath his tan olive skin. His thighs and legs began to retract inward, shortening, while his feet stretched impossibly long, with scaly talons where his toenails had once been. He thrashed around, the foreign parts of his body flopping, and half-formed. He was dying, ebbing away…to give birth to something else, something otherworldly.

He thoughts screamed…but he could make no sense of them. No longer words, or coherent ideas, but more akin to feelings, impressions of reality…instinct and patterns of expression. His mind no longer tried to understand the freakish metamorphosis seizing his body. His mental process struggled instead to survive it. A wavering image of a great bird flickered within his mind, like a candle flame caught in the draft of a swinging door. He couldn't quite hold the image, and some new level of instinct told him that it was imperative that he do so.

The boy, Gabriel, awoke to a beastly sound. He breathed deep. His first thought was of his hands. He brought them up to check himself, flipping his palms over front and back. He sighed. They were normal human hands, his skin also was smooth and normal when he pushed back the nightshirt's sleeves…

"CAHHHH!!"

His head snapped to the source of the half-human sound, midways between the screeching caw of a bird and the panicked scream of a child. His brother was not in bed.

"Giddy!" The boy leaped up, flung the covers aside, and ran around to the opposite side of the bed. What he saw, startled him so that he stumbled. His brother, his twin or at least he thought the freakish creature flailing around on the floor beside the bed was his brother. It shrieked, a malformed beak of sorts where his mouth had been.

He tip-toped toward the half-avian tangle of feathers, talons and dislocated limbs. The boy treaded slowly, not wanting to worsen his *brother's already frenzied panic. The oddity of his dream so perfectly mirroring reality wasn't lost on him. The dream boy hadn't been him at all, but Giddy...trapped in the half-bird transformation. The dream was real, a preview of sorts.*

"Giddy?"

The flailing paused, and the halfling thing twisted around...a single crazed bird eye caught his.

"Cahhh!"

ABOUT THE AUTHOR

D. Alyce Domain. Is a long-time lover of creative fiction. She learned to read with Dr. Seuss, grew up reading Sweet Valley High, James Howe, and Lois Duncan, and graduated to category romance with Harlequin and Silhouette in her teen years. Ms. Domain started out writing fan-fiction after her favorite fictional characters met with death and cancellation on network television. Inspired by the entertaining, multi-layered storylines created by so many female romance, young adult and television writers, she began to experiment with her own characters. Coupled with her own unique brand of genre-bending romantic fiction, Ms. Domain was able to create a whole new world within the pages of her books.

Ms. Domain was born and raised in Houston, Texas, the youngest daughter of Charles and Eunice Domain. She has one older sister. She earned a BS in Biochemistry and a MS in Biomedical Sciences. She worked in Patient-Based Biological Research before switching careers and opening her own fashion boutique, The Aesthetic Domain. In addition to fashion apparel and accessories, she sells her own original jewelry creations and runs the Boutique & Blog website, which is based in Houston, Texas. Ms. Domain also has avid interests in inspirational music, art/entertainment, and history.